I0743509

An Official Killing

A tale of

Cruelty
Perseverance
Strength and Empathy

Hester Garner

First published in Australia, 2024
NSW, Birpai (Birrbay) Country

ISBN: 978-1-7636692-0-8
Cover image generated: Author
Photograph courtesy of Lindie Kolver Photography
Typeset in Adobe Garamond Pro
Printed and bound in Australia

Dedication

For everyone who carries Nelie's blood in their veins –
this is your story too

Acknowledgements

Without my husband, Ernest's encouragement, this book would not have been possible. The calm, happy place our marriage creates is where ideas and dreams flourish – thank you.

To my close friends, Gail Morgan, Mariaan Wagner Michau and Lindie Kolver – I am most grateful for your attention to detail, your kind guidance, and eagle eyes. No one could better understand the urge and need to read comfort prose about Africa than ex-South Africans. The many hours you've spent reading and dissecting chapters speak of your kindness – the willingness to tread forgotten and sometimes cumbersome paths.

An Official Killing has been one of the most enjoyable novels to write, especially since the main characters took me to the Bushveld - the place that always paints my heart with a special brush.

Reviews

Hester transports us to another time and place in history in her book. She is an excellent wordsmith with that unique ability to paint a character or scene vividly with words. A great storyteller who has breathed life into each character, making it a rich, raw, and very real story woven in a time gone by. A compelling read.

Gail Morgan, Author

This book by Hester Garner, set during Afrikaner history when the country's politics were turbulent, is masterfully written. We experience this dark period in the history of South Africa through the eyes of a family who have been taken from their farm and made to walk to Irene Concentration Camp. It is a deeply moving and disturbing account of the trials and tribulations this family endured.

An Official Killing is a must-read for anyone interested in the history of South Africa during the period of the Boer War and subsequent Concentration Camp internment of their womenfolk.

Lindie Kolver

Author Notes

An Official Killing is Nelie's story. The tale of a young Afrikaner woman caught up in the battle between Boer and Brit during the Second Boer War (1899 – 1902) in South Africa.

This story is a recount of history from Nelie's perspective.
It is a work of fiction. However, the main characters, Nelie, Ampie and Edward, are real. They kept their identities, whereas many place- and family names are fictitious and a product of my imagination, or have been changed out of respect for living relatives.

Nelie's journey begins on the family farm, Morgenster, near Klerksdorp in south-west Transvaal (now North-West Province), where fierce fighting raged at the time. I follow her on a path of bewilderment after the farm was slashed and burned – a path most captured Afrikaner women were forced to travel, including hellish incarceration in concentration camps.

The devastation, displacement and destitution after war are honestly portrayed as they happened for her and thousands of disillusioned Afrikaners like her. The joy of love and family also found its way into this story. In addition, details of an Australian connection are revealed.

Between the first and second World Wars, Nelie ventured into the Bushveld and frontier territory of north-western Transvaal (now Limpopo Province), untouched by world events. Her journey encompasses the full range of human experiences before, during and after war.

The story showcases the humanness of Africa's people and the significant events that shaped their world at the time. The empathy and strength of the Afrikaner people influenced Nelie's character depiction, and their sacrificial compassion comes to the fore in scenes of concentration camps. But war and loss also highlighted man's extraordinary wickedness.

I have allowed for a measure of artistic freedom and creativity to yarn events into a readable fabric.

Glossary

agterryers	informants/goods carriers
alles sal regkom, Oom, alles sal tog regkom	all will be well, Uncle; all will eventually be well
bakoven	outside oven built with clay bricks
bekslaner	gate made with barbed wire and wood, literal meaning: hit on mouth
Biesiepan	a farm, pan with reeds
biltong	dried meat strips (like jerky)
blinkblaar-waggen-bietjie	buffalo thorn bush, Ziziphus mucronata
bly kyk	keep looking
Boekevat	reading from the Bible
boere opskop	dance party
boerseep	handmade farmer's soap
boeppens	fat stomach/bend in river
boet/boetie	brother/little brother
bokwa	ox wagon
bulala	to kill
burghers	Afrikaner civilian soldiers
bywoner	subsistence farmers
daar	there
dankie, Mammie	thank you, Mummy
dom	dumb
Driefontein	farm, three fountains
duiker	small antelope, subfamily Cephalophinae
Elandsfontein	farm, fountain where eland roam
God is mijn herder, ik zal het niet willen	Dutch for: God is my shepherd; I shall not want
grafblommetjies	tough flowering plant, bitter taste
Groot Doornlaagte	a place called Big Thorn Flats
Groot Tommie	Big Tommie
haas	rabbit

hartbeeshuis	small daub and reed thatched house
Hartebeestfontein/ Hartebeest Poort	a village; a place where hartebeest roam
hier sal ons doodgaan, Cornelia	here, we will die, Cornelia
hottentotsgod	praying mantis
huisapteek	portable medicine chest
hulle is skelm	they are thieves
juffrou	young woman/female teacher
ja	yes
kaffer	person from Africa, usually black
kaiings	speck cutlets fried in a thick-bottomed pot
Kameelfontein	a farm, where camel roam
kappie	cherished, old-fashioned, wide-rimmed Afrikaner bonnet for women and girls
khakis	soldiers from England
khaki duwweltjies	paper-thin brown thorns
kinta	child
klein	little
kleinhuisie	outhouse/farm toilet separate from house
Klerksdorp	a town, established by magistrate, Jacob de Clercq
klim af, my sussie	come down, sister
knobkierie	black man's fighting stick
knoppiesdoring	knob thorn tree, Senegalia nigrescens
kolhaas	rabbit
kom, die Here is nou met ons	come, God is with us now
kom nader	come closer
Kremetartpan	a farm named after the baobab tree
kyk hulle ore	look at their ears
Landdrost kantoor	magistrate's offices
Langkloof	a beautiful valley north of Nylstroom
Leeuwpoort	a pass, where lion (used to) roam

liefeling/liefling	darling/sweetheart
loof, loof de Heer met lofliederen	Dutch for: exalt God with songs of praise
mamba	black mamba, highly venomous snake
mamma	mother/mum/mommy
manne/man	men/man
maroela	marula tree, Senegalia nigrescens
meester	male teacher
miesies	missus
meneer	sir
Meneer	Mister
mevrou/mevrouw	ma'am/mrs
Morgenster	a farm, morning star
my kind	my child
my hartjie	my dear
my liewe tannie	my precious aunty
my meidjie	my dearest (child)
my ou maat	my old friend
naand, niggie; goeiendag, my kind	good evening/good day, child
nader my God aan U	nearer my God to thee
nee	no
neef	cousin (male) or good friend
Nederduitsch Gereformeerde Kerk	Dutch Reformed Church
Nelie	short for Cornelia
niggie	cousin (female) or good friend
Nylstromers	people from Nylstroom, a town in North West Province
Nylstroom (now Modimole)	a town named after the Nile rivulet
oom	uncle
Oom Ampie, kom kyk die tarentaaltjies!	Uncle Ampie, have a look at the guineafowl keets!
ouklip	type of rock used for concrete
ouma	grandma

oupa	grandpa
pensklavier	accordion
Pietersburg (now Polokwane)	a town established by Hendrik Potgieter
Pikanien	common name for a little boy (usually a black child)
Potgietersrust (now Mokopane)	a town, named after Piet Potgieter
riempiestoel	fold-up chair with criss-cross leather seat
rinderpest	an infectious viral disease affecting hooved animals
rinkhals	venomous cobra snake, genus Naja
rooibos	a medium-sized tree, grows in Bushveld region
Rooibokvlei	a place, named after impala
rooinekke	English soldiers (red necks)
Rooipad	a farm, Red Road
Rustenburg	a town in North West Province, City of Rest
seun	son/boy
Skilpadfontein	a farm, fountain (pan) where tortoises live
skippies	kangaroos found in Australia
springhaas	a rabbit lookalike rodent, Pedetes capensis
soetgras	curly-leafed sweet grass
sus/sussie	sister/little sister
Sterkspruit	a creek, Strong Creek
sepela gabôtsê, Mma	go well, mother/friend, SeSotho language
Soldaat	Soldier, popular name for a dog
stampmielies	crushed maize
steenbok	small antelope, Raphicerus campestris
suurknol	a plant, Watsonia family
spoor	tracks
sitkamer	lounge

Sandrivierspoort Nek	a pass north of Nylstroom, Sand River Neck
stoep	veranda
tante/tannie	aunt/aunty
toemaar, my boetie	don't worry, son
tokoloshe	mythical figure like a ghost, SeSotho language
tolbos	tumbleweed
totsiens	goodbye
tot wedersiens	until we meet again
Truiatjie	little Truia
Tweespruit	a river, Two Creeks
ululating	a high-pitched celebratory tune
vaalbos	a tree, mogonono, Terminalia sericea
Vaalwater	a town, grey water
vastrap	an enjoyable dance
velskoens	farm shoes made of soft leather
verdomde	darn/damn
vlakhaas	rabbit
Vlieërg Pas	a pass named after flies
voorbereiding	a religious sermon of contrition and preparation
voor een iegelik die dit Testament zullen zieu of booren lezen zij het kennelijk, ondergeteekende getuijgen verschenen	Dutch statement, freely translated as: the Will has been sighted and duly signed by witnesses
Vryburg	a town, free town
waar gaan ons, hê, Pa?	where are we going, ey, Dad?
waar gaan ons, hê, Nelie?	where are we going, ey, Nelie?
Waterberg	a mountain range, water mountain
Weltevreden	a farm, contented
Witkerk	white Dutch Reformed church in Nylstroom town
word wakker	wake up

Wondergat	a large water hole obscured by mountains
Wonderkroonessens, Witdulsies, Levenessens, Paragorie	Lennon's liquid medicine
wilde-als en buchu	medicinal herbs
Zeerust	a town, Dutch for Rest Close to the Sea
Zoutpan	ancient salt pans in North West Province

Table of Contents

Part One: Scorched Earth

1- Burning Farms

'Since we are with Clements, we have had plenty of work burning farms. It is very hard sometimes. Last Sunday, six of us went out with an Imperial officer to a fine farmhouse, giving the occupants five minutes to clear out all their goods as well as themselves. There were an old grandmother, three married daughters, and several children, crying and asking for mercy, but no, when the time was up, we burned it to the ground.'

Trooper Morris, Brabant's Horse (Australian Volunteers)

Winter 1900, Klerksdorp, South African Republic

It was a night like any other.

The barrenness of a Highveld winter's night lay white in the full moon's gaze over the homestead and the vegetable garden, which offered long-armed onion and spinach to its light. Sheep huddled for warmth in their pen behind the outbuildings, while chickens, geese and turkeys slept head-under-wing.

The dam out front waited without a ripple for dawn, when mist usually hangs above its cold waters – its silvery arms folding and unfolding in a quiet dance. Without a breeze disturbing the lemon tree's branches, *oupa* Dewaldt's grave underneath rested peacefully, while the rise behind kept watch. All was quiet.

Yes, it was a night like any other.

But this time the silence had a life and body, a presence which I could not name. Someone was there, not in the bedroom where my sisters breathed deeply, but out there in the cold.

My stockinged feet found the cold floor to the kitchen, where coals were still glowing a faint red in the hearth, waiting to be stoked and fed. As I poked through its embers, the aroma of yesterday's baking mingled with that of a fire coming to life. I breathed it in deeply, kept it there, and felt the familiar odours calm the unsettled feeling that something was moving silently outside.

I already knew that the 'something' would come, never of certainty, but a foreboding, which had been my constant companion since birth. 'Born capped, is what it is,' older folk explained its existence, but whatever they chose as an explanation, it had woken me in the death hour to sit here, fully dressed in the warming kitchen to wait for the inevitable.

Time ticked by slowly, interrupted only by the grandfather clock's hourly strikes - twelve, one, two, three, four, and then they came when the full moon made way for the morning star. In the bleak pre-dawn light, horse and rider moved silently, turning the bend at the old skeletal leadwood tree that had been our patient gatekeeper since the first day our people came to live here.

Ma Sophia appeared quietly to stand at the table, resting one hand on the family Bible, the other idly on the yellow stinkwood table. Even with the dangerous enemy nearby, the remember of life's journeys and a time long gone came to sit fresh in her amethyst eyes. In those fleeting moments, she calmly walked the paths so oft revisited by my grandpa, *oupa* Dewaldt. I could tell she was with him, like in times of old, as his mind travelled with his young self into the Knysna rainforests far to the east of the Cape Colony, where the majestic yellow stinkwoods grow.

There, he braved snake, elephant, buffalo, leopard and the ferocious caracal among the tentacles of dense forest to fell one of the giants. With four trusty oxen, he negotiated the mighty Vaal River and daunting Drakensberg mountains, moving north-north-west towards Morgenster, to this farm on the other side of the country. Here, it lay fallow for two seasons to dry.

Then he started the labour of love, creating this most beautiful table for his new bride, adding a chair for each of their seven children as the little family grew.

On the day the last chair stood proudly on ball-and-claw feet, he thanked his heavenly Father on bent knee and took his last breath, right here where I was sitting – a good place to be still and feel his presence.

'It is time, Cornelia,' *Ma* said, then turned to wake the others, her long nightgown swishing around slender ankles in a nod to a German heritage. Her sleeping bonnet framed a beauty, the envy of many - high cheekbones, friendly eyes, and a wide mouth, always generously smiling.

In the warmth of down overthrows, my two older sisters, Lettie and Hannie, and six children were still fast asleep in the near bedroom, unburdened by foreboding.

Along the quiet passage, four orphaned children and our three younger sisters, Johanna, Martha and Sara, shared a bed for warmth and lack of space. In the corner stood a single cot where my body's shape lay permanently etched in the coir mattress.

Furthest from the kitchen, our disabled grandma's bedroom looked out over the back yard towards her gentle mate's final resting place and to the mountains beyond. Five households' joy and suffering clumped together under one roof.

If we were asked a few years ago what extraordinary circumstances could have conspired to bring us all together, the answers would've varied between 'drought, death, misfortune, God's will,' but certainly not 'the English.' Such was our unpreparedness for the greed of gold, which saw England and its allies swarming our precious country.

Like their fellow *burgher* soldiers, our menfolk were defending our country from the English invaders at our door. Fatigue was pushing them beyond endurance in this second Boer War, which seemed determined to wipe the Afrikaner off history's page. Our people's suffering, be it God's will or not, was worn with mute acceptance and a firm belief in pre-ordained destiny. And through His will, we women, bound by a common past, were safe on the family farm, Morgenster - named for the morning star which always appears directly over the dam out front.

During the coldest winter months, armed black bands were roaming the outlying farming areas near Klerksdorp. Commandeered and armed by the British army, they burned to the ground Boer homes and crops, killing all farm animals and moving swiftly like a pestilence sweeping the land.

'They come when least expected,' a visitor had warned a week prior, adding to the limited knowledge women and old people on isolated farms had of enemy soldiers' ways. But like a fierce forest fire, knowledge travelled fast of these armed blacks roaming the countryside - a danger no local could have guessed at.

After all, these were our fellow citizens - labourers, landowners, and most often servants who understood the demands of living off the land during drought and plagues.

'*Ja,* the English armed these heartless devils to do their bidding,' I overheard at the general store in Klerksdorp, and my heart became cold at the thought of local black people, angry at whites for personal reasons, drawn into a conflict.

Noticing my interest, the informant had turned to me, 'Now the enemy has another army who knows the veld, where people live and what they own. They can better plan to slash and burn to the ground our homes and crops, and kill, maim or steal our animals.' But the speaker left the worst result unsaid: in the aftermath of and mostly in conjunction with these bands, the foreign soldiers gathered and systematically removed women, children, older people and loyal blacks to intern in concentration camps far from their beloved farms. Occasionally, a few managed to escape capture, but at great cost.

After receiving word that neighbouring families had been left homeless and taken away, our two older sisters, both close to confinement, fled with their young children and hid in the hills for many days during the enemy's merciless advance. There, they endured the bitter Highveld cold with little food and drink, to slowly make their way in the dark of night here to Morgenster, some thirteen miles away.

Sensing their coming and waiting at the yellow stinkwood table did not prepare us for the wild-eyed despair they brought to our back door, but questioning the essence of humanity that allowed it, *Ma* said, is not what Afrikaner people do. 'Never, never question God's will for his people,' she reaffirmed our focus and brought our crying to an end.

'Did you cry about Maria's orphans?' She pointed to our brother's four orphaned children, not one older than ten, now living with us after an English splinter group killed his wife.

Clear in our minds the night just after the cock had crowed the first time, when old Jacob, their loyal farm worker, brought the frightened children to our back door. The old man stood ashen-faced as he cradled the tin coffee mug *Ma* steadied in his knobbly hands. His eyes wide and glassy with the horrors of a single day, to supersede all horrors known to a simple, honest soul.

'Did we besiege an Almighty when *Ouma* lost the use of her legs?' she continued, referring to our grandmother, Susara, who fell off a horse, doing men's work in the years after *oupa* Dewaldt's sudden death.

'We do unto others as we want them to do unto us,' and with that, our household grew from a few to twelve.

We worked the fields, planting and sowing in the men's absence. We tended our large sheep flock and fattened the piglets for slaughter, should neighbours or the men at war need sustenance. Even my older sisters, their bodies heavy with the nearness of giving birth, led bullocks while tilling the soil.

As the horses came into focus out front, old Jacob and his little grandson stood fully dressed in the back door. After he had delivered the orphans, he would not leave for his people across the border in Bechuanaland, even though we pleaded with him, he stayed on in our barn, 'To look after you, *Miesies.*'

It was while hunting in the hills one day, shortly after Jacob's arrival, that I came across his grandson. The overwhelmed, starving boy tearfully gave life to the day of our sister, Maria's brutal rape and murder. Something shifted in my soul that day.

'Let's go home, Pikanien,' I said and lifted him onto my horse, where he clung to me until our return late in the afternoon. Feeling his scrawny body, so vulnerable in trust, my heart hardened towards those people intent on changing our lives forever. What kind of person would do such an evil deed while a child watches on?

For months, news had been spreading that the English *khakis* were coming, leaving a trail of destruction in their wake. After a British slash-and-burn proclamation in early 1900, which left not a single four- or two-legged soul behind, the Transvaal and Orange Free State principalities were rapidly turning into a wasteland. English troops and their brutal black armies followed directions to turn women and children out of farmsteads mercilessly, burn them to the ground and leave nothing to eat and nowhere to go, except far-off concentration camps.

Who could believe such callous cruelty? Certainly not defenceless Afrikaner women, old folk, and children who believed in a sense of decency and lived it as well. Yet, as we were about to have coffee, the *khaki*-clad riders' boots crunched gravel at our front door.

It was our turn to pay for our men waging war with the invaders. We did not want this war, and neither did Afrikaners deserve it.

There was no reason to expect a civilised knock, but the loud rifle-butt banging on the front door made us jump, and *ouma* Susara cried out from her bedroom while the young ones hid fearfully behind their mothers. Pikanien uttered a heart-wrenching wail, remembering a cruelty etched forever in his mind. The other children started crying in sympathy with the boy who had to endure such pain without the comfort of a mother's arms.

'Jacob, take Pikanien and leave nów,' *Ma* said, proffering a freshly baked loaf of bread. 'Go unseen. Gather ten ewes and the ram and move up into the high country where no horse can go. We'll come for you one day. God's hand is on you,' she said, urgently pushing his bent frame out the back door.

By now, all except *Ouma* were waiting in the kitchen. Young Sara was already reaching for cups - always welcoming in nature and believing others to echo such behaviour. But this day the door was flung open with force, and there, without asking, stood the wild-eyed soldiers - eyes such as I had seen before in hunters given to a merciless hunt.

Ma moved unobtrusively between the children and soldiers. She had a good command of English - the benefit of some years at boarding school in the Cape Colony before *oupa* Dewaldt's death – which she then passed on to us. Loathing for the evildoers kept me seated, and I did not care whether it was good manners or not.

'Get your things. You have five minutes to be outside!' a red-faced soldier ordered. His face and neck were severely burned by the harsh African sun, with only a pale, untouched forehead beneath the pith helmet revealing an insipid English sun's effect.

Six soldiers pushed their way into the kitchen and started looking through our personal belongings. 'Those are our things, Soldier. I'm offering coffee and nothing else!' *Ma* warned, quietly moving my sisters to shield our rifle on the wall. Without a rifle, a woman on her own cannot survive long on an African farm.

My younger sisters and I had been using the remaining firearm and bullets sparingly when out hunting, as it was becoming increasingly difficult to buy bullets. Even though we were first-class shots, nobody could handle the .22 or .75 better than *Ma,* who, in essence, became the breadwinner at a young age.

She could shoot a bird in flight from 200 yards. During New Year's festivities in Klerksdorp village, young males eager to impress a beautiful girl often walked away red-faced losers. Prizemoney was generally a turkey, so *Ma* built a good flock, which now roamed the yard around our house.

'Ma'am, don't waste time. Get your things and move outside!' the soldier said without introducing himself. Behind him, a quiet blue-eyed soldier tried to hold back the others who were intent on searching the pantry, all the while throwing cutlery to the floor.

The kitchen was filled with the scent of veld and unwashed bodies, telling of days on horseback and rough sleeping. One soldier found the remaining loaf of bread on the wood stove and was tearing at it like a ravenous animal. Others were already ransacking bedrooms.

'Soldier, take command of your men – there's an invalid in our house!' The quiver in *Ma's* voice revealed outrage and concern. But after a lifetime of holding the reins, she was not given to idle acceptance, and determinedly set off to *Ouma's* bedroom, pushing soldiers out of her way as she went. 'Cornelia, come!' she beckoned while Sara was still shakily pouring coffee in mismatched cups.

'No coffee, Miss! I'm trooper Morris, I give orders – now get your things!' the soldier said and swiped cups and kettle off the table to join the much-needed articles scattered on the shiny floor. 'Now you have four minutes!' he helped the women and children along with his rifle-butt. In the busyness of the moment, my sisters managed to stow away our gun under layers of petticoats, then scrambled for suitcases, already packed and stowed under our beds.

As the English approach became certain, we carefully considered what we might need in concentration camps, for which there was little detail on the ground.

From *agterryers* – our *burghers'* informal war supply and support network - who came by, we learned of shortages in what was quickly becoming the most horrendous places of concentrated incarceration for women, children and old folk - even blacks.

We packed what we thought was necessary and could be carried even by the orphans and sewed money into our hems and bodices, which not even the trained eye could detect.

By the time *Ma* and I reached *Ouma's* bedroom, two young soldiers were shouting at her to get up, hitting the bed repeatedly with their rifles and laughing wildly as she struggled to sit.

For a slender beauty, *Ma* was surprisingly strong. In one fluid movement and as fast as a *mamba* snake, she cuffed them behind the head with fingers spread wide, recognising their youthful need for guidance.

'Cornelia, take *Ouma's* arms,' she said, and stepped over a soldier to help lift and wrap our grandmother's frail body in a down coverlet. 'Now, you two devil's children, take her outside!' And in that moment, she became the mother longed for at night in a strange land where jackal howls and lion roars.

In the kitchen, we were met by chaos. Crockery, cutlery and all manner of household goods were strewn on the floor. The blue-eyed soldier stood motionless at the table, and with sad eyes followed *Ouma's* rough journey out the front door. 'I'm so sorry, Miss, I'm so sorry!' he said over and over as I walked by while the sounds of fowl and sheep in distress wafted from the back yard. He offered his hand, 'I'm Presgrave, Miss,' and when I took it, my heart recognised the meeting of souls.

By now, dawn and mist had all but gone, but the icy wind was whipping up dust swirls, which changed *Ouma's* blanket from white to brown in an instant, where she was dropped unceremoniously.

The two soldiers scampered to the back yard to join their comrades; all but one, who stood motionless at the kitchen window. Others were already caught up in the chase, crying out with glee as they pursued our animals. *Ma's* prized turkeys ran wide-winged from bayonets, and chickens lay lifeless, strewn everywhere, while the wind rustled through feathers which would never again warm and protect plump bodies. The butchers moved on to the sheep pen and pigsty.

Never had I seen such barbaric behaviour among those believed to be civilised. Blacks, yes. They do not share the white man's habit of naming and loving animals. Yet even old Jacob was often seen talking animatedly to Sara's pet sheep as if arguing a point and then sealing the argument with a pat and toothless smile. His absence thankfully spared him this destruction.

Screwing up our eyes to the dust only made it easier to follow the butchery happening behind our house.

Everyone was crying – the children wailing in chorus as Sara's pet lamb came charging around the house to the safety of his master, just to be felled at her feet by a soldier adept at wielding a bayonet. To worsen the dreadful situation, a tame piglet escaped towards us for sanctuary, prompting a chase-and-kill which ended abruptly in its shrill death-cry. Distress hung thick around us.

Dust, blood and tears mingled with the sorrowful cries of women and children who clung to each other in powerless grief. 'Oh, merciful God! Where is your soul, Soldier?! Do you have no feeling!' my sisters cried out in disbelief and fell to their knees in the dust, pleading for mercy.

Just then, Trooper Morris rounded the corner with pickaxe and hammer in hand. 'You don't need this where you're going!' he shouted while smashing wooden window frames and ordering the furniture to be dumped outside. 'Load what you can and burn the rest!' he said, and without a backward glance at our pitiful group, set fire to the house. On top of the pile was *oupa* Dewaldt's yellow stinkwood table – its four legs reaching heavenward for the respect it was entitled to.

Not until the day I lay down my head in eternal sleep will I forget *Ouma's* distressed cry at the sight of her beloved table, and as if in response to her sadness and despair, the fish eagle sounded his mournful cry from the leadwood behind us.

My heart became heavy with rage, and a terrible sense of foreboding overcame me when soldiers started loading fodder from our stores onto wagons that had arrived during the cacophony. They piled dead sheep and slaughtered hogs on top. A team of blacks started herding the remaining animals towards town, *ululating* a spiteful, high-pitched celebratory song as they walked past.

I looked sideways at our dishevelled little group. The burning farmstead clearly highlighted the horrors of the moment in every face, forever printed in our memory.

In the stillness which followed, the smouldering embers' warmth deceivingly invited us closer, but our abandonment was complete. Against its glow, *ma* Sophia stood erect - a single teardrop hanging defiantly from her chin while the soldiers' departing hoofbeats faded to the north.

It was a night like no other.

'They sent a bullock waggon to load us up for the journey.
We didn't go very far when the side of the waggon gave way.
We almost fell between the wheels.'

Mrs George Moll. 1900

The dust of a thousand hooves hung in the windless air. It was a cold day to wait for the enemy's return but return they surely would.

With no suspicious movement for some time in the bushes and along the gravelly road, we made our way to the grain store, which was spared the fires that wiped out our haven and lifeblood. In their haste, soldiers defied the order to burn everything and left behind enough fodder to make beds and keep warm for the night.

They will be back in the morning for more fodder, and when they do, we will have to go, of that I was certain.

None of the choices before us was palatable. We could follow old Jacob and Pikanien into the high country but would have to carry an invalid while on the run from those who could track us down before reaching the first ridge. Or we could walk to the next farm, which might've been ransacked as well. Or go with the English and be the strong Afrikaner women we were known to be.

With dust rising beneath our feet as we moved to the grain store's safety, we came face-to-face with our own feelings: not one was given to easy surrender, least of all to red-necked foreigners. *Ma* was determined, though. 'We will go when they come,' she said. We didn't question her wisdom, years in the making and born from a character long chiselled by a harsh and unforgiving land.

As dusk settled around our burnt-out home, Johanna, Martha, and Sara scoured the devastated vegetable garden for food and came back with a few carrots and potatoes they had dug up with bare hands. 'The *khakis* trampled all our vegetables!' they informed with eyes blazing indignantly.

It was easy to sympathise with them, as many hours of backbreaking work had gone into digging over soil that stubbornly resisted three young girls and two pregnant women's efforts.

In late autumn, the children carried buckets of sheep manure from 200 yards away, spread it evenly and meticulously to sustain a winter crop. And hands, more used to needlework, raked the life-giving soil and sowed seeds from dawn to dusk.

In the men's absence, everyone had a job to do. Apart from old Jacob, there was no one to replace *Pa*, Daan, Jan or young Andries. *Ma's* German culture, even though two generations removed, determined our work quality. 'Do it well the first time,' she would often say, hands on hips in oversight of every task. So, we learned to plan with care and execute thoroughly. Soon the vegetable garden wore a green coat, dutifully nurtured by daily watering from the well a hundred paces away.

During this time, *Ma* became the homemaker and *Ouma's* carer, and I took over as stockman and hunter – a task I relished and was used to. But dresses were not ideal clothing and made the job cumbersome, leaving me hot and irritated most of the time. 'You will grow into these; you are only sixteen,' *Ma* often consoled when dresses were passed on from well-endowed older sisters. Her sewing skills seldom satisfied my youthful yearning for mature curves, and soon it became more practical to wear my brothers' clothes rather than fight ill-fitting petticoats on horseback.

Before the English came, at least two ewes had been kept close to home as a milk supply, while Pikanien spent his days watching over the herd in the far fields. I wondered if the milk would leave a bitter taste in the soldiers' mouths, or if they would laugh and enjoy what was meant for children. Remembering the callous burning of our home, a deep anger at the unfairness of life overcame me.

We could hear the occasional hiss and crack from our house, which was now just a red smouldering skeleton. 'Our dear home's ashes will give sustenance,' *Ma* declared, but with heavy hearts we set about plucking and roasting two young turkeys over its cinders. 'Two turkeys – that's what they left behind in their haste to the next farm plundering, *Ma*. How long will this last?!' Lettie said and turned away angrily. She was the only one brave enough to defy *Ma*.

Our silhouettes stretched long in the embers' glow, reaching toward the dark that was upon us. But once we lay down on our hay beds, sleep was just an illusion in the knowledge that the English were close by.

There would be no rooster to wake and no coffee to sustain us at daybreak. We waited in silence – an owl helping to count the hours with its mournful cry.

And then they came. Again, in the hour of stillness. This time, an old ox-wagon's creak-and-thump announced their slow arrival. We were ready.

Four scrawny bullocks pulled the oldest wagon I had ever seen. Steamy breaths spurted from their tired nostrils. The wagon seemed even more tired. It was so dilapidated that, if it had belonged to us, my brothers would surely have spent weeks repairing it. More likely, they would've used it for firewood.

The quiet Presgrave and another soldier who introduced himself as Williams rode beside the wagon. A black boy led the bullocks to a standstill in front of us. There was nothing to say. We loaded our few belongings and provisions onto the wagon and made *Ouma* comfortable on the good side. Still, splinters and cracked beams made up most of its rump.

Holding her hand, *Ma* said, 'Let's pray,' and on our knees we thanked our Father for our farm, for sparing our lives and for His guidance during the uncertain journey that lay ahead. The soldiers did not speak but looked on in silent unease at the reverential display.

'Now, let's go,' she said, and we dusted our knees to fall in next to the wagon.

All the way down the road, round the bend at the dam and old leadwood tree, we kept turning for a last glimpse of our happy home, now ash. The bullocks kept a slow pace, burdened in old age by a task quite forgotten.

We knew the route well, knew where to steer horses to avoid potholes, but on foot, the potholes seemed much bigger. The children hopped and skipped back and forth for a while in childlike enjoyment, but soon they tired of the game and sought shade in a landscape where it was not to be found. Nothing to do but walk - one foot following the other in the early steps of a long journey.

I hung back. 'Are you taking us to a concentration camp?' I asked Presgrave, screwing up my eyes to the Highveld sun's brilliance.

When no answer was forthcoming, 'Soldier?' Presgrave dismounted to walk beside me. 'Klerksdorp and Potchefstroom camps are not ready, Miss Cornelia,' and as an afterthought, 'We are pushing through to Irene.'

Just the week before, a Dutch merchant from the Cape Colony had visited Morgenster, his wagon carrying hardly any goods worth the long trip north. 'Missus, take to the mountains when the English come,' he said, 'but don't let them take you to Irene.' From his telling, hunger, disease, and tremendous suffering reigned in that dreaded camp, sitting uneasily on its south-facing bare and stony hill.

'Such misery, Missus, such misery,' the merchant said. Upon delivering soap to the camp on the English Consular Corps' insistence, a sea of black-clothed women and children in threadbare clothing stared hollow-eyed at him from behind high barbed-wire fences – a mute testament to daily loss of life.

No hawkers, family, doctors or nurses were allowed to enter the concentration camps, which were run by soldiers never tasked with looking after human beings. Food staples, 'Mostly flour and condensed milk, came from meagre excess army supplies,' he said. That night, sleep evaded us; yet no one was fully able to imagine a situation so dreadful.

I looked at the two lean soldiers and, remembering our animals' slaughter the day before, could only surmise that rations were in short supply.

The next day, we walked side-by-side in silence - captor and captive, conscious of a feeling we dared not make sense of but shared some thoughts in the moment. 'I am sorry, Miss Cornelia,' he said, fiddling with the reins. 'In Australia, we do not treat women like this,' then he veered off to the right and spoke to his fellow soldier, pointing to a lonely tree by the roadside. Even though not dense, there was shade where we could rest. The children were hungry and had been complaining for a while.

Again, Presgrave came to walk with me. 'Why our farm?' I asked, content in his calm presence. The quiet soldier began explaining the immense difficulty of scouting, the numerous encounters with our *burghers*, and the severe wounds and casualties in a war he was keen to join but was less able to understand as time went by.

From June to August, his Brabant Horse regiment fought valiantly while moving north.

Still, many Australians like him were adventurously engaging an enemy similarly used to shooting from the saddle and free from rules.

'Major Henderson sent Williams and me with five others to your farm. The rest of our regiment was in pursuit of your General De Wet. The 'why' of it, I don't understand, Miss. Only, that two brothers Niemandt helped blow up a railway, killed two people and injured one. Your farm had to be burned.'

Our menfolk sometimes came home from a war fought guerrilla-style over vast areas. Because they roamed far and wide, we learned that a supply train was derailed at Klip River, south of Johannesburg. Apparently, Daan and Jan had led the small commando who waited for hours in bitter cold to blow up the railway, cutting off the enemy's lifeline. Blowing up the line too early would've given the *khakis* time to call a halt, and so they had to wait until frost outlined the snaking iron tracks in the moonlight. 'Fighting for your country is a bloody business,' they said when *Ma* asked whether people were killed.

Out on the veld, food consisted of stale bread eaten on the go, dried meat - the *biltong* loved by country folk – and chicory root brewed hastily over small smokeless fires. Invariably, it didn't last long enough between home visits, or bread became mouldy. But it was food in a war where every Boer *burgher* supplied their own, unlike the British army, which increased its food supply by confiscating and stealing fodder and provisions from undefended Afrikaner farms.

The *burghers*, hungry for good food, coffee and company, visited at night to make sure their women were managing on their own, knowing that black armies watched many farms. Our men told of efforts to derail the enemy's progress, their loathing for the English, and admiration for Australian and Canadian volunteer soldiers who understood frontier people's hearts and shared their love of the veld.

Daan and Jan had covered the distance to Irene on horseback many times while on war patrol. Riding their hardy Boer ponies at a steady pace, it was a two-day ride with hardly any rest kin between.

'A week,' Presgrave said, and when he noticed my doubtful eyes scanning a cloudless sky, 'Maybe two.' With a war raging in the hills around us and women and children of all ages in our group, *Ma* declared that only a miracle might get us to the nearby Klerksdorp in a week.

Glancing at Hannie and Lettie's bodies, swollen in expectation, she quietly confirmed all our thoughts, 'Never Irene, Soldier; never all the way to Irene.'

In answer to her doubts, the ox-wagon swayed sharply left on the rutted twin-track and unbalanced the oxen, already unsteady on old legs and fatigued after the distance travelled.

Like a fierce clap of thunder in a Highveld storm, unique in its ability to appear when least expected, the calm was shattered as one wooden wheel slid into a deep pothole, cracked and gave way.

We rushed forward like a swarm of bees to catch *Ouma* as she slid down from the far side. Everyone was shouting and crying in distress, and as another wheel gave way and the wagon came crashing down, a few children were caught between axle and bullocks. The horses milled wildly in a dust cloud, whinnying shrilly at the sudden change while bullocks bellowed in pain, kicking furiously in the air.

'*O, liewe Jesus*! Oh, dear Jesus!' my sisters wailed in anguish, trying to free the little ones from between broken axle and hooves while wood splinters rained down on them. With the smell of blood and dust hanging thick in the air, they managed to drag the children free from danger to huddle in a shivering little group. For long moments afterwards, dust and bellows blocked out any sense of reality, but as the noise died down, the horrific scene around us took our breath away.

One bullock bellowed weakly, and upon hearing this mournful sound, the frightened children wailed loudly in sympathy. Another scrawny bullock lay awkwardly beneath wood and chain, kicking in slow motion like a windmill stoically awaiting a breeze.

Ma's pale face was barely visible, where she sat obscured by dust and the upturned wagon, her hands clenching and unclenching in anguish. '*Ma*! Do you have pain?' I touched her dusty head and rubbed her arms with shaky hands. One foot stuck out at an unnatural angle, and I could tell that bone and muscle had given up the task of movement in a single moment. My hands shook, and fear kept me anchored at her side.

I looked around, and there, close to her bloodied foot, was our beloved *Ouma*, securely pinned under the heavy wagon. My older sisters tried to shield children in the folds of their dresses from what could never be forgotten, while dust settled in the unnatural quiet that followed.

My ears started ringing and, in the distance, a single cicada echoed a shrill, tuneless song, unchanged by years of isolation underground. What else was this than a sign of our aloneness and the desperate times to come?

We were left with two able-bodied men and one woman to lift the wagon when a dozen would have struggled to do so. Then there was the horrific task of freeing *Ouma*. That fell to Johanna, Martha and Sara.

Presgrave sucked his lips in doubt while young Williams stood dazed at the roadside, unable to comprehend the situation. "We can do it together,' I said, and with unfounded belief and all our might, we bent down to the task. At that moment, the wagon creaked and slipped further from our hands in defiance of our desperate efforts, burying *Ouma's* frail body up to her neck.

My breath was sucked from me, and I folded double in grief and disbelief while the cicada continued his lone song.

After a while, I heard Williams' far-off voice, 'We should leave both here,' but Presgrave silenced him and motioned we should at least try one more time to lift the wagon.

I held my cupped hand lightly over *Ouma's* nose and felt her warm breath. Slight little dust puffs mixed with blood in her struggle to breathe. 'No, we will never leave them here!' My whole being recoiled from the callousness expressed so casually.

'Come, Miss Cornelia,' Presgrave said sympathetically, hand on my shoulder. 'It's not done yet.' We strained desperately again to free *Ouma,* whose eyes opened in a sudden surge of clarity. With the disabled's unawareness of pain reflected in her toothless smile, she looked from one to the other, then slowly heavenwards, and said lovingly, 'I am coming, Dewaldt, I am coming,' and took her last breath.

Johanna fell to her knees next to the only grandmother she had ever known, and with a tenderness she had not displayed before, wiped away dust from *Ouma's* face. Then she falteringly started singing *Ouma's* favourite hymn, '*God is mijn herder, ik zal het niet willen,*' praising God in the face of overwhelming sadness. As one, we encircled her and lifted our shaky voices in unison to a cloudless sky and unseen Giver of all good.

Williams stood to the side, unaccustomed to raw emotion and an invisible god, unsure what to do. Presgrave's blue eyes welled with tears in sympathy and recognition of a time of closeness and love forever gone.

'One more word about the women and children, who are now the chief sufferers in this sad war. I think there are between two and three hundred brought away from their homes round Potchefstroom, no proper provision whatever having previously been made for them, mostly all deposited on the veld....'
Englishwoman in Potchefstroom

We stood in the middle of the road like cattle at sale yards. The children milled around, hungry and distressed, while the soldiers seemed indecisive, faced with the moment's sadness.

'Take my petticoat, Cornelia,' *Ma* said, her voice revealing much pain. I did not hesitate and removed one of her wide, full-length petticoats, tore it in half, and gently wrapped *Ouma's* head, securing it with stones, which were in abundance next to the road.

'We could dig a grave,' Presgrave offered doubtfully - his kindness crossing war's divisions. 'No, she will be safe from predators here,' I said, touching his arm gently in recognition of his humanity.

The lone tree in the distance was already casting a long shadow, and we could feel the night's frosty fingers approaching.

Flour and sugar dusted the road with a fine white coat, while blankets and bags lay strewn all around us. Our medicines lay scattered among the brown winter grass where the children searched and recouped some, but most of our staples lay trampled on or securely buried underneath the wagon. By the time we had gathered what remained of our belongings not claimed by the wagon, it was cold.

But it was the loss of water that worried me most. What remained in our water bottles was all we had to share. We also needed to move off the road.

Soon, beast and man would discover the bounty left so tragically, and I was sure before sunrise, vultures with crops bulging from war's spoils would be waiting in the lone tree for yet another easy feed. Most of all, we needed to avoid skirmishes between Boer and Brit, which were bound to happen when they discovered the wagon.

Presgrave and Williams moved around restlessly, unsettled by events and a situation they had no answer to - it was clear we should not wait for decisions from these inexperienced soldiers unfamiliar with the African bush.

'Get your rifle, Soldier,' *Ma's* voice was trembling as we bandaged her mangled foot with the petticoat's remnants, and when there was no movement from either, I pointed to the bullocks. 'You have to shoot thém; they need not suffer more,' I said. Noticing Presgrave's eyes growing wide in dismay, I stood and fetched the rifle from his saddlebag, went up close and shot each bullock between the eyes. Every shot rang in hollow finality. Killing precious livestock was the last straw for women and children not accustomed to animal cruelty, and they started crying again. Not a single bullock was saved from a dusty grave.

The nearest ridge was at least two hundred yards towards the west, its slopes sparsely covered with low-growing thorn trees, but its crown dark with tall trees. Sporadic rifle fire could be heard in the hills to the east, telling of ongoing skirmishes between warring parties. If we were to survive the cold and stay safe, we had to head for the ridge where the trees were denser, then move west-northwest towards Klerksdorp.

For years since the discovery of gold around Klerksdorp, the inexperienced, the unkind and merciless had hunted beautiful bosbok, duiker and rooibok to near extinction on the flats. With the British army moving ever north in pursuit of evasive Boer commandos, the veld was left mostly trampled to dust. Few wildlife dared stay, and only the occasional hare and jackal made an appearance during the cover of night. Not even the stoic tortoise, regarded as a delicacy and aphrodisiac by blacks, escaped the armies sweeping the countryside. However, the hills gave sanctuary to the last and most cunning antelope.

I had scoured these hills on horseback over time with my father, Andries, who knew every secret hiding place where antelope sheltered from an increasing number of hunters. Warier antelope hardly ever ventured down into the valley to feed, preferring to stay on the crest where sweet grass grew undisturbed, making this dwindling food source exceedingly difficult to reach for those caught up in war's busyness.

Yet the ever-cautious antelope were able to find a path down into the valley at night to drink undetected from Schoonspruit's clear waters.

These secret paths were our passage to Klerksdorp and a doctor for *Ma*.

With less than an hour's light left, our meagre rations had to be carried uphill to sustain us as long as possible, as no shot could be fired for fear of detection by war's multiple players. At least the antelope would be safe in our presence, I thought as we divided the goods between us.

Hannie and Lettie, born to practicality, gathered the children, our belongings and scant provisions, and nodding their willingness, started the demanding climb with heavy bodies moving duck-like uphill.

'Left out in the open, these bullocks will be devoured by jackal and caracal or taken away by the roving and hungry before dawn,' I told Presgrave and Williams.

All Afrikaner women and even children carry knives of some kind. 'You can help us with the meat or starve later,' I said and joined my younger sisters who were busy slicing sinewy chunks of meat from a bullock's hind quarters. While hastily cutting broad steaks, I had Williams remove the saddles and packed the bloody slices between saddle and horse.

Johanna, Martha and Sara found the wagon's wooden side panel and piled it with meat slices, then followed the others uphill, taking turns with the heavy panel.

'Good Gawd!' Williams uttered, surprised at our effort to stow away meat. 'You can help, soldier!' I urged, but he stood to the side with distaste, and I had to explain that our survival depended on whatever food we could find. The horses moved around restlessly at the smell of blood, their nostrils wide and eyes rolling apprehensively, and with difficulty, we fitted saddles over the meat. Presgrave and I cut a few branches from a nearby thorn bush and attached these with the axle chain behind Williams's horse.

It was time to go. 'Now, take the reins and follow us,' I ordered Williams, exhausted from our effort to lift *Ma* onto Presgrave's horse, who was skittishly moving about under a changed rider.

I walked out front, showing the way, and Presgrave was leading his spirited horse at a slow pace. With no choice or plan, Williams followed, thorn branches swishing behind to erase our tracks as we headed towards the ridge in twilight.

We followed Lettie and Hannie to the top, where they were resting under an overhanging rock with a good view of the escarpment and shelter from an icy wind blowing from the south.

The children huddled around a small fire, and in a clearing beyond, a blanket that held the promise of sleep waited for our weary mother. By the time we had negotiated the stony hillside, *Ma* was consumed with pain and swaying in the saddle.

'She would've been without mishap on our farm!' I could not conceal the sharp edge to my voice when *Ma* collapsed from the saddle into our arms. My anger was further strengthened by the unexpected joy at a fleeting brush of Presgrave's hand against mine. He was the enemy after all.

'In this war, doing and liking are not the same,' he said thoughtfully, the discomfort of a cold night in the wild seemingly furthest from his mind. There was a gentle, yet unsettling energy about him that people living close to nature know well. I've seen it in pacing caracal when trapped - appearing calm, but ready to strike at the wrongdoer. 'Not born to be caged,' *Pa* had explained as we rode through the countryside, freeing these beautiful cats from hunters' traps. 'Caracals kill not for fun. They take only the weak.' I listened and learned about fairness and empathy in the hunt – qualities seldom witnessed in war. Fairness and empathy had certainly not brought us here to this cold, inhospitable mountain.

'It is in sharing everyday tasks that we learn best about sameness and differentness,' *ouma* Susara's wisdom came to me, and here, around the fire, we practised exactly that. We roasted meat, and Johanna explained why it should be cured under saddles, 'So it would not rot in the hot African sun,' and when the men looked on in distaste, 'This is how it is kept edible, and this is how you survive on the run like our men.' Both soldiers grew up on Sydney's streets in homes that were always denied the joy of having plenty. Both were well-acquainted with competing with many for access to food, but neither knew much about living off the land.

'Sweat and heat from your horses will cure the meat and boost our supply on this journey, however long it may be,' Hannie and Lettie elaborated on the preservation process, which saw our menfolk sustain themselves for weeks and months away from home.

Williams, barely eighteen by my reckoning, shook his head vigorously, 'I will not eat it!' His horrified expression told the truth about an opposition army's reliance on and belief in a never-ending food supply.

There was nothing more to say, but we heard our sheep's bleating again as they were driven away from Morgenster to feed the enemy.

The children fell asleep without complaint, their arms and legs lashing out occasionally, cradled by mothers restless in pregnant half-sleep after the previous days' horrors.

'Tether your horses and get some sleep,' I spoke softly, not to disturb others or draw attention from those wandering around in a war fought wherever it presented itself. When that was done, Presgrave and Williams came to sit around a lifeless fire. A rare communal spirit among enemies made itself at home; a spirit as evasive and secretive as the mist dancing on Morgenster's dam.

We sat in peace for a long time, each contemplating the day's events, but were brought back to the present when *Ma* cried out in her sleep. When I touched her forehead, I knew immediately the dark days behind us paled in comparison to the course that lay ahead.

Out in the sparsely populated countryside, a home pharmacy, or *huisapteek,* in effect, becomes a doctor in every home. Apart from medicines that could be bought from any general store, home-made remedies for anything from whooping cough to cuts and abrasions found a place in the *huisapteek.*

Afrikaner women have been sharing practical medicinal recipes and remedies for generations, with no remedy too absurd or far-fetched to follow and try at least once. Ours contained the best tried and tested remedies of salves, powders and elixirs to relieve all ailments. From our *huisapteek,* my older sisters and I selected Lennon's Turlington, a brown liquid that was said to prevent infection, and Wonderkroonessens for pain to ease *Ma's* discomfort.

I tried to wake *Ma,* but her eyes seemed blank and unfocused. '*Ma,* you have to drink this,' I said, helping her into a sitting position. Lettie held her chin, rubbing her throat rhythmically like you would for an animal unable to swallow, but most of the medicine ran down her neck and was absorbed by her blouse. We tried again and again, to no avail.

I felt my heart shift with a deep sense of helplessness, and an overwhelming sadness came to sit like a stone in my chest.

I held *Ma* tight and rocked back and forth, back and forth. *How long would she hold on?* I did not know and did not care. For now, all I wanted was for her to sleep and get well.

But sleep, the eternal tease, became just a dream, as the evening star took charge in the west and the morning star faded in the cold of early light.

*'I feel very anxious about J., but I know the dear Lord will take care of him.
Oh! You cannot think what poverty and misery there is in the Transvaal, not
so much in towns as in farms. It is dreadful to see the homes burned down,
and not a living thing about.'*

Mrs John Murray to a relative. 1900

I was running in the long grass with the melodious lark's chirping and
singing so near, I could almost touch the flirty little birds in their loopy
flight. *Up the hill we go, up and over!* Their happy song guided my feet to
the top of the hill and over, jumping weightless into the dark abyss as the
ground gave way to nothingness.

'Wait for me, little bird!' I called, floating deeper and deeper into the
dark, following the lark's song, *This way, Nelie, this way!*

I woke with a start in the semi-dark to find Hannie and Presgrave
speaking in hushed tones nearby, cautiously getting ready to go. I looked
around sleepily and could see women and children outlined, crouching.
Williams, gagged and bound, lay on his side at the back of the shallow cave.
My eyes met Presgrave's, but he shook his head. A few larks' alarmed tunes
reached us from the grassy plain below.

'Nelie, we have to go,' Hannie said close to my ear, her breath warming
my cheek. Between her and Lettie, they gently removed *Ma* from my cold
arms while everyone else was clearing away signs of our stay. Presgrave held
a finger to his lips as he lifted a wriggling Williams onto a horse, and then
Ma's seemingly lifeless body onto his own.

'Ride with her,' he said and helped me up to lead side-saddle, arms
around *Ma*. The others formed a human snake behind.

A swarm of larks flew overhead with their happy chirping now a shrill
warning. Presgrave held up five fingers, pointing to the valley below where
we left *Ouma*, and followed that with a shrug - too dark to know who was
following. In the moment of quiet communication, loyalties shifted, and I
sensed he could be trusted with our wellbeing should we meet up with the
khakis.

I touched his hand to confirm his own wellbeing should we meet up with *burghers; now was a time for* safety and speed.

A chance encounter with soldiers would severely curtail our efforts getting to Klerksdorp's newly built hospital.

Ma leaned heavily against me, and Hannie walked next to my horse to explain in hushed tones how they had found Williams scrambling downhill from where we came to find the British Army, without even knowing which soldiers were swarming in the valley below. It didn't escape me that if they were black, we would be dead now. Known for their tracking skills and brutal treatment of prisoners, they had to be avoided at all costs. It was a simple truth, observed without malice.

I knew the sun-facing cliffs well, but not the rocky western side. 'Stay behind me,' I said and held the horse on short rein, then guided the group towards the western slopes where *Pa* and I had seldom ventured and on their nighttime visits to Morgenster, Daan and Jan had described them in detail. As they had said, the stones soon turned into boulders, and visibility dropped to just ten feet. One antelope pathway skirted the boulders, trodden mostly by the shy and agile Cape bushbuck. As we moved slowly where sunrays seldom fell, the sheer drop of my dream-abyss was made real by wet, slippery stones and inaccessible antelope paths that led nowhere and forced us to back up and reroute. That our journey would be difficult, if not impossible, was sure.

Afrikaner children are born into a culture of respect and obedience, and that has stood us in good stead now. Their silence behind me, interspersed with dull hoofbeats, was their patient acceptance of adult wisdom and the unusual circumstances no amount of crying would change. If nothing else, respect, obedience and faith would win this war.

My spirits lifted in celebration of our faith, which dictates that no burden would be laid upon us that we would be unable to bear. As a nation, we took heart in the belief that an outcome was pre-ordained.

For five days, we negotiated the treacherous antelope path, which seemed never-ending. Where the tree canopies fought the sun for ownership, I dismounted and carefully led the horse until we came to a clearing. Along the way, we often rested to eat so as not to overexert Hannie and Lettie. It was safer on the western slope, and we could make a fire and brew coffee with no fear of being detected.

On the sixth day since we had left the cave, we dismounted several times.

During a stop, we inspected *Ma's* foot and found it purple and swollen, twice its normal size. I leaned forward and pressed it gently. Yellow pus oozed from multiple scars, with the smell of decay rising offensively. 'Gangrene,' Presgrave said close to my ear. 'I've seen this happen to injured soldiers, Cornelia,' he said, wiping his face resignedly, sighed and sat beside me. 'How many days to Klerksdorp?' he voiced my deepest concern.

'That I do not know,' I explained, glancing at the sun, which faithfully guides feet to their destination. 'Maybe three,' and with that unsettling guess hanging over us, we made camp and settled for the night.

Every evening when the others were asleep, Presgrave came to sit at the fire. First, there were no words between us, and then his life before war took on form in the hesitant telling of a boy, always concerned about the defenceless, the shy and the meek.

'I was born in far-off Tonbridge - a small town about thirty miles south-east of London. My parents, Edward and Elizabeth, left the miserably cold and wet shores of England behind for sun, sand and sea.' My heart felt heavy as he explained the hungry years after their sea voyage to Australia. His hands and scarred knuckles clearly bore evidence of many street fights. He looked down, hands wringing. 'The bullies often took our food,' he said, and told of similarly hungry immigrants from all over the world who had made Sydney their home. 'We were always hungry, and food was scarce. Many people speaking languages we could not understand, fought us for food at Sydney's markets.'

Life was hard with two older sisters and two younger brothers to feed. 'My mother slaved away in a fashion she would not have in England, and Father changed jobs often and drank away what little there was to spare,' he painted a picture of a family indisputably different from mine. But the story sprang from lips used to laugh at life's challenges, and eyes confirming an inner strength not ordinarily found in someone so young.

'My friend and I learned food was there for grabbing. That's how we filled our stomachs,' until war broke out in South Africa when he was nineteen. He bore the unsafe Atlantic Ocean journey resignedly, and his father, who proclaimed, 'War is food and freedom, Son.' But war proved much worse than fighting bullies.

'Is it not time to call me Edward?' he changed the subject with eyes downcast, and I took his hand and held it for a long time that night.

In its warmth was a promise that wiped away any lingering strangeness between us.

We woke to a brilliant sun the next day. Mid-morning, the horses suddenly became skittish, and even though we covered their eyes, they would not move forward. Ahead, a narrow pathway led into dense undergrowth where it was impossible to see much. With no other route to escape capture, we had no choice but to forge ahead.

I reined the horse in sharply. 'Leopard,' I said, pointing to finger-like brown scat at the path's edge. Had a sunray not fallen on it for the shortest of moments, I would've missed it altogether. My scalp crawled at picturing this elusive, cunning hunter, strong enough to hunt and carry a human of Sophia's size. Everyone remained still, hearts beating in our ears.

To scan the bush ahead was senseless - the veld's disguise king would not reveal itself, and more so when on the hunt.

Pa and I had sometimes come upon big cat scat, but never face-to-face, as these wily spotted hunters became wise to the gun's unfair advantage during encounters and chose hunting grounds far from humans.

'You have to appear tall, Nelie,' he had explained how to escape a leopard. On those occasions, we stayed on our horses, waved our arms and held our hats high, while shouting at the top of our voices, but the cats never once revealed their presence.

On another day, we had discovered a half-eaten bushbuck high up in a camelthorn tree, the favourite pantry for mountain leopard. The smell of the wild hung thick in the air, and our horses became fearful like Edward's, forcing us to backtrack slowly and leave before dark when the leopard hunts.

According to *Ma, oupa* Dewaldt had often relayed tales of the time after the First Boer War in 1881, the year before I was born. Leopard had roamed these hills in larger numbers then. It was a time of great suffering when man and beast competed for food, even though war produced many dead and left-for-dead feeds. 'Once a leopard has tasted human flesh, it won't go back to hunting antelope,' he had warned. There was no credible reason why some would not be alive and sheltering in these hills now.

'Gather the children to walk two-by-two in line between the adults and bring up the rear with the other horse,' I whispered and dismounted, holding tightly onto the reins.

The leopard would already have been aware of our presence, more so if used to the smell of injury, and *Ma's* foot was like a beacon on the hill.

'Now, don't stop, no matter what,' I said, looking over my shoulder. Then we ran straight into the dark, dragging the horses with all our might, shouting and waving our arms like windmills. The din we made was deafening, but in the face of a deadlier foe, the noise was irrelevant. When the woods suddenly gave way to a sun-bathed grassy clearing, the children sagged to the ground, laughing wild-eyed in high-pitched relief. *Ma* sat bent while Williams moaned loudly in his uncomfortable face-down position. Hannie stumbled to the nearest one, leaned against it, and circled her heavy stomach with one arm. Lettie cried out in alarm and rushed to her sister's aid, helping her sit more comfortably on the ground.

This journey has only just begun, I thought, as Hannie kept rubbing her stomach at this first warning of a baby soon to arrive.

Edward busied himself loosening the straps around Williams but watched me closely. I nodded in agreement. Williams would not run back through the woods, but there was no telling what he would do downhill towards Klerksdorp. That was a chance we had to take. Already, the ridge began to give way to a gentle decline. If we travelled at a steady pace, our journey could be over by evening, I estimated.

Used to hard work and many challenges at Morgenster, Hannie straightened, hand on back, and called the children. 'This is our day,' she said in a tired voice and started walking. Seeing my concerned face, she said, 'I know my body. Let's go,' and we stood, dusted ourselves and started downhill, stopping often to scan the veld for unwanted attention.

A sad little group, uneasily bound by necessity.

'When the troops came, they were ordered to give up all their supplies.... "If anyone is to suffer, you must be the ones to suffer, not we," they said. If she had not previously secreted a little meal under a mattress, the baby must have died, as she was not nursing him herself.'

Mrs John Murray to a relative. 1900

We continued our journey towards Klerksdorp, the town which straddles Schoonspruit River, aptly named for the beauty surrounding its clear waters. Many buildings lined both banks, creating a beautiful yet peaceful scene. It took many hours before the triple-story stock exchange building came into view through a far-off haze.

From our vantage point on the lower slopes, the last few miles seemed an impossible journey.

When the cooler air on the plains touched our tired legs at last, we had to support Hannie, getting her to shelter under the umbrella-shaped shade of a camelthorn. 'The baby is near,' she said, panting, her usual tightly platted hair hanging in wet strands beneath a wide-brimmed *kappie* – our cherished Afrikaner bonnet that shields faces from a fierce African sun. That unfriendly sun was now directly above.

'Ride to Klerksdorp for a wagon; any transport,' I urged Edward, whose hesitancy questioned the wisdom of leaving women and children with Williams. 'We will tie up the pony,' Lettie said, keeping a watchful eye on the young soldier who had displayed no loyalty but to himself during our journey.

As the long winter grass swallowed Edward's horse, and the sun withdrew in the west, a tiny little girl was born without so much as a whimper, forced into a hateful world far too early. She lay swaddled in the only baby blanket she would ever own, her unseeing eyes squinting at a mother exerted to breaking point.

For a moment, *Ma's* eyes opened. '*My meidjie,*' she said softly, expressing a grandmother's love completely with the endearing term, before falling into a feverish sleep.

'Eva. I name her Eva,' Hannie whispered, kissing Eva tenderly. *The Living One, but for how long?*

Following tradition, the second-born girl in a family should have been named after the maternal grandmother. The baby should have been named Sophia, after our mother, who blessedly, in her other-worldly sleep, knew no hurt at the unintended slight.

While wiping the tiny forehead with tired, shaking hands, Hannie noted, 'Where is Williams?' In the busyness of the moment, he had vanished into the semi-dark. *What if he took some of our things?!* The children gathered our bags and counted them. We still had our clothes and medicines, but no provisions or water. Nothing to eat or drink, and Klerksdorp so near; yet so far.

The sharp '*kwêh*' of a go-away-bird in the branches above warned about movement nearby. Hunters loathe the company of these slow-flying birds, but from experience we knew they are loyal to the weak and defenceless, and what else were we? Used to its ways, we immediately fell silent, crouched and huddled around *Ma* and Hannie, secure under the bird's watchful eye.

We could hear many hoofbeats approaching, then they stopped no more than twenty yards from us. The go-away-bird was running from branch to branch in its cat-like manner, stopped, cocked its head and watched the *Khakis* on horseback. 'I left them here!' we heard Williams, as he directed the English troops. The uncertainty in his voice transferred to the horses milling around in confusion.

'Spread out to Klerksdorp!' came the order, giving the go-away-bird respite from his intense watch. We waited a long time, cramped and exhausted, for Edward's return, but there was no sign of him. We waited some more. Later, Jackal started howling and yapping on the gravelly slopes behind us, and an owl took over the night watch high up in the tree, but still no Edward.

'I will fetch help,' I said, my uncertainty about a woman by herself in the dark hidden by a firm voice, 'And will come back for you,' I promised. 'God be good to you until then.' We needed transport, but a few miles can seem far in the dark, and finding transport in Klerksdorp, even more difficult than crossing the mighty Vaal River's grey waters. I was the only one in our group who had travelled this far at night.

I stood and slung the rucksack over my shoulder.

Lessons learned in youth seem to take prominence when faced with a dire situation. Being a son of the veld, *pa* Andries could hunt in far-off fields at night, then follow the stars to find his way back to Morgenster. On the day I turned ten, he handed me the .22 rifle and said, 'Nelie, the expanse is your map at night; always look up for guidance, never down where others have trodden.' After that, he would remain at our campfire while I hunted alone and learned about the dark's trickery in distorting the veld.

Remember, this is just another night hunt, Nelie. With the moon hidden behind the sun in its new moon phase, darkness came suddenly and fully, but its trickery soon waned as the stars grew brighter without competing with it. To find Klerksdorp in the semi-dark, I first had to find south. 'Find the Southern Cross. It displays five bright stars - the brightest at its tail points south,' *pa* Andries had explained, his finger tracing the crosslines between the four outer stars, which, when followed, are true north/south, east/west pointers.

I looked heavenwards and found the Southern Cross pressing down on me in its closeness. Without the moon's help, it was the best guide for feet born to the Highveld's grassy plains. There was no time to waste; their light would fade soon.

I adjusted my rucksack and, moving slowly, followed the Cross north – firm in my belief that I was watched over.

'Only a few lines to tell you that I was taken and sent to Sanna's Post.
Now we are all here in a tent; old Aunt N. and my sister also.
The latter they brought here with her three little sons.
They would not even allow her to bring her baby.
Oh! Unless God come to help us,
I do not know what is going to become of us.
I must perish in my misery.'

A mother, Bloemfontein Female Prisoners' Camp

I sensed some presence close by, barely 200 yards into the journey. 'Always take a moment to listen, Little Bird, and your path will become clear,' I remembered *pa* Andries's lessons and listened.

In obedient sympathy, the night opened its arms to the grandest song. Close by, the *tok-tokkie* rhythmically tapped out its beetle mating-call, undisturbed by human movement. A cricket choir near and far joined their soprano voices, with the spotted eagle owl taking up the base with its *hoot hoo-hoo buhoohoo-hooo*. Far off, a few jackal howled their hungry despair, scouting a landscape already stripped bare by the gun.

Relief flooded me. I could hear only familiar night voices. Then all fell silent mid-song.

Hunters know the chilling split-second when hunter becomes hunted. Inexperience and indecision in such moments littered a thousand miles of African soil with sun-bleached bones. Here, knowledge mattered.

I stood still, one foot in the air, my breath a mere whisper. 'Storks stand on one leg to catch fish,' Daan took over the lesson. We, the younger ones, learned how to be storks and stand still for a long time, moving only our eyes until the fish swam between us in the dam at Morgenster. 'That's when you strike!' he said.

The slightest human odour revealed an enemy close to my right. *Closer, a little closer.* I held my breath, then struck out with my strong arm, but stronger arms caught me from behind, one hand over my mouth.

Like a cornered lioness, I tried to fight night's enemy but was held firmly. *What will become of the others if I don't return?!* I struggled wildly.

'Little Bird, be quiet,' *pa* Andries whispered my name reassuringly, then slowly attack became a gentle embrace. 'What on God's earth are you doing here by yourself?' We sagged in the long winter grass. I could tell we were not alone by the soft rustling as other weary bodies sat down in the dry winter grass.

The mystery of Edward's disappearance became clearer as *Pa*, Daan and Jan explained in hushed tones how their small commando, together with others in the area under General De Wet, was moving south towards the Cape Colony. Around us, *burghers'* shiny German Mausers became distinguishable in the starlight. My heart stopped racing in the assurance that their excellent marksmanship and the Mauser's 2000-yard accuracy would keep us safe.

The unwarranted and bloody First Boer War of 1880/81 taught *burghers* many valuable lessons - now refined, tried and tested. To move around undetected in numbers among the enemy was made possible by the commando formation, which drove home an attack as a loose swarm, intent on outflanking the opponents. With the dark moon its faithful helper, the system worked in their favour tonight, and I knew many others scouting the English movements would be nearby.

Joining the First Boer War as a youth, *pa* Andries had the experience and knowledge of his old hunting grounds. His intent tonight, heading the scouting expedition that included my young brother Andries, was to find the enemy, then, just before daylight, the commando would approach under cover of dead ground to get within effective rifle range.

The *burghers,* in their everyday clothes, would gallop into the nearest dead ground, dismount and open individual fire. Speed, initiative and self-reliance were the keys to their ongoing success against a foe still focused on columns and formations, and all their movement decided on from afar.

It was while scouting the valley floor one mile shy of Klerksdorp earlier in the evening, that *Pa's* patrol came upon a British war-horse tied to a thorn bush and its owner shielding underneath. On this occasion, nature treated a foreigner unkindly - the dark moon's unwillingness to guide this humane soldier to his destination made my heart ache for Edward.

'The *Khaki* was sleeping, Nelie!' *Pa's* voice sounded incredulous that any soldier could be so careless.

'That's how they are,' he spoke the language of Boer soldiers, by now used to British mounted troops who were mostly deficient and constantly changing. 'Always waiting for the big generals' telegrams, they are,' he explained with a note of sympathy for an enemy robbed of their strength on the ground where it matters most.

'Where is he now, *Pa*?' I could not keep my concern out of my voice. His hand rhythmically rubbed my arm, warmly spreading the message that all was well. *How could you not see them coming, Edward?!* 'But where is he?' *Please be nearby! Please!*

'Nelie, and nów?' *Pa's* hand stilled, questioning my concern for a *Khaki*. And I explained our journey, Williams's traitorous behaviour, and Eva's arrival - another precious grandchild born in and of the veld. Words leapt sad as the fish eagle's cry from my lips in the telling of *Ouma's* departure from this life. He sat still for a while, then said, 'God be praised for her life,' his voice breaking with emotion. We wept quietly.

Like the hard crust that forms around an oft-beaten ox's heart until he accepts it stoically, so a soldier's heart becomes hardened at death's senselessness.

'We shall kill the swine!' he said with feeling, got up, slung the Mauser over his shoulder and motioned that we should go — dismissing unknowingly my chance to see Edward. 'You lead the way, Nelie.'

I turned towards the hills, where the camelthorn tree kept vigil in the stars' light. The knowledge of *Ma's* dire situation burned like a coal of fire in my stomach. How could I tell him such pitiful news now?

I retraced the Cross and judged the road to the camelthorn tree. The occasional clank of metal horse bits behind us was the only evidence that a larger group followed us. 'It is close to midnight,' *Pa* said close by. In my mind's eye, I could see his head tilted to judge time by the stars' position.

Within the hour, the camelthorn appeared like an elongated ghost just a few yards ahead. I reached back for *Pa's* stocky frame and pulled him close. 'They are under the tree,' I said softly, but he held me back as a warning against possible danger. 'Let me go first.'

In the fading light, dark swallowed him and left us behind in quiet agreement.

A short while later, a fiscal shrike's warning call forced an ingrained emergency lie-down in the long grass. I could hear riders quietly forcing their horses down behind me. We were in extreme danger. As daytime callers, shrikes reserve their warnings for seen dangers.

Only human mimics would do so at night, and *Pa* was the best one I had ever heard. We waited.

First came the *whoop-whoop* sound horses' stomachs make when filled to the brim with water. Then a hundred hoofbeats approached, muffled by sandy soil so close to the river. They stopped, unseen on the flat stretch between camelthorn and river.

'There is always a sign, Nelie, always,' Daan had explained the patience required while waiting for fish to reveal themselves. And then the sign came. From our low vantage point, we could see a tiny red glow moving up and down between hand and mouth. *This was not a hunter!*

I remembered the early hunting lessons learned well before a gun was placed in my hands. The night before a hunt, soap stayed dry in the soap dish, and *pa* Andries's pipe rested on the sideboard for more than a day so scent would not announce our arrival to a wily prey. We breathed easier – a careless foe could be avoided. Nature stood still for many minutes while we waited.

A horse's leather seat sighed and creaked as the rider dismounted and walked right up to our position to stand not more than twelve inches from my bent form. Small grunts came from above while the rider relieved himself in the grass. 'We've got to catch that bastard De Wet,' he spoke thoughtfully into the air, then turned and left. 'Southward, men!' The order came in muted tones, but to homegrown ears, it was a trumpet announcing the enemy's departure.

When the last hoofbeats had died down, Daan said, 'A hunter like that won't ever catch De Wet.' No one could argue the point while standing among the very *burghers* the enemy sought. I stood and led the way.

We found *Pa* sitting under the tree, arms wrapped protectively around *Ma*. In her arms, little Eva disappeared altogether beneath *Ouma's* soft down blanket, which kept the icy wind at bay. The dark's masterly skills hid the rest of our group perfectly.

'Where are the others?' Daan whispered in my ear, stirring a faint worry.

We walked cautiously around the tree, but there was no sign of the women and children.

I sat down next to *Ma* and took her hand. '*Ma. Ma,* what happened to the others?' She turned her head slowly. 'The *Khakis,*' she said. I squeezed her hand when the unimaginable became reality.

Kalahari Bushmen, on their eternal food-gathering travels, leave the old and weak behind out of love to die in peace. A heartless enemy on their mission to destroy Boer soldiers, abandoned *Ma* and Eva out of hate, but took the healthy who had the ability and potential to provide sustenance to *burghers.* After all, that's what Lord Roberts's scorched earth policy was all about - Boer republics were deliberately and systematically devastated to deprive *burghers* of food and shelter.

Pa Andries's cheeks were wet, and his eyes hard as crystal in the changing light. He knew, and he hated. I knew, and I hated with equal strength.

The stars were already withdrawing their shining - it was time to go.

'The method of taking these women from their homes was truly conspicuous for its barbarity. They were literally robbed of everything they had before being sent away; and I know women, once well off, who were carted about the country for months without once being able to change their dress.'

G.W. Goodwin

For two long hours, we travelled north towards Klerksdorp, scanning the landscape in dawn's early light. The two scouts *Pa* had sent ahead caught up with us when the sun sat above the treetops and reported that the town was abuzz with British activity. The sandstone station building quietly watched soldiers as they poured out of the early coal-dust-puffing trains from Krugersdorp to the north.

'The *Khakis* have taken the Transvaal, *oom* Andries!' the tale spat out wearily. Lord Roberts had achieved what others couldn't - proclaiming the entire South African Republic as British territory. The scouts' bent shoulders carried every *burgher's* disillusion. 'When?' *Pa* knew timing was crucial, not only for the commando's movements, but more importantly for *Ma's* wellbeing and my safety. What chance does an orphaned baby have, then?

'Yesterday, *Oom*. The trains brought the news,' the scout said, standing still for a moment in reverence, as the newly erected Nederduitsch Gereformeerde Kerk's bell announced Sunday service. *Pa* pondered with a far-off look in his eyes the likelihood of the British being organised while so euphorically celebrating. 'Today, the ox is in the well,' he said after a while, declaring his firm intention to get us women to safety even on a Sunday, the day of rest.

Daan and Jan, secret-sharing partners since youth, looked at each other, with the unspoken question of what to do about Edward, hanging expectantly in the air. *Pa* sighed deeply in recognition of love's inexplicable paths - once trodden, never forgotten – and relented. 'Bring the *Khaki*,' he said, his fatherly eyes watching a blush creeping unbid up my neck.

My heart's desire came to me, hands bound tightly. I stepped up and rested my head on his chest, where his galloping heart matched my own. 'My girl,' he said simply and rested his chin on my head.

Not given to grand displays of affection, the *burghers* shuffled their feet and lightly coughed their embarrassment to ants and beetles on the ground. 'Cut him loose, Daan,' *Pa* said, then held out his right hand in greeting. 'You have been good to my people, *neef*,' he used the familial term of acceptance.

In Afrikaner culture, *oom, tante, neef* and *niggie* intersperse conversations, whether they are related or not. By calling Edward' *neef,' Pa* invited and uplifted him to the status of a cousin within our family. In that happy moment, I thanked generations of Afrikaners who had fostered a respectful attitude in the endearing use of these terms.

When the church bell tolled its second call to worship, our rescue plan was firmly in place. Klerksdorp would be overrun by British forces intent on destroying the remaining Boer commandos, denying *burghers* free movement or access to the only hospital, built on countless church bazaars' gains and begged-for donations.

Ouma, always willing to give freely to society, knitted baby blankets and warm mittens until late at night while confined to a bed. The rest of us baked, canned and preserved for hours to support the effort. We sold and auctioned livestock as our family's contribution to the nation's health. We needed that care now but were unable to access it.

"Gather round, *manne*,' *Pa* called the men to attention. Each day started with prayer, as it did at home. Quietly, hats came off to give thanks and seek guidance in a war that refused to die down, 'As long as we live, Amen,' *Pa* promised in conclusion, and his voice was gruff in imploration for the nation's needs.

He explained our plight, which, in some way or other, was the plight of every *burgher* around him. Many trusting eyes turned to him for wisdom born of experience, and his tired voice revealed the price paid for this honour. Barely a year into the war, and every minute spent defending their country against a vastly superior enemy that outnumbered Boer soldiers six to one was slowly eating away at their strength. But never their resolve to succeed.

Never.

Edward would accompany *Ma*, Eva, and me to Klerksdorp to make sure we were treated at the hospital as a family unit and not separated. He could keep his horse, and I would have Williams's tenacious Burmese pony.

Edward was granted freedom for this duty - a gift from Boers who never willingly offered gifts to the English, least of all their country. The *burghers* would fight on and dared not risk capture.

Pa hugged the mother of his children for an eternity as if to pass on his strength. He tenderly wiped hair from the still beautiful face and kissed her gently. I embraced this strong man, crying wildly into his shoulder, with premonition's knowledge that his eyes would never again dwell on her beauty.

Daan, Jan, and young Andries said a solemn goodbye and helped me onto the horse, sitting behind *Ma's* saddle, holding onto her as before. Edward shook hands from the saddle, then lifted his slouch hat in silent greeting to the *burghers*, his left arm awkwardly cradling little Eva. With a light 'tsk-tsk', he spurred his horse into a slow walk.

We travelled slowly. *Ma's* face was as pale as a sun-bleached sheet, her once womanly body now reed-thin and swaying back and forth in the saddle. We had not eaten for two days and drank sparingly from our water bottles. What she needed was the life-giving maise porridge we used to have at Morgenster - cooked to a smooth, creamy texture over a slow fire. Time was not on our side, though. Klerksdorp was already close enough to see the church steeple and the three-storey stock exchange building, but *Ma* needed rest more than food.

Eva was making the kitten-like sounds hungry babies make, adding urgency to our journey. It had been nearly twenty-four hours since her birth. Babies born early just fade away without milk, not even crying much for it. I've seen it happen with sheep. 'We have to keep going, or she will die,' I said, trying to judge if we should go faster. 'Tell me what happened to you while we go.'

He explained how he became disoriented in the dark. Unfamiliar with the African veld, he became confused as the sounds of horse and man mingled with those of the wild - the source of which he could not guess. Fearing he may get lost or captured by his own people, he decided to wait for the sun to show the way.

According to *Pa*, it was a fate that had previously befallen many of Edward's fellow soldiers. A warm glow filled my soul when he said, 'I missed you, Cornelia.'

He continued, 'This cursed war will kill us all. Come with me; we'll go west,' he expressed a heart-wish with no future. I reached out to touch his arm in agreement, realising the futility of make-belief on a day like this. 'Best to remember what we have in our hearts,' I said, and we talked and made plans to be together as soon as his assignment was over in March the next year.

Before our horses left behind the thorny scrub for Klerksdorp's smoother streets, he laid out plans for building a life together under new British rule, which was bound to happen after the recent annexation. Workable plans if you're English; unworkable if you know an Afrikaner's heart, that will never let go of their beloved country. Fighting might not end for many years, and I told him so.

In the soldiers' hurry and scurry, our entry into town came unannounced. Before, my family had often come to town while the new hospital was being built. My younger sisters and I had played hide-and-go-seek among various rooms, just to be chased away good-heartedly by *oom* Abraham Bergmann and his sons, the builders living not far from here. 'Not a better builder for a thousand miles, Nelie,' *Pa* used to say, walking along the neatly built walls. 'Drunk as a lord in the morning, but never a skew brick,' he complimented the old man. 'Young Ampie has already learned the skills,' he hinted at a courtship carrying his approval. But in my bones there lingered the excitement and promise of the unknown.

Finding the hospital now was not difficult. Finding it without being noticed where traffic eased off, was a difficult task with severe consequences when caught. 'If we can get there unseen, the battle is half-won,' Edward explained.

With Edward leading my horse on short rein, weaving casually through pedestrian-, buggy- and horse travellers, we made it to the hospital unobserved. He helped me strap Eva to my back, and I waited on horseback, holding *Ma's* swaying body while he went inside to find a wheelchair.

Even though it carried the day's name, the sun was unkind and showed its face angrily even this early in the day.

I waited for a long time, not daring to call a passerby for help, but *Ma* was hanging limply in the saddle and sorely needed help. Then Edward emerged through the front door with a *Khaki* on either side, speaking animatedly, arms pointing first south, following the sun's path and coming half circle to point inside. Even deaf people would've known we were in serious trouble, but this is where we were – dependent on the ruler's goodwill. Rough hands helped *Ma* off the horse and carried her inside.

'Cornelia, we have to go nów!' Edward urged as he mounted his horse, sensing a few minutes' grace before the soldiers returned. 'They'll take you to Irene's killing fields!' he urged. 'Please, please, I've seen that place your God has forsaken,' he said over his shoulder before skirting the low horse trough out front and disappearing around the corner, leaving me with little choice but to follow.

Oh God, why do I have to choose between the one who gave me life and giving life to the little one?!

'Always choose life, Little Bird. In death we are near our Carer, but in life wé must care,' I heard *Pa's* voice. And we rode hard west among the thorn trees' hindrance and help, not looking back once.

In almost every case, these women, with their little ones, had been taken by force from their homes at a moment's notice. They have not even been allowed to take with them a morsel of food, or to be removed in their own carts.

Mrs Bodde, an English woman

For at least an hour, we rode through no-man's land west of Klerksdorp, galloping at first, then tired hooves slowed to a sluggish walk. Edward's round-hipped English charger swerved continuously through flesh-tearing thornbush, and Williams's little pony faithfully obeyed the stronger horse's call with a willingness that evaded me.

The veld's vicious disregard for foreign horses was evident all around in dozen upon dozen vulture-stripped carcasses. Horses in the allied forces' armies, so unaccustomed to the dry African landscape's sparse yield, perished in their hundreds each day wherever the war took them. As war's ever-willing participant, imported from the earth's four corners to their peril, showed in pursuit that their breeding had little value. 'Underfed and thirsty, 500 horses were ridden to death in one day earlier in the year at Kimberley's relief,' Daan said. 'Fools and brutes, all of them,' he gave his opinion of foreign soldiers used to lush climates and abundant forage.

As we rode on, I missed nature's voice, which was all but absent on the desolate flats. All around, lay a country stripped bare by a multitude of grass-eating animals, forced by war onto an unappetizing dry grass diet; a veld mostly trodden to dust. But the signs of insufficient water belonged to this moment as well. It showed clearly in the well-bred charger's protruding ribs and hip bones.

'It's not what sprouts from the soil that gives animals the will to live – it's what comes from the sky,' *Ma* had explained on a pancake-weather day, sunken deep into her favourite chair, coffee in hand. Rain came down in grey sheets around the veranda where we always had pancakes to celebrate the first spring rains.

A peaceful silence hung in the air, while big raindrops played *old-maidens-with-knobkieries* on the dam out front. Every drop showed off with big splashes until they danced together in continuous rain.

In silence, she relived why *oupa* Dewaldt had chosen 2000 morgen of land stretching over the mountains, from the high country in the west where old Jacob was tending the ten ewes and ram now, to the valley floor below the dam. All sentences were preceded by a sip of coffee, a slow run of tongue over full lips, followed by the minute details and sweetness surrounding *oupa* Dewaldt's love affair with Morgenster. The story was made more poignant in its mirroring of her own life journey - water-rich Morgenster always at the centre.

Between the sway and bump of a pony ride, I thought about my grandparents' tale, part of which all Afrikaners have since claimed as their own – the *Voortrekker's* arduous journey south to north across a harsh land.

Together with 400 Boer families, the *Voortrekkers* had left the picturesque Graaff-Reinet in the Cape Colony in 1835.

'The greatest pests in Africa are drought, locusts and *Rooinekke*, even today,' *Ma* described the English. The intense dislike of a meddling English government made her voice sound tinny and hard-edged, as if she were part of the trek. 'I was not even born yet,' she said, rubbing her neck cautiously as though she could feel the English *Rooinek's* sunburn.

'They trekked into the inhospitable hinterland, crossing fearsome and fast-flowing rivers and mountains where no wagon had ever made its imprint. It was on this trek that we Afrikaner women learned to be self-sufficient, Cornelia,' *Ma* explained the origin of a *huisapteek* in each wagon.

Her voice became raspy as she recounted the hazardous conditions in the open veld, where wild animals abounded, and how the Trekkers struggled to reach a site suitable for peaceful existence.

She also described how the *Trekkers* fought the vicious Matabele tribes in their path. The way she put her cup down with precision was reflective of the common-sense approach to life adopted by Boer women - refined in the moment of loading and reloading old Sanna rifles and heavy elephant guns in these fights, where the bond of love between man and woman was cemented in passing and receiving loaded rifles.

Ma's eyes became hard, and determination made its home around her mouth. 'That journey tested our forefathers' faith, Cornelia,' she said and continued telling of the most important day of the trek.

Early on the morning of 16 October 1836, *oupa* Dewaldt and his friends - the strong and youthful backbone of the party - drew the wagons in a tight circle, lashed wheels and filled the gaps with thorn bush.

With 5000 Matabele warriors waiting and hissing their displeasure outside the laager, a vast silence opened time for prayer inside. For many hours, the sun looked on, and then, suddenly, they charged. The way she told the story, I could follow the warriors, ostrich feather headdresses and animal skin furs flying, and *assegai* spears beating shields in rhythm with their killing song, '*Bulala, bulala*!'

A tough spirit was born on the day that was finally spent at sundown. 500 Matabele and two Boers lay dead on the dusty ground. This time, *oupa* Dewaldt said a prayer of thanksgiving and led the shaken group in singing Psalm 118, '*Loof, loof de Heer met lofliederen.*' One day's hand changing a youth into a man.

By the campfire, with the evening star bright in the sky, he went on one knee in front of *ouma* Susara. First, proposing and then wedding the only love he would ever know, sealed hand-on-Bible in front of those present. 'Their souls were pure white like angel wings,' *Ma* described *oupa* Dewaldt and *ouma* Susara, who adopted her as a baby and, with love, made her their own.

Years of endless trekking ended for many when Potgieter, their stubborn leader, continued his explorations, leaving most behind. But on a tired, disillusioned day in 1838, the remaining group came across a meandering stream with clear, sweet water where *Oupa*'s horse, Abel, walked into the river and stood chest-deep, snorting his pleasure, throwing back his head and breathing deeply in true reflection of one who is called Breathing Spirit.

No whistling or calling could move him into action. Then he started swimming downstream.

Oupa and *Ouma,* with earthly belongings still on their backs, followed him on the riverbank, their youthful legs carrying them around the bend and up a rise where Abel finally stepped from the water - his soulful eyes looking south along an imaginary path to a lush, green valley in the distance where the river flowed unhindered.

'He is showing the way, Susara,' *Oupa* said, helping her to mount, and sitting behind her, he held the reins lightly, giving Abel freedom of choice.

About thirteen miles south-west, with the morning star already asking permission to sleep, Abel came to a halt. He nodded as if to say, 'Here is our home.' Their Morgenster.

The beautiful morning star vantage point still carries its name proudly after all these years. 'Until the *Khakis* came to take our pride,' *Ma* said in afterthought. After having heard this conclusion to the love story so many times, I got up to bake pancakes. But the wistful look in her eyes held me back, and I guessed there might be a never-before-heard chapter to the story. But I was wrong. 'Another day, Cornelia, another day,' she said softly and looked dreamily out over the dam.

In front, Edward's horse took a sharp turn, and the rounded hip's interrupted sway brought back the harsh reality of an angry landscape. The growing heat was chasing away all thought of a time and place born of love and devotion.

We left the thorny scrub behind to enter a pleasant plain, scattered with pink-blooming sickle bush, which cast their shadows on a once inviting green carpet. Over time, the invasive bush had changed to become a food source and shade. Here, they grew in abundance, seemingly pleading forgiveness for taking advantage of the space left by so many dead trees and shrubs all around.

'Why would they grow here?' Edward contemplated, sweeping the plain full circle.

'We are standing in an ancient riverbed where ordinary trees had given up hope of quenching their thirst over millennia. Even though farmers dislike the tough, invasive sickle bush, it is the medicine chest of the veld,' I explained and continued that not only could every part of the tree be used for one medicine or the other, but its leaves gave sustenance to animals in times of drought. As firewood, it was rivalled only by the rooibos that grew in the Bushveld to the north.

'Our horses may not like to feed from treetops, but we can help them,' I said wearily. My arms were heavy with exhaustion, but I indicated where we should cut the soft, feathery leaves for fodder.

Our priority, though, was feeding a weak newborn, then only could we rest.

Edward spread *Ouma's* blanket in the shade and gently took Eva from me. My tired legs carried me to the shade.

We sat, total exhaustion just a breath away.

Eva's tiny little body looked so still. I rubbed her cold, clammy skin, but hope for signs of life faded when she didn't react. This was the hour of truth: *The Living One will cry no more.*

Oh, God, this war has taken infinitely more than its share! I lay down beside her, and my soul gave up the fight.

I heard someone call me again and again as if from afar. I opened my eyes. A butterfly flitted past on fairy wings - tentative and near imperceptible - its flight seemingly the only promise that life was more precious than death.

'Nature's milk,' I spoke the words to bees swarming around the pink canopy above. But the silent workers took no notice, not even of the butterfly.

'Cornelia, don't give up - she needs milk,' I heard Edward, as he gently shook me to the present. The unbelievable had happened - Eva's little butterfly hands were doing a slow dance right in front of me! No, it could not be. Would God be so cruel as to take her away and then, without warning, bring her back to life?

In my dream-like state, I heard the monotonous cry of the honeyguide closeby. The sound was real, unlike Eva's moving hands.

My head cleared, and then my heart stopped. Eva was moving! And the honeyguide was calling. I sat up.

'Edward, stay still!' I warned, now fully awake, and scoured the sickle bush for signs of movement. Almost imperceptibly, the insignificantly coloured beeswax-eater revealed himself on purpose, darting from branch to branch, every time a little further from us.

'Stay with Eva,' I pleaded and unhurriedly followed the veld's teaser, tightening my *kappie* as I went. 'Slow down, slow down!' I informed him of my tired legs, but he danced, swerved and dived out front, deciding the pace with no consultation, yet telling the world he was in charge with his unflattering song. Up a slight rise and over stony ground, he led to sit in the low branches of an ancient, gnarly camelthorn; at its base, bees buzzed in a dark swarm.

I had witnessed firsthand how a weak honey-tea could save lives in this unforgiving land.

In the mountains of the high country where old Jacob and Pikanien were looking after the sheep, wild honeybees have been making their homes for an eternity.

There, we had often raided their hives as children.

'No bee colony shares its bounty willingly,' Daan had reminded us for the umpteenth time in spring when pollen-laden bees flew past our home from dawn to dusk. 'Always leave enough combs for their survival,' he said when we came home with hats and aprons bulging and laughed good-naturedly when cramps left us sorry for our thievery.

Hannie and Lettie's swollen faces always carried the deed for all to see, but angry, wild bees were not selective and made victims of us all. For days, they would sulk and complain, while Daan and I merely scratched a few red patches after having smoked vicious colonies into submission.

Today, there was no escape from the smoke. Today was made to save a life. I removed the *kappie* and loosened my hair to hang like a face-covering. With a penknife firmly in hand, I boldly stuck a hand into the opening. Inside, row upon row of old honeycomb seemed alive with enraged bees. With one hand cutting and the other steadily pulling, dark brown combs came loose, dripping with honey the colour of a leopard's eye. I wrapped it hastily in the *kappie,* leaving a thank-offering for the honeyguide, and found my way downhill as fast as I could.

In answer to Edward's question, I explained that, between deep breaths, we needed a small spout, and for that, his army-issue spoon would do. My fingers trembled as we uncorked his water bottle and mixed some honey in the tin food bowl issued to all allied forces. Eva only needed to swallow. That would be a miracle, but once a weak lamb had lost their ability to suckle, the will to live was already forsaken. We could not allow this little lamb to give up.

'Hold her up,' I said, giving direction to hands more used to war's rough tasks than handling a baby. Eva's little bald head looked so fragile in Edward's cupped hand. Her tiny rose-petal lips opened and closed slowly, defying life's eternal thief in its silent cry.

Drop by drop, the honey tea found a new home, and all the while Edward rubbed her cheek softly until she swallowed. Her unfocused eyes opened for a second, but that was enough.

With foreheads pressed together, we cried silent tears of gratitude. Exhausted and without much hope for our future, Eva's small feet walked into our hearts to make us one.

Here, among the bones of the dead, life received a chance.

9 – Unforgiving Veld

'This little brown wooden box, together with a larger black lacquered box, which has a dark red interior, was made in China. It was meant for a Chinese woman who was intended to travel to the United States to join her new husband, Lee B. Lok, who had immigrated to America with an uncle in 1881.'
Cornelia Bergmann

We lay on our backs, shielding Eva between us from a late-season cold wind that was creeping uninvited into our warm, sunny place, stealth and menace foremost in its mind.

'This is how we'll find water,' I shifted to give shoulder blades a softer bed and indicated with a lift of eyebrows where his focus should be. 'The birds will tell us,' I sighed an acceptance of a city boy's ignorance. The cold wind had already announced its intentions, and night was drawing near. I knew from experience that we should take note, find sustenance and warmth in what was promising to be a bitterly cold night on the riverbed.

'Follow their winged path, and we will find water,' I explained the birds' daily routine. 'They always quench their thirst before finding a branch for the night.' We felt contentment in the routines of those around us - a mellow moment when nature eats, drinks and rests. The horses added to it as their heads moved rhythmically up and down, sharing a sickle bush feast - one elegant, the other stocky. 'They have good parents, bred from strong bloodlines,' Edward commented. In an instant, contentment had disappeared, and an unwanted memory stepped into its place.

'Even good parents can't always protect their children from harm,' I heard *Ma*'s long-ago voice, as she gently removed two trampled chicks from a nest late one afternoon when out gathering eggs. 'Why couldn't she sit on her own nest?' she bemoaned the careless actions of young hens, unaccustomed to fowl etiquette.

At that moment, the last sunrays shone a light on tears which quietly found their way over cheek and chin. She flicked them away with an irritated hand, but the hens' squawk and tuck-tuck allowed space to speak about her adoption.

She never revisited the topic again.

'It all began with chickens,' she said, shooing an old hen away with more force than the moment demanded. The story took us to Driefontein in the Marico district, her birthplace in 1853. With eyes looking inward where pain was seated deepest, she told how, on a balmy spring night, just after farm animals had gone to sleep, her parents were woken by a cacophony in the chicken coop a few hundred yards away. Thinking it may be a fox, her father grabbed his gun to investigate. After a while, her mother heard two shots in the distance.

The chickens were still unsettled, and the sheep were restless in their pen. *Ma*, barely able to crawl, woke and could not be soothed. She was still crying after half an hour.

'Shhhhhh, Sophia. Mummy will find out what has happened,' the mother promised and hurriedly went outside on that exceptionally dark night to look for a father who should've been home long ago. But an evil hand was waiting at the back door. One vicious blow to the head cut her life short but spared her eyes the sight of a slain husband, shot twice with his own rifle.

'All for the want of chickens,' *Ma* said, bending to gather more eggs.

I learned of concerned neighbours finding the weak baby Sophia in her crib after days on her own. 'Yes, even caring parents bring harm upon their offspring,' she said, her twisted view of parental care bound to the moment but revealing her unbelievably deep loss.

Oupa Dewaldt and *ouma* Susara were busy milking cows when an exhausted young man came galloping up the path, spreading the terrible news far and wide. By the grace of God and others' goodwill, baby Sophia found her way from Driefontein in the north-west to Lichtenburg, then to the farm Hartebeestfontein, where a kindly Lombard family took her in until a family of her own could be found.

Ouma removed her apron, smoothed her hair and said, 'Let's go, *my man*,' and without needing an explanation, *Oupa* left the milk pail where he was sitting to find Abel.

With precision and speed, Abel was inspanned and given the lead. That same day *Ma* came to Morgenster and a new home with *oupa* and *ouma* Niemandt.

'No baby was loved more than me, not then and not ever,' she concluded the story.

I looked at Eva's crumpled baby face and knew that could be said about any baby who is surrounded by loving parents. In this tiny, broken body lay the promise of a love that had the makings to cross oceans and climb mountains. And she was ours to love and cherish.

'They're flying upwind to the south,' Edward said, straightening to saddle the horses. It was so. Birds of all sizes strained silently against a southerly, flying low with determination. Where did so many birds come from in this barren veld? In the day's busyness and struggle, I did not once ponder the existence of winged life, but now these riverbed chameleons revealed themselves in flight.

Edward helped position Eva on my back, and we wrapped and fastened her with *Ouma's* blanket in the way black mothers carry their young – comforted skin-to-skin, leaving me hands-free. Then we followed the birds on horseback before dusk had settled in.

Any travellers venturing out this far into no-man's land would surely not have a choice or a planned journey and certainly be travelling light in haste. We were the fortunate ones travelling at a slow pace along the sandy snake's back. What meagre belongings we had were strapped to the saddles. My bag contained a few necessities and my precious Afrikaans Bible, small and thin in its leather coat, that swaddled the first three translated chapters. Bound, 'For a new generation's language,' *Ma* had said, happily paying at the church office for SJ du Toit's mammoth task. At the bottom of the bag was *Ouma's* handkerchief, which had fluttered forlornly on the ground the day she died.

Edward's mare carried a bulkier soldier's supply - rolled-up sleeping mat, eating utensils and equipment fastened to the saddle, and clothing, similarly rolled up and pinned in front of his saddle. A small oblong shape in its own bag made itself at home between baggage and saddle. Often during our journey, Edward's protective hand rested on what seemed to be the same shape and size as *Ouma's* jewellery box.

I patted my pony's neck and marvelled at a well-bred horse's strength and endurance. While fatigue sat heavily in our bones, the horses willingly stepped neck-on-neck where we directed. I leaned over and touched the oblong shape. 'Tell me about this,' I said, the gloomy day forgotten in expectation and inquisitiveness.

He sucked his bottom lip, as you would when thinking deeply on the wisdom of sharing what is hidden in your heart.

Eva made little noises and moved slightly in her heated blanket cocoon. I waited. 'His name was Lok Lee,' he looked fondly at me. My anticipation grew.

We kept following the birds while a story of human patience and love unfolded.

Lok Lee went to work as a dishwasher in New York City, and by 1891, after ten years of monotonous labour, he had worked his way into a management position at a general store in Chinatown – a store of mystery, selling dry goods, silks, porcelains, teas and herbs. Once a manager, he was allowed to travel freely to and from China at a time when travel by Chinese labourers was severely restricted. His longing for Ng Shee Lee, the patient bride-to-be, was made more palatable by these frequent visits.

Sailing the Atlantic during a return journey on a steamship overburdened with goods, they encountered a severe storm. 'Most of the passengers were lost, but Lok clung to a crate with a few earthly belongings strapped to his back,' Edward clarified and continued. Lok's bad luck turned into fortune, as a steamer from Australia with many volunteer soldiers on board was less than a day's sail away.

'The wind was howling, and mountains of water chased each other, but most of us were hanging over the rails to scan for survivors. Yes, me too. And my father.'

Understandably, living close to the beach in Sydney made Edward a strong, fearless swimmer with a good understanding of the sea's moods and whims. So, without hesitation and timing the waves perfectly, he dived overboard to save the barely breathing man.

Once rested, the short Chinese man came to stand close to Edward on the deck where sunlight gave life to weary bones. He squinted into the sun and said, 'You take; it make happy.' In his hands was an oblong wooden box, simple in design and made with care.

More than twelve years in America had exposed Lok to enough English to explain the Chinese lore that promised good luck to the family who looks after the prized wooden box. A box intended for the American house where his bride would eventually settle.

'Thus far, this wretched war has not taken the luck that came with the box. Look, I met you,' Edward said shyly, shifting in the saddle.

We came to a bend in the river where the horses took the lead at a canter. 'They can smell water,' I said and held the reins tighter. To our right, the riverbed was hollowed out, showing its once mighty flow. To the left, a few willows hung their arms over a waterhole, not much bigger than the tin bath *Ma* used on washday. 'People had once lived here,' I said of the surprise find.

'Willows are from the north,' Old *Meester* Riggs had told us. He knew all about the water-loving tree, having been a soldier from England in the First Boer War. His love for Klerksdorp called him to stay after the war and teach in the local farm school. Wisdom dictated his knowledge, not book-learning.

That's how we came to know about indigenous and non-indigenous trees, where they naturally grow and how seeds are carried around the world to become pests. Yes, people had once lived here.

Grateful to be unsaddled, the horses competed ankle-deep in the mud for water. Large numbers of birds flitted from branch to water - their skilful manoeuvres between hooves a lesson in warfare. Surprisingly, clear water rose to the surface from a spring that was most likely fed from deep underground.

As the wind died down and the sun dipped behind the riverbed's high side, different customers came to quench their thirst – the shy duiker, *its* big ears turning clockwise and anticlockwise in anticipation of a predator; guinea fowl, sounding their loud chatter in deafening excitement; the tough honey-badger, there for a more solid meal, showing no fear as usual.

We watched on in silence, and when the dark spread its fingers across the veld, Edward hog-tied the horses and led them away to the high riverbank that unselfishly shared a hollow large enough to protect us from the cold. There, we used Edward's sleeping mat and *Ouma's* blanket for a bed. Snuggled up, it was a good shelter.

With care, we fed Eva - now more alert after her warm passage - and tied the horses to a timeworn tree root, bent to the ground in its forgotten search for water. Roots lay scattered everywhere along the riverbed, disclosing a time of plenty, but now just a plentiful firewood supply.

We sat huddled under the blanket's protection, soaking up the fire's warmth, content in each other's company.

Edward reached into the dark behind us, and when he turned to the firelight, the wooden box was in his hand. He searched for mine and held it protectively to his chest, then placed the cherished box on my lap.

'I will wait forever for you; longer than Lok waited for his bride,' Edward promised, and in my heart, I knew I would wait more than a lifetime to be with this gentle man.

He patted the wooden box and said simply, 'This is yours now, my Cornelia,' and in that moment Ng Shee Lee's good luck was transferred.

10 – Rinderpest and Starvation

'…the order came for no oxen to cross the river on account of the rinderpest having broken out here. So these poor women are stranded on the flats with hardly any food and next to no shelter. They had been there for days when I heard from them, and I can't say if they have been taken on to Bloemfontein yet.'

Mr Rowntree

The stars were still bright in the sky when hunger and premonition forced me from our warm nest, premonition winning the race with nightmarish dream-visits of people never met.

'Why don't you learn, Cornelia? Never eat *biltong* before bed; it just causes nightmares,' *Ouma* had often scolded, totally ignorant of the unwanted premonition gift bestowed on me. At times, I greeted the day drawn and exhausted after a night's visions, but she had no patience with this. Never in her long life did she understand the supernatural. I could see her now, wagging an all-knowing finger to emphasise her point - a frown cutting her forehead in two. However, I had to reluctantly acknowledge that the culprit could indeed have been eating *biltong* the night before. Johanna, Sara and Martha's effort to preserve *biltong* weeks ago had been our only sustenance until the honeybird had shared his honey feast.

Our vegetable garden at Morgenster was regularly raided by rabbits, and it was up to my younger sisters to protect their hard work. They had learned the hard way how to thwart the wily scavengers, but once their methods had been perfected, the pressure was off me to hunt for hours at night. Before that, there was a lot of crying when the rabbits got away.

'The catching lies in stealth and patience, just like fish,' I said, while setting a tempting trap. 'What you need is timber, wooden spikes and a decent length of *Ouma's* wool.'

Out here in the wild, cunning was the only trap; here, the rabbits made the rules.

At the waterhole, a thin strip of green defied the elements. Closest to the willows, springhare burrows sat squat in the low riverbank, which allowed them to stay clear of trampling hooves.

Here, they could feed in the mornings when all was quiet.

The wildlife was not at all afraid of humans. The previous night, they drank unhurriedly and moved away at leisure, not skittish and wary of guns like the antelope hiding up in the mountains. I was hoping the springhare would be at ease too, as we had not seen any sign of human movement for many days. It made sense that most fighting should happen close to food and water sources, but this life-giving spring was so far from main roads that it was there solely for nature's use.

I approached the waterhole carefully with Edward's rifle already cocked and crept forward cautiously. Springhare, especially those conscious of intrusion, could jump six feet, just like the kangaroos in Australia which Edward had described, and be swallowed by the veld before the first shot. I blinked a few times to take aim, as there, in dawn's soft light, four grown hares tended the grassy patch, confident the day would be without predators.

Edward came running, while the two successive shots still echoed from riverbank to riverbank. I could hear Eva crying faintly, and a horse whinnied, sharing their alarm with birds that had made their home close to the waterhole. 'How can you take my rifle?!' he asked roughly, hair pointing in all directions, but his eyes showed more concern than outrage. I held up two springhares as a peace offering.

He relented, bent, looked closely, and with surprise said, 'They look like *skippies*,' comparing the springhare to kangaroos. He touched their long back legs and lifted the short front legs one by one, muttering something about rabbits not being rabbits. To me, it was only a meal to break the night's fast, but I explained the difference between a springhare and a rabbit anyway.

'It has to do with language,' I said, slowly pronouncing the Afrikaans word *haas*, and why all rabbit-looking creatures are called *haas* – *kolhaas*, *springhaas*, *vlakhaas* – not the same, yet the same in our eyes. 'Both *kolhaas* and *vlakhaas* are rabbits, one just bigger than the other, while a *springhaas* is not a rabbit at all, but grouped by many a farmer as the same nuisance in gardens and on the cornfields,' I explained.

'The springhare lives here at the waterhole because its long jumps are helpful to quickly get away from predators,' I said while deftly stripping skins.

'To my reckoning, Wolmaranstad lies south-west from here,' I calculated the logical route we should follow in between mouthfuls of roasted hare, but deep down wished we did not have to leave our peaceful spot. After Eva was fed, we discussed whether it was wise to enter a town that was established only nineteen years ago.

Logic dictated that its isolation far from service-rich towns would make it less attractive to soldiers from both sides. Our thinking was supported by sickle bush, which petered out the further south we travelled, taking sustenance with it. There was no other choice, and we had to leave for our own survival.

The sun was already five fingers into the sky before we started packing up. I bent over to pick up Eva, and in that half second, a slight movement downstream caught my hunter's eye. *An antelope!*

Two skinny hares could not feed us for long on this arduous journey, and not without water either. I put a hand on Edward's arm in warning, and slowly straightened, squinting for a focused look.

The antelope moved hesitantly, shy to reveal itself in distance-haziness and too far to be in any danger. The horses stood still, accustomed to waiting in silence when war required, with ears only turning to catch the sound of movement. Eva was content in full-belly slumber, so we waited and watched.

The well-known hands of foreboding held my stomach tight, as the figure slowly came towards us, stopping at intervals to listen and sniff the air. After each stop, our vision became clearer until Edward exclaimed, 'It's a human!' at the exact moment I recognised it as a boy.

'Take care of Eva,' I said, and he understood the necessity to comfort the boy in his own language.

My feet struggled to keep up with impatience, driven by a fear that was still gripping my stomach, but I ran as fast as I could through the thick sand. Early spring's heat was already upon us by the time I reached the boy, where his feet gave up the race – his body barely covered by tattered pants and shirt.

Oh, dear God, what had happened to him?!

The boy's old-man face hid his youth, and when I touched him, he opened the vacant eyes of one who had seen too much of life's wickedness.

'*Boetie,* where is your mummy?' I said and gently put my arms around him. A body that should've held onto the nourishment of wholesome farm food felt bony and cold. He leaned into me and sighed like someone letting go of life. '*Tannie, dáár,*' came his hoarse whisper. He pointed downstream towards Wolmaranstad.

Edward and Eva kept their distance as the two of us sat together for a while. Then we slowly made our way to the waterhole, where I fetched a portion of the morning's springhare meat. I felt deep empathy watching the boy take small bites – sparingly eating a feast which had clearly not been available to him recently.

Shame washed over me. Each day of this journey had provided us with its own nourishment, yet we became angry at our circumstances as soon as hunger struck. I stroked his hair in a plea of forgiveness for such selfishness.

When he had finished a piece of meat the size of his palm, he asked to keep some. 'We'll shoot another springhare,' I promised, but he shook his head vigorously, looking downstream. I touched his shoulder, and when he looked at me, the boy within was revealed briefly in his life-weary eyes.

He was not alone!

'Who is this for, my boy?' I asked, folding the leftovers into one of Edward's handkerchiefs, but something forbade him from saying more. He just sat there, rocking back and forth.

We rode downstream faster than on our approach to the waterhole. The horses were refreshed by muddy water and a respite from war's duties. Within the hour, we came to a bend where the long-forgotten river narrowed, carving high banks on both sides. The boy leaned forward in the saddle with anticipation. His breath came heavily from lungs constricted in agony, like someone eager to know the truth, yet unwilling to face it full-on.

There, under a camelthorn's sparse umbrella and the bank's hollow hand, a makeshift tent sat forlornly. An old blanket strung from tree to makeshift driftwood walls tried in vain to provide a semblance of protection from the elements. A crooked cross higher on the riverbank pointed to sadness and loss in this unspeakably desolate place.

As we came closer, the wind carried tidings of decay accompanied by a swarm of eager blowflies. Edward dismounted in one movement, holding Eva in the crook of his arm.

In concerned haste, the boy followed, fell in the soft sand and scrambled in a fatigued crab-like run to the nearest person. He threw his arms around her body, shaking her to and fro, causing blowflies to fly off in pursuit of a new home.

'*Mamma, Mamma!*' he cried, shaking her harder. '*Mamma, word wakker!*' he tried again, but her limbs were slack and her eyes blind to another day. He held her fiercely and cried the heart-wrenching wail of an abandoned cub with such sadness that I turned away. Deep down, the memory of abandoning *Ma* at the hospital would always remain to haunt me in such moments of child-like tenderness.

'Cornelia, help me,' Edward said, and gently turned me around to face the full reality. A dreadful scene of human suffering lay before us. Underneath the blanket's meagre protection, four adults and seven children lay on clean-swept ground, their belongings neatly stored around the edges to strengthen and support the flimsy walls. Each person rested in their own preferred position – a baby snuggling against a mother's breast; a grandmother with a Bible open on her chest; siblings holding hands with foreheads pressed together; mothers with protective arms around their young. The angel of death took them in the quiet moments with their God.

This was too much to bear, and I felt something tear inside. Was there even a God of mercy, one that would remove this suffering from our people!

But that God remained distant and did not listen to such disrespectful lamentations.

An awful task was assigned to us. With heavy hearts, we buried the family in loose sand where water would never flow again. The boy never once spoke until the last body was covered and given into the Lord's hand with prayer. Then he stood and slowly turned in a circle, scanning the area with more determination than a burial site justified.

'What are you looking for, *my kind?*' I asked, possessively and intentionally making him mine. He came to stand close to me and explained hesitantly that there were not enough graves to account for everyone in their party. An aunt, slightly older than me, was missing. And so was her baby.

'We have to search in circles,' I suggested and pointed to the sun that was already moving steadily west.

Eva, strapped to my back, was crying to be fed and would not be consoled. We too felt the lack of food and water, and more so after the day's hard work. Exhaustion, made worse by an all-consuming sadness, was never far away, but we hastily fed Eva with honey-water and left her in the boy's tired arms.

It was in the half-hour before sunset that we found the woman, curled up under a bush and clinging to her lifeless baby. She looked at us with the veil of starvation shrouding her blue eyes, but willingly allowed our supportive arms to walk her the few hundred yards to camp - the baby content in eternal sleep.

As we stumbled to a resting place under the blanket cover, the boy jumped up and cried, '*Bettie!*' nearly knocking us over in his joy. There, surrounded by the walls that gave shelter for five weeks, we made her comfortable against the wooden wall and fed her like an invalid with the remaining meat; her own baby silently cemented to a mother's protective bosom. The boy, eager to talk in the happiness of the moment, told how English soldiers *en route* to a concentration camp left the family to fend for themselves when more exciting war efforts beckoned.

'Dirk,' he introduced himself when I pressed him once more for a name and shook my hand solemnly.

Bettie cried out in her half-sleep, and as I sat beside her, she opened her eyes and, bewildered, pulled away. She looked at her baby and softly stroked the unresponsive little body until the light of understanding was lit in the deep blue pools. Sorrow has no measure, but in those motherly eyes a nation's sadness rested deeply.

I closed my eyes. No one should see such sadness. *No one* could ever be whole again after having seen such sadness. I held her tight until sleep took us both.

11 - The Vast Highveld

Contrary to the announced intention, Lord Kitchener states in a memorandum to general officers the advantages of interning all women, children and men unfit for military services, also Blacks living on Boer farms, as this will be 'the most effective method of limiting the endurance of the guerrillas (burghers) ...'
South African History Online

A cold wind found a path south to north across the barren veld.

I looked at the sky from my high-side riverbank position. During the night, strata clouds were painted in neat white lines as far as I could see. The southerlies often pick up pace at night, leaving the skies with feather-like clouds drifting without much competition. Just as often, the winds died down and left a stillness instead.

'Whistle, Nonna, whistle,' old Jacob had always advised on days when the wind stood still, and clouds echoed those now looking down on me. 'It comes, you see,' he would say with confidence in a superstitious belief, which required only patience to confirm its truth.

Not a day went by at Morgenster without a farm worker waiting patiently at the windmill behind our house, whistling a tuneless song to call the wind. We younger ones, tried it when no one was around, being surprised when it worked, and not realising that no day is without wind. Old Jacob would slyly look on, then slap his thigh and do a little dance which mimicked, 'There you go, it worked.'

Today needed no whistler. The wind held the promise of becoming stronger, and the clouds pledged no rain. It was going to be a hot and thirsty day. In all directions, the veld lay flat and barren, becoming undulating towards the blurry south, many miles away. We were already too far south to travel back for water at the spring, and to continue along the dry river towards Wolmaranstad might take many days.

Like other travellers before me on these African plains, the Highveld's vastness came rushing from all sides and put doubt forward as the only option for the day. My dress played along with the strong wind, making me feel more insignificant and needing help.

We had been travelling for five days since leaving Klerksdorp, accompanied by the forces that separate life and death. That we had survived this long was a testimony to the goodwill and care of a Higher Force – that I did not doubt. But here on the high riverbank, remorse for not reading my Bible once in all this time also took its rightful place beside me.

The gusty wind carried a lone go-away-bird overhead. I followed his path north, but as the wind slowed before gathering strength, he turned west, flapping vigorously in anticipation of another path-changing gust. But why turn off the waterhole path? I narrowed my eyes, but with a loopy dive, he disappeared over the horizon like birds often do - they fly and circle until something entices them, then dive down without warning.

If our little group had any chance of avoiding the misery of those now resting beneath a wooden cross, we had to find the sustenance hidden by these desolate plains. Under the blanket-tent, Bettie sat withdrawn in a curled-up cocoon, and Dirk had tired of fussing over Eva, who had fallen silent in undernourished sleep. The life-giving morning sun fought the ever-present fatigue that sat heavy in our bones. We moved wearily and without purpose around the camp in the aftermath of the burials.

'When there's nothing left to fight for, your soul will speak,' *Pa* had explained the hopelessness that injured soldiers feel after defeat in battle. He did not often revisit the First Boer War but kept the upsetting tales for life-lessons on our frequent hunting quests to the high country. The stories always came easier to him in the rhythmic roll of horse and rider among nature. After the men had departed for war duty, I remembered his guidance during the bitterly cold winter months, when lambs succumb to heavy frost and snow. That was the time *Pa*'s wisdom sustained and helped me to accept what was outside my control.

Now was such a time. I stood still for a while and waited for that elusive voice, and after a while, certainty grew about how to move forward.

'I have to know where the go-away-bird went,' I informed Edward, leading my pony in crab-like fashion up the steep bank, then mounted and unhurriedly made my way west. On the windy plains where the cold stirred up dust from the pony's path, and where war's cruel hands had seldom touched, a wholeness of mind was bestowed upon me - unsolicited, handed out to a weary soul.

I held my face to the sky and felt my Maker nearer than He had been in a long time. In the immenseness of the veld, prayer, which I had so often avoided, came freely at last.

At the point where the go-away-bird had disappeared, the land sloped down into dried-out grassland. The pony lifted his head and found a reserve of energy which took us on a gallop to the grassy plain's furthest reach. Like an omen, the wind suddenly changed direction to surge with a gust from the west, forcing the pony's ears back and my bonnet to fly in tandem with its windy tentacles. In that moment, I remembered *Ouma* Susara's attempt at imparting the wisdom surrounding the inevitable: should we run away from punishment, a strict mother would not let up. 'Running away from danger is always running towards a bigger danger,' she preached her truth. It didn't make sense at the time, but often when *Ma* caught up with us, the punishment was more severe.

Just as this valley was hidden from us on the higher ground, the deep ravine that opened and just about swallowed us was not visible until the last breath-grabbing moment. Its northern arm opened into a wide, shallow valley, becoming deeper and carving out a narrower south-western path. In front of me, a stand of tall trees held hands in the deepest part of the ravine. The pony circled and decided his own advance from the north, skirting the steep embankment as if pulled by an invisible magnet. On our way down towards the tall trees, a swarm of birds took flight, with the go-away-bird lagging in his loopy flight.

The pony's urgency became clear as we approached the dense undergrowth that formed a wall in the trees' shadow. We could feel the cool, damp breath while circling the trees for an entry to what could only be a waterhole. At the south side, the undergrowth was more forgiving and strangely flattened. When the pony deftly stepped over it, he was instinctively following the path antelope had pegged out.

If paradise was to be found on earth, this was its origin. Ahead, quite at variance with the surrounding countryside, lay a pool so pristine and still that one could easily imagine mystical beings. The water's pull was so strong that my weary body ached, and I yearned to share its calm.

In its eagerness, the pony took us knee-deep into the cool waters. I dismounted, and with no eyes to watch, I undressed and floated undisturbed. Free at last from clothes worn for weeks.

While the sun and wind played catch-me in the treetops, I pondered water's endurance out here where drought and barrenness ruled.

Could this be the origin of the Maquassi River, which flows through Wolmaranstad? If so, following the creek's path would lead us to town, where it becomes a slow-flowing river.

My clothes dried quickly, spread on a thorn bush. With the water bottle filled and the pony happy to leave the magical waters, we set off east to fetch our despondent group. The sun was already on our backs.

My heart ached to see that the camp's picture stood still in the time we were away. As I dismounted, death's clingy odour wafted up to linger in my nostrils. Eva did not move when I touched her cheek, and Dirk looked out over the riverbed with dull eyes to where Edward was digging a small grave. *Or was it more than one?!*

I shook Eva lightly and was overwhelmingly relieved when she opened her mouth in search of a long-lost mother's breast. I held her close and curled up next to Bettie, who was still holding onto her baby.

'She will not drink,' she said brokenly, 'You try,' and then held her baby out to me.

My whole being recoiled from the request, but somehow, I found the strength to exchange Eva for the baby and said, 'See if mine will take to your breast.' For a heartbeat, Bettie froze, pupils dilated in indecision, then, as I began to unbutton my bodice in mock-feeding a baby with no need for sustenance, she put Eva to breasts engorged with milk. As I looked on, she bent and kissed Eva's downy head and cradled her in an age-old act of nursing.

I stood and walked away from such intimate emotion with Dirk by my side, empty and hollow after the unspeakably sad betrayal. Now we had to commit an even more brutal and sorrowful act, burying a baby who would be forgotten and forever resting in an unmarked grave.

12 - *Bereft of Everything*

'Large numbers of homeless women and children are being drafted down continually. There are about 3000 bereft of almost everything, but a bundle of bedding and a box of some sort. The authorities begrudge rations to those who have any means. The British Government has confiscated most of these people's effects.'

Mrs Rowntree. 1901

The morning sun found us halfway to the spring with the pony eagerly taking the lead in anticipation of the sweet waters.

It was with difficulty that we convinced Bettie to leave her tent-home. In silent resistance and clinging to Eva, the bizarre bond with a desolate place that brought death and so much despair, found expression in pursed lips and downcast eyes. We stood silently for a while, knowing choice had no part to play in this struggle, but it was Dirk's youthful generosity of spirit that found a way to her heart. He wrapped their family Bible in his grandmother's shawl and tied it to his back, then said, '*Kom*, Bettie, *die Here is nou met ons,*' promising God's hand on them - a promise which appealed to her deeply religious core. And I thought, *This war has created adults with feet still firmly in infant shoes.*

Edward and I turned away, emotionally drained after one too many displays of raw emotion.

We travelled slowly during light hours and made camp close to the spring.

In the middle of the night, I woke to my old premonition foe, ensconced in Edward's arms, uncomfortable and stiff on earth's hard bed. In my dreams, demons came galloping from nowhere on shiny red horses, flames spurting from wide nostrils, and raspy breaths carrying the sound and message of death in their wild flight. Our little group was standing in the middle of a corn field – guarding the forces of peace behind us, where the spring waters rested quietly between the tall trees.

Overwhelming in their multitude, the horses were driven straight at us, and as they leapt in an extraordinary high jump, I woke to Edward's reassuring touch.

The unsettled feeling stayed with me, and not even the cool spring waters could wash it away. Later, it came to ride with me as I tried to find the meaning of such an upsetting vision, but it remained a mystery.

'I think this spring is the Maquassi River's source,' I told Edward and pointed out the logical path to Wolmaranstad and why the ancient river we had left behind would not have led to civilisation.

Even though we were surrounded by a paradise, it was time to go. '*Tannie* Cornelia, I can kill birds for food,' Dirk pleaded his case to stay at the spring. Looking into his trusting eyes, it was nigh impossible to say no, but with Eva showing few signs of improvement and us unable to survive on meat only, leaving was the only answer.

After two days' sun-filled peace at the spring, we followed the gravelly river road south, stopping often to feed Eva and for the men to rest weary legs. Dirk's shoes had given up their journey months ago, and although we had bound his feet with petticoat strips, they started bleeding around the toes a short distance onto our path.

I dismounted, and we exchanged places, as the shoes *Pa* had so diligently made to *Ma*'s precise specifications had thus far held up to her standards. I lacked the will and energy for walking, but could still do it out of love and caring.

'We don't need shops, Nelie,' I heard *Pa*'s explanation why shop-bought shoes might be better-looking, but not better-wearing. Whenever farm work eased, he would spend time in the tack room forging shoes for the family, whistling old Dutch songs learned as a child.

The enduring picture of a father lovingly stretching leather over a boot-last, cutting, sewing and polishing *velskoens* that would last until fast-growing feet demanded a new pair, now forged warm tears. How I missed his wisdom!

The further we travelled, the more a feeling of doom grew, and I became convinced the premonition would become real around each bend. All around, the veld lay in heatwave silence with the occasional bird waving a goodbye on its northward sojourn to the spring.

I forced myself to revisit the quiet talks between Edward and me on our journey - intimate moments of planning and wishful thinking of a time that might not eventuate but never considering its futility in the circle of love that surrounded us.

Under the stars' patient gaze, he explained the six-month periods that most volunteers signed up to – his with the Brabant Horse's 2nd regiment, an irregular unit just six months old, but already with 600 recruits from Australia and Canada at the time when he joined. The six months would end in Cape Town in the south on 16 March the following year. It would be a good time to travel to Upington, the isolated north-western town far from war's unwanted attention.

'There we can start building a life together until the war is settled and build a good nest-egg with my five shillings a day war-pay,' he said. His plans carefully avoided and ignored the question of how he would rejoin his regiment or the path my feet would travel now with Eva, Bettie and Dirk.

But love does not ask or answer many questions, and I continued counting each step my *velskoens* made, scooping loose sand as we went.

The sun became an angry red ball, forcing us to stop often to seek shelter among thorny scrub on the western riverbank. The horses became hang-eared, and the heat filled us with despondency.

The flat surroundings slowly changed to gentle hills, leading to the mountains in the distance where Wolmaranstad was laid out next to the Maquassi River. My stomach grumbled at the thought of good food served on a plate. How I missed the comfort of being with my people!

Nature generally positions its living creatures in their rightful place, and nowhere do humans realise more keenly where they fit into the scale of things than on their backs. There, eyes designed to look forward and sideways, are suddenly presented with a deep blue sphere that seems to cover everything like a blanket. There, bird types we had never noticed before, share paths without much effort, unobstructed by mountains or rivers and quite unconcerned about war's killing fields.

Edward pointed to vultures high up - their family type clearly revealed by the typical circling. Even Bettie seemed interested while cradling Eva in relaxed arms. Dirk sniggered like a child at how big the horses' nostrils looked from below. Then he stopped abruptly. '*Kyk hulle ore,*' he drew our attention to their ears, now pricked and alerted to sound.

'Lie still,' I said and lifted my head cautiously to scan the veld. There was no sign of movement, but the horses moved restlessly, insecure in the thorn trees' sparse cover.

My second scan picked up ant-like figures far to the south, the faint scent carried to the horses on the upwind breeze. 'Horses use their noses and ears to avoid an enemy,' *Pa*'s voice came to me. 'Always trust horses and dogs – they are nature's guards,' he said. I knew that to be true.

'Those travellers are the enemy,' I said, and looked around for a better hiding place, which was hard to find in a hurry. I estimated the travellers were less than half an hour away, allowing little time to conceal our presence, so we moved the horses to a dense thicket nearby. Between Edward, Dirk and me, we hobbled the horses and made them lie down. I marvelled at how tolerant war horses are of this command. With the riders already clearly visible, we lay down in the wide mouth of an old warthog hole and waited.

There was no time to erase all our tracks, just those leading up to the riverbank. We stayed low while I kept my eyes on the small approaching army with dread now drumming in my ears and taking shallow breaths. It was obvious from their tense demeanour that fear of the enemy was a prime concern. Their low chatter carried faintly on the wind. I put my hand reassuringly on the pony and felt the muscles' nervous trembling under his coarse coat, but he stayed still. This was a time to be patient and quiet.

From our hiding place, we looked down on the squadron where a few scouts walked bent over like San trackers in the Kalahari Desert. To the masterful San trackers, our presence would probably seem like the colourful signs outside Mosam's shop in Klerksdorp. We could only hope soldiers from far-off countries lacked such skill.

'I know these men,' Edward whispered concernedly. When I looked sideways at him, I saw my own fear reflected in his eyes. He took my hand, and in the silent rubbing of thumb and forefinger, I knew we were in extreme danger.

The soldiers came to a stop, and only then did I notice some were wearing slouch hats, one side pinned up like our own *burghers'*. Others wore wide-brimmed hats, unlike the pith helmets worn by the British. 'Australians and Canadians,' Edward pointed to the different soldiers, and said, 'Brabant Horse – my contingent.' What were they doing so far off the main road between Wolmaranstad and Klerksdorp? And in such a small group?

Two dismounted and inspected the ground minutely, bent double and hands pointing north towards the waterhole. They straightened and turned around slowly. It was obvious they were looking for tracks up the riverbank and finding none. Then they mounted their horses, which seemed hardy and of good lineage.

A third soldier in red uniform, sitting stiff and upright on a much spindlier horse, addressed them from under a bushy moustache. 'General Bruce Hamilton - a dog with a bone,' Edward said and rested his head resignedly on his hands in acceptance that we would be found.

The soldiers chose a riverbank each and steered their horses up and over for a better view, with Hamilton joining the search on our side. He sat silently in the saddle on the near riverbank, waiting. *A cunning hunter used to catch his prey.* My heart felt cold, but we kept still. After a long time, he clicked his tongue once and turned his mount around.

Who knows the ways of babies? Until I take my last breath, I will not know why Eva chose that moment to cry. Why not a few minutes later, sparing us a life-changing future? Hamilton reigned in his horse, shook his head, unable to marry the idea of a baby and the barren veld. He stood frozen for a second, then whistled sharply and swung his horse around.

The whys came by the dozen: why after all we've endured; why now that we've found love; why now that Eva is better; why so close to escape; why us, oh God of mercy, why us?!

What a picture we must've been to a hardened soldier high on his horse. Two dishevelled women and children, two trusty horses and a soldier in a dirty uniform now awkwardly standing at attention in front of me – both protector and enemy.

'Identify yourself, soldier!' came the order from above, and in the staccato answer that followed lay the shards of our plans and the road we would travel.

I watched as if from afar, my ears deaf to the sound like a bomb had exploded nearby. Soldiers leapt off their horses and grabbed Bettie by the arms, pulling her to the ground - her mouth wide open in a silent scream. Eva lay in a pathetic little bundle, and as Dirk fell on top of her for protection, he was kicked mercilessly. Edward's frantic efforts to help Bettie were like butterflies darting from flower to flower, and her threadbare dress was ripped off by uncaring hands.

Edward's horse whinnied in a high-pitched tone and skittishly milled around with the rifle sitting in its rightful saddle holster nearest to me. 'Wait, Nelie, wait – now, shoot!' *Pa* had always cautioned, and I did not wait any longer, but grabbed the rifle, cocked it without looking and fired a single shot in the air. Time stood still.

In my fury, I charged up to the red devil general and shouted, 'You vile man! Again, waging war against women and little children?!'

He sat there, breathing heavily and chewing an imaginary morsel, his cold blue eyes taking in the helplessness of unequal roles so callously taken advantage of. Then he looked down into my eyes and said, 'Miss, pick up the baby and do as I tell you.' And with a shrug, 'Stuart! Horn! Take them to Irene,' he forced two Canadian soldiers into unfamiliar roles. Edward instinctively moved forward but was held back by others.

Like cattle at a show parade, we walked stoically past the onlooking soldiers. As I drew level with Edward, he reached out and touched my cheek. I cupped his hand with mine for the briefest second before being forced forward, but in that moment, war was forgotten, and humanity won the day.

13 – Captured

'I personally, on visiting some of the poor families at night who were brought into Pretoria, have seen a father, mother, and eight children huddled together in two tiny zinc rooms, nothing either above or below them for warmth and protection…. who were left in this neglected state for weeks at a time.'

Mr H.A. Cornelissen, Irene Camp

Stuart and Horn became two eagles, staring from above on their scraggy mounts, who, in turn, looked on with gentle horse eyes.

We followed the direction from which the soldiers came, walking single file between the horses – Bettie, with Eva on her back within the folds of a torn dress, and me protecting Dirk from behind. Our pace was determined by horses already exhausted by war's demands. The purple setting sun lingered longer on this spring day, waiting for us to find a bed to rest.

I had witnessed firsthand how a choice to be positive in the face of great difficulty could determine life and death. Many a day, I came upon *Pa*, sitting head pressed against the cow he was milking and lips moving in silent prayer. Although I could not guess at the sadness that prompted a lone prayer, I felt its devastating depth. Once, he looked up with sad eyes to find me waiting and said, 'Little Bird, God gave us a brain to choose. Choose to be happy; always choose to be happy.' And as the purple hour dragged on and Eva wouldn't stop crying, *Pa*'s words rang in refrain, which enabled me to ignore the soldiers on horseback's indifference.

Later, when nightfall forced a rest, I watched the soldiers' struggle to get a fire going - moustached Stuart, blond and lanky with kind eyes, and stocky Horn, hot and bothered in tight clothes and knee-high leather shin-guards. The cold-climate army uniforms' inappropriateness fixed his face in a permanent scowl. Both were in their early twenties with deep lines between eyes that had seen life from death's point of view.

I stood and left the others in the comfort of their close huddle to kneel at the smoking fire where sticks far too thick stuck out at odd angles. 'Let me do it, else we won't eat tonight,' I said and rearranged the sticks, blew on them, and stood back when flames licked into the air. I sat down again with Bettie and Dirk. *Now the hunter will watch and wait.*

Bettie turned away to nurse Eva, but Dirk and I watched the soldiers' every move. '*Bly kyk*, Dirk,' I advised him quietly to keep watching. Stuart and Horn busied themselves noisily with spoons and food pans while tough-looking meat fried over scorching coals. We followed each bite from plate to mouth and back again in silence.

Halfway through their meal, Horn threw his plate down and said, 'Stop staring!' so we looked down briefly, then up again as soon as he started eating. With a thud, his plate landed on my lap, and he walked away in disgust.

'Eat up, Dirk, there may not be more to come tomorrow,' I said, keeping a portion for Bettie. I smiled at Stuart but felt no joy at taking from an unwilling giver when his meat too landed in my hands.

When pheasants announced the sun's arrival, I woke the others and followed *Pa*'s advice. I took their hands, and we prayed quietly, giving our problems to God and choosing to be happy on this day and all the days He may grant us. Our travels had already changed Dirk's feet from painful to hard and calloused.

Bettie, withdrawn after the soldiers' attack, chose to live in a world exclusively furnished for her and Eva. But with two guns close-by, scary as it may be in the wrong hands, we would have food, and that was enough for me.

Why we were travelling south-west while Irene was north-east as the crow flies, I dared not ask. Yet, that's exactly what my tempestuous tongue decided on. The soldiers looked from one to the other, and Stuart declared, 'We know where it is, so be quiet and walk on,' with the seed of uncertainty already planted in his voice.

'Not one of those poor women wants to be in Irene camp,' Daan's words came to me, slowing my feet and dampening my spirit. Thoughts of Edward and the harshness that was sure to be meted out to him set the tone for the paths my soul would take for the day.

With time on our hands and the days becoming warmer, I recalled a more pleasant time and a day when *Ma* had willingly shared how she came to love and adore *Pa* – a situation that was frowned on at the time but decided on anyway.

'Love determined everything in *Oupa* and *Ouma*'s lives. I believe that's why they were blessed with so many children.'

Not of their own, I learned, but made their own with love. It was on a hot summer's day while stirring a big three-legged pot filled to the brim with lard over an open fire, that the story spilled forth unhindered from a mood in need of upliftment. 'He was my brother,' she spoke of *pa* Andries as if he had passed away long ago, but I understood her word choice. What he was and what he is were two quite different people.

Wiping her face between sentences, she told how our neighbours closest to Klerksdorp had lost their lives in unthinkably sad circumstances. First, the father died when his horse slipped and tumbled down a deep ravine, and then all sanity deserted the mother, who hanged herself from the rafters with his church tie the same day. 'Jacobs was their name,' *Ma* explained, and went on to tell of the only son, Andries, an eight-year-old who was tending the sheep and returned home to the horror of total loss.

She wiped eyes far too wet to account for a smoky fire. 'My mother did not ask questions when he stood on our doorstep, tears still wet on his cheeks.' *Ouma*'s warm embrace left him clinging to her, forming the foundations of a bond that could only be broken by death.

'Yes, he was my brother,' *Ma* said again. 'I am the oldest, and your father, Andries, is three years younger.' Five more children became their siblings in short succession, always leaving behind lives less favourable than at Morgenster. *Ouma had* insisted they know their birth names, 'Because they have to know who they are and one day go back to their roots.'

Soon after, the last chair found its place under the yellow stinkwood table, and *oupa* Dewaldt took an eternal rest from carpentry on the hillside behind our house. Under his watchful eyes, *Ma* and *Pa*'s love received his approval, if not in society's eyes.

'It was *Ouma* who had sent him away to Bechuanaland. Far enough for society's memory to fade,' she said, her voice sharing the loneliness and longing felt until he returned four years later to take her as his bride. 'At last, people had changed enough to accept we were meant to be together,' she said.

My steps became lighter in the recall of a happier time, and I willingly trudged along the hot path chosen by soldiers who were unaffected. It was only when Dirk stumbled and fell in the heat of the day that Stuart reigned in his horse. He looked down on Bettie, who had no alternative but to feed Eva on the go.

Then his eyes wandered to me, and I felt resistance rising like bile in my throat. I stepped over Dirk and took his horse's bit firmly in my hands.

'Surely you have no mother, soldier. If you did, you would have manners!' My hands shook with rage and fatigue, but I held onto his horse until he dismounted, grabbed me by the arm and brought his face so close to mine that I could smell the warm breath of dirty teeth.

I held his stare, and he let go abruptly and uttered, 'She died,' and in those words lay the future and quality of our journey to Irene. I nodded and sat down to explain which way we should be travelling. To everyone's surprise, he shared water with the group in acceptance of the directions while Horn stood indecisively on one side.

Horn was the dark horse not to be trusted. He was the one to watch.

Part Two: Concentration Camps

14 – Interned

'The high mortality of women and children can be attributed to three causes: the exhausted condition in which they arrived at the camp, to be housed in tents – no Boer would ever think of living in a tent in winter on the South African veld - and the inadequate medical aid and bad quality and insufficiency of food supplied.'

Mr H.A. Cornelissen, war correspondent. 1900/1901

It was in the quiet moments before sunrise that my soul yearned most for answers to our suffering.

Long gone were the senseless questions of why my people had to suffer so. Now they were replaced with sinful questions, why a God who had declared himself to Moses in Biblical times to be a God of compassion and pity, not easily angered, and showing great love and faithfulness, has now deserted his people. A people whose first and last thought of the day always faithfully included Him.

No answer was forthcoming except the memory of God's admonition, so often quoted by our pastor, *Meester* Jacob Strasheim, 'But I will not fail to punish children and grandchildren to the third and fourth generation for the sins of their parents.' Sleep became an illusion in the hours of wrestling with my Maker. How could He not know that at sixteen, my wisdom was shallow and inadequate?

For seventeen days, we followed the road to Irene. The soldiers sat comfortably in their saddles, and we were squeezed between four pairs of hooves, front and back, barren land left and right. Compassion, the word least visiting my thoughts during this hungry and dangerous trek, was all but absent in the treatment our Canadian guards meted out.

Our humanity, from sunrise to sunset, was stripped in the simplest tasks – being watched over when nature called or feeding Eva, which became a cat-and-mouse play between roving eyes and a simple motherly act.

Their craving eyes were always alert to a chance sighting of womanly flesh.

Dirk bore the brunt of these frustrations created by war's unequal relationships. He was sent ahead of our party in the mornings to search for water and food and beaten when returning empty-handed, weak, thirsty and hungry. Yet he remained unaware of the sly ploy to send him away while planning intimate acts. Bettie and I took to carrying walking sticks, secretly sharpened in the dark of night. 'That one is evil,' she whispered into the loaded night air when Horn was nearby.

For days, we felt Horn's eyes on us as we trampled along, until his brooding mood spilled over and he jumped off his horse, grabbing me by the shoulders from behind. Stuart, in front, kept going, not aware or choosing not to be aware of Horn's actions. I fought him with what strength I had, but strength became a fight between lust and will, and eventually my heart stood still and accepted the inevitable.

'Relax, Nelie, just relax if you are the weaker fighter. Think - that makes you strong,' Daan had taught me how to get the upper hand in wrestling matches with young Andries, and I forced my body to become limp with Horn's face only inches from mine.

In that moment, I readied to give over. I could see Bettie crouching like a cat behind him, eyes wide and body taut. Our eyes met, and then we struck at the same time. Her walking stick pierced his shoulder just below the left shoulder blade while I rolled away in the silent seconds that followed. We waited and watched as his passing was announced to the veld in quiet spasms.

Every Boer child grows up learning to respect life and to humanely let go thereof. To kill an animal is to eat; to eat without regret is to kill in honour of the gift of food.

'Never trust or marry a man who hurts an animal and takes delight in it,' *Ma* used to say when young men came courting my older sisters. Admittedly, life sometimes showcases women who are cruel, but Bettie was not one of them. Her walking stick had found the perfect path to a humane kill, but her shaking hands showed that honour was nowhere to be found.

'He was evil,' she reiterated and walked away. 'It was necessary,' I breathed and stood slowly with Horn's unseeing eyes watching me dust myself and claim his horse as a survival trophy.

There was no room left to feel shame in taking what wasn't mine, but now having transport for Bettie and Eva helped fill the growing void in my heart created by war's unkindness.

We followed Stuart without looking back in an act of defiance. Out on the inhospitable Highveld plains, two defenceless women were empowered and would pass that on to the children who were entrusted to us.

When the sun was at its fiercest, we chose a few thorn bushes that had survived the drought as a place to rest and wait for Dirk's return, emboldened by our experience and the knowledge that the vultures would find Horn before sunset. We watched Stuart shrinking in the distance and much later growing again when he realised we were not following. We waited calmly, assured the vultures had, without doubt, already erased much of our unthinkable deed, like they had done to so many others on this war's trails.

We offered no explanation and none was asked, but the next morning, Dirk was not sent ahead again. Spirit-sapping days travelling north-east followed, resting briefly in the shade cast by young oaks lining Potchefstroom's dusty streets. After this respite, many more days filled with hopelessness went by unnoticed, plodding on roads furrowed by numerous wagons and surviving on the meagre rations obtained in Potchefstroom. And then, on an unpretentious day, we reached Johannesburg's busyness.

There, we lived off passers-by's scant goodwill – soldiers sharing with a fellow soldier and food gifts from the occasional concerned civilian. On many occasions, we stood mute witness to a nation's generous spirit, showcased in the hands of those who shared unselfishly what little provisions they carried.

Hawkers of every persuasion had set themselves up roadside on the city fringes with wares plundered from farms to the north. We passed them by with longing beggars' eyes, where they sat listlessly in the dust, waiting for customers. Their misery seemed no different from ours.

One evening around a dismal wood-fire, I surveyed our little group with fresh eyes. Gaunt faces and dull eyes returned my stare. Our dirty, threadbare clothes were the silent proof of cruel ordinances issued in a far-off place by a government that had never been exposed to suffering in their civilized world.

What a sad and defeated group we were.

As if our dusty journey was not enough to break a spirit, our will to persevere was shaved thin by the thought of being incarcerated in concentration camps. Avoiding such a fate seemed beyond our ability, controlled by Stuart's watchful eyes and gun. Eva seldom cried, and Dirk sat around listlessly whenever we rested - sadness and solitude found a welcome home among us, and silence became the norm.

On a day that had lost its name in the flatness of our thoughts, we arrived at Irene Camp, sitting high on barren, steep sloping ground and fenced with barbed wire.

The guards at its entrance were uniformed soldiers with guns at the ready, but with no enemy in sight needing to be kept out.

Against the fence, dozens of dirty children stood wide-eyed, bodies pressed hard against each other in the early morning chill. Row upon row of flimsy round tents lined up like white ghosts flapping their arms in the dusty wind, which lifted their skirts to expose bare ground where furniture should have been.

'Pitch your tent away from the cattle's run-off,' *Pa* had once told his receptive audience where we sat around the yellow stinkwood table. The time after dinner and *Boekevat* was always made special with Bible reading, followed by storytelling so vivid, we could taste the food and breathe the air where his characters had been.

A master storyteller, he often relayed some of the more hilarious tales of times long ago when he and *oupa* Dewaldt used to pasture the cattle on the high country. Always stories to remind us of who we were and where we came from - his calm voice continually firming and keeping alive our view of a gentle grandfather whom most around the table had never met or touched. Now those tales came back to teach and guide.

From the hilltop to the gate, tents at Irene Camp ran parallel – each the recipient of a neighbour's refuse. Even the impractical could guess at the result should it rain.

The Highveld is notorious for ferocious storms where thunder and lightning do not wait politely on each other but wreak their fury on everything in their path. The clouds had already started building the night before as if to say, 'We're on our way, Irene, just you wait for our show.' I shivered.

Dread's cold hand touched my back while queueing at the gate as the wind took on a more ominous tone. But it was the contemptuous look in the guards' eyes that competed with the menacing wind for first place. 'Name!' one said, pulling me roughly to a make-shift table. An open book with scribbled notes lay on top and told the tale of a thousand names becoming numbers.

I scanned the scrawny children's faces behind the fence and shivered again. Their dull eyes and hollow cheeks shone an ominous light on the future of our treatment in this bleak place. How I wished Edward were near!

Heavy legs and tired feet carried us into camp and a tent of our own at the bottom of a long row. '*Hier sal ons doodgaan, Cornelia,*' Bettie declared our demise, and sagged down wearily on bare ground to nurse Eva, while the soldiers congregated at the sturdy gate which stood guard over this forlorn place.

Stuart was waved away, but he lingered, looking from our group to the hungry children. Then, shaking his head as if his mind was made up, he mounted his horse and rode up to the fence. I ran to the fence, called by the

strange affinity that made its home among us during our trek.

'Tell him we're fine,' I said, my voice the mouth-peace of uncertainty and despondency. Would Edward even get my message?

'Tell him this is fine, I'm fine,' and I looked over my shoulder at the miserable tent city.

'Tell him, please tell him,' I sobbed and held onto the barbed wire, which cruelly denied freedom and humanity.

He sat silently for a while, opened his mouth to speak, but eventually decided against it. Then he slowly turned his horse around and left with words still hanging unsaid in the air.

15 – Irene Camp

'While the shelter is miserably inadequate, the rations are very bad. The rations supplied by the contractor, consist of flour that is often bitter and unfit to be eaten. The food is quite inadequate for adults, and the poor children simply starve and die. From one farm alone, ten children have died, and there are cases in which every child in the family has perished.'

Mrs Bodde. 1901

The wind was playing havoc with the tent flaps. The bell tents billowed and swayed in a strange dusty dance which reminded me of the early morning mist's dance on our dam at Morgenster. Longing for the familiar came to me, wringing my empty stomach in its own pain.

Staring at the tent rows bending in unison to the wind's mood, my foreboding heart recognised that of all the hardships we had endured the previous months, this forlorn place could be the worst, similarly forcing us to bend in unison to someone else's moods. By the time I reached our tent, big raindrops were mingling with equally big tears, and in this way, nature kindly spared me an explanation.

Expecting to find Bettie, Eva and Dirk settling in, I stepped into a tent full of strangers, squashed tightly upright like *Ouma's* preserved cucumbers in their glass bottle-houses. In the sudden cool of pounding rain, a heavy warmth emanated from the tight cluster. I inhaled their earthy odour - the sweat gone cold from days and weeks' travel and the heartache of lost homes wrapping them like a blanket. And I cried more, for my people, for the innocent and those too young to know what fate may lie ahead.

A greeting murmur of, *'Naand, niggie; goeiendag, my kind,'* went up respectfully from the group. Looking at the weary faces with lines of worry etched deep between their eyes, my heart softened towards them. Who was I to resent the old, the bent and the young's company? I spread my arms wide to embrace those who were sent to share this tiny space.

'Life is not meant to be complained about, but to be endured when the going is tough,' I remembered *Ma's* admonitions. Resignedly, we stood shoulder-to-shoulder, muddy water finding a path from the top of the hill to swirl around our ankles and precious *velskoens*.

Unlike our sturdy tents at Morgenster, these army tents harboured no goodwill and clung jealously to their meagre protection. '*Kom nader*, Dirk,' I ordered him to squeeze between us for warmth and protection from the rain that was coming down in torrents through thin canvas. With night's dark hand outside, I feared the Highveld chill would creep up like an unwelcome guest and take the frail.

Within the hour, the rain stopped as suddenly as it had started, but by then the starless sky ensured that we could not see each other. With hands outstretched, I found the tent door. Outside, feeble light emanating from two light bulbs that hung dejectedly at the gate was the only light close to us. Among the tents lining the hill, only a few showed the flickering light of a candle. These cast strange human shadows on canvas walls and opened a window to the occupants' private struggles. From what I could tell, those in our tent had no belongings. The contents of the rucksack on my back were most likely all we had to share.

Behind me, Dirk clung to the tent flap, wet like clothing forgotten outside on a rainy day. 'Dirkie, hold this,' I handed over my rucksack while searching for a candle and matches. My lips decided of their own accord to make reassuring clicking sounds, as if pacifying Flower, our restless milk cow at Morgenster. 'Don't despair, my boy, this too will pass,' I said. His need for a mother showed itself in the quiet sobs that came in fits and starts, and I waited to give the tough young boy with a man's heart time to grieve for what had been and what is now. A life so distant that it seemed not to have existed. Then I lit the candle.

The miserable scene that stared at us with big, tired eyes spoke of a broken spirit, crushed and dull with despair and helpless misery. In that moment, my heart cried out to the only constant in my life – a god that seemed to fade with every sunset, a distant god, unreachable now.

Oh, God, will we suffer and die together as broken people in this war?!

Even as I beseeched Him, I knew it was becoming more difficult by the day to remember parental wisdom, words which were fast fading from memory like the messages from my Bible which I had chosen to ignore when life became hell.

With no chairs or beds to rest a weary body, we stood together mutely until sunrise, with Eva's cries to remind us of the horrors inflicted on us by the untouched in distant lands.

I focused my hate on their heartless messengers sitting at the gate. A faint whiff of coffee was carried into our tent, and with no tents downwind, it was obvious the soldiers were enjoying what we could only remember from a previous life.

I did not wait for the sun to warm us, but lifted my skirts and covered the 200 muddy yards to the gate, slip-sliding, a red-hot fury driving me. I found the two soldiers sitting wide-legged, coffee in hand, laughing and slapping thighs in derision of my effort. What a spectacle I must've been to them. Only half-a-day ago, they had insulted and bullied us into a bare tent with no regard for our wellbeing, and now we acted as entertainment. Everything about me shouted the night's suffering, but in their eyes, I was an object worthy of scorn.

My heartbeat sounded like gunshots in my head, and the throbbing in my chest was worse than running after cattle for many miles in the high country. The soldiers faded in and out of vision, and my mind was in a place where no sane reasoning could be found.

Even in this all-consuming rage, I thought, this is what *oupa* Dewaldt must've felt like when his heart became tired of this world. *Ma* had found him on that bright sunny day, as he slid slowly to the ground next to the last chair he had ever made, one hand still holding the cloth for a final polish. His face, contorted by pain, slowly relaxed, and a gentle smile exchanged places. '*My* Sophia,' he recognised *Ma*, 'Teach the children to be gentle,' he whispered and closed his eyes. He knew her impatience well.

The memory brought some clarity. I should try to be that gentle person now and bring some sanity to the camp's unfairness.

Looking the older soldier in the eye, I said with forced calm, 'Why do you laugh, soldier? This situation is not of our making, yet you think not feeding us and forcing everyone to stand in the rain the entire night, is a fit and proper way to treat women, children and old folk?!' There was so much more I wanted to shout out, but a tightness in my chest warned that tears were near, and I waited, breathing heavily through my mouth.

The soldier stood slowly, his uncertainty scarcely veiled. 'Come see for yourself,' I invited and started the wet return journey to our tent, not expecting compliance, but feeling better for having said it. He followed some distance, then turned back.

Outside our tent, at least fifteen people stood in inches of mud, trying to warm themselves in a dreary early-morning sun. An old grandmother was supported by her teenage granddaughters; mothers with young children on the hip and others clinging to their dresses; a grandfather with a wooden leg and a skinny middle-aged woman holding his hand. This was the sorrowful group that shared our tent. A tent big enough for six people. 'I'm Cornelia,' I said and shook hands with the old man and kissed the women, as is our Afrikaner custom.

A matronly woman introduced herself and the others as '*Tannie* Prinsloo and my girls, Sannie and Gertie. This is *oupa* Van der Westhuizen - just call him *Oupa* - and his daughter, Kotie.' Then she continued naming everyone else.

That's how I learned that the group was divided into four families: Prinsloo, Van der Westhuizen, Goosen and Steenekamp, all from the same area, many miles north-west of Johannesburg. 'There were more people when they took us,' she explained, eyes downcast.

'We lost many people on the way, *niggie*,' Sannie whispered, and I had to lean in to hear her words. Between mother and daughter, their journey took on shape. 'My *pa* and brothers are still fighting. *Oupa's* sons, too,' she pointed to the old man and went on, 'One son's wife and three children died on the way here. The children just gave up after days of travel with barely any food or water,' the softly spoken young woman said, resignedly wiping away tears.

'We buried them along the way,' *tannie* Prinsloo explained, then told of another woman who now lay beneath a wooden cross. Death spared her the knowledge of a husband interned as a prisoner of war at St Helena, a son losing his life in a skirmish, and two more still fighting for a mother whose fate was already sealed.

The older Prinsloo woman's son-in-law was killed in combat not far from their farm. They learned of his fate a few hours before the *Khakis* burned everything to the ground - the crops, bales of wool, implements, farm animals and the home they had built with sweat and tears. 'From the start, we were herded like animals in the terrible heat. Since then, ten children had died, four of mine too,' she said brokenly, sadness shrouding her eyes. I touched her arm softly, and she covered my hand with hers without hesitation, hungrily accepting my inadequate gesture.

Then she straightened and said, 'Believe, as God is my judge, I am not exaggerating. No one can make things worse than they are. Our land is desolate, and we can build it up again, but we cannot bring back the dead.' The others nodded in agreement, and again I was made aware of the enduring Afrikaner spirit. We had nothing except a tent without lining and threadbare clothes clinging to our unwashed bodies, having to sleep on the bare ground and denied our freedom; yet we would not give up.

While we were talking, I felt a human presence closeby, but when I looked, there was no one. Dirk followed my gaze, and in silent agreement, we jumped over tent pegs and ran around the tent. Swift as the waterhole *springhaas* that was our meal weeks before, giggling children ran criss-cross between tents, bare feet carrying them out of sight. 'They'll be back, Dirk,' I promised, knowing curiosity would win the day. Dirk laughed out loud in anticipation of a good chase, and his face was transformed in child-like delight. My heart ached as I realised he had never laughed in my presence before, but there was no time to dwell on war's thievery, as the children came bounding from behind, grabbed Dirk by the arm and playfully dragged him along their muddy path. 'God's grace at work, Cornelia,' *tannie* Prinsloo said, hugging Sannie and Gertie with much force.

We had hardly soaked up enough sun to warm our bodies when black-clad women started arriving at our tent, each sharing whatever they could spare – a pot, a spoon, lard, a hat, a freshly washed blanket and even a straw mattress so we could take turns resting.

'Not much,' they called it, 'So much,' we called it. They showed us how to take up the tent's sides to dry the inside, and how to hook our belongings overhead and not lose them when the Highveld storms came. 'Irene's tent city is just a few months old. The soldiers hammered in the first peg on November the second,' they explained, and that's how I knew how long we had been away from Morgenster. We were already in 1901. Christmas came and went, and so did the new year.

The best gift came from two sisters who had been taken ill at the time. 'Generous God-fearing women, Cornelia,' the women who carried it said, and unfolded a canvas groundsheet, 'That'll be a barrier between you and the mud. They must be from a wealthy household, my dear,' an older woman explained while rubbing it between thumb and forefinger for quality.

I bent down to straighten the canvas, and that's when I noticed the writing, burned deep into the triple-folded corner and faded with age: DN, Morgenster.

My legs felt week and I sagged to *oupa* Dewaldt's canvas. The coarse material under my cheek felt ike the softest down blanket.

16 – Death and Misery

'They have been dragged by force from their homes, their food and clothing destroyed by fire, and are now dying by hundreds weekly for want of these necessities. To compel our brave men to surrender, their families are tortured and on the way of being rooted out. You are sufficiently aware of what is taking place at Irene Camp, and thus enabled to give an account thereupon to your Government.'

Committee of Boer ladies. 1901

Ankles thick, thin, old and young surrounded me, supporting their hosts and finding balance on feet cast in all types of leather – brown, black, ripped, torn, unpolished and bare flesh. All bearing witness to a unique path trodden against their will.

'Where are they?' I sat too suddenly and held my head for a while between shaking hands. 'Who are you looking for, *liefeling?*' I recognised *tannie* Prinsloo's voice, her warm hand rubbing my back in slow circles like *Ma* used to when I was little. 'The women who sent this canvas,' I explained and tried to get up, but her strong hands kept me down.

'No need to thank them, child. They wouldn't want that; the canvas is only loaned to you,' another motherly voice cut in, and when her grey hair and kind eyes came into focus, she went on to explain Tent 4's circumstances briefly.

Apparently, a small family occupied a tent by themselves – some of the first emaciated arrivals to this miserable place. The lucky ones at the top of the hill, where the winds cleared the air and stormwater found no home.

'They even smuggled in a gun, hidden in tattered dresses, and that under the guards' noses,' said the older woman, then kissed me like a sister, introducing herself as *tannie* Botes, a long-term resident. She spoke in a hushed tone, often glancing over her shoulder at the gate. 'They are mine,' I blabbered and took the older woman's hand. 'They are my family.'

Her eyebrows shot up, and her lips firmed, but she helped me up, and together we cautiously set off on the slippery uphill path.

My eager feet tried to carry me between pothole and puddle with much haste, but my mind knew to slow down.

Surely *tannie* Botes was mistaken. Mine was a large family. But if they were mine, where were the others housed?

With a steady hand, the determined woman guided my impatient journey between tent pens, accepting without question my need to be hopeful. By the time we stood on muddy feet outside Tent 4, many thoughts had shared my imagination, none of which made sense.

Tannie Botes patted my arm as if to say, 'There now, take a deep breath,' and I stood still for a moment, then called out in a scared stranger's voice, 'Hannie, Lettie, are you in there?!' We waited for long moments. 'It's me, Nelie!' We waited longer this time. 'Johanna, Sara, Sophia, answer me!' I started sobbing, not wanting to believe the lie from within.

After a long while, I was convinced this was not the tent I was looking for, but as we turned around with heavy hearts, a life-weary voice spoke from deep inside, 'Go away, little sister. We can't touch you; it's the measles,' and as an afterthought, 'Make sure to boil your drinking water.' *Tannie* Botes squeezed my hand, and all I could say was, 'Thank you, thank you!' She motioned for us to leave, then said, 'Come, child, let's take care of it,' and started hurriedly downhill towards a big oblong building sitting in the middle of a clearing and surrounded by hundreds of tents. 'The camp hospital,' she explained, wiping stray hair from her friendly moon-face.

Inside, double rows of single beds lined the entire length on both sides. Close to the entrance, a nurse, head bent in earnest paperwork, could easily be recognised in her dark dress, crisp white apron and starched pillbox hat. A red cross badge was proudly displayed on each forearm. 'Red Cross volunteers. The good ones,' the older woman hinted at the existence of bad ones.

Tired eyes framed by a pleasant face looked up. 'We'll come to your tent, ladies,' she mistook us for patients. There was a strong antiseptic smell hanging in the stifling building, trying its best to camouflage what *Ma* used to call 'Death's breath' - an odour recognised even by those never exposed to it. My empty stomach complained about this added burden, and bile rose quickly in a throat parched beyond tolerance.

True to its nature, retching was instant in front of the nurses' table, causing papers and books to join her surprised flight. She rushed around the table and held me at arm's length.

'Which tent are you from, Miss?' I heard through ringing ears, and then her face faded.

The fish eagle's call came clear from across the dam – long and mournful, not once, but repeated a few times. *I'm not ready to get up yet, big bird; just a few more minutes in bed.*

Someone shook me lightly. I turned around and felt the clean crispness of sheet and pillowcase against my cheek. 'Cornelia, wake up,' *tannie* Botes's voice spoke from far away. Mist was hanging dreamlike behind my eyelids, and I rubbed my face to make sense of it. 'Wake up, Miss!' This voice was nearer, and as the mist lifted, the friendly-faced nurse was bending over me with worry signed on her forehead.

Closeby a whistle shrilled long and loud three times. 'They're blowing the escape whistle; I must go. Sit, please!' she said, her movements were urgent and fearful. As a shot rang out close-by, her hands flew up to press hard over a trembling mouth. Then she held me close to her trembling body, wailing softly in despair. With my face in her apron's folds, I heard *Pa*'s voice, 'Even the mortally wounded lioness will protect herself, Nelie, do not go near. Trembling is usually the final straw before she strikes.' I kept still.

Three *Khaki* soldiers burst noisily into the field hospital, looking under beds and overturning whatever could be a hiding place. 'Where are they, nurse, where?!' a stocky soldier said, his rough tone revealing a backstreet upbringing. His unkind eyes scanned the place erected for kindness – an emotion that obviously avoided the neighbourhood of his youth.

She shrugged once, then turned briskly and walked up to him, speaking as she went, 'Get out of here at once, you ruffian, or I'll report you to Captain Hime-Haycock today!' Changing instantly from fearful carer to stern teacher, she shooed the soldiers away as you would fowl. *Pa's trembling lioness!*

When she stood in front of me again, she measured my pulse as if nothing had happened, but in the shortness of breath I read months of frustration dealing with insensitive soldiers, lack of medical provisions and uncaring camp managers. 'The captain is caring, but not towards the vulnerable ones in this camp he was ordered to manage,' she explained to my raised eyebrows.

She looked me up and down, and recognising a kindred spirit, said, 'We will fix this mess. But now you must eat and then go,' and a sandwich from her knapsack was placed in my dirty hands, leaving me to wonder how to share this meagre meal between fifteen people.

'There will be more. I will bring some,' she promised outside, her eyes following *tannie* Botes's arm towards our tent and the muddy road leading to my new home.

At Tent 457, fifteen pairs of eyes came to rest eagerly on my hands, and when I unfolded the dishcloth, *oupa* Van der Westhuizen said, 'Let's say grace,' and, head bent in prayer, he thanked a Father of all good for the simple meal.

Then said simply, 'For the children,' and as we watched them eat the small gift with eyes closed, hope and faith made themselves at home among us.

17 – Forced Together

Sickness broke out in the camps--scarlet fever, measles, whooping-cough, enteric, pneumonia, and a thousand ills brought by exposure, overcrowding, underfeeding, and untold hardships. Expectant mothers, tender babes, the aged and infirm, torn from their homes and herded together under conditions impossible to describe, exposed to the bitter inclemency of the South African winters and the scorching, germ-breeding heat of the summer, succumbed in their thousands, while daily, fresh people, ruddy, healthy, straight from their wholesome life on the farms, were brought into the infected camps and left to face sickness and the imminent risk of death.

The Petticoat Commando, 1913

Our haste to escape the disorganised soldiers' search for escapees and the eagerness to share Nurse Ratcliff's offering prevented *tannie* Botes and me from reporting the measles in Tent 4. It was up to the two of us to do so.

Oupa Dewaldt's canvas underfoot was a timely reminder that nothing matters, not even dry soil, if measles spreads among the camp's weakened residents and takes life with it.

A slid in the tent flap allowed me an outside view. Soldiers and residents crossed paths without plan or consideration for each other, many leaving hasty footprints in the mud. All the while, loud whistles were adding to the confusion and fear.

At the first shrill whistle, crows took flight and, unsure of their safety, chose a fence lookout from where their beady eyes jealously guarded food scraps at the nearby refuse pile. An old woman was caught in ropes; others tried in vain to stay on muddy feet in their haste, and soldiers, rifles at the ready, forcefully ordered people from their tents where they were cowering, arms over heads.

Chaos was happily taking charge of the situation.

'Someone could not take this anymore,' *tannie* Botes said when another shot rang out, the tremble in her voice completing the sentence. Hunched, she waited a while, swallowed a few times with effort and then explained how, for some, hopelessness determined the path of escape-at-all-cost. 'The cost is high, always too high,' she reflected.

We heard about secretly hatched plans, but with no certainty of success attached to them. 'Such are the actions of a hungry, desperate and downtrodden people,' she said, and a slow, despondent sigh escaped from deep within her matronly chest.

A few shots were fired some distance away, and soon after, the camp became deathly quiet. The escapees were found!

I felt eyes on me and found *tannie* Botes's pitying gaze on our tired, motley group gathered here in our cloth home. 'Rest now, it's over,' she said, stood and left me behind in a tent that now looked quite homely with gifted articles neatly arranged to surround the canvas, while she retraced our journey to the field hospital.

Behind me, the two oldest occupants shared the coir mattress head-to-toe. *Tannie* Prinsloo's sturdy frame filled the only chair, and the rest of us stretched out on the canvas as much as space allowed to rest during the midday-heat.

Behind the veil of eyelids, my thoughts found a quiet place to retrace the long road from Morgenster to Irene. The demands made by others on this road fell far outside the moral and physical boundaries set and lived by *Oupa* and *Ouma* Niemandt, passed on to us through *Ma* and *Pa*'s guidance. I felt lost in a world with no guidance and where we had no choice. Would our forebears be proud of our effort to survive? Even astonished at what circumstances demanded from us?

'Everyone sins and falls short of God's glory, Nelie, but we must try living by His commands. Love Him, but also your enemies like yourself – that is the one that will test you most,' *ouma* Susara's gentle voice came to me over time and space. My heart squeezed remembering her kindness, and a dark guilt cloak at falling short came to rest gloomily on my mind. A mind, already dulled by hunger and weariness, now lacked the will to worry about God's judgment, too. I doubted there was any love left to share with enemies.

My thoughts flitted between my seeming loveless betrayal of *Ma* when her need was overwhelming; my selfish abandonment of Eva to another mother; failing to be a good mother to Dirk and killing Horn on the barren road of despair. Even now, the unforgivable failure to remember for even the shortest period my own sisters in Tent 4, leaving the reporting of measles to *tannie* Botes. I will be judged as lacking, I was sure.

But without much notice, sleep approached softly with glimpses of Edward on his horse to replace the dark thoughts.

'Come, Cornelia, it's not far to go,' Edward motioned with a flick of his head and prompted his horse into action. With the setting sun in our eyes, our impatient horses chose the way, hearing an urgent call our ears were deaf to. Their wild gallop disturbed guinea fowl busily hunting for the last snack of the day. Their sudden noisy flight to find succour among a mopane tree's butterfly leaves, virtually unseating us and unsettling our horses on the set course.

We kept going due west until saltpetre layered our horses in white, and the sun's compass was set on dark. When we finally slid from the saddle, Edward reached for my hand and said, 'If anything happens to me, my precious Cornelia, continue west until reaching Upington – that's our home,' and he held me close for a long time.

It was two four o'clock shadows that intruded on this tender moment. They cast themselves deep into our tent, accompanied by brisk movements and skirts rustling. 'Time to wake up, people!' Nurse Ratcliff's voice hastened my return journey, leaving Edward to ride on unhindered towards his dream home. With pencil in hand, she counted big and small, mouthing the number, and noting it in her pocket diary while *tannie* Botes patiently stood by.

'When did you eat last?' she asked, scanning the tent for evidence of a meal. Silence. I reached up and handed over her sandwich dishcloth, which she accepted with recognition flooding her dark eyes. *Tannie* Botes stood behind her, forefinger on lips. Who had it?

The kind nurse was determined to find the recipient, and when met with more silence, she shrugged and went on to explain the rules around food and fuel distribution; how important it was to eat, 'Whatever you are given.' *Tannie* Botes stared at the sky.

Nurse Ratcliff kept talking, all the while taking temperatures and examining skins. 'Meat rations are handed out once a week, which is tonight for your tent. Eat it!' she ordered. At this point *tannie* Botes was hands-on-hips, shaking her head, but smiled sweetly when the nurse turned to leave.

Sixteen pairs of eyes followed *tannie* Botes's cumbersome effort to sit among us.

'Well, now,' she said, leaning close to reveal the secrets burning to be released. 'The meat is not fit for a pig,' she shared and pointed to Kotie and me, 'Bring a bowl at about four, and we'll go together for the best meat.' In her low conspiratorial voice, she relayed the residents' difficulties in securing enough food, meat and milk. Not having adequate rations of wood for fuel – a constant source of discontent - meant hunger, sickness and starvation.

'The camp manager is a soldier who does not know hunger or cold,' she coloured the picture of well-fed officers and emaciated, food-starved camp residents.

'You will see them soon enough. They are thin as *biltong,* having to survive on refined flour, sinewy meat and tinned condensed milk,' *tannie* Botes described women and children, not long ago, healthy and energetic on a plain, yet wholesome diet of mealie meal porridge, meat, creamy cow's milk, butter, eggs and produce from their own back yards.

'Sadness invaded our camp,' she said and explained how it was reinforced day after day when little children were carried away by the undertakers. 'Hands-uppers,' she spat out the name for turncoat Boer men who pledged allegiance to the British forces in exchange for sparing their farms from destruction. *'Ja,* those live here in the camp on good rations. The lazy who now bury their own people. Vermin, that they are!' she said, cheeks tainted red in anger and eyes feverishly bright.

As the unbelievable plight and human misery in Irene Camp became clearer, fear moved into Tent 457. It sat on each face, except those too young to understand, saving their innocence for a more generous future. How a future may be possible after a war where the dead already counted higher than the living, was the question in the frowns around me.

But in a single afternoon, *tannie* Botes had prepared us and strengthened our resolve to live, 'Longer than those taken away on stretchers.' Her labour-worn hand reached out to rhythmically stroke a little girl's hair while continuing to share advice. These were the lessons learned on an empty stomach in a cold tent.

'Always be first,' she said, looking to each for acceptance of such an un-Christian deed, but was met with downcast eyes. 'The dead would want you to live to rebuild our nation so their sacrifice is not in vain, and this is how you will survive,' she uttered guiltily.

Like gravestones speaking their message in silence, we sat there, not wanting to believe *tannie* Botes's truth. The little girl moved away from her stroking hand, sensing a discomfort among us.

Then *oupa* Van der Westhuizen said, 'Cornelia, bring your Bible. *Mevrouw* Botes need not feel guilty. Even though Scripture says that he who is last on earth will be first in our Father's house, in this hellish camp, we have to be first to stay alive and live that truth one day.'

He opened the Bible, searched for a while and started reading with the unschooled's slow emphasis, 'Pay attention to what you hear! The same rules you use to judge others will be used by God to judge you, but with even greater severity,' then lifted his head and looked at each of us in turn.

And ashamedly, we learned anew to heed the wisdom of age and soak up the kindness that flowed from it - the kindness that now released *tannie* Botes from her burden.

18 – *Irene Camp's Hidden Soul*

Mortality continued to dog Irene camp. The repeated influx of new arrivals, who could not be isolated, and who had no immunity to the disease, meant that the measles kept finding new hosts. Pneumonia and bronchitis were also continuing sources of concern, especially in the cold winter of 1901. Few of the children were admitted to hospital so they continued to suffer in the tents, treated by their mothers.

Database, Welcome Trust. No date

Like Harry the magician's swift hands, which brought the wonders of trickery within inches of enthralled children-eyes, walking magically delivers the veld's hidden soul close-up. The smells, the sights, the thoughts, the heat, the feelings it evokes, seem just inches away.

Kotie and I waited outside our tent, then boredom walked us uphill past a few tents to look for *tannie* Botes. The camp's hidden soul was delivered close-up in a foul-smelling breath, more so as the quiet girl stopped often to examine the unhealthy surroundings. 'It smells like our outhouse at home,' she stated frankly without distaste. All rural households had a *kleinhuisie* – an outhouse to cover a pit latrine, always a fair distance from the homestead and complete with a wooden seat and lid to keep flies at bay. Yet, on our short walk, we could not find an outhouse. Flies, however, soon showed the way.

Forced in between two tents, a few rusted corrugated iron sheets held onto each other like drunkards, their innards precariously leaning in the same direction, which invited flies and blowflies alike. 'I have to go, Nelie,' Kotie said urgently, her words spurred on by need, not want. How she could deny bodily functions for so long while the rest of us sneaked out to the refuse dump during the night was still unanswered.

While I spread my skirt wide as a door and with eyes scouring the sky in mock ignorance of passersby, the outhouse chose to drop. Even more dramatic and comical was how it slowly folded Kotie in its metal arms and then sagged to the ground.

Its loud sigh and dramatic slide to the ground would've earned Harry the magician's admiration.

'This is God's house!' *Ma* had often reminded us in church when giggling mirth for no reason overtook us, bringing the promise of punishment to her frown. Looking at Kotie's muddy boots and bare bottom from above, the same uncontrollable laughter took over. 'It's no laughing matter, Nelie!' I heard her muffled reprimand, but the laughing devil was already in control. Others came running, and they too were soon ensnared by the same spirit. The more we tried to free Kotie, the more we slipped and fell. Our strength was altogether drained by laughter. Many more hands joined our effort, and after much hilarity, Kotie emerged from her smelly cocoon with wild hair framing a red face. Anger at her role in our amusement saw her sloshing back to Tent 457 with *Ma*'s frown firmly in place.

To laugh out loud in surroundings that had only witnessed sorrow and despair, weaved its own magic in our hearts. Passersby stopped to help, surveyed the flattened fly-infested outhouse hands-on-hips, and every so often they doubled over with amusement as laughter took hold anew at Kotie's fate. The camp struggles that were signed in every ruddy face were now softened in merriment. I could only imagine how *Ma* would've admonished these adults.

'Let those lazy hands-uppers dig another hole. They can do the stinky job,' a woman my age said, wiping away happy tears. I introduced myself as a newcomer, and old and young came to hug me to bosoms full, flat and growing. Meat-bowl in hand, they introduced themselves as from odd-numbered tents, on their way to 'Fight for the blue cut,' which perfectly described meat so lean as to appear blue.

A woman of *Ma*'s age came to walk next to me. The grey at her temples confirmed my calculation, but the warmth that glowed in her unusual honey-coloured eyes made her appear much younger. Her body odour brought a lemon's freshness to my nostrils, and her skin felt soft as a child's when I touched her arm in sudden recall of *Pa*'s much-valued lemon tree at Morgenster. On a return trip to Pietersburg in the north when I was still young, he brought the small tree, wrapped carefully in hessian, and planted it close to *oupa* Dewaldt's grave where it 'Would be protected from the cold winds.' Why he came back with a tree instead of cattle was never explained with more than a shrug but marked by a quiet withdrawal into a secret world that no one was keen enough to enter.

A subtle conviviality grew in the silence between the woman and me without being invited. 'Where flesh meets soul, Nelie,' *Pa* would've explained the feeling only a few were able to recognise and even fewer able to explain. At Tent 457, she leaned closer and promised, 'I will help with whatever you need; just call, and I will come.' She pointed to a tent uphill, and while I stood there wondering about the inexplicable affinity between us, she joined others on their way to the meat lines.

Tannie Botes found me deep in thought outside our tent, but in her busy manner, she missed the emotional undercurrent and called out to Kotie, who was still smarting over the outhouse incident. 'We have to be quick,' she said with eyes on the setting sun and others pushing and shoving to be first in line.

The meat distribution point was towards the east and best approached from the second last row of tents, which sat next to a run-off trench. 'Not a practical man,' *tannie* Botes described the camp manager who probably had scant knowledge of drainage. The problems an easterly wind and oppressive heat could generate were therefore ignored when he ordered a trench to be dug for bloody run-off. A late afternoon breeze started from the east, and while these winds were, for the most part, favoured for their cool sweetness, they now wrapped their rancid arms around us from the meatworks. Kotie heaved and clenched her stomach as she retched at our feet, adding to the overwhelming smell that seemed to line our throats.

I questioned *tannie* Botes, who nodded angrily in confirmation and said, 'Yes, Cornelia, the undertakers remove more than one every single day from those tents close to the ditch,' and added, 'Here we need more than faith to survive.'

With handkerchiefs clamped tightly over our noses, we joined a queue that already held the promise of becoming long. But we were lucky to be about twentieth in line, flanked by others stoically waiting their turn. 'Without a will, like donkeys waiting at the plough,' *Ma* used to describe the world's followers. From what I'd seen in a single day, Irene Camp had already managed to change many into followers in a short time. What stood out, though, was their clothing's threadbare state. Some garments were quite obviously of poor quality to start with, but others were the product of good craftsmanship and excellent material, albeit faded by constant wear and full of holes and tears.

Somewhere behind us, a rowdy few shoved and pulled for a better place in line. 'Those women are from Nylstroom and Pietersburg,' *tannie* Botes said without looking at the fracas. Staring straight ahead, she explained under her breath how even the poor whites in areas surrounding these northern Transvaal towns were forced from their mud-and-dung homes by the British. 'Here they fight for what they never had at home,' she spoke, the corners of her mouth pulling down in distaste. She continued describing the terrible lack of necessities many families were used to and which they accepted as their lot in a world of servitude as *bywoners* on Boer farms – cottiers who worked and lived alongside black servants, often indistinguishable from their fellow workers in habits, cleanliness and customs.

I peeked over my shoulder to where a full-scale fight was going on. Other women moved away from the screaming, punching and hair-pulling, but kept their place in line by holding hands. I had never seen any white woman resorting to physical means to settle an argument, and *tannie* Botes did not help much either, saying, 'Cornelia, stay away from those cats. They come from malaria country and bring the entire Waterberg's diseases to this already filthy place.' She went on to describe the Waterberg region as one of the most beautiful in Transvaal, where 'Antelope roam in their dozens, and the skies are clear and blue. There, hawk and falcon ride high on the airstreams.' Her eyes scanned the clear Highveld sky for the silent gliders, and her frown changed from stern to longing. I realised she was on the Waterberg cliffs, flying with the raptors, where the air is fresh and cool on the skin.

'Malaria?' I prompted, and the talkative woman didn't disappoint. 'People from the south like you who are never plagued by malaria, do not know the devastation it causes up north where the sickness is carried across the border from Bechuanaland and Mozambique,' she said and continued as if I had asked many questions. 'Just like the rinderpest wiped out nine out of ten cattle and antelope before this hellish war, malaria will kill nine out of ten in this camp if we don't separate those Nylstromers and their Pietersburg friends from the rest of us. And they carry measles on them and in the folds of their dirty clothes too!' she declared her take on these illnesses' spread. It was only much later that I learned *tannie* Botes knew people from Schoemansdal, a small village to the north.

The first time I had heard of malaria was when *Pa* returned from Pietersburg, lemon tree in hand. During his travels north-east of this spread-out rural town where more than 800 people made their home, he came to recognise the sickness by the number of blacks who sat around listlessly, or lay prone with death in their eyes. 'Most live in huts close to water – stagnant waterholes or creeks which cling desperately to the summer rains' leftovers,' he said pensively, and explained how most whites whose water source was either a borehole or a pit, did not suffer from malaria.

'There's something in the water or close to the water, Nelie,' he remarked, 'The blacks are often taken to witchdoctors, but many traditional healers and their helpers had died too, so now they throw bones and cast their spells from afar.' I prompted him for more information about these far-off places, but he became silent, except to say, 'You would not like the mosquitoes which attack in big, hungry swarms up there, Little Bird, especially to the north-west where malaria had taken so many.' Who then could blame *tannie* Botes for being scared?

My thoughts kept me quiet while we moved slowly towards a long row of low wooden counters on which whole sheep carcasses, off-cuts, intestines and hooves struggled to hold onto the wood. Behind the counters, a small team of hands-uppers wielded axes and meat-cleavers without much concern for safety and even less for cleanliness. Even in this late hour, blowflies in their blue-green coats were swarming with determination, then settled quickly on the meat and blood to lay eggs.

'Oh, my poor mother would turn in her grave if she saw this,' the woman in front said, and I felt my stomach turn when another who had already received her cut, scraped the eggs off as if that was what you do, and left hurriedly.

'Close your mouth, Cornelia,' *tannie* Botes said and pushed me ahead with, 'Take whatever you're given, and do not complain.' And when my legs wouldn't carry me towards the dirty counters, she took my hand, smiled at the butcher and held out her bowl. 'She's new, *broer*, give her a nice cut,' and his dirty hands sorted through lungs and liver to come up with half a leg of lamb.

She thanked him profusely, winked and walked away with more sway to her hips than befitted the moment.

Outside earshot, she stopped to wait for Kotie. 'Do not judge my methods, child, but learn and learn quickly that a promise to him is not a deed, but in that promise lies your food and your survival.'

She straightened and walked away without sway while Kotie and I tried to make sense of our first lesson in camp morality.

19 – A Hopeless Struggle

'During the winter of 1901, a blizzard passed over the High Veld, the site of so many Concentration Camps, and overtook a young lieutenant, W. St. Clare McLaren, with his men They were without shelter and crept under a tarpaulin for protection from the fierce and bitterly cold blast When morning came, they were found dead, stiffly frozen, and around them lay the bodies of six hundred mules Small wonder to us then, when tragedies such as this were brought home to us, that in the camps the thin tents, torn to ribbons by the storm, afforded no protection to the scantily-clothed, half-famished inmates.'

The Petticoat Commando, Johanna Brandt

'**W**e need a table,' *oupa* Van der Westhuizen said, his eyes already making space for it in the tent's centre where Kotie and I stood indecisively with the meat. The others grunted their agreement, like menfolk seconding a suggestion with 'hear-hear,' at meetings. Loud enough to be authoritative, but soft enough so that even the best ear could not pick an individual speaker.

'Well, *Oupa*, that is a splendid idea; now it needs a good plan where we will sleep tonight,' I said impatiently, placing the meat unceremoniously in his hands and gathering the children to find firewood. It was already dusk. My leaden legs harboured no more strength for yet another task 'There is no firewood anywhere,' Dirk confirmed my worries. During the day, children played and explored outside among the tents where not a grass blade remained. Dirk would know. Water was distributed from a wagon at the gate once a day only, but no such arrangement was in place for kindling and firewood. We've had nothing to eat since our arrival two days ago, except for nurse Ratcliff's sandwich. As the bearer of that welcome gift, all eyes rested on me for another meal.

I sighed, and whie the children waited trustingly on me, my feet found a path forward. While the children and I walked uphill, the smell of cooking spoke angrily to our empty stomachs. 'Where are we going, Nelie?' Dirk's voice came in fits and starts, as food odours added wind to his feet.

I pointed in the general direction of the honey-eyed woman's tent.

'We'll have to walk faster so dark would not overtake us,' I said, but was unable to tell by name whose tent we were looking for. Why did I not ask her name? In this tent city, not even *tannie* Botes's name was known to me.

What good was the meat if we had no wood, and how did it become my problem? had no answers, and those I had were as good as the man in the moon's!

I felt the hopelessness of our struggle clamping its dark hand over my heart, and my legs refused to go on. '*Kom,* Nelie!' Dirk spurred me on, but my ears started ringing, and my knees became weak. From somewhere far away, a woman's cry mingled with the easterly wind – the anguished wail of someone who had nothing to lose. Faces peered from tents, hardly recognisable in the grey of dusk. One with lion-eyes came running, calling urgently, 'I'm coming, I'm coming!' She sagged to her knees by my side and wrapped her arms gently around me. 'Do not cry, Little Bird, I'm here now,' she said and stroked my hair as a mother would. The wailing stopped.

We sat there for a while until Dirk coughed and said, 'We can't cook our meat, *tannie*, and we are so hungry.' She patted my head and spoke in undertones to Dirk, who called the others and set off towards a lit tent not far ahead. On their return, each carried firewood. She nodded and said, 'Make sure everyone eats; Cornelia stays with me,' then helped me to her tent.

I was lying on my back in an orchard, the likes of which I had never seen Overhead, orange-, lime- and lemon trees' green skirts cast a pleasant shade over me – their flowers' fragrant scent calling honeybees who were busily flying about 'From the weak comes strength,' I mused, closed my eyes and breathed in the heady scent 'They can't do it on their own, Nelie,' a nearby lemon tree said and brought the lemony smell to my nostrils, stroking my shoulder with its leaves 'We nurse each other,' the tree said I had to twist for a better look and found honey eyes resting calmly on me as the dream let go of its grip.

'Who gave you the lion eyes?' I asked when she came into focus, and she laughed a velvety laugh. My mother did. he could see things normally hidden from others with those eyes,' she elaborated, then leaned forward and whispered, 'So can I, just like you.'

And like peering through a looking glass, everything became clear, needing no explanation - *Pa's* precious lemon tree, his withdrawal into a secret world, and this stranger who did not seem like a stranger. he kept stroking my shoulder, but her eyes looked inward, taking their warmth to a place known only to her.

'Sleep now, Little Bird,' I heard *Pa's* voice and fell into a deep sleep.

I woke when roosters started crowing somewhere on the outlying farms surrounding Irene Camp. How brave were they to reveal themselves in a war that had already stripped all farms bare? till, I knew how difficult it was to catch a rooster who doesn't want to be caught After each hatching when chicks ran around long-legged and feathered, *Ma* assigned the task of catching surplus cockerels to us children

That's how we learned that not even Soldaat, our snake-catcher terrier, was a match for these sprinters who could fly like guinea fowl to sit high up in the trees, puffing out chests to crow for hours spitefully That's how these crowers have survived the war thus far.

A cool breeze wrapped Irene Camp in deceitful quiet, as people clung to the warmth togetherness brought. Winter is close,' the lion-eyed woman said and held her knitted shawl a bit tighter while the tent flaps clapped hands in the wind.

'Tell me about my father,' I said, wanting her to unlock the secrets *Pa* carried with him. he sat withdrawn for some time, then her shoulders relaxed, and a softness came to play around her mouth before she revealed what had been hidden for so long.

'If, at the end of my life, you should ask: *What made you a better person* you would expect me to say it had something to do with surviving three wars which caused me to become more caring and loving But I won't say it because it's not true That made me cynical and bitter and hateful No, I would say: '*Come, walk with me in a citrus orchard, and you will go away a person better able to survive your own wars.*'

'There are no wars to fight or battles to win in life, that can't be solved by the memory of a slow walk with nature,' she said softly.

'To feel the soil beneath your feet, smell the flowers, see the birds and bees, and hear the wind's quiet voice that brings scent as a gift – thát has made me a better person,' she continued.

'Meeting your father on this slow walk where lemon trees grow and then losing him among the sweet scent, made me a better person. It was infinitely better to have walked, than not to,' her voice trailed quietly.

Her eyes deepened to honey pools, recalling a home far away and a time long gone.

I waited And she told of growing up on a farm close to Pietersburg - the first where citrus saplings found a home about a hundred years before large citrus farms started covering hill and valley around the town Their family moved from the Cape in the south some years after the restless Voortrekkers bumped their way into the area with *bokwa* and oxen.

'We changed from being French *Du Toit* to *DeTooit* among the Afrikaans-speaking first-comers, *Papa* said He was only a boy then There they planted the citrus cuttings *Papi*, my grandfather, had kept alive for months on the long journey from France.'

'Other farmers scoffed at their efforts, but the valley *Papi* had chosen as their home was perfectly suited to those precious trees, rather than the sorghum and corn – the crop of choice in the area at the time - that struggled to grow in poor soil on the flats.' Even as a baby in the 1840's, she would ride on her father's shoulders among the rows of scented trees, and when she could walk, that's where she spent all day, following birds and bees

As an only child, she became the son who learned the secrets of pollination and fruit from the older men. 'I even believed for a while that I was born among those trees,' she said and continued telling how she used to disappear for hours in the orchards, rubbing leaves and picking flowers, darting like a little bird here, there and everywhere until they started calling her *Little Bird*.

I shot up. My name!' I said breathlessly, and her honey eyes laughed at my surprise. How could she know my pet name? But then I remembered - she could see things hidden from others with those eyes. 'No, Nelie,' she said laughingly, 'I think you reminded him of me,' she explained the coincidence, removing superstition from the equation.

Still, when I asked how shé knew, I was greeted with a shrug and that soothing, velvety laugh.

'Little Bird was infinitely better than the Afrikaans name I was given at school,' she said.

'On the first day of school, the schoolmistress said *RéAndriese* will have to change to *Regina* because nobody would be able to '*rrrrr*' and '*jza*' such an outlandish name. So, I became an Afrikaans *Regina*,' she spoke the guttural 'g' with contempt.

'I shall call you by your real name,' I said and rolled the soft r's of *RéAndriese* between palate and tongue. hen waited to learn more.

'She had honey-eyes as well,' *RéAndriese* said after a while, the words staccato and measured Her wounded eyes completed the story of a short period in life when paths crossed on a forbidden journey which changed her and *Pa* forever 'Her grave lies under the lemon tree that gave life to the one overlooking your grandfather, Dewaldt's resting place,' she whispered and pressed her forehead against mine.

An icy wind came rushing into the tent – its chilly fingers spreading dread in the already cold space created by *RéAndriese's* story.

From General Maxwell the committee of investigation got permission to inspect the Camp at Irene, called the "Model Camp," and with the statistics obtained there, as well as the official statistics of all the camps in the Transvaal, the Diplomatic Corps drew up a report, which went to prove that unless immediate steps were taken to arrest the appalling deathrate, the Boer population in the camps would be extinct within a period of three years.

The Petticoat Commando, Johanna Brandt

Of those in Tent 457, Bettie, Dirk and I were the only ones who came from the colder south. For us, co-sleeping with siblings was as natural as having coffee in the morning. For the others from the north, beds were hot and steamy places associated with sweat and bad dreams, winter and summer.

'This is where you learn life lessons,' *Ma* had always said with discipline's steel in her eyes. he was right. In the cramped, uncomfortable space of a single bed, we learned to fight, be fair, use force if needed, speak quietly, and be gentle if possible. If not, we quickly learned how to, as the same toes joined our beds every night.

In the short time since we had arrived at Irene Camp, we had already learned valuable life lessons which had nothing to do with co-sleeping, not the least of which was the camp's thievery of date and time.

Between *Boekevat* in the morning - *oupa* Van der Westhuizen willing us to persevere another day with short Bible passages and long prayers - and bedtime, days lost their names and hours became empty spaces filled with hunger and despair.

'The sun comes up and the sun goes down on our sorrow, and always God's grace is there for the taking,' I remembered *Meester* Strasheim's words, said so often at funerals that it had lost its meaning.

To my child ears it had no meaning to lose, but here in camp, we clung to the many promises flowing from the Bible as dateless days rolled by.

From the moment, 'They need me in our tent,' reluctantly passed my lips in explanation why I was leaving the comfort and warmth of *RéAndriese's* tent, I knew those thankless and hollow words were driven by the same dread that had me waiting for the *Khakis* at Morgenster so long ago.

At least here, *oupa* Van der Westhuizen became our moral sergeant, spending many light hours finding Bible verses for our quiet time, that would lift us out of our daily misery and fear.

On my return to our tent at sunset, I found Bettie and Dirk busy tightening ropes and hammering in tent pens in dusk's sparse light – a task familiar to southerners before a snowstorm or strong winds. Tonight', Dirk spoke into the breeze when he saw my worried face. Sniffing the air like Soldaat, he beckoned Bettie and me, and with haste we took off towards the refuse heap nearby. Go in from the side,' he said. We moved against the barbed wire fence behind the heap to avoid everyone else's outhouse. *Sies*, people are such pigs!' he said, scraping the unmentionable from his foot.

By now, it was quite dark, and the risk of falling and hurting oneself greatly had multiplied. Dirk was like a springhare, disappearing hastily into the gloom and stink that hung thick in the air. Nelie, Bettie!' his muffled voice carried from the dark. Bettie and I held onto each other but almost lost our footing when a few stray cats rushed past.

'Beelzebub and holy hell!' Bettie cursed under her breath, and forgetting the seriousness of our situation for a moment, we clung to each other in uncontrolled mirth at the quiet woman's word choice. In the most unlikely place and time, I realised again how the hard realities of life most curiously sharpen the gift of humour.

'*Kom nou*!' Dirk called us to attention, holding onto the fence and following his whistling, we found him with the corrugated iron sheets of Kotie's outhouse at his feet.

By the time we arrived at our tent, totally exhausted from struggling with the heavy metal sheets, a strong wind was blowing up dust, deepening our dread. Inside, we found the others curled up in pre-sleep slumber, threadbare blankets barely covering them.

'We have to strengthen our shelter if we want to see the light of day again,' I explained when they were fully awake.

'Put on all the clothes you have and move your bags closer to the middle,' I said.

When they were ready, we made them lie head-to-toe, tightly packed in the circle of bags and furniture. Even the two old people had to lie on the ground. We wrapped them in their blankets like the Egyptian mummy pictures I had seen at school, leaving just enough space for us three to fit in. Bettie crawled in next. Then Dirk and I tightened the tent flaps, moved the bags, table, and two beds even closer, and fastened one corrugated iron sheet windward inside the tent. When that was secure, we fixed the remaining sheets to the structure as a roof and crawled into the 'bedroom', plugging it with a bag from inside.

'Breathe into your clothes and do not move,' I ordered, as we listened to the wind's howl outside. The little children, unfamiliar with blizzards, started crying at the wind's shrill whistle, but were soon silenced by the storm's wrath, lost in our cocoon, so inadequate against nature's whims.

What seemed like hours passed, and afterwards an unusual quiet settled over the camp. Dirk and I made our way outside to find snow and moon working together to cast a soft light on everything. Where our tent walls were meant to be, ribbons of canvas hung limp in the windless air, opening a window to devastation. All around us, tents were either torn from their pegs or aimlessly struggled to stand up straight. A few people walked around with lanterns, calling out to loved ones. Belongings lay scattered in the snow. A shiver ran up my spine as I looked towards the camp's entrance, where the gates were torn off their hinges, and the guardhouse lay on its side. Whoever has the strength and desire should leave now from this hellhole,' I spoke my thoughts aloud, ignoring the sympathy even ruthless guards deserve.

Dirk and I walked around our tent, but the cold drove us back inside. '*Kom*, Dirkie, there's nothing we can do in the dark,' I said to comfort. We went inside to release the others from their prison. One by one, we pulled our bewildered and disoriented tent family from the shelter. At the sight of the dishevelled group in their thickly layered skins, a long-forgotten feeling of gratitude took its proper place in my heart.

We were alive.

In my mind's eye, I could see many others who might've met their fate alone, so totally unprepared for nature's cold hand.

'It will be a long night,' I proclaimed, feeling utterly helpless. *What about RéAndriese, tannie Botes and my sisters?!*

Kotie gathered the others with arms wide, like a dog gently herding sheep. 'And it will become even longer thinking about others out there,' she said, and came to stand close to me. 'We are safe. Can't we try to help our brothers and sisters?' he spoke for everyone. I imagined women, children and old folk lying hurt and suffering as if on their last bed of pain. I put my arm around her shivering body and explained to a group unaccustomed to snow the danger of trying to find people in the cold and dark. When understanding came to them, we cried together, thinking of others we could have saved, but now lay friendless and alone as they awaited their lives' untimely end.

We moved the furniture against the torn walls and used the metal sheets to make a stronger barrier against the freezing southerly, which was picking up pace.

'Never be fooled by the quiet after a storm, Little Bird. It is a devil that will swallow you in its anger,' *Pa* had warned whenever snowstorms ravaged Morgenster. These came unannounced every 8 to 10 years. I've lived through only two. Still, their ferocity left me in awe and scared for my life. The last hit a year ago when old Jacob, Pikanien and I were grazing the sheep in the high country. We hurriedly herded the sheep into Solomon's Caves, leaving Soldaat to manage the stragglers by himself as the storm rushed at us uncaringly. All night we listened to their bleating, magnified by the cave walls. At sunrise, we found many latecomers dotted on the hillside in their white graves. If not for the caves' protection, we would all have perished in the cold wind that stepped into the storm's footsteps. In the caves, sheep huddled and warmed each other, and we brewed coffee over a wood fire to keep warm.

Living off the land goes hand in hand with grazing livestock away from home. Like the comfort of well-worn shoes, accepting a hard bed on the ground, having maize porridge and bland meat cooked over an open fire while in the high country, was as easy as co-sleeping at home. Here, in the tent, sleeping rough was no discomfort to me.

Still, the cold would bring severe discomfort to others if we let it. We had to keep busy.

So, we cleared the floor canvas away and started a fire in the middle of our tent for warmth and coffee. When the flames started playing hide-and-go-seek on our faces, the worry about others in the snow world outside became just a fleeting thought in our overwrought minds.

When the stray roosters started crowing, Kotie, Dirk and I set off to look for *RéAndriese's* tent and then Hannie's higher up the hill. In the semi-dark there were no neat tent rows to guide our way; instead, we were faced with such ruin as to overwhelm the mind. Here-and-there flickering lanterns marked the living, but we held onto faith that others might be saving fuel and could be alive after all.

Kotie stumbled and fell. When we helped her to her feet, the moon shone unkindly on a lifeless body. 'Oh, God Almighty, have mercy on this soul,' she uttered shakily, and we hastened along in the general direction of *RéAndriese's* tent. There was no telling what awaited us, or whether we would be able to find them at all.

Dirk suddenly grabbed my arm, and when I followed his gaze, I realised the cold wind was faster than us. In front of us, only a few pegs and belongings marked what *RéAndriese's* tent had left behind in its flight. Everything was covered in a thick white blanket. I rushed forward and started scooping up the snow from where her bed used to be, calling out to her, but, together with the others around her, she remained quiet. Dirk and Kotie were digging furiously beside me in loyal support. *No one could have survived this cold, no one!*

As I was about to give up, Dirk, who was digging as if possessed, shouted, 'Here she is!' and held up a cold hand.

When we lifted *RéAndriese* from her cold grave, she was thickly dressed like others in Tent 457. Even her face was covered by a thick blanket, and her feet stuck out, swollen and fat in several pairs of knitted stockings. 'Open her up! Open her up!' Kotie urged tearfully, and our anxious hands dug and rubbed and moved faster than a lion on the hunt while blood roared through my veins with anxious speed.

As if from another world, I heard Dirk crying, 'Don't die, *my tannie*, please don't die!' His anguished tone spoke of the sadness of long-ago loss. Someone much more powerful heard his cry and listened. *RéAndriese* started moaning softly and moved her hands.

We kept rubbing her body all over, and when she tried to speak, I hugged her so hard that Kotie shook me by the shoulders, saying, 'Come, Nelie, let's get her to the fire.'

Close to the fire and with willing hands exchanging their warm clothes for her frozen ones, *RéAndriese* chose life.

Slowly, her cheeks and lips regained their pink colour and when she tried to speak, I held warm coffee to her lips, 'You are safe now; drink up and then we can talk,' I promised, but knew there would be no talking for a while When we were sure she was warm enough, we made her curl up with the children around the fire 'Don't let her get up,' I begged *tannie* Prinsloo who was rocking Eva on her hip.

Those strong enough - Sannie, Gertie, Kotie, Bettie, Dirk and I - put on our gloves, had coffee and went outside where the sun made sure the utter desolation was there for all to see. Looking at the ruined camp a second time was an even bigger shock than the first. 'Where do we start?!' Sannie said, eyes wide, and I explained that we would start from the hilltop where Hannie's tent was. After all, she was a relative. With the sun as a guide to our east, we set off to find a tent that might have been blown miles away.

Snow did not often visit this part of the country, and if not for the sadness all around, the way Sannie, Gertie and Kotie slip-slided in the melting snow would've been a source of great hilarity. 'Hold onto each other,' Bettie said and took up the lead.

According to nurse Ratcliffe, much was said outside camp about the Afrikaner women's stubbornness, dirty ways and loveless nature. But whoever spoke such untruths had never been interned with few resources or been witness to their generous spirit, always sharing in the face of disaster Like bees at a hive, those who had survived the storm were helping others in distress.

Many an older woman was caring for little children without shelter or food to speak of, while others waited patiently for mothers who might never return. An old man was struggling against the breeze to pull a tent upright.

Without being asked, Dirk and Gertie set off to help. We saw two older women offering steaming soup to those who trudged by.

Sharing their meagre potato and onion rations, they nourished others who had no means of feeding themselves.

Women were busily cooking over open fires in self-sacrificing generosity, and children carried it in all directions where the wind had not been so kind.

We passed several bodies already neatly laid out for the undertaker. We bowed our heads in sadness. Of their last night on earth, nothing will ever be known. Towards the top of the hill, the tents were pegged close together, and even though much more exposed to the wind, they held hands to protect themselves, with only a few blown over or sitting awkwardly.

'Where is your sister's tent, Nelie?' Dirk wanted to know, and at that moment I realised I could not tell which way to go 'What is her name?' he asked again, and then we stood together and called, 'Hannie Hannie, show yourself!'

Two tents up we heard Hannie's forceful voice, 'Over here!' and we rushed over to find her and Lettie standing in their tent door, weak and pale, but with heavenly smiles lighting up their faces 'Don't come near, we're not well yet,' Hannie said, but when I asked about Johanna, Martha and Sara, their eyes became veiled, and joy left their bodies 'Do not ask now, Nelie,' Lettie whispered and turned away

When I opened my mouth to question, Hannie shook her head and slowly turned away as well Sorrow washed over me, and part of me didn't want to believe the unspoken truth Where could my gentle sisters have gone Were they sleeping in a place known only to God's all-seeing eyes Wherever that was, I will find them; yes, I will.

'That the inborn sense of humour of the Dutch South African race should have been stunted in its growth, if not completely crushed by the horrors of the war, would be small cause for surprise to most people who have given the matter a thought But to those of us acquainted with the facts, an entirely different and wholly comprehensible aspect of the case has been made manifest.'

The Petticoat Commando, Johanna Brandt

From the hilltop, the camp's layout as it was before the blizzard was so much clearer than the view from Tent 457. The brilliance of a Highveld winter's day made it possible to see far into the distance, but with close-up sharp focus inside camp borders, and I thought, *'Just like eagles, seeing far and near with equal clarity.'*

We stood in silence, somehow strengthened by our ability to comprehend the changes forced on us. To the north-west, I imagined the hazy mountains of Rustenburg, their peaks and ridges pointing skyward as they guarded the farming town from severe cold.

Johannesburg, this terrible war's birthplace, tried unsuccessfully to hide itself in feigned innocence to the south, where the eye could see forever, unhindered by hill or dale - the true high veld.

Behind us, Pretoria, the quiet town of few homes and friendly people, was overrun by the British and the hordes who were involved one way or another in the war. The Magalies mountain range that we could not see from our vantage point, wrapped its northern border in long arms and petered out many miles away, close to Rustenburg.

To the east lay a vast plateau all the way to Witbank village, which Daan and Jan described sourly as, 'Like saltpans – cold, flat and unfriendly.' Inside the eastern camp borders, the meatworks echoed those characteristics. Snow outlined the blockman's tools like fairy wands, and white humps of leftover meat lay frozen for another meal.

'That's where we'll start,' I said and pointed to the long meat tables, sterile in their white covering. Five frowns questioned my wisdom to start a clean-up in the dirtiest place.

With forefinger I traced our east/west path from the meatworks, around the bloody run-off, and past Tent 457 towards the gates which now smiled toothlessly at us There, my finger lingered in explanation, then moved on to the refuse heap west of the hospital Only a few people had the strength and inclination to wander far from their tents this early At the unmanned gates no eagle-eyed guards were watching.

The frowns eased in understanding – in chaos lay opportunity; its window would not last long.

'We could escape, Nelie,' Dirk said, yearning for a time long gone My heart ached and I squeezed his shoulder in sympathy There was no sense in escaping to a landscape that had surely felt the storm as severely as we did, but feeding our people and giving shelter when no-one else would, was our duty, even though our hearts longed for the freedom that was on offer Our captors had won again, only this time it was our hearts.

We hastily found our way to the meatworks, and on our way, other feet joined our journey. I stopped, divided the group into meat carriers, wood gatherers, people finders, and tent locators, and said, 'We'll meet later at Tent 457.'

At the meat tables, *tannie* Botes was already busy filling a bag, but in her haste, she slipped and fell heavily in the melting snow, one leg pointing east and the other west. Behind me, someone whispered, 'Serves her right for stealing,' but when I searched for the speaker, she was hidden among the others, so I pointed out that you can't steal something that already belongs to you.

'It was for everybody,' Bettie spoke close to *tannie* Botes's ear, and others clicked tongues and 'uhm-phed' their agreement.

'Would you kill a bird with a broken wing?' I asked the loudest supporter – a long-legged youth with hardship and pain written in his shoulders – and when he stood silent with no remorse, Sannie said, '*Boetie,* you know if it's a bad break, the bird suffers for a long time, then dies,' and motioned to *tannie* Botes's legs.

He considered it for a while, then stepped forward and announced, 'Not this bird. There is a hospital,' and with that, he took off his jacket, straightened her legs and bound them together with care.

All the while, *tannie* Botes's screams rang shrilly in the still air, as she cried out to visible and invisible gods to 'let me die like your bird.'

But four pairs of hands carried her off to the field hospital, leaving us shaken and with anguish in our hearts.

We gathered as much meat as we could in aprons and moved south to spread the bounty on our tent table. It was May. The cold had already set in firmly. Winter would make itself known loudly this year and would not be easily convinced to make way for spring. Our team started arriving with news of the tent-less; others dragged in whatever wood that did not belong to someone, until the pile was waist-high. With each new report, the mood and outlook became more miserable and bleaker.

At the gates, they said, two soldiers lay frozen in their eternal sleep next to the guardhouse ruins, and I thought of coffee beans so jealously kept, which would now be blown far from the cups that held their brew just half a day ago.

'No beds at the hospital; people are lying everywhere on the ground,' Dirk explained on their return from the hospital after delivering *tannie* Botes into care The brick building was untouched by the angry winds His team scoured the surrounding tent sites and counted 45 mostly old people, huddling in what was left of their tents, and 31 others with nowhere to go Some were little children He told of tents on quite sturdy and strong anchors close to the refuse dump, now home to the dead People we knew, became frozen statues overnight.

'We'll make way for the living,' I said, and in teams we went out to help clear tents and gather the cold wanderers. By the time the strong tents had new occupants, wood and meat, our hands and feet were numb, and our hearts were overcome with despair. 'Life and death are twins,' I remembered *Ouma's* words at the funeral of a dear aunt. It didn't mean much then, but now I witnessed first-hand the fragile breath that separates one from the other.

Halfway down the hill, beef and onion soup's tangy smell met us before *tannie* Prinsloo came into sight, her posse of cup-carrier children beaming in self-importance as they bounced uphill, soup in hand 'There's plenty at home,' she said, giving our draughty tent higher status, then trudged uphill to feed others with greater need than us.

The bell-tent we were dragging to strengthen our own tattered home, became heavier the nearer we got to Tent 457, but in its canvas skirt lay our survival and sense of belonging.

The task of lifting the new tent over what remained of ours, became the straw that nearly broke the camel's back. Several times we tried to drag one side over, just to find it pulling the structure skew until *oupa* Van der Westhuizen said, 'No, children, anchor two pegs first, then slip the bell over with the centre pole We will help,' and with, 'Pull Pull Rest Pull!' as his contribution to the team-effort, the canvas fell into place to create a space for warmth and comfort.

Dirk and I left the others who were still admiring the new walls for the guardhouse. 'They had more than coffee, Dirkie,' I said, and while confusion hung over the camp, we found the guardhouse foundations. With sticks, we dug without dignity for gifts which might soon be denied us with a change of guard. We had no faith in finding the stock that used to line its shelves – coffee, tea, sugar, sweetened gumdrops, liquorice, and peanuts in paper bags – a delight seldom encountered even before the war. Still, I trusted a child's focused ability to find the smallest of treasures. It was not surprising that Dirk found layer upon layer of these articles hidden under the wooden walls. There was no need to tell him how to stow away such treasure.

We left the ruins seeming twice our size with articles filling our clothes. Not once did we look at the guards in their quiet sleep, as if it was natural to ignore the dead.

On our way back, we could hear hoofbeats rumbling, their numbers rendered unrecognisable by soft snow. We walked on, heads bent against the cold wind. 'The *khakis* are back,' Dirk said resignedly. New guards would be in place before sunrise.

The creak of wagons in the distance announced the arrival of more women and children destined for this miserable place. 'Where do you think they'll go, Nelie?' Dirk asked without looking at the approaching travellers. I had no answer and just kept going until we reached our own tent, conscious that we must hide our find to savour later.

Dark was upon us when a wagon came to a standstill close to our tent 'Stay here,' I ordered the others and went outside where soldiers were busy loosening the yokes from two pairs of scrawny oxen, then led them away and left the wagon's occupants in the freezing wind.

At least 10 people looked down mutely from the inadequate protection a dilapidated wagon provided.

Even they knew up there they were sure to die in the cold of night.

They climbed down, stiff and dusty from travels that so obviously had sapped their spirit. Old and young carried the same weariness in their eyes, and hunger was painted in dark rings around those blank pools of mistrust and apprehension.

'*Kom in,*' I invited them to our tent where soup on the open fire drew them in quicker than any word could There they stood like cattle ready for the slaughter, seemingly accepting of death after suffering a long arduous journey It was *oupa* Van der Westhuizen that softened the moment with, 'Let's give thanks for the gift of friendship brought to us by our brothers and sisters,' he welcomed them and prayed long and hard to a forgiving God for mercy and acceptance When 'Amen,' passed his lips, they sat down cautiously and waited for our generosity, so seldom felt on the long road to Irene.

We learned that they were from Biesjespan, Kimberley and Elandsfontein in the south-west, and that their *Khaki* captors spoke a distinct English '*Niggie,* even our young ones who can speak some English, could not understand them,' an older woman said, and then described their uniforms and horses By the time she took a breath, we had a good description of the Australian soldier 'There were some good ones; not like the English,' she said to soften somehow the horrors they were exposed to My heart raced and I wanted to ask so many questions, but she fell silent and slowly slumped against the woman next to her 'Sleep now,' I said and made sure the fire was burning high as a token of goodwill towards these poor people With so little space, many breaths would help warm our tent.

That night, sleep became a ghost that teased and angered, but never reached out to draw me in Edward visited my thoughts for hours while Eva fussed in teething discomfort Empty hours ticked by in which I revisited times which had been, could have been and might never be These took turns to haunt me until my whole being yearned to stand on a rock high above Solomon's Caves There, the quiet soothes the mind and the ear hears what no-one else can.

While others found comfort on the hard canvas, I went outside to join the cold wind, which was also searching for a place to rest. At least we could find solace in our shared discomfort. I breathed deeply, feeling the frosty air clearing the last cobwebs from an overwrought mind.

I sensed her presence by what every wagonload brings to camp – the odour of hard travel and few conveniences Long gone were the smells of carbolic soap and freshly washed clothes so synonymous with living a simple life on the land We sat together After a while she said in a quiet voice, 'Cornelia, maybe this is for you,' and held out an envelope with *Eva's Mother* written in curly cursive on its face. My heart stood still. My hand trembled as I took the letter from her. 'A soldier with bright blue eyes gave this to me when we were captured,' she said, and explained that he was the one who determined that her family should come to Irene Camp. 'He said you are waiting for it,' and went inside before I could thank her.

I waited some time behind the ox-wagon for the sun to show the best place to read in private. When the white pages with Croxley stamped at the top lay open on my lap, the wind died down, and Edward's world came to me.

The 22nd day of May of the year 1901.

My Cornelia,

It is my twenty-first birthday today My mother would say I'm a man now, but little did she know about war and how we became men long before we should have My day was empty without you, and I long for the day we can be together I have started praying to your God to keep you and Eva safe and well Also Bettie and Dirk.

I am now part of General Dixon's forces, charged with fighting Koos de la Rey and his three thousand troops We are but a small contingent and I am scared; scared to lose my life before it has become one with yours Soon it will become one, I promise I am making plans for us to be in Upington which I have told you about.

But first, let me tell you what has happened in the half-year since I last saw you. So much had happened!

On that fateful day, they had taken you away to Irene, and I was obliged to be loyal to my regiment, Brabant Horse, 2nd Regiment. The soldiers who took me away were part of the bigger regiment in pursuit of De Wet across the Vaal River in the Cape Colony. They were waiting south of the Klip River. From there, we chased De Wet for endless days and nights until the end of February without once laying eyes on him.

Then our regiment was divided, and my division was operating in the south-west of the Cape in the Lamberts Bay area Quite a pretty place so close to the sea They told us to find and fight Hertzog and Kritzinger who had been fighting there since about December I don't know why; fighting was supposed to be in the northern provinces But a soldier does not ask; we just follow orders.

My second six-month placement was up, and I went to nearby Cape Town city There they discharged me on a Saturday in the middle of March; honourably, you should know I had put away all my soldiers' pay, but it was not enough for us to start a new life I decided to join again to earn more.

To be honest, I am tired of our soldiers' shameful drinking when we are not fighting All of them — the old ones like me, and the new ones fresh from the boats - they are bad, bad Drinking day and night like dockers in Sydney Even breaking into the SA News offices and shops - there is no-one to pull them up Not the South Africans, no, they go to church on Sunday and drink a bit of wine at home.

When the Marquis of Tullibardine's Scottish Horse regiment put out calls for volunteers, I signed up with their 1st regiment four days after being discharged from Brabant.

I thought of you every day of our long journey to Elandsfontein. After that, I travelled with other soldiers to undergo a training course, but I don't know what it was for. Then we were transported by rail to Pretoria, and then on to Middelburg. So much time spent thinking of you and longing for you!

Then we did general patrol work and no fighting, which was good. This war is hideous. I do not wish to fight people like your brothers and father. It would be like killing my own father, even though he has disappeared. I tried to find him, but the war office said they think he went to England. An old friend of his said he went back to Australia. That, I do not believe, because my mother, who writes to me every week, did not mention it.

Easter was in Middelburg for me, so close to where the blizzard was at its worst We came upon the poor young lieutenant, St. Clare McLaren, with his men on the same patrol route as us We counted six hundred mules that lay like frozen ant-heaps in the open You know how flat and open it is at Middelburg Those of us blessed or cursed with the divine and cruel gift of imagination, saw in our mind's eye the suffering on those desolate planes.

I have not been able to sleep since that cold day, thinking of your fate at Irene Camp. It is my fervent wish that this letter finds you alive and strong, and to remain so until I fetch you; and fetch I will.

From here in the Magaliesberg, we will still destroy farms and transport the goods to a central headquarters depot in Johannesburg. I will see you as soon as I can. Do not try writing to me. It is far too dangerous. I will come to you.
All my love and devotion. Until we die.
Your Edward

The sun was high in the sky by now, but I didn't care whether it shone on my tears or not. The day was born in sadness and will go down in yearning and tears – another bead in war's sorrowful necklace. At least my heart had lost its burden, and my steps would be light until I see Edward again.

'He was replaced by G.F. Esselen, a man who inspired little confidence Johanna van Warmelo, one of the Pretoria women, had little time for him 'I think we are going to bully this new man — he looks so small and sickly and afraid', she wrote The Ladies Committee agreed They thought him 'weakly amiable; he has no authority and no force of character.'

BCCD, 1901 - 1902

It was a friendly sun that rose the next day, marking the first day of July with promise and goodwill, and a new guardhouse.

One by one, the others in our tent came to stand outside to observe the ant-like activity at the gates, as soldiers hurried here and there to mend fences and carry provisions to its new wooden home In the centre of the hum stood a small, skinny man His feminine high-pitched voice carried clearly across the 300 yards but had little effect on those around him.

'War left thát one behind on purpose,' Bettie said in her usual blunt way.

She saw the world through a black-and-white lens; there were no greys in her life But that made her an expert judge of character - how fair and good she would've been as a magistrate at Klerksdorp's court A court notorious for welcoming the most unwilling judges to its largely rural community since the upheavals of the 1880's gold rush 'If only we had good magistrates like Jacob de Clercq,' *ouma* Susara had announced on a day when a few sheep mysteriously disappeared from their pen

She spoke fondly of a time when the rule of law was king and accompanying punishment under De Clercq severe, yet fair What would she have said about the English That they were strict but fair Thankfully, death spared her the injustices heaped on our nation.

We watched the goings-on for a while longer. I wondered why Mr Scholtz was replaced as camp superintendent after only a few months. 'I knew his family in the Cape,' an older woman said in response to *tannie* Prinsloo's explanation that Scholtz came like a saint in working clothes a few months ago in February.

'Not many of our people liked him, but he was good. Changed the camp from a dirty, unhealthy cesspit to a place that was acceptably liveable,' she said I thought about the dirty meat blocks and bloody run-off and couldn't find enough reason to agree with the older woman The Afrikaner's natural aversion to wealthy English colonialists was understandable after the Great Trek saw many living in poverty in the north, but Scholtz was also a farmer with order in his blood and didn't deserve their scorn.

'And now we have this *hottentotsgod?*' she put the little man in the same category as the stick mantis 'Be careful; he has big ears,' Bettie warned against the wily mantis's outstanding ability to hear sounds that most humans can't 'The *hottentotsgod* has no ears,' Dirk pointed out, which left the conversation open to interpretation of why and how the mantis knew when bats were on the wing in the dark for a mantis feast *'Hulle is skelm,'* *oupa* Van der Westhuizen declared them thieves to conclude the idle talk and went inside.

Edward's letter rustled in my pocket, and I touched it, pondering the reasons why and how it ended up in the hands of a woman at Biesjespan, if he was supposed to be on a train to Pretoria at the time Only Edward will know that answer *I will ask him soon enough* For now, we had to brace ourselves for new rules put in place by society's weaklings.

Oupa van der Westhuizen sat quietly at the table. Concern about a new order at our gate was deeply etched between his eyes. 'You must hide the goods you and Dirk brought here last night,' he said in a hushed voice and pointed to soft earth underneath his mattress. 'Use my leather suitcase and then cover it well.' Then he got up and stood wide-armed guard in the tent opening until I was finished and straightened, hot and dirty from scooping soil by hand. He nodded to seal our secret and lay down with much feigned sighing and coughing. No soldier would move him unless he wanted to be moved.

RéAndriese, who took over Eva's care, came to stand next to me. 'Little Bird, send the others to find another tent; I have a bad feeling,' she said, her voice trembling. We watched the increased movement at the gate. Outside its borders, a few wagons were drawing near, and far in the distance, dark specks announced more to come.

Arrivals were typically revealed by dust spirals long before coming into sight, but melting snow hid the latest.

Dirk and the young ones left unseen to find a second home for the families who had moved in with us the night before, while we moved the abandoned wagon out of the way. Once a tent was pegged in place, I ordered the newcomers to stand three-deep in its entrance, 'So soldiers would imagine double the number,' I explained Overcrowding was the main spreader of disease in Irene camp, combined with a limited number of medical staff That killed more vulnerable people than hunger or cold We were hardly finished, when soldiers marched two groups of bedraggled women and children up the hill in search of empty tents, but we stood firm in our rows, forcing them away.

'But what about Hannie and Lettie's tent?!' Dirk asked. Ten of us took a shortcut uphill to the east, and by the time soldiers came into sight, we were already filling Hannie and Lettie's tent entrance to the brim. 'More tents there!' Dirk shouted in his broken English and pointed towards the refuse heap in the west, as the soldiers moved from tent to tent looking for space, I looked him in the eye. However, he seemed sincere, so we moved away from a tent that still harboured the dreaded measles. Soon, the soldiers took a new direction.

Hannie and Lettie were safe for now.

Not long ago, *RéAndriese* explained the dreadful circumstances in the camp when she had arrived many months ago There was a severe doctor and nurse shortage, almost no food and water with disarray and incompetence ruling their days She told of the delight at having volunteer nurses and how glad they were about Henrietta Armstong, a compassionate nurse volunteer who arrived with the sickly Apies River camp residents, most of whom came from malaria-riddled Nylstroom and Pietersburg in the north. At the time, there was one trained nurse – Nurse Turner – who took 'French leave' whenever she pleased, which was often.

A Dr Woodrooffe visited irregularly and had no sympathy with or understanding of the unforgivable circumstances the poor women and children were subjected to. Some came over to Irene with sacks tied round them for lack of better covering. 'God have mercy on those evil English decision-makers!' she uttered in disgust.

RéAndriese's voice was raspy and her eyes fierce at the memory of farm children, used to clean air and good food, but in captivity covered by fleas and skin disease 'That's when doctors from Pretoria discovered their hearts and started looking for volunteer nurses in town,' she explained the presence of Nurse Ratcliffe, the dismissal of Nurse Turner and the arrival of Johanna van Warmelo and five other young women able to speak Afrikaans and with an understanding of the Afrikaner ways.

'These poor people will go to Johanna's ward close to the hospital,' *RéAndriese* said calmly and explained that Johanna van Warmelo's ward always contained the new arrivals, mainly poor people of the lowest classes For some reason, this wealthy young woman had a special feeling for the poor and oppressed 'She lives with her mother in a huge mansion close to the Apies River,' *RéAndriese* said thoughtfully and went on to describe the park-like grounds surrounding the house, now dotted with English soldiers and war equipment. 'People say her mother is a forceful woman,' *RéAndriese* whispered secretively, and I wondered at her changed tone and how she could know so much detail.

We brought the wood inside It was best to preserve these for the colder nights 'wood, not food, could be your saviour,' *Pa* used to say when out with the sheep on the high country where the cold winds could strip the will to live The first time I had spent time in Solomon's Caves, he led me deep into its dark interior. There, he pointed to a few skeletons huddling close in their musty coats. There was no firewood, and thus, my best life-lesson was learned wide-eyed from skeletal bones.

I veered off towards the field hospital on our way downhill A scene much worse than that in Solomon's Caves greeted me inside its doors Death's odour rose thick from those on the ground I did not have to be a nurse or doctor to recognise the peril contained within these four walls A young woman in a nurse's uniform cautiously stepped over bodies on the floor, administering what seemed like tea from a spouted medicine cup Her hair was taken up in a pleasant roll which framed a kindly face.

When I went up to her, eyes with a directness to them looked me up and down. 'You are the one people call The Organiser,' she said matter-of-factly without introducing herself and shook my hand like a man.

I recognised the kind of person that most likely grew up in a household ruled by a forceful mother.

Her grip was firm and lingered longer than it should have, and I recalled *RéAndriese's* secretive tone earlier. I shivered involuntarily and felt an unease and sense of foreboding taking a firm hold of my feelings.

She led me hand-in-hand to find *tannie* Botes. 'She's not in a good place,' she said and left me standing next to a pale *tannie* Botes who had pain written boldly on her face. The nurse didn't speak. *Something's amiss here,* but there was no time to dwell on the unseen.

'Take my things – they are yours,' *tannie* Botes said in a voice that had already given up the will to live. When I protested, she shook her head slowly in resignation and squeezed my hand. 'Look in my Bible, dear child, look in my Bible.' With sadness, I realised her eyes would not see another sunrise. I kissed her forehead and left to find what was so important to her while it was still light enough for a return journey to her bedside.

I found *tannie* Botes's tent with tent flaps bound tightly shut despite the storm's fury Inside, everything was neat and ordered, even a single bed stood proudly with a multi-coloured bedspread covering crocheted from leftover wool, and a good quality carpet lay in plush thread underfoot To my surprise a solid bookshelf stood to the side, lined with various books – some thick, some thin – and in the middle an extremely old family Bible took pride of place Hesitancy kept my hands in my pockets To intrude felt like walking on holy ground, but I heard *tannie* Botes's urgent request again, and knew I had to find what she desired.

The Bible smelled faintly of apple blossom and pine needles I breathed it in deeply to a place where body and soul meets, then opened the Bible at an oft-visited page There, a pressed apple blossom lay fragile like fairy wings, and wedged in the book's spine a small hand of pine needles rested As if wanting to be read, the words from a small note jumped up to meet my eyes:

> *'Under the apple tree I woke you,*
> *In the place where you were born.*
> *Close your heart to every love but mine;*
> *Hold no one in your arms but me.*
> *Love is as powerful as death;*
> *Passion is as strong as death itself.*
> *It bursts into flame and burns like a raging fire.*
> *Water cannot put it out;*

No flood can drown it.'

I immediately recognised the words from Song of Songs in the Bible – a love song so tender and yet so bold Somehow the image of a dumpy woman didn't quite match such a lyrical song, but then a photo, yellow with age, fell from the Bible to land face-up at my feet A tall man was holding a young *tannie* Botes protectively in his arms On the back, a simple sentence: *Sannie, my apple blossom.*

Was this the 'it' she wanted so badly? I sat and searched the Bible for more clues, but there were none. On the last page, someone had written the names of all the siblings in the Geertze family. Having a family tree noted in your Bible was customary. I didn't think this strange, but this tree was different. Two children were named as Geertze - two girls, whose names were followed by their married names. *Tannie* Botes's was noted first, making her the oldest, but no date: Susanna Susara Geertze (Botes). Then my eye caught the second name: 1842 - Sophia Aletta Geertze (Niemandt), and my world stood still. *Ma* Sophia*?!*

I ran back to the hospital with the photo in my hand, not caring about the cold or others on my way, to find *tannie* Botes near death's door 'I found it, *my liewe tannie,*' I said kindly and folded her hand in mine For the briefest moment she looked at the photo, smiled and whispered, 'The testament is there; find it,' and closed her eyes for the last time I held her fiercely and when there were no more tears to shed, I left her with the precious photo in her hand.

The sun will shine again on another day to search for the truth – the truth of this woman; the nurse's truth; *RéAndriese's* truth.

And search I will.

23 – Secrets and Promises

The two people chiefly concerned in this story, mother and daughter, lived in Sunnyside, a south-eastern suburb of Pretoria, on a large and beautiful old property, appropriately called Harmony, one of the oldest estates in the capital. This historical place consisted of a simple, comfortable farmhouse, with a rambling garden – a romantic spot, and an ideal setting for the adventures and enterprises here recorded.

The Petticoat Commando, J van Warmelo

The dark hours of night dragged its feet like a drunkard until the wild roosters announced the day to a cold camp and at last brought my wandering thoughts to a halt. Whichever way I looked at *tannie* Botes's unfinished story, it made no sense, and when light dawned, I slipped out quietly to revisit her tent.

A thick veil of smoke hung over the tent city, but I hardly noticed so totally engrossed was I in my own thoughts. In *tannie* Botes's tent, I lit a candle and sitting on her bed like she would've many times before, I surveyed what she held dear and surrounded herself with. A homely warmth was reinforced by the slight smell of Lennon's home remedies which sat unobtrusively in its *huisapteek* within easy reach. My heart cramped at the thought of *ouma* Susara who kept her home remedies equally close to her bed.

The candle's flickering light could not hide the quality of the surroundings. The bookshelf was hand-carved and stood on squat feet, elaborately adorned with flower images while the side panels grew apples from branches winding over the top shelf like a grapevine. Even *oupa* Dewaldt's handiwork could not compete with what was clearly a work of art and carved with love. It drew me closer, and I sat on the floor to read the titles. Many were leather-bound. A new world of writings in English and Dutch unfolded in front of me and I recognized the reader as a deep thinker and lover of knowledge, someone quite unlike *tannie* Botes; yet these belonged to her.

The thickest and heaviest book was the family Bible in its prominent position. It lay easily in my hand when I reached for it and I stroked its leather jacket softly, then held it close like you would an old friend. I felt the guilt of not holding my own Bible like this for a long time, and now it took a dear person's death to bring me back to the Word that had always sustained me.

The memory of the pressed apple blossom willed me to open the Bible and visit the Song of Songs again. Maybe the answers to *tannie* Botes's note were hiding among the lines of Solomon's beautiful love poems.

The sun had coloured the eastern tent wall orange and was moving overhead by the time I closed the Bible on a fruitless search. There was no reason to feel so bereft, but a sadness eased itself into the tent and took advantage of the space where *tannie* Botes's good nature once ruled. I rested on her plush carpet, Bible close to my chest, as if to wrestle some comfort from it. That's when I noticed its thick leather jacket, quite out of proportion with the cover pages which nestled inside. I was not to know then, that the papers my trembling hands pulled from the jacket contained notes on a life journey fit for poems.

My stomach rumbled along with the sounds of a camp going about its daily business, but I paid it no heed and gently unfolded the first paper. It came from the same pen as the note I had found the day before, written in an elaborate cursive style such as we had learned at school. It was not a letter, but more like a poem written in half-sentences which didn't make much sense except to express devotion. At the bottom, I found the tall young man in the photo's name, signed formally and somewhat at odds with his poem's love-style:

> *When apple blossoms are no more*
> *Don't forget their promise,*
> *My Apple Blossom*
> *Be true to generosity*
> *Sand and tree belong to thee*
> *Give, give, give*
>
> *Your only love, always,*
> *Paulus Botes*

I will make sense of this one later, I thought.

The second was written on thicker paper with the Transvaal Republic's crest in the middle, and underneath, *Testament.* The rest was in High Dutch, '*Voor een iegelik die dit Testament zullen zieu of booren lezen zij het kennelijk, ondergeteekende getuijgen verschenen,*' which I could not understand, except that it was a testament signed by three people: Antoon Botes, J.J. de Villiers and an officer of the court in Nylstroom whose signature was more fanciful than Paulus's.

The document was written in even more elaborate cursive and by the forceful placing of letters', I could tell it was the work of a man, and one in authority – probably the local magistrate. It contained the transfer of ownership of the farm, Elandsfontein, Section 334, district Waterberg, to Paulus Johannes Botes, only child of Antoon and Gertruida Botes, previously from Driefontein, Marico district, should they pass away before Paulus. In the event of the child's death, ownership passes to his living spouse, should he have one. It occurred to me that *Section 334* would have no owner returning after the war if something happened to Paulus. It would just be another burned-down farm in a country that was sure to be a black shell from north to south when this madness was over. Would *tannie* Botes be the spouse then, even though there was no life in her now?

I had a vague recollection of *tannie* Botes saying she grew up around the Waterberg area north of Nylstroom where so many women and children in this camp came from. Was she confused then? It was clear from the testament that Paulus grew up in the area. Still, it did not explain how the Waterberg featured in her childhood.

That she had intimate knowledge of it, was undeniable. Nylstroom, she said, was a gateway to outlying villages north, east, west, and south. The Waterberg to the north, Johannesburg to the south, Rustenburg west and Pietersburg, where *Pa* met *RéAndriese,* to the north-east. 'This is where I spent the coldest night I've ever experienced under the stars,' he had described Little Nile River's grassy banks which stretches through Nylstroom village.

Tannie Botes once said her husband had joined the war effort, and if Paulus's love-poem spoke the truth, someone would have to let him know of his wife's passing.

Is that what she wanted mé to do? But where did Ma fit into this, and why was tannie Botes so set on me finding the deed?

At the back of my mind a niggling thought kept knocking on memory's door, but like the mist on Morgenster's dam, it danced away before I could remember.

The third paper was as white as freshly bleached sheets. When opening its arms to draw me in, it smelled like Mosam's store - liquorice and Lennon's remedies all in one. To my shock, it was addressed to me and written only a few months ago! An eloquent handwriting talked to me:

Dearest Cornelia,

How long have I searched for you - a strong woman, worthy of the gift she's about to receive. And here, in the foulest of air and harshest of circumstances, I have found you. I fear this place will kill me before my story is told, and so, I'll write it down for you to treasure.

I have lived an interesting and full life — one of love found and lost, one of travels north and south, one of loneliness, grief, and the passing of youth. If only I had known you for more than a few months.

My love for Paulus had borne no fruit, and when he was taken away from me in the first month of the war, I longed to pass our beautiful farm to someone as honest and caring as you, child. A large section of Elandsfontein is yours by birth and my goodwill. You will find it stretching south to north over the mountains which the blacks call Thaba Mêêtse — the water mountains, or what us Afrikaners call the Waterberg.

The deceivingly calm waters of Tweespruit runs between Section 334 and 333 of the farm. Old Abraham Bergmann put in an application to buy Section 333 before the outbreak of this terrible war, and now he and his two sons are chasing the khakis somewhere. In the dry season, it's easy to cross the creek between the two sections, but the Bergmanns could not yet build on a farm they had not paid for, and so the old man settled his family north-west behind the Waterberg to live on Weltevreden before setting off to war. Dear people with hearts of gold who would help with whatever need you may have. I pray fervently for the menfolk's safe return to help the three girls and their mother run such a big farm once it's in their name.

I met Paulus Botes in the Marico district, the only child of poor farmhands on the Geertze's apple farm after circumstances and bad luck had driven them north from the Cape Colony. It was the Geertze hearts that opened doors for his family, that became my family through the saddest event and cruellest deceit.

On a bright summer's day, my parents sent me to play at Paulus's house. Oom Botes was away delivering apples in Zeerust and the five-year-old boy was quite lonely without his father. Sophia, my baby sister, was only a toddler then, and stayed at home. That evening, the two of us were so exhausted, that we fell asleep during Boekevat. Tante Botes made a bed for me and that's where I slept until two rifle shots woke the household. It was she who found my slain family and Sophia crying in her crib when the light of day revealed the gruesome scene two days later.

Then the devil took hold of Oom Botes who reported the Geertzes' death and put the word out for Sophia's adoption but could not part with me. And so, I stayed with them. Tante Botes removed the best furniture, all the books you see on the carved bookshelf and the family Bible from my parents' home and surrounded me with these so that I would 'feel at home.' She influenced the old man to keep all funds from previous years' apple sales, which my real father kept in safe storage. It was enough to buy a farm. Shortly afterwards when Sophia was taken in by a childless couple at Klerksdorp, Driefontein was sold. We packed up and left overnight for the Waterberg. There, Oom Botes bought Elandsfontein Section 334 with Geertze money.

Everything I know about the world, came from those books. With no schools in the area, tante Botes hired a retired schoolteacher to tutor me. Old Mrs Sandingham whose husband used to be a lawyer in Pretoria, chose the quiet of solitude after his death, but never lost her love of reading. I was lucky.

From the time I was little, I had loved Paulus, but we were forced to get married far away from Elandsfontein; after all, we were brother and sister in the community's eyes. The logical choice was Zeerust, close to Driefontein where our hearts became one in the first place. We spent quite a few years at Driefontein which was bought by the Transvaal Government as a community-run orchard. I will never forget those years among the apple trees. When my adopted parents died, we moved back to Elandsfontein until this war broke out. I need not tell you more, except that you became my child in this short time, and that's why the farm belongs to you should I die.

Go live in the shade of those beautiful mountains if I am not here anymore, Cornelia, and find the peace that's been missing from your eyes since you came to camp. Hopefully I have given some comfort to you as well.

Your loving aunt,

Sannie Botes

Hours passed and people in the camp went about the business of surviving, but I was lost in a world that was mine alone. Until there was much movement outside. I quickly reinserted the papers in their leather home and returned the Bible to the bookshelf.

'How many in this tent?' a soldier asked loudly at the entrance, giving me the opportunity to make a space for Bettie, Dirk, Eva and *RéAndriese* in Sannie Botes's home. 'Five families live here!' I shouted, feeling no guilt about omitting the numbers in each family. We were overcrowded in Tent 457 and so indescribably tired of eating little and sleeping hard. I prayed that this lie would be forgiven.

Around me, *tannie* Botes's belongings cried out to be left in place, and I had an overwhelming feeling to protect it and preserve the warmth she had created around her.

From across the divide, I heard her again, 'Take my things – they are yours.' I stood, certain of what should be done. With determined haste I walked to Tent 457 to fetch my camp family.

'If ever a Concentration Camp was mismanaged, Irene was, and the six volunteer nurses, not being paid servants, but having taken up their work for love and at no small sacrifice to themselves, left no stone unturned to bring about the necessary improvements. How futile their poor little efforts were! How powerless they found themselves against the tide of wilful misunderstanding, deliberate neglect, unpardonable mismanagement!'

Johanna van Warmelo. 1913

'**I**t's all about the eyes,' *ouma* Susara said, and turned her milky-grey eyes with towards *Oupa*'s grave, resting quietly in the apple tree's late-afternoon shade. She patted the bed, indicating there was a story wanting to be told. She waited until my frown had faded and the well-known deliciousness of her slow storytelling had called me to her bed's warmth to give it life.

'It's like this, Nelie, *my kind* - a family's wealth lies in happy eyes,' she started with a statement that somehow seemed more like a riddle. I waited.

Then her telling turned inward, as she recalled a time when *oupa* Dewaldt started crafting chairs for each destitute child that came to Morgenster, broken and sad, but most of all, angry at life's cruelty. 'At first, they shout and cry in a quite unbecoming way. Then they turn from their new parents and fight with the other children. Sometimes it took years to calm down,' she remembered child rearing's push and pull.

'When the mist hangs thick on the water, an exhausted heart takes your feet to the gate and back, to the mountains and back, to the Bible and back, and delivers only despair at a parenting effort that would surpass even those of blood-parents. The constant guidance, trying to love a child who did not come from your womb, for that, one needs more than human effort,' she spoke the true sadness of childlessness.

Unlike other stories *Ouma* had told, this one brought pain and suffering to our conversation. She took my hand and comforted, 'At the point where despondency takes over your being, the child looks at you with this special shine in their eyes. And you just know – the strangers' child is yours at last,' *Ouma* concluded with love's soft tremble in her voice, and I took on board the life-lessons hidden in the story's nuances.

Fetching my camp family – Dirk, Bettie, Eva, and *RéAndriese* – for the comfort of *tannie* Botes's tent, was the easy part of getting used to it being mine.

'*Waar gaan ons, hê* Nelie?' Dirk wanted to know our hasty uphill journey's purpose. His excitement forced the question at least five times until we stopped at *tannie* Botes's tent. 'This is where we'll stay now, Dirkie,' I explained the reason for bringing our belongings. Just like *Ouma*'s sad story brought life to a child's eyes, this happy reason snuffed out the light in Dirk's eyes.

In the weeks to come, getting Dirk to accept the tent as his home, was strangely difficult. The child I came to love like my own, withdrew into the silence that he came to us. Bettie and *RéAndriese* looked on mutely at my efforts to make him feel at home, but he was living in the past's dark spaces, crying out in the night at invisible enemies. I took to walking the camp in the dark where the Highveld cold had no intention to console. Reading *tannie* Botes's Bible while Dirk remained cocooned in his own world did not bring relief either.

'Come inside, Little Bird,' *RéAndriese* brought me home one cruel cold night and stoke a fire. 'Now tell me about her,' her hand swept the tent. Up to that point, I had not given or felt like giving any reason for claiming the tent as our home. And now tears took an acceptable explanation's place. She drew me close, and we sat quietly until the fire had burned down to ashes. Only then the truth of my family and Elandsfontein farm fell readily from my lips. I felt curiously unsettled afterwards and transferred that to Dirk's sleeping body. He coughed in his sleep and turned over with a grunt. We remained sleepless.

Dirk woke me early the next day from a short, unsettled sleep. The sky was an unwelcoming grey, and the August winds reminded us that winter was not ready to leave. I followed him uphill, obediently trudging behind like a sheep ready for slaughter. How the dumb of the animal world knew when death was near, no farmer was able to tell; yet us humans lacked the same insight. Knowing that I was feeling despondent and unsettled did not deliver the answer to it.

Behind the top-most tent row, Dirk led me to a lone camelthorn which was covered in sweet-smelling woolly round ball flowers, and towering with branches held wide from at least fifteen feet above the camp.

I was astonished at the tree's ability to thrive and be lush compared to the barren veld around it. Dirk stood with eyes closed, inhaling the sweetness, then said, 'You too, Nelie,' and I closed my eyes and breathed the unexpected scent gift. We sat on the ground where shade would soon join the tree's half-moon seeds – seeds so hard that even giraffe gave up on it.

'Many of these grew on my *oupa*'s farm,' Dirk said after a while. I sensed the space he needed for what was to follow. Slowly the story unfolded of a life I could not have guessed. The picture of an abused child took shape; a child beaten and denied self-respect by a violent stepfather. His telling shifted to good memories of a caring grandfather living many hundreds of miles from the scene of abuse; his love for this old man who rescued him, clear in his changed tone. 'He said God wants us to be honest and not take what's not ours, like you took *tannie* Botes's tent,' and when I tried to explain, he added the reason for abandoning his silence, 'But I heard you last night – it is yours.'

After the old man had died, word filtered through about the stepfather's death and kind-hearted travellers delivered Dirk to his mother. Soon after, the *khakis* came, rounded up everyone sheltering with his mother, just to abandon the group on the dry riverbed where we found Dirk. I could not believe how much this young boy had to endure; infinitely more than me, but his trust in others remained.

The sun crept over the horizon and shone into Dirk's old-man face, and with surprise I realized that *ouma* Susara was right – it's all about the eyes. I pulled him into my embrace, knowing that the strangers' child was mine at last.

Our first stop downhill was Hannie and Lettie's tent. 'But they have the measles!' Dirk protested and I had to explain that it's been many weeks since they had pinned a sign outside their tent. When we got there, the sign was still pinned to the tent-flap. I went inside and found both quite well and reading quietly, forcing me to explain against my will to an open-mouthed Dirk, that everyone finds ways to ease our discomfort – we stood five-deep in tent entrances, and my sisters kept the sign outside.

Another much less palatable emotion was added to the morning's intensity. I purposefully and stubbornly made myself at home on a bed.

'We're not leaving until I know what happened to our sisters and the children!' My voice dared them to argue, but Lettie stood to make tea and in the homeliness of the act, Hannie leaned forward for the telling. Her folded arms told me that doing so did not come willingly; that there would be a personal price to pay for it.

'The *khakis* came in the dark shortly after you had left on foot for Klerksdorp,' she started, and hand-on-forehead went on to describe the soldiers who had surrounded the little group that night. 'It was unforgivable and harsh beyond belief! They ripped Eva from my arms saying they are not taking small babies or old folk,' she sobbed, revealing the price she was paying again for reliving the nightmare. 'After that, they left Eva in *Ma*'s weakened arms and marched the others in front of their horses in total darkness.'

She told how young ones kept falling. Johanna, with Martha and Sara clinging to her teenage frame for comfort, bore the brunt of their brutality. 'One angry *khaki* got off his horse and whipped Johanna mercilessly until she let go of the two girls and then our Sara disappeared like dust before a broom under hooves in the dark,' she painted the distressing picture. I closed my eyes and imagined Hannie, weak after Eva's birth barely a few hours before, together with Lettie trying to protect the young ones from the savagery delivered to undeserving innocents.

'When we got to Klerksdorp, the bleak streetlamps showed only a weakened Johanna was still with us,' the unspeakable truth fell from lips that would never smile again. 'We were exhausted. But when we woke the next day, she too was gone.'

The jubilation in Klerksdorp about the Transvaal Republic's fall a day earlier, siphoned most *khakis* to other duties, leaving a few junior soldiers to transport the group. 'But then pace was much slower. With no sense of direction, they took us to Hartebeestfontein village in the north instead of Irene in the north-east,' she said, and elaborated how a Reverent Winter, noticing the confusion, volunteered to escort them to Irene. 'He loaded these beds and goods onto a ramshackle wagon that was donated to the church, but his plan was to free us like he had freed others who had come to him before. In this time Lettie's baby was born, but no cry was ever going to come from him,' she said, while Lettie's hands stilled on the kettle.

After a few days in Hartebeestfontein, the soldiers became anxious about their decision, reclaimed their duties, and thereby denied the reverent an opportunity to help the captives. 'But he promised to give the baby a good burial. And that's how we ended up here,' she concluded with a sigh.

Would our children and grandchildren even believe that a time like this existed? That human beings could be so heartless?!

'So where is Johanna then?!' I spat out my loathing for the English. Hannie straightened, and showing the strength that got her here, she delivered good news, 'We later learned that a *burgher* patrol found her shortly after she had escaped, but where she is now, nobody knows.' I thought about how Bettie and I had killed Horn to free ourselves from his torment, and somehow knowing Johanna may be free in the unknown felt more acceptable.

Lettie poured tea from a tin kettle, blackened by repeated open-fire use. A contented calm came to sit among us. 'No-one will ever return to Morgenster,' she said pensively, instinctively knowing the path our thoughts had taken.

'Rebuilding this country requires strong men and boys, not girls like the baby that came with your friend, Bettie. She will surely die in this place,' Hannie uttered. The tears that found its way over cheek and chin explained her anguish and longing, and in her wringing hands lay the devastation this war had brought upon our people and continued to wreak on all who were exposed to changed circumstances.

'No-one could ever love and have children again with this darkness in our hearts,' she said brokenly. A silence followed, and in that gap, sharing that Eva was alive, became mine. But Dirk took it upon himself when he offered innocently, '*Tannie,* you can play with our Eva,' looking from one crying adult to the other.

Until the day God takes me to his eternal home, will I remember how sadness made way for hope in Hannie's eyes.

As if in our midst, *ouma* Susara's voice spoke from beyond the grave, 'It's all about the eyes, Nelie.

Part Three: Escape

25 – Well-laid Plans

From the Boer point of view the greatest problem was the meat, for they were accustomed to generous quantities (as were many Victorians, black and white). The quality of a ration scale was judged by the meat and the livestock was sadly thin and scrawny. Tinned and later frozen meat were alien to Boer bywoners and always seemed a poor substitute. Esselen tried to remedy the situation by giving away the heads and 'plucks' (innards) free to the poorest camp people. Even this had its problems, for the Ladies Committee was appalled at the condition of the slaughter ground, where the young children went to collect the blood and tripe from the slaughtered animals.

BCCD (no date)

'This is a good-enough camp, *niggie*,' a new butcher at the meat-works declared, measuring me with a stockman's discerning eye. The practiced way he wielded axe and cleaver with both hands, revealed a decisive person, used to getting tasks done meticulously.

On this miserable windy afternoon in late August, the dust-trampled area around the meat-works with tents sitting forlornly in the background, 'good-enough' was about as bad a description as I had ever heard. 'Good enough is not good enough,' I said like a spiteful child while our struggle to stay alive played out vividly in my thoughts. How could the new person know the daily battles to feed, care for and nurture the disheartened, down-trodden and widowed?

From first light, the day's hours moved stubbornly and with slow intent between intense longing for Edward and senseless thoughts of escaping the awful camp. Neither left me open to discussions about the merits of the things which kept us separated from our humanness – the barbed wires, the uncaring soldiers, the lack of basic necessities and food.

'Best to walk away from an unwinnable fight, Nelie,' *Ouma* used to say, and she was a wise woman. I walked away.

'You forgot your meat, *niggie!*' the blockman's voice followed me, but it was Dirk's plea for meat that morning while forcing down dry, stale porridge, that made me turn around.

On the wooden trestles the cleaver lay idle next to a choice leg of lamb. The blockman's hat shielded his eyes, but with a near imperceptible head-shake he mouthed quietly, 'All the goodness is inside, young Protector; go and protect your people.' He touched the meat as if to explain a job well done, then turned to the next in line. Goosebumps spread slowly to cover my arms and legs and I hurried to our tent.

A peaceful quiet hung over *tannie* Botes's tent. Dirk had found a good piece of corrugated iron at the refuse pile on which a three-legged pot now contentedly waited over hot coals for the meat. Inside, the heat of bodies and coal shielded us from the August winds.

RéAndriese was nowhere to be seen, Bettie and Eva were spending the day with Hannie and Lettie, and Dirk went to camp school which kept its own undetermined hours. The space to think about the strange blockman was waiting patiently in the quiet, and I started cutting the meat while I, too, waited for insight.

My hands automatically found the job they were trained to do at Morgenster, and I cut along the meat's grain and natural lines, separating sinew and steak. It was covered with a thin layer of fat and obviously a good cut, quite dissimilar to the lean and inedible cuts we had become accustomed to. Like meat from an animal fed on the sweet grass of the high country.

My hands waivered, remembering a time so long gone, that it seemed a few lifetimes ago. I wondered how old Jacob and Pikanien were faring in their mountain haven. On occasion when the old man had refused hot cake straight from the oven, *Ma* reminded us that he grew up with few wants, 'Do not confuse his sentiments with your own.' They would fare well on the high veld.

Close to the bone, my knife struck an unfamiliar object which clung to the blade with invisible hands. I pulled harder and then it came loose with the sucking sound of a calf at its mother's teat. I looked in surprise at a piece of cloth stuck to the blade, and when I unfolded its slightly bloodied innards, a message read, 'See Afrikaner nurse.'

Whoever chose lamb to send the message knew about blood and various meat types. The blood-sparse lamb hind quarter was the ideal hiding place for its rolled cloth passenger. Each letter was burned into the cotton, probably by warming fencing wire over an open fire, but legible, nonetheless.

Later when Dirk burst into the tent with, 'I'm hungry!' the meat still had not found its way into the pot. 'What's wrong, Nelie?!' he came over concernedly to sit next to me on *tannie* Botes's bed and would not accept the lie of being late from the meatworks.

I retrieved the message from my pocket, 'See if you also understand this, Dirkie,' I said and watched him try to understand such a simple command's meaning. 'You have to see Johanna van Warmelo,' he offered in explanation, 'But whatever that means, I go where you go,' he swallowed the last words. I took his hand and squeezed my promise, but we were no nearer to unravelling the full meaning – the blockman, the good quality meat, the suggestion hidden inside, and why me.

Night came suddenly as it does that time of year. I said our thanks for the bountiful gift of good food without being questioned about its origin by the others who ate with abandon. As it was, Bettie's thoughts lived in the new world she was busy creating with Eva, Hannie and Lettie, but what about the receptive *RéAndriese?* She appeared happy and relaxed. Dirk looked away which only confirmed that he very much doubted the secrecy of our new-found knowledge.

I went to see Johanna van Warmelo, the only Afrikaner nurse I had met before. I found her doing the rounds among the previous day's newcomers, talking with respect even though it was doubtful the dirty, constantly scratching, poorest of the lower classes that came from the north, appreciated her calm and patience. According to *RéAndriese*, these *bywoner* families were no better than the uneducated blacks they worked the fields with. Their fighting, biting and extraordinary bad language shamed anyone calling themselves a Boer.

I paced her steps until she had scribbled the final note of the morning and put away a dog-eared notebook. She leaned back against a tentpole with a slight glint in her direct gaze, 'Well then, Miss Protector, what is biting you this morning?'

And when the cotton lay snugly in her palm, she said, 'I'm having good Pretoria coffee at midday,' then walked away as passers-by came into sight.

'Coffee tastes better out in the open,' she said when I arrived and patted a short-legged *riempiestoel* next to hers. I doubted that taste came into play, looking from our vantage over the refuse dump and dusty hills beyond. The typical Afrikaner back-less leather chair creaked as I sat down in a sickle bush's pretend winter shade. She moved even closer, and with her left holding the coffee, her right searched a pocket to produce a pure white envelope. 'Open and read,' she said, eyes searching my face while I looked inside. There was no letter or clue to its emptiness. 'Keep it low,' her hand on my arm warned, as people milled around the refuse, but to me the empty envelope had no purpose and I folded it again.

'Finish your coffee and go home. When alone, hold this over a fire, read, remember and burn; we will talk here again tomorrow,' she promised, and I stood, aware of a strange foreboding that forced to the front thoughts of the secret undertones I had detected a while ago. *RéAndriese's* face came to mind, but I shook off the feeling, rearranged my skirt and walked back to our tent with purpose in my step.

The words appeared in the heat like the darting butterfly I had noticed earlier outside our tent – some clear and others dull and showing itself only when good and ready. I sat back on my haunches, surprised to have received a message and excited about the light-brown letters' possible meaning. The longer I sat there, the faster my heart raced and the sweatier my hands became. I read the message again and then burned the envelope.

'How long is long?' we had always asked as children when *Pa* made us wait in anticipation of a gift, and he would always say, 'As long as my patience,' which could be long or short. In this case, my patience had to be seven days long: '*Be ready, three o'clock, night of August 30, meatworks.*'

Never had I heard of or seen such a secret ploy to convey messages. The next day before I could speak the question, Nurse van Warmelo shifted on her *riempiestoel* and said, 'There are certain things you don't need to know, Cornelia. What happens in secret outside these fences are not your concern,' then her shoulders relaxed, 'Know that you are appreciated, not only for helping and protecting others here, but by those working quietly outside.' Then continued, 'It's lemon juice,' clarifying the question of invisible ink.

We sat in quiet companionship for a while, and I sensed she would not be drawn further on the subject. The ground coffee she brewed was freshly roasted and tasted like home and carefree days at Morgenster. When I swirled the last few drops onto the ground, she stood. 'There's more. Tomorrow?' She took my cup, and I was left with the warmth of promised friendship.

In the days to come, as we went about our daily jobs, I realized patience needed flexibility. A few days later when the menfolk came to build a *bakoven* outside our tent for baking bread and rusks, it already felt like I had waited two weeks since the note's discovery. When Eva cut two more teeth the day after, I had carried the crying toddler many times to the camp's four corners, expending nervous energy. My temper was as fragile as the peace between Boer and Brit. Even a distracted Bettie felt the brunt of my impatience and took over cooking duties to be out of the way.

But the hours took their time and taught valuable lessons on their way. Nurse van Warmelo didn't hesitate to press these on my heart, 'Time is the only freedom you have here; don't waste it with resentment.'

Friday, August 30, dawned with the promise of spring rain. A north-westerly wind brought clean air and swallows on their return journey from the north. My sleep-deprived eyes watched their flight's ballet, swooping and swerving high and low on quiet wing. 'A good omen, Little Bird,' *RéAndriese* predicted as she came to stand behind me, and I wondered again about her confidence in the unknown.

From where we stood, the meatworks were hidden behind multiple tents which had gone up over the last month. Still, I could clearly picture a path to the meatworks in the night, avoiding tent pegs and loose objects in the dark. That decided, I went inside for our morning *boekevat* and prayers, but this morning *RéAndriese* took *tannie* Botes's Bible from my hands and read from Psalm 23: 'The Lord is my shepherd, nothing I shall lack.' I knew then with certainty her involvement in whatever was waiting at the meatworks.

Whoever chose the night and time, was accustomed to working with nature - in a full moon's brightness there was no need for a lantern. I found my shoes easily next to Dirk who was in the deep sleep of pre-dawn when even loud noises and activity would not wake the sleeping. Yes, the chooser was clever that way.

Death's breath hung over the meatworks, made more intense by the night-dew. Bettie's stew rose so quickly in my throat, that there was hardly any time to bend over, and so it happened that between unladylike heaves, two *velskoens* appeared silently and unexpectedly. I followed their path up a slender, yet muscular body to wide-set eyes framed by the new blockman's smiling face. 'Krause,' a strong hand shook mine and led me away towards the darker south-eastern fence corner. We stood still for a while until rustling outside announced someone's presence.

'Nelie, *my kind,* don't speak,' *Pa's* voice whispered from the dark. Then he proceeded to outline a most daring escape plan and ended with, 'Be ready, same time and place. There is a new moon on October 11, so the night of the 12th will be darkest. Come then and come alone.' But I remembered my promise to Dirk and said, 'Dirk is my child.' No confirmation came.

He coughed softly, 'Old Jacob says the grass is sweet on the high country,' and my heart swelled at the thought of the old man's love that reached us here in a leg of lamb. I waited, but after a while I realized I was alone. The blockman was nowhere to be seen and I found my own way between blood sludge, discarded bones and potholes.

Dirk was waiting in the dark outside our tent. I held him tight and promised again, 'We stay together, Dirkie,' and when his body melted into mine, I said in afterthought, 'This is a good-enough camp after all.'

Pursuing an Anglicisation policy, the British were often oblivious of the profound objection of the Boers to the loss of their own culture. 'Education was another source of conflict. Although Irene camp had schools from early on, they seem to have been used by the inmates to instil their own culture... In addition to the manual training classes, it was hoped to open a cooking school.'

H. Armstrong, 1901

Meester Strasheim had chosen his sermon carefully on a long-ago Sunday to admonish and punish the 'forbidden' elements tempting his flock. 'A secret is to keep one's thoughts and activities hidden from others, and to hide is a sign of guilt!' He pounded the lectern with extra zeal that day. Every word was spoken to inflict the most guilt which caused his flock's eyes to turn inward.

To a ten-year-old and the 'guilty', that message might have been perceived to be true, but here in camp, it was somewhat hard to swallow. Still, the thought stayed with me, counting the days to 12 October – six weeks and one day witnessing more suffering and keeping secrets. 'Or six weeks and one day helping those in need,' *RéAndriese* had reminded me only the day before after we had witnessed a serious fight between women from tenant farming families. 'It will take a lifetime to pull them up, as now their children will learn the whole spectrum of the lower classes' values among the diverse groups in camp,' she said sadly.

Having coffee at midday with Johanna van Warmelo became a daily routine. 'We have to teach the adults too,' she declared on a day when exhaustion was bending her back and casting dark rings around her eyes.

I learned about the struggles to heal 'her people' and their unwillingness to visit the hospital or to have seriously ill children admitted for treatment. 'They fear dying alone, or having to pay, or the English poisoning their food with Condy's crystals. And when there are no more excuses, they say we'll starve them to death like the typhoid patients, who, of course, must go on a limited diet,' she uttered helplessly.

RéAndriese was right, we had to break the cycle to avoid teaching the children these misguided ideas, acceptable as they may seem when dozens die daily. I've seen mothers sifting maize meal, searching for the dreaded blue crystals with little children attentively watching, believing without question the presence of non-existing poison.

A few weeks ago, on the day the camp 'undertakers' had trudged *tannie* Botes's body past black-clad mourners along the dusty path, Dirk and I stood outside her tent – guardians of a life lived in secret. From there the make-shift schoolhouse behind the hospital was clearly visible, and so was a sizeable adjoining patch of bare ground. That was a good place for a school to teach adults. Six weeks and one day won't be wasted.

In his struggle for acceptance, Esselen tripped over himself to improve a camp-director image which had never truly existed. To him, approving a school was such an image booster. Soon, thatch piles and wooden poles waited on-site for menfolk who had nothing much to do but build a school during the long daylight hours.

Word spread faster than their labours, and by the time the last thatch found its allocated place, women had become used to the idea of coming together for a chat. That's how we drew in the unwilling, the uncouth and unwise. Soon the Afrikaner women, known for being industrious, found a new purpose showing others how to knit, sew and bake. Through singing and being read to, many softened towards the language of the oppressor.

With two days remaining before our escape, there was hardly any room left under the thatched roof during get-togethers. I looked with pride at the heads bent over simple tasks, and a sense of joy in witnessing how those who were fighting or listlessly sitting around a short while ago, were now eagerly learning from women they would normally not mix with.

The day before, Johanna van Warmelo commented pensively, 'Did you know, Cornelia, there are women on commando with our men - that unknown band of heroic women, fleeing north, south, east, and west with their men - for whom they cooked and sewed and prayed throughout the long war years.' Until now, their existence was unknown to me.

Most of those toiling away in the shade and contented company of newly formed camp friendships, probably had no inkling either.

Such extraordinary dedication to a cause again reassured me that the Afrikaner nation would never be broken, but that also brought despair about the length of a war fought guerrilla-style.

RéAndriese was always there to guide and inspire the women, and on a few occasions, I even saw Johanna Van Warmelo paying close attention to *RéAndriese's* precision needlework stitches. Their quiet, animated talk dried up whenever I wandered over and the busy nurse always left to do her rounds, before I could join the conversation.

On the 12th, Dirk and I said quiet goodbyes to my sisters and tent family.

In the sadness of parting hugs, I realized *tannie* Botes's tent haven had in fact become a prison within a prison. The pain I felt having to leave it behind only served to emphasize that truth. 'You must go, Little Bird. I will look after them,' *RéAndriese* reassuringly promised to put the seal of success on our plans. I did not feel reassured at all with little Eva's downy hair against my cheek. Her softness was a reminder of the long journey we had travelled to be here, and I felt an overwhelming sadness. Maybe there would never be a reunion. But my obstinate mind ruled that if two people could be freed, surely others could similarly find a way.

At the right hour, Dirk and I found our way to the south-eastern corner. Our journey could have been light with one rucksack each and sturdy shoes to walk many miles, but our bodies had taken on gigantic proportions because of what we had on our person – several layers of clothes, woollen garments, socks, and the threadbare coats that had served us so well during the last year.

We passed the meatworks which had become a bloodier cesspit since my last night-time trip. The day after meeting with *Pa*, a stocky farmer had taken Krause's place – an unpleasant man of few words. Because he had no sense of cleanliness, we started cooking meat far longer than necessary. One morning on my way to meet Johanna van Warmelo, I imagined seeing Krause disappearing behind the hospital, but by then quite a few *hands-upper* men were living in camp, all wearing slouch hats which made it difficult to distinguish between them.

Our shoes sloshed softly in the mud and blood, but once at the unguarded fence, someone was holding it aside and we walked to freedom in silence.

Deft hands helped us onto a Boer pony's sturdy back to follow in the moonlight. I could distinguish the outline of a lone rider who skilfully and swiftly found his way towards the west.

At first light, Irene Camp lay far behind the Magaliesberg mountain range where the horses found narrow antelope trails high above human activity. Edward had written about these mountains from which his commando, The Marquis of Tullibardine's Scottish Horse, trekked back and forth for supplies to a central headquarters depot in Johannesburg, constantly destroying Boer farms on their way. All the more reason to be careful.

The occasional scrape of hoof on rock was the only sign that humans were about, but enough to disturb pheasants hiding beneath the shrub. A cool breeze visited us among trees that grew sparsely on the mountainside, and which were quite different to those close to Morgenster. Bare-root trees grew flat against the rockface with contorted roots creeping into crevices and cracks. 'A rock fig,' Dirk whispered, and I remembered the grandfather who rescued him from a tortured childhood lived here in the north-western Transvaal. Aloes, with red winter flowers dancing on delicate legs grew in abundant numbers without a care for humans' senseless fighting.

The man, hat pulled deep over his face, dismounted below overhanging rocks hundreds of yards above a beautiful valley, that stretched far to the south. The first hesitant sunrays coloured the valley floor a soft green, and hartebeest could be seen on the banks of a river which ran south to north through a shadowy gorge at the mountain's foot. 'The Crocodile River,' the man named it and elaborated in hushed tones, 'It first runs away from the sea towards the Limpopo River,' he pointed north, 'then turns towards the Indian Ocean 1000 miles that way,' and pointed east from where we came. When he looked up, it was Krause's brown eyes that met mine.

He smiled knowingly, sat on his haunches and we followed suit. Sandwiches of the kind that nurse Van Warmelo has in the morning, landed in our hands and between bites he explained the path forward, 'Down towards the gorge, sidestepping all the usual British trails and then to Rustenburg.' He looked west-ward.

He leaned forward and motioned to the gorge below, 'That's where the locals used to drive hartebeest for an easy kill, hence the name, Hartebeestpoort.'

'With the Crocodile River running between its shoulders, it would be a good place to build a dam,' he said and left the obvious question hanging in the air: who would have money for building a dam after this war?

By now it was quite light. Krause scanned the mountains and valley below. There was no sign of life. Without waiting for my questions, he said, 'I was a blockman on the behest of others more important to the war effort than camp people,' he shifted uncomfortably, 'and they wanted you freed.' Then changed course, 'Wear less clothes and a hat from here onwards,' and turned away so we could change clothes.

Our descent to the valley floor was arduous. The horses moved slow on shale ground and around ridges too steep to negotiate. We stopped many times to listen. There is something awe-inspiring about a hardy war-horse, that could wait patiently and quietly for long periods, then with a touch of the reigns go into full gallop, totally ignoring bullets flying about. The two Boer ponies were not exactly the best-looking horses, but I could tell by their quick response to the slightest touch, that they had lived through many-a-skirmish, guided by a caring owner. Once, a leopard coughed not far away and soon after baboon barked their displeasure at its presence but the ponies stood still with hardly an ear-flick.

By the time we neared the gorge, an angry sun was already baking the valley which was now deserted by the few remaining bullet-shy hartebeest.

Krause dismounted and led us within the trees' protection until the river panned out into a shallow stream with many possible crossings. Still, he waited until the midday sun was ready for its journey to the west. 'Stay directly behind me,' he warned and pointed to a distant log on the riverbank, 'It is called the Crocodile River for a reason.'

Where we crossed, deep layers of pebbly stones formed mounds and ridges in the shallow water, and although cumbersome to negotiate, it was the safest place to be. Once clear of the water, we mounted, and Krause's pony forged its own path. I looked back and could not find a sign that we had been there, as the long grass swallowed us.

This time, we rode at the foot of the Magaliesberg to our left and kept at it until nightfall when Krause guided his pony into a shallow, abundantly treed tear in the mountain. It became so dark that it was nigh impossible to follow.

Dirk and I smelled it at the same time as our pony who came to a dead stop. Tobacco's faint smell hung in the windless air – the local leaf tobacco which reminded of *oupa* Dewaldt's pipe tobacco. I heard leather creak as Krause dismounted to take our reigns. 'From here, you're on your own, young Protector. May God protect and keep you and make his face shine upon you,' he said softly with a quiver in his voice, his hand resting on my arm fleetingly. We waited, but he was gone.

'What now, Nelie?' Dirk whispered. I had no answer. Mountains are the best hiding places for big cats and that fear alone kept us on the patient pony's back. 'The horse will warn us of danger,' I reassured. What choice did we have? Not even in the camp did we have to deal with such uncertainty – the darkness, the mountains, the smoker, the English who could be anywhere.

A match flared ahead. For a split second the smoker's cupped hands shielded the tiny flame, but that was long enough to recognize an Australian uniform and slouch hat. Dirk stiffened and leaned back against me for protection, but I knew there was none to give.

May God protect and keep you safe, refrained like a song of abandonment in my head and we just sat there in the dark, unable to move.

Army boots crunched dry leaves on their way over and a firm hand patted our pony. 'It's all-right, I'll take over from here,' a familiar voice spoke in the dark. That voice sucked the air from my lungs.

Edward! My Edward!

My head found a haven against his shoulder, and I breathed his earthy scent deep into my lungs and held it there. It felt so good and safe and warm in his protection.

Meester Strasheim was wrong all along – to hide during war is not a sign of guilt. Edward hid for my freedom, not out of guilt. Our escape hid everything but guilt.

27 – Freedom

A party of the regiment being under fire of Boers and of our men, voluntarily crossed a most difficult kloof under heavy fire from both sides to stop the firing of our own men, thereby saving many lives. Also, on June 15 crossed the Crocodile River under fire and burnt some Boer waggons and stores on opposite bank.

AngloBoerWar.com

The September night was like an angry, cold hand against my cheeks. More so, this close to the mountain. September is the month that's always angry for no reason, and harbours changeable weather.

We mounted our horses, and Edward led us deeper into the Waterberg's crevices and gullies. As we pressed forward, I suddenly smelled burned wood. 'Burned-out Boer wagons,' he said, explaining the scent, as a clammy cold greeted us. I guessed that we were close to water and deep in the heart of the mountain.

Here, where no human eye could see a path, we pushed on for a long time.

'Come,' Edward touched my leg. Then he helped us dismount after hours on horseback. Dirk's teeth clattered, and he nudged close to me in the dark. A match flashed ahead to reveal a small alcove and a woodpile. It was ready-stacked for a fire, which began immediately to cast red tongues against the walls. 'This was planned,' I stated the obvious, and Edward smiled and motioned us closer. 'Sit. Here, we can talk unhindered.'

We wrapped ourselves in our coats and sat huddled close to the fire. Edward had his arm around my shoulders, and the odour of his war journeys wafted up strongly, but there was comfort in his closeness. In our little circle, many questions waited patiently, some of which ignited hope in my heart for something better than the finality of killing fields and concentration camps' despondency.

'Truthfully, I cannot face another farm burning, or taking stock, wagons, and rifles out of women's hands. They so desperately need it for survival. The endless burning of homes, slaughter of livestock, and the heart-breaking cries of the defenceless, while we bully and ransack and gloat in their desperation,' Edward said bitterly.

The bitterness borne of a war waged against women and children dripping from his words. I squeezed his hand in agreement. We learned how he became involved with Krause through a chance encounter with *Pa* one wintery day when he had lagged after one too many of his regiment's house-burnings.

'My heart was bleeding for those poor women and children who stood wailing, homeless and with nothing but sand beneath their feet, just like your farm, Nelie,' he whispered with anguish so clearly etched around his mouth, that I reached out as if to wipe it away.

Then, with anger, 'I hate this war, I hate the English!' I sat up, surprised at the traitorous remark. 'There is a better life for us to the west,' he proclaimed with a certainty that I didn't feel. 'I'm taking you to Upington, and will return to Pretoria to take on the long journey to Cape Town for a discharge,' he offered a mind-map. In the long silence that followed, we made a bed from our clothes and settled to sleep around the small fire. Everything always seems worse in darkness; tomorrow will reveal more, I reassured myself.

First light couldn't reach us deep in the mountain's bowels, but our inbuilt body clocks and stiff joints woke us to an icy wind that blew fine ash from the once-welcome fire. Edward revived it, brewed coffee and explained that our journey was long and arduous, 'To the west where friends are waiting in Upington.' We led the horses on trails barely visible, and after hours, we arrived at a small clearing where the sun most likely shone for a short time during the day, if the small patch of green grass was anything to go by.

There, in the opening, three sturdy Boer ponies stood tethered to a tree. Saddlebags were filled with *biltong* and rusks – the dried meat sticks and hard, dry biscuits the Afrikaner is so fond of. 'The Secret Service's doing,' Edward said with a warmth I couldn't gauge.

And so it was that while we rested, the secretive undertone in Irene camp, the hushed talk, *RéAndriese* and Johanna van Warmelo's whispers, the comings and goings of nurses and those delivering supplies, took on form. He coloured a picture so brave, daring and risky that the hair on my arms stood up and my heart raced in the story's unfolding.

Dirk sat, open-mouthed, and totally engrossed in a tale that would enthral any youngster. 'Yes, Krause is no ordinary man,' Edward explained. 'As captain of the Secret Service, he leads a network of *burghers,* who secretly enter the heavily guarded Pretoria to help local men, to escape by secret passageways. These men are anxious to join the Boers but are contained in town by the British forces,' he explained.

Pa entrusted Edward with the knowledge of these secret underground movements for three reasons: his love for me, gratitude for rescuing *Ma,* and a belief that Edward could ensure my wellbeing once freed from Irene. He risked being hanged for revealing these secrets to an enemy, but I was certain that such unconditional love would be rewarded and not misused by Edward.

Over the following days, Edward revealed the Secret Service's daring exploits and smooth dealings with three old Boers, who, because of their various states of bad health, were never suspected of heading the most powerful underground movement - the Secret Committee. They worked tirelessly with conspirators, including Johanna van Warmelo and her mother, to send coded messages to and receive replies from President Kruger, who had escaped to Europe earlier in the war. They organised many camp escapes and kept the Boer generals in the field informed of British movements.

How could I have been so ignorant of the clear signs that ordinary folk were cleverly orchestrating such daring activities, especially since I had borne witness to its workings in the juice-scribed letter! Who would ever expect such well-oiled machinations among the poor and infirm?

I marvelled at the young man beside me; his humane heart and deep love for me that could see him court-martialled if caught as a collaborator. My love for him was complete.

On the fourth day since we had crossed the Crocodile River, we left the shelter of Magaliesberg Mountain Range behind. When entering open grasslands, Edward's urgency began to show. 'A strong man would travel six days from dawn to dusk to reach Upington,' he explained quickly as we adjusted to the new landscape. I understood that Dirk and I would lengthen this journey considerably. 'Even with fresh horses, it'll be 12 days, which I don't have,' he added, as we paused at a familiar rendezvous marked by waiting fresh ponies and full saddlebags.

The north-western Transvaal is not an area my family had often explored. Even though Lichtenburg, which lies on our route, was quite close to Klerksdorp and Morgenster, we didn't visit it often. As if reading my mind, Edward drew a map in the sand. 'From here, we'll cross open country towards Lichtenburg, then on to Vryburg – an English stronghold – towards Kuruman's thirsty plains, and then to Upington. We must keep north of these towns for our safety.' He didn't have to explain the danger, the thirst or the hunger that had killed so many before us who had tried to avoid the war in the east. It was certain we had to travel at night and as fast as hardy war horses could carry us for him to be back with his regiment before they head south.

There were hardly any antelope on our way, which reminded me of another journey, having to contend with the burden of precious little Eva. I realised that time spent with Edward had always meant urgency, wariness, hunger and fear. At least now we were free and out in the open with only nature around us. The stars once again guided our feet over veld that neither of us knew well. Edward's compass showed our path towards the west coast, many hundreds of miles away. By day, we rested in the shade, and by night, a chorus of crickets accompanied our ghost-like passage, stopping their chirping for just a while so we could pass.

Once we had turned north, I could tell by Edward's cautious manner that we were close to a rendezvous point. He dismounted and chose his path forward with care. Dirk and I followed his example, and the next moment we were standing on a precipice overlooking an enormous expanse of water.

In the full moon's metallic light, we looked down on the lake's deep black waters. 'I have misjudged the location of our meeting place,' Edward said. 'This is the sinkhole your father had warned me about. No one who falls into its cold arms comes out alive,' he said. I remembered a tale *Pa* had told of a place called *Wondergat,* which is filled with the wonder of changing colours but also swallows people alive. Now I understand why.

As the moon's light moved across the waters, the rays played hide-and-go-seek in its depths. No wonder people referred to it as Wonder Hole. *Pa* also filled our children-hearts with fear when he explained that, according to legend, a local chieftain had kept his charges in line many years ago by offering the disobedient to *Wondergat*'s water gods.

We felt an unease and quickly left its shores, turning south, and when a horse neighed close-by, our own increased their pace to find the rested ponies we came to rely on. A note stuck out conspicuously from a saddlebag.

In the firelight, Edward's features became drawn, and weariness, instead of laughter, cut deep lines in his forehead. He held the note over the fire, and it burned brightly for a second or two. Dirk and I waited expectantly for its message. 'Krause may be dead,' Edward said in a voice to match. 'He was caught with two others the day after delivering you, and they are now in prison.' Sadness kept us quiet, contemplating the war's capacity to inflict even more harm on this vast land's rightful citizens.

'In the concentration camps, menfolk are spat on as traitorous hands-uppers,' he said, looked into the fire and wearily wiped his face, 'But they are not the bad ones.' Dirk moved closer to me while Edward explained the three kinds of Boer traitors he had identified through direct contact. 'Those with a mistaken sense of duty who surrendered themselves to the enemy so the war could end with less suffering; those tired, despondent and demoralised who only longed for peace. And then the vilest of them all, those who lusted for gain and didn't care whether they had to fight against their brothers to stand side by side with the enemy. They are known as the National Scouts, the 'Judas-Boers,' who would sell their souls for money. We call them cattle rangers because they're even worse than the English. They spitefully gather in the livestock from their Afrikaner brothers' farms and protect them from recapture by the Boer commandos. These are the men who deceived and caught Krause.'

Through shock and tears, I noticed his wet cheeks, and again felt the strength of my love for this man from across the waters.

There was no more travel that night, and when the grassland pheasants called before sunrise, we erased evidence of our stay and headed towards Kuruman. 'An oasis in the desert,' Edward described the lush little village that sits squat on an enormous spring on the Kalahari Desert's edge. 'That's the last of our readily available water sources, and from there it'll be hot and dry to Upington, not to mention the danger from the local Border Scouts who are armed and provisioned by the British.' Seeing my surprise about war activities so far from active fighting, he elaborated.

Many mixed-race coloured people were recruited as a mobile border protection force. Those local men were excellent riders and shots and not at all loyal to the Boers. Whoever paid the most had the scouts' loyalty, which, of course, made the English their paymasters, as *burghers* are volunteers without pay. 'The farmers you'll be staying with are neutral and provide the much-needed food the English rely on, not by choice, but the money buys survival. You will be safe,' he said with conviction.

From Kuruman, our travels became cumbersome over high sand ridges, brackish salt pans and with limited feed for the horses. 'The Scouts roam this desert country night and day and do not miss anything, because of their excellent eyesight and knowledge of the terrain,' Edward said. We travelled with extreme caution, as these far-flung habitations harboured much danger from Boer, Brit and scout.

At midnight on the eleventh day since our trek had started, we neared a farmhouse which stood like a skeleton on a hill. No trees, shrubs or garden could be seen in the light of a waning moon. Dirk sat hunched on his pony, but premonition kept me far behind. An owl called its sadness to the empty night, and we sat frozen on our mounts for many minutes. Then Edward imitated the owl twice, and a dim light flickered soon after in a window. 'It's safe,' he said, and we approached the house from behind.

The back door led straight into a homely kitchen and *sitkamer* – a large lounge, kitchen and scullery combined, as you would find in most Afrikaner homes. Unlike the floors at Morgenster, these were clay, 'polished' with a dull green cow-dung slurry which caught and hid every footstep as we entered.

Edward introduced the occupants as 'Mr and Mrs Kleynhans' - a middle-aged man with the directness of his German ancestry to his eyes, and a matronly woman, sturdy like her Dutch forebears. '*Oom* Roelof *en tante* Katrien,' she gave their preferred names. In their warm embrace, I knew we had found a home.

'We kept it on low burn,' *tante* Klatrien said, stoking the hearth and readying a tin kettle that was identical to ours on the farm. Smells of home-made soap, bread and aniseed rusks filled the room with memories of childhood pleasures, love and kindness. She looked at Dirk and me with knowing eyes and said reassuringly, 'This is your home now,' squeezing our shoulders with hands accustomed to hard work.

Edward held me tenderly before Dirk, and I went to sleep in a room with two single cots – one of only two bedrooms. The sun was already steadily approaching midday when we woke to soft murmurs in the kitchen, where we found the older couple in relaxed conversation. Outside, there was no sign of our horses, and when I asked, *oom* Roelof just shook his head and continued drinking his coffee.

From where I stood at the window, there was an uninterrupted view over hills, valleys and the Orange River to the south. A few sheep grazed not far away near low-slung outbuildings, which presumably shielded them from the cold at night. A lone Boer pony stood tethered at its entrance.

'He left when you were in deep sleep,' *oom* Roelof explained how Edward spared us the sadness of parting. And I understood that long, lonely days and nights would be my constant companion from then onward.

28 - *Loneliness and Longing*

There was peace in South Africa—peace "with honour" for England, peace and defeat for the Boers. PEACE, PEACE—AND THERE IS NO PEACE!
But let us (Burghers) in future live in such a way that nothing may be lost of the honour which is our inheritance from the battlefields of South Africa.

The Petticoat Commando. Johanna van Warmelo

Bleak loneliness and longing came to inhabit daily activities and followed each step I made on the farm, Rooipad – our new home, whose acres stretched from the simple hillside homestead, south across wagon trails between Kuruman and Upington, to thirstily touch the Orange River in the south.

From the front porch, it was evident why it was named Red Road. Crossing the oblong stretch of farmland towards its southern horizon lay many wheels' criss-cross tracks, carved into the powdery red sand - far enough from the house on the hill not to invite inquisitive eyes or blanket everything in dust. On a clear day, the river's wide ribbon could be seen where it flowed past *oom* Roelof's ploughed fields, now waiting barren in anticipation of early spring rains.

I imagined that sowing wheat, corn, pumpkin and watermelon to supply the warring parties would require many hours of sweat and toil in the semi-desert heat. Watering our own crops on Morgenster required much hard labour with man-made irrigation from the dam. To supply water along furrows and channels to the low-lying fields tested our strength, especially after the menfolk had joined commandos.

It was no different on Rooipad's fields. Ploughing was ox-driven, and manning the river-channels was hard work for an ageing *oom* Roelof and a few Herero men from neighbouring German South West Africa. Anyone labouring in the fields had to be brave with strong nerves to work where rifle shots could be heard on any given day.

'Most days I work by myself,' *oom* Roelof explained wearily, but true to his inborn determination and willingness to do whatever it takes, he saddled his pony in daylight's early rays every morning regardless of the weather and rode the few miles to the river.

The months came and went while I stayed at home and Dirk accompanied *oom* Roelof everywhere, never venturing into town or presenting ourselves when visitors came by. British soldiers came by day and roaming *burghers* at night, and without exception, they were in desperate need of food.

On a summer evening when mosquitoes circled us hungrily, a lone *burgher* rode in from the north and was made at home like any other visitor. 'Venter,' he introduced himself and gratefully accepted coffee and rusks with shaking hands. There was no hiding the many hours on horseback, but he held himself with pride and authority. At last he said, 'Our Secret Service men were betrayed,' and went on to confirm Krause's capture weeks ago together with a Judas-Boer and a youth, 'Peet Venter, my cousin and a mere boy.' Three or four days after that event, we were staggered with news of both men's execution – like bandits, they were shot in the old Pretoria jail's prison yard while the traitor Judas-Boer turned King's witness,' he uttered with loathing.

I remembered Krause's kindness and dedication to do the right thing by our people, but my mind was already on the dreadful time to come, stirred by such callousness. Surely the *burghers* would retaliate, and how would these events influence my own future with Edward on the enemy's side? No comforting words came to me for this poor man who so clearly had been pushed to the last thread of endurance.

Oom Roelof's fields turned from brown to green to brown again before we received word from Edward. Unlike the sad news of Krause's death, a note from Edward, which we had found wedged in the back door a month ago, simply read, 'Soon, Cornelia, soon.' From that moment, my heart sang, and my steps became light. *Tante* Katrien and I baked bread, biscuits, rusks and whatever we had no need for.

Barely a week later, at the end of May 1902, to my surprise, the devastating war ended, and if it wasn't for the far-off celebratory shots in Upington, we would not have known. But we knew with certainty it meant that our *burghers* had succumbed to the constant threat to their families, the dreadful displacement and the burning of everything they had worked so hard for. The life-sapping guerrilla war our men were forced to wage to protect our nation from the invaders had at last taken its toll. The fear I harboured after Krause's death now had no sting.

For days, we went about our tasks without enthusiasm, robbed of our very essence and sense of fairness. 'The big struggle to survive will start now,' *oom* Roelof said quietly around the dinner table in early June, and my thoughts turned to Morgenster and the effort it would take to rebuild the once thriving farm. Would old Jacob and Pikanien even know the war was over where they had been sheltering the sheep in the high country? And what would Edward and I have to build a future with?

'Where will we go now, *hê* Nelie,' Dirk asked in his half-man voice one *brisk morning, stopping his wood-chopping while I was hanging washing with cold hands. At 11, his body already revealed the strong man he was to become, but his heart still belonged to me – the only person he could rely on to comfort and protect.

'You will always be with me, Dirkie,' I assured him as a rider came up the hill. 'The *rooinek* may not want that,' he said quite uncharacteristically short and pointed to the rider who dismounted, strode up and without hesitation took me into his arms. In the protection these arms afforded, there were answers to every question, I thought, but in truth, it was more a wish.

Edward stayed for two days, and in that time, we learned about the many adventures he had had after his discharge in 1901. 'Now I am a long-haul trader between Cape Town and Upington. I am staying permanently, Cornelia. This is my country that I have fought for.' That turn of phrase brought an awkwardness to the conversation and an unease that I could not explain.

Wasn't it his plan to stay all along? Had we not planned a life together?

Everyone became quiet and avoided my eyes to fix theirs in the distance. But soon we felt reassured when Edward explained that he had already saved a substantial amount of money and would be able to buy a house in Upington. 'Now that the war is over, we can start looking for a house,' he said before leaving the next day, and with these words, my last concerns were wiped away.

Six months, Dirk and I scanned the road for Edward's return. Christmas came to us hot and spirit-sapping, and still no rider came on the dusty road. The kind Kleynhans pair turned conversations towards a positive future for everyone and never went to bed without making it known that Dirk and I would always be their treasured guests.

In my heart, I knew that they were sincere, as I could tell that their childless lives had taken on new meaning since we had arrived.

The only riders that came by after the war were families trudging wearily to their once flourishing farms. One day, a single rider with a trailing pack mule leisurely rode up to the front door. I could not believe my eyes as one of *oom* Abraham Bergmann's boys dismounted. Seeing a familiar face from our previous life brought unbidden tears of joy to my eyes and a slow smile to the tall man's handsome face.

That night, we celebrated what was good in life before war and what good could come from our experiences. 'We have to hope, and then pray to the good Lord that our hopes will be fulfilled under the English,' *oom* Roelof said and then prompted young Ampie Bergmann for the knowledge he had gathered on his way. The quiet man never stood a chance of retiring early, and between generous helpings of dessert, his family's war journeys were told simply and honestly.

I learned anew that his family had moved before the war to Weltevreden, a farm in the northern Waterberg district. This confirmed *tannie* Botes's letter, which had already explained the family's journey.

Ampie continued, '*Pa* was shrewd and knew about business,' he said and went on to tell about the old man's ever-present ear to the ground through which he learned about and then acquired a government-backed promise for a portion of an enormous tract of land called Elandsfontein. The farm stood with one foot in Langkloof valley, straddling the Waterberg mountains to pan out north close to Vaalwater village - the district's best farming land. The steep mountains could be crossed along Rankin's Pass and north through Sandrivierspoort Nek - a narrow pass that gave way to a beautiful plateau where livestock could graze in future. 'A farm in the valley would have the benefit of both sides,' Ampie said.

'And how did he get his hands on this land?' the older man said, and Ampie explained patiently that because of 1886's Occupation Act, the government acquired land free of charge in the North-Eastern corner of the Waterberg District. Thereafter, the Zuid-Afrikaansche Republiek could control the distribution of land in the Transvaal.

Regarded by the government as useless mountainous country, and keen to settle white farmers as a buffer against black people, the Bergmanns were able to buy as much as they wanted for a few shillings an acre or make a claim to such land for tenancy or purchase.

Elandsfontein was the official name noted for the entire area, which would, in time, be cut into portions and made available to potential farmers. But who could know the future, and so old *oom* Bergmann ensured the official papers were in writing. The fine print was read and re-read and then locked away in his tin trunk. '*Pa* knew best; he was clever that way,' it came with pride from a firstborn son. What form of ownership it entailed was locked in the High Dutch documents and served as testament to good planning and foresight.

The family settled and built a modest house on Weltevreden farm, while *oom* Abraham and his two sons, Ampie and Gert, took on building work, often travelling far from home. Then the English came, and the three men set off to war, leaving the women behind – a mother and three older sisters with families of their own and husbands who had also joined the local commandos. It was a full household, made even busier by a sickly fourth sister and her four children.

Sadness crossed Ampie's face as he relayed his father's death at sea in 1901 on their way to St Helena as prisoners of war. He stared into the candlelight for a while, shoulders bent under the burden of witnessing a beloved father buried with little ceremony at age 62. Now that he was the provider, the building skills he had learned from *oom* Abraham took him across Transvaal for work that was desperately needed. But with no funds allocated by the new government, which struggled with an insurmountable war debt, it was an uphill battle to find work and survive. Then he sighed and said, '*Alles sal regkom, Oom, alles sal tog regkom,*' expressing his hope and desire that all will be well in the end.

Over the next week, Ampie searched for building work in Upington and on surrounding farms. There was much to do, but little that he could do, except for free. War made beggars of us all, and Ampie, too proud to ask for hand-outs, was happy to sleep in the outbuildings, 'For a few nights,' but the ever-hospitable *oom* and *tante* Kleynhans would have none of it. That's how it happened that the two of us talked into the night about a world that may have little generosity for its next generation.

When he saddled up, Ampie promised to visit again after riding south and before returning to Weltevreden. 'It could be months, Cornelia, but I will visit,' he said and held my hand a fraction longer than necessary with his long fingers - fingers too elegant for a builder's rough work.

Midway through January 1903, a dust storm brought Edward to our front door. For a glorious week, we looked at the possibilities of owning a house in Upington, but with so little available after the war, we decided to buy land instead. We rode out to a piece of land outside the town boundaries, 'Where the river meets the front *stoep*,' the desperate farmer who needed to sell a section of his farm for his family's survival, said. After hours of fruitless search, we came to a bend in the river, and there, hidden behind two enormous willows, a tiny shack leaned forward to meet the river. 'This is ours,' Edward said softly, and echoed my own feelings.

Inside, a rough-hewn wooden chair stood at attention, and in the furthest corner, a single bed on spindly legs barely held onto a coarse mattress. But this could be ours!

Edward took my hands, and we danced the dance of happiness, laughing loudly and shouting *yippees* to the river.

Then, in the coupling of our dreams, we came together for the first time – fierce in many years' pent-up desire, and tender in our love for each other.

Part Four: Secrets and Deceit

29 – Distressing Choices

There were still 10 000 women and children who were not in camps (just before peace). They were in shocking condition – their homes and all food supplies were destroyed, and, while their men were able to supply them with food, the British sent out at once to rob them of these fresh supplies, and did this by means of bodies of armed natives, who took away all food and clothing and broke up the women's cooking utensils. The women were then entirely at the mercy of these natives, with results that one dare not dwell upon. Many women were almost naked when their men arrived, some had on only blouses. Many of the women were found in Kaffir huts.

Emily Hobhouse

In the contented afterglow of finding a home and each other, January passed quietly. Whatever I touched had a purpose and direction to it, and the lonely days without Edward became dream-filled. I stacked corners of my mind with the happiness so rudely denied during war.

On the cool front porch, *tante* Katrien and I spent hours sewing and mending, until my mind turned to the note in *tannie* Botes's Bible, which called to be read and understood.

I read it again, and the half-sentences talked to me expectantly in their elaborate cursive curls:

When apple blossoms are no more
Don't forget their promise,
My Apple Blossom
Be true to generosity
Sand and tree belong to thee
Give, give, give
Your only love, always,
Paulus Botes

'Whatever could that mean?' My thoughts spilled aloud into the quiet, forcing *tante* Katrien's hands to stop their task. I handed over the note.

'Well, now, the way I read it, it is a wish to be fulfilled. Maybe it's about something the writer owns,' she ventured. I thought on that for some time, and then it came to me like lightning on a dark night – *tannie* Botes's farm, my farm in the Waterberg district! It was waiting for me to do something.

But how could I share my ownership of this far-off property when it didn't fit into our plans to be in Upington? No, it had to remain a secret.

The desert heat became unbearable in February, and many-a-day I did not feel like getting up in the morning. My longing for Edward added its cruelty to the empty hours. *Tante* Katrien, who had become used to the heat over a lifetime, suggested bathing in the morning and spending more time out on the south porch.

One particularly scorching day out on the porch, she said calmly, 'Cornelia, *my kind,* if wisdom is not exercised, wisdom ceases to be.' She wiped my forehead and arms, then took my hand, 'I too have to remember that the very nature of knowing things is an instruction on my heart to do what wisdom expects.' I looked at her loving face but could find no answer to this strange statement.

With thumb stroking my hand softly, she said kindly, 'You may not have a choice but to tell me what the note is hiding – together we may be able to find an answer to your situation. Soon your body will tell others what I already know.' I pulled my hand away in shock and protested, but no sound came forth.

'Edward will be back soon,' I proclaimed weakly, knowing full well the enormity of being with child in a society not yet willing to accept man-made rules' transgression.

We sat quietly until the sun turned its face towards the west, then I shared *tannie* Botes and *Ma*'s story - the intricacies of circumstances so often forced on parents, that can change lives forever. *Tante* Katrien waited patiently until the last whispered sentence. 'Your discretion and vision will be the wisdom that will instruct your heart now, Cornelia. Use it to fulfil the note's wish and to fulfil God's will for your unborn child,' she said, and together we started planning my life, which would always be entwined with Dirk's and this baby's.

How I longed for *Pa*'s wisdom and *Ma*'s practicality! Now that I needed them most, nobody knew whether they were still alive and if my sisters had escaped Irene camp's hell, or where they could be, should they have survived war's brutality. My quiet time with our Maker grew longer and longer until Dirk commented, 'I can pray for you too, Nelie,' which just brought tears and despondency. How could I explain the pain associated with waiting on promises made and not being able to wait much longer? 'We will be fine, Dirkie,' I tearily consoled the boy who became a man far too early.

'Walk with me,' *oom* Roelof invited me to the ridge behind the house one morning when the desert mist drifted quietly before the rising sun. Up on the hill, the landscape's beauty was soothing to my burdened soul. 'God's beauty is everywhere, Nelie. He shines his light even on the problems you now experience – take it, it's yours through his grace.' We sat down on the rocky ground, and I sensed he had more to say.

After a while, he said in his direct manner, 'Your path is not with Edward, child. I know this because word has filtered through of his involvement with the Herero and the war-thirsty Jakob Morengo, who is leading a revolt against the Germans across the border. That's why he doesn't visit or write. Your child should not wait on a father with fighting in his veins,' and with that, he got up and pulled me into his strong arms. 'God will provide,' he promised. It was a long time before I followed him home.

The house became a place of silence and concern. Dirk spent many hours in the fields until *tante* Katrien scolded him with warranted sharpness about the sun's harshness. But I felt unable to throw off despondency's heavy veil.

Visitors were mostly a few stragglers on their way north, while hundreds upon hundreds could be seen in the distance, trudging the red path between Upington and Pretoria.

Sitting on the front porch, not a day went by that the misery of human suffering was not pressed on our hearts by those wandering aimlessly and dying of thirst on their way to a better place – a place not to be found on scorched farms or across the border in war-torn German South West Africa.

'The hell which the English brought on our nation will be with us for generations,' *oom* Roelof said, pipe in hand. '26 000 women and children lost, and our nation forever filled with hatred towards the English vultures,' he sighed, knowing we were the fortunate ones who felt fighting's softer touch.

Many who came by told of horrendous treatment by the British soldiers, but even more degrading and soul-destroying were the barbaric treatment of women outside the camps by blacks serving their paymasters. Many nights, I could not sleep, imagining what their lives would be like now. How could I be so thankless and bemoan my situation day and night, when thousands would never know the joy of happiness?

When we woke the next day, Ampie Bergmann's horse and mule were tethered at the outbuildings. Dirk was out the back door like a hare, and through the kitchen window, we could see him talking animatedly to Ampie, windmill arms adding colour to his pent-up stories. 'The father he never had,' *tante* Katrien said quietly, and I wondered what caused Dirk to blossom in Ampie's company yet become withdrawn in Edward's. Both men had a great capacity to love and be empathetic, and both were at ease with an orphaned boy who would always be with me.

That night, Ampie took us on a tour to Klerksdorp, where the *burgher* leaders had decided to lay down arms, and south to Morgenster's burned-out farmstead. 'In Klerksdorp, I ran into a farming family who said they were your neighbours. They suffered greatly in the camps but were trying to rebuild their farm. The old man said your father had returned to Morgenster and later passed by with a small herd of sheep and two blacks – one old, one young. They were on their way to Kameelfontein, a farm between Rustenburg in the north-east beyond the Waterberg mountains' westerly fringes. Not far from Weltevreden, where my family had settled before the war. You could easily travel between the farms by crossing the Vlieëberg Pass,' he described the pass known for flies' annoyance.

My heart leapt wildly at the knowledge that my family had survived the war. 'We should go, Dirkie! Maybe all are alive,' my happiness spilled over. For the first time in weeks, I felt hope taking hold, but Ampie just smiled his slow smile and sat back in his chair. 'We'll talk about that tomorrow, Cornelia,' he said calmly and went to bed without discussing the possibility further.

Dirk and I lay awake most of the night, talking about a place that held no meaning to us. A place where even flies were cemented in names. 'Well, Nelie, on my grandfather's farm, the flies were so bad that they would crawl up your nose if you let them,' he said and laughed at a long-ago memory.

I woke to a quiet house. Coffee was brewing on the wood stove, and its aroma came to me in bed. Outside, Ampie was mending a leather stirrup, whistling in the enjoyment of simple tasks. I watched him for a while; his hands' strength barely masked their sensuality. He stopped for a moment only as he smelled the coffee I brought outside, and we drank in silence. Then he said matter-of-factly, 'Marrying me will be a good thing.' I stood speechless, but when I looked into his kind grey eyes, a great calm came to sit in my chest, and a longing for better days settled in my bones.

Ampie's words, mundane though they may appear out in the back yard, were significant of greater things. It would be a promise for a life of unswerving loyalty 'until death do us part' - altogether the most significant promise a man and woman can make - a promise before our God. Is such a promise not worth a million times more than Edward's promises that never seemed to reach fulfilment?

I nodded slowly with quiet certainty. God in his wisdom had indeed provided.

30 – Northwards

The devastation of both Boer and black African populations in the concentration camps and through war and exile were to have a lasting effect on the demography and quality of life in the region. Many exiles and prisoners were unable to return to their farms at all; others attempted to do so but were forced to abandon the farms as unworkable given the damage caused by farm burning in the course of the scorched earth policy. Destitute Boers and black Africans swelled the ranks of the unskilled urban poor competing with the "uitlanders" in the mines.

Van Onselen. 1982

'**D**isappointment is part of life, but we have to get up and become encouraged again to be able to live the life of gratitude we're called to,' *Pa* had said one winter's morning after black frost's icy winds had killed many dozens of sheep overnight.

Of all *Pa's* sayings, this one came to me when Ampie returned from Upington the day before our departure - his lanky frame bent under an unseen weight. 'Let him be, Cornelia,' *oom* Roelof said, and we carried on with our tasks. Around the dinner table, it suddenly sprang from his lips like an uninvited guest, bringing worry and unease to the onlookers. 'I've had word from home,' Ampie said, and with effort told the news that killed any hope and plans he may have had for our future.

He explained that his father's will was read during his long absence; a will that was drawn up in 1892, shortly after his youngest sibling was born, and long before the family had moved to the Waterberg district. It was confirmed to those present that they were merely tenants on Weltevreden farm but could soon be required to pay for land use.

The land had lain fallow after Resolution 159 of 1855 had prohibited anybody who was not a *burgher* from owning land. Because black people were specifically prohibited from having *burgher* rights, many farms became uninhabited. However, since the 1890's, some areas had become havens for destitute whites to settle, and that's how the family came to live on Weltevreden. Everybody present knew Weltevreden was theirs on loan only, but what came next was a surprise.

The officer of the court who read the will informed the family that the old man had no immovable property, not even what they had believed to be their permanent home - Elandsfontein in the Langkloof valley - for which his father had apparently only lodged an expression of interest, but had lacked the funds to buy at the time. Therefore, the family had no legal claim to any land. If only he had paid a deposit, their future would've been secured.

Movable belongings had to be shared equally among his mother, each surviving child, and each grandchild. Their only income would be an indeterminate war widow's allowance once the estate was finalised. With a new government, it could take many years. How an inheritance of unknown value at an undetermined date could practically sustain them, he would have to find out. The letter simply said it was an enormous disappointment to the family, who had believed their lives were secure.

His face became dark, and his jaw clenched determinedly. 'I will buy Elandsfontein one day, but I can't ask you to go to a place of struggle, Cornelia,' he uttered unhappily. But *Pa's* words came to me: 'Disappointment is part of life, and we'll find a way.' *What option did we have?*

On the morning of our departure, *tante* Katrien took my hand and led me to their bedroom. On the bed lay a dress like no other. Layer upon layer of ivory lace adorned the full-length skirt - the kind and quality I had only heard of. She picked it up and held it delicately against me with measuring eyes.

The lace skirt reached to my feet and was held together in the back with a pretentious satin bow. The bodice was a see-through material that any seamstress could only dream of, and the narrow middle carried a wide satin belt that fastened in the back. 'For your wedding,' she said, deep emotion trembling in her voice, but I could not even imagine touching an object so precious or dare to accept such a gift.

She ignored my protestations and folded the dream dress into a calico bag, took me gently by the arm and said, 'For you, my daughter.'

My tears knew no limits, and together we cried for what was, what we would never have and what would be.

Then *tante* Katrien said, 'Be a tree, Cornelia. Let the high winds rustle your branches and your roots rest deep in the soil – there you will not lose who you are, but labour with all the force of your life to remain what you have always been – a strong protector.'

T*ante* Katrien held me with such force when we were ready to go that my sobs became dry spasms of inner pain. For more than a year, she had been my constant, my friend, my patient teacher. And now the parting was more distressing than leaving *Ma* to her fate. 'This is a good choice, *my kind*, albeit a bitter one,' she said softly and wiped away my tears. In her sorrowful eyes, I saw my own deep loss. Blood does not make a child more real - I was hers as much as Dirk was mine.

'We know where your family lives, Cornelia,' *oom* Roelof promised gruffly to keep in contact, and helped me onto the one-horse carriage he had stored away years ago and 'have no need for anymore.' At my feet, a canvas that would be our shelter at night.

For days, the older couple had scurried around in their search for that elusive 'something else' they supposedly did not need. Practical articles that would make our lives easier: knives, a spirit level, ladles, crockery, but most of all a little bag of delicate lace and beautiful buttons that would shape a baby's christening dress. Tiny buttons fit for the girl who was never gifted them. I could imagine them in Edward's button box until needed.

Dirk stood to the side, scanning the far-off fields, but when *oom* Roelof formally shook his hand, he let go and hugged the older man fiercely with a hollow cry. '*Toemaar, my boetie*, all will be well. It is your turn now to look after Nelie,' *oom* Roelof said and helped Dirk mount.

Ampie waited patiently for our parting to take its course, and then it was time to go. Down at the crossroads, I looked back, and there the two old people stood like two beacons on the hill, waving us on our way.

Ampie calculated that it would take 16 days as the crow flies to reach Kameelfontein, my parents' farm. 'But we have to eat and rest,' he explained. 'I have sent word to the post office in Nylstroom that we are on our way. From there, it will travel to the outlying farms, and our families will know we're coming,' he voiced his plans, using words sparingly as usual. What he didn't say, and I understood without explanation, was that the two families would work together and start preparing for our wedding in Nylstroom.

Over the next few weeks, I learned that a beautiful new church had been built in town before the war and became the envy of passers-by. A building fit for a wedding.

Our travels followed backroads, often just faint tracks left by farmers many years ago, and at times, evidence of troop activity stood out clearly in the trampled earth. From Upington, we immediately trekked north-north-east towards Mafikeng, a British stronghold during the war. We skirted the town, whose inhabitants were once mainly traditional black pastoralists but had become home to soldiers who had no intention of returning to England's cold shores. From there, we turned north-east towards Zeerust, then over sparsely populated countryside through Leeuwpoort Pass, and across Rooiberg's granite mountains where caracal and baboon fought for dominance and survival.

Standing between those mountain boulders, Ampie pointed north and east, saying, 'See those mountains? That's the Langkloof where our home will be one day.'

We arrived at Weltevreden halfway through March. My body ached, and my spirit lagged, but I was lucky not to have become ill with morning sickness. Thankful that my secret was safe, hidden amid the heat and discomfort. Four barefoot children with wild hair came running, and a strongly built boy, slightly older than Dirk, was chasing them from behind.

'*Oom* Ampie, *oom* Ampie, *kom kyk die tarentaaltjies!*' they shouted over each other in their excitement about the guinea fowl kits, as he dismounted stiffly and then greeted each with a kiss. Together they disappeared behind a sturdy farmhouse to inspect a brood of guinea fowl, leaving Dirk and me behind.

The house was quite unlike any in the region where I grew up. It was firmly planted, facing west, with a wide *stoep* surrounding the square structure. There was no garden to speak of except a lone flowering plant that I've seen before in graveyards, sustaining itself in the harshest environments. '*Grafblommetjies*,' *Ma* called the tough flowering plants that ensured survival through their bitter taste.

A motherly woman came towards us, removing her apron and brushing back grey hair in her stride. She hugged Dirk warmly and kissed me full on the lips, then held me at arm's length. 'Ampie chose well,' she said pleasantly and led us inside with, 'Call me *tant* Gertruida.

Come, there's coffee and jam tarts in the kitchen where Truia and I have been baking for days.'

Freshly baked bread and cake's aroma met us at the front door, which looked across a wide passage through to the back door and outside, where the children and Ampie stood surrounded by all kinds of fowl. 'Go to them, Dirkie,' I prompted the child in him when I noticed his yearning eyes. He needed little persuasion.

On the kitchen table, a sweet feast was lined up to entice even those without a sweet tooth. 'Oh, have as much as you like, *kind*, the pantry is already full,' *tant* Gertruida said with a sweep of the hand that included many shelves in the pantry leading off the delicious-smelling kitchen. Truia, Ampie's oldest sister, brought the wonderful odours from the pantry with her. With arms wide, she welcomed me to the family. Without warning, tears overwhelmed me, as my weary soul recognised the goodness and comfort of a loving family.

Tant Gertruida wrapped me in her arms and said, 'You are home now, Cornelia. Soon you'll be with your parents, but now is our time,' and stroked my hair softly. I rested my head on her shoulder and felt calm flow between us, and thought, *here I can be a tree whose branches rustle in the high winds.*

Around the scrubbed dinner table that evening, when it was just Ampie, *tant* Gertruida and me, she answered all our questions and some we couldn't ask. She explained that, apart from Truia's family of four children and a second husband, Ampie's older sisters and their families had moved away towards Nylstroom and Pietersburg in the North-East in search of a better life. The three adults, four children and sixteen-year-old Gert had to survive on what little they had until Ampie's return.

'If we live frugally, a good life could be had, Ampie. Because your father died at sea during the war, his war pension will be paid in full without me having to fight for it like other poor widows. According to our will, everyone will receive equally.' For our benefit, she calculated on paper how much each would inherit once the will was settled.

Apparently, after the will was read, a War Office representative arrived from Pretoria to inform her of the exact amount she could count on. His visit gave her hope that life would become less cumbersome.

From the £51,266 pension, a £44,000 lump sum would be paid once the Will's terms had taken effect. The seven children would each receive £3-1-6 as a child's portion, while she would receive £21-11-6 as a widow's portion, with ongoing payments on the remainder until it runs out.

'I can buy my own farm if I so wish when the estate is finalised,' *tant* Gertruida said, 'but now that you're back, I might move with Truia to Pietersburg.' Then she whispered, 'She hasn't been well since little Rachel's birth in '97, and the new husband is no good,' she mimicked someone lifting a glass.

'I have no money yet, no husband and no home. Whatever I decide will be independent of others' needs. To help with the paperwork, I have appointed Hendrik Kroep in Nylstroom as my attorney and agent to act on my behalf. Just promise me you'll look after Gert; he is already doing building work here and there in the valley and can learn much from you.'

That night, I pondered our path forward. While no one could survive long on the promise of 3 pounds, 1 shilling and 6 pennies, Ampie and I were young and strong with dreams in our hearts.

Although my heart ached to be with Edward, with the desire of a first love, with this gentle man, I could let my roots rest deep in the soil.

I will learn to love Ampie and not lose who I am, but labour with all the force of my life to be a good wife and mother.

Why did the Boers give in? How could the Boers give In and lose their independence?' 'The National Scouts – the Judas-Boers. They broke our strength. Not by their skill in the use of arms, not by their knowledge of our country and our methods - no! They broke our strength by breaking our ideals, by crushing our enthusiasm, by robbing us of our inspiration, our faith, our hope----'

The Petticoat Commando. 1912

'**E**veryone has secrets stored away. That is not a bad thing,' *tannie* Botes had whispered in my ear the day she died.
Was my secret then a good thing, or just not a bad thing?
How long would I be able to keep my secret? Surely the women in my family would be able to tell – they had a keen sense about such things. How would I explain the deception that accompanied my situation?

Sleep vanished in these questions' wake, and when morning came, my limbs felt heavy, and I could not get out of bed. I heard someone at the door, but *tant* Gertruida hushed them away with, 'The journey was tiring for her.'

When I woke again, the sun had already shifted overhead, but I felt refreshed and eager to visit Kameelfontein, a 'few miles away,' according to Ampie. As it turned out, a few miles were nearer to 20 with a cumbersome trek across the Vlieëberge Pass due west.

The buggy rolled dangerously on its two wooden wheels, designed for smoother surfaces. My hands automatically cradled my stomach, protecting the germ of life so sweetly sown and so bitterly resented now. How could something so small kill off the only dream worth having after the pain of war?

We rocked on, and soon I learned why flies were honoured in a name, as our body heat drew them in swarms to every wet orifice and offered a free ride to the valley beyond. From the escarpment, the veld stretched out ahead. As far as the eye could see, sickle bush and camelthorn stood side-by-side in a dense blanket.

The beautiful Waterberg mountain range dropped off to our right, and the lush vegetation of the Langkloof valley was replaced by overgrown, inhospitable bushland.

From up high, we saw wagon tracks below, left by long-ago frontier peoples, cutting a narrow path south to north. I wondered at the endurance and bravery needed to journey into unknown territory and avoid wild beasts who, Ampie said, still roamed mountains and valleys alike.

Summer's long days allowed enough time before sunset to reach Kameelfontein – named after the numerous camelthorn trees dotted from horizon to horizon, spreading their wide canopies for shelter. The temperature changed from mild to hot as soon as we reached the bushveld, and I had to wipe my face constantly. A gate fabricated from wooden poles and wire invited us to my parents' farm. After a few tries to open the unusual gate, Dirk gave up.

'A *bekslaner*,' Ampie said with a twinkle in his eye, and demonstrated how to negotiate the gate with a tightly sprung bow-lever that's feared by everyone as 'the devil's sjambok.' He laughed good-humouredly at our disbelieving faces. I had never seen anything like it before and knew for certain that I would never be able to open such a gate. But it was strong and vowed for the maker's ingenuity and practicality in a time of scarcity.

A simple farmhouse with wide verandas greeted us. As if called by a bell, *Pa* came through the front door, followed by Jan, Daan, young Andries and a few children of differing ages. By the time I had straightened my dress, Lettie, Hannie and Bettie had joined the group. At that moment, a small child came running from behind and grabbed hold of Hannie's skirt.

'Eva?!' Bettie nodded to confirm my suspicion. I could not believe that she had grown so much or that she had survived all that life served her. She was bound to become the typical strong Afrikaner woman who could overcome the worst humanity could dish out. I felt overwhelmed with gratitude and had to hold onto Ampie and Dirk for support.

Then everyone laughed the happy laugh of freedom, and we hugged and cried for an eternity. With hat in hand, Ampie shook everyone's hand, even the children milling at our feet. They liked him instantly, and although my heart still yearned for and belonged to Edward, it recognised the kind soul in Ampie and beat warmly at the thought of him as a father.

Pa guided us inside where the cool of day was settling in. In the *sitkamer's* comfort and a grandfather clock's measured time, we sat to learn about each other's journey. I looked at what was left of my family, the heads sitting around me - small, medium and large, wheaten, brown and black, and then there was *Pa's,* whose lush mop had given way to wispy grey and sparsely sown hair and beard. Each head carried its own story, deeply buried in the recesses of memory. The adults' lined faces were the only evidence of a painful path that might, in time, become overgrown by goodness.

Between cups of coffee and generous servings of baked goods, the concentration camps' sadness and war's terrors were sewn onto the blanket of gratefulness that it was over. No one mentioned *Ma* or my traitorous actions, leaving her to others' mercy. My shame would not let me ask the question either. It was Ampie who innocently asked about her.

A hush came over us, and then *Pa* said with anguish swirling around every word, 'By the grace of God she is here, but resting.' He squeezed my hand, and his eyes promised an explanation later.

By the time cows came home to be milked, we had completed Hannie, Lettie and Bettie's travels from Irene camp. Against the *sitkamer's* wall stood *tannie* Botes's elaborately carved bookshelf, and on the floor her good-quality carpet adorned an otherwise unpretentious room. 'There was space on the wagon,' Bettie said matter-of-factly, but I knew she would've carried it on her back if needed be.

Theirs was a harsh road to travel, but the three women took turns telling of the chaos following the British's decision to abandon camps, and how they survived on the goodwill of others while trying to find their menfolk. 'It was *RéAndriese* with her contacts within the *burgher* network who directed us to the Waterberg district,' Lettie said. 'And then we travelled together to Nylstroom, where we split up. We took Eva to the Waterberg and *RéAndriese* went to Pietersburg in the north,' Hannie elaborated.

'She knew how far we had to travel but told us to find her if we needed anything, anything,' Bettie added. In the silence that followed, we imagined how they held onto each other, their unwillingness to break away from the shared kinship built up in the cruel concentration camps' confines.

'When I asked how we would find her, she said we just had to ask around,' Lettie said, shaking her head at the improbability of needing or finding *RéAndriese*. But they did not know the lemon tree's secrets.

Pa stared at the floor for a while, sighed and then told his story. After the war, as part of peace deliberations, he was chosen as a Boer negotiator at Klerksdorp, close to our farm, Morgenster. There, he spent weeks gathering information about *Ma's* hospital stay. A brusque nurse, overworked and emotionally drained by years of facing maimed and dispirited soldiers and *burghers* who had filled the hospital to the brim, pushed him out of the way with, 'Why would a woman find herself here?!' There was little he could do but rely on word-of-mouth.

Passing him for the umpteenth time one day, she stopped and, with a softer expression, said, 'Try the cemetery.' When she noticed his desperation, she mentioned as an afterthought, 'If she had survived, they would've sent her to the church's welfare office.' And it was at the church where *Pa* ran into our old minister, *Meester* Jacob Strasheim. After having seen death and destruction for more than three years, there was nothing left of his admonishment and high-handed condemnation. He remembered well when a Canadian soldier brought my weak and disoriented mother to the church.

'I could not care for her, but the school master took her away,' old Strasheim said wearily and pointed in the once thriving farm school's general direction. *Meester* Riggs, bent double by a back ailment, led *Pa* to a tiny backroom with a single cot. There, hiding behind a curtain, he found *Ma*, conscious but paralysed, and eyes which refused to focus. We could not believe that the once-strong woman could have become so frail. Everyone started crying, and the tears seemed to point their fingers of blame at me, but *Pa* stood and took my hand, 'The war caused this, Nelie. You made sure that she stayed alive, and for that we praise our Maker.'

He left *Ma* in the teacher's care and rode to the high country to find old Jacob and Pikanien. After arranging suitable transport, he fetched her and led the others to Kameelfontein, which he had secured before peace negotiations, and where young Andries was waiting.

In Irene camp, Hannie and Lettie had withdrawn into a quiet world whenever I asked about the children and our younger sisters, Johanna, Martha and Sara.

An unspeakable trauma did not allow them to talk much about it then, and I did not expect them to repeat the heartache now. It was Hannie who hesitantly started reliving the horrors of their capture by the British and their unbelievable callousness to leave *Ma* and Eva behind on that darkest of nights. As if to guard and protect the unmentionable, she explained in a few sentences for the menfolk's benefit, how our once carefree sisters were wrestled from her arms and never seen or heard of again. She was quiet for a long time, struggling with emotions that spilled over into silent sobs, 'I could not save them! I could not save them!'

Children who came from separate farms were loaded onto a wagon bound for the north. It was Jan and Daan, who had located the remaining members of their families at Nylstroom's concentration camp, known to have been one of the most mismanaged. Their heartache at the neglect and mistreatment was compounded by the loss of two of Daan's orphaned children and all of Jan's. Their precious children's graves stood side-by-side among war's victims at a specially dedicated area in the local graveyard. Now, Eva and two cousins were the only ones to fill the void in their parents' hearts.

My eyes searched Lettie's. She looked down and shook her head slowly. I knew in time she would have the confidence to speak about what had happened to her baby, whom she so laboriously carried over the mountains. I could still see her heavy body negotiating the hills after *ouma* Susara's accident at the wagon trail. A little cousin to Eva that could've given meaning to Lettie's life now after the loss of so many others.

Jan did not mention his own wife or children, and no one was brave enough to ask. He explained that Lettie and Hannie's husbands, Stephanus Pretorius and Michiel Horn, were alive and well, but hunting towards the interior along the Crocodile River that was in full flow after seasonal rains. I remembered crossing the same river with Dirk and Krause on our way to Upington and was surprised to learn at the time that it flowed away from the ocean to join with others before turning towards the sea, many, many miles to the east. 'Oh, there is plenty of antelope to hunt, and soon we'll have the best *biltong* hanging on the *stoep*,' *Pa* said.

The similarities between the Bergmann and Niemandt families' pain and joys struck me again, and I wondered whether any Boer families were left intact after the war.

I realised that, even though I had suffered, my people had suffered more yet remained optimistic in the face of sadness. How wonderful that the human heart could be happy and heartbroken at the same time.

Lettie stood, wiped her hands on her apron and declared, 'We have a wedding to plan, so no more crying and living in the past!' And we dutifully followed our practical sister to the kitchen.

32 – Peace at what Cost?

The principal speaker was a very tall, finely built woman, with eyes that were capable of a great variety of expression. (She said) 'There will be no peace unless we get what we want – unless we get what is right. We may get it still more bitter, still more hard; I may be without a petticoat at last. But if everything is gone – that day that we get our independence, I will dance and play like a little child.' Then the same strange, beautiful light again spread over her face, and filled her eyes.

The Brunt of the War and Where it Fell. Johanna van Warmelo

I found him head-on-forearm next to *Ma's* bed. 'It is our humanity and the pride our women carried throughout this war, that will give us back our land,' *Pa* spoke quietly, stroking her hand, 'How proud you were.'

One look at *Ma's* hollow cheeks and sunken eyes told me that pride would not accompany her again. The memory of what she used to be made his tone husky in tenderness and respect. I recognised the privilege of sharing the moment with them. But like a thieving intruder, *RéAndriese's* image came unbidden to sully the moment. Was his love for her equally deep as it was for *Ma*? How was that even possible?

As these thoughts crowded in on me, I realised that I already loved Ampie while my love for Edward was without doubt unquestionable. Who was I to question *Pa's* devotion then?

I stood back against the wall and felt the afternoon sun's heat through the bricks. We might complain about the heat's harshness here in the north, but it shines on all humankind and shares its rays with the same intent that it used to at Morgenster. Surely *Pa* would know if love could be shared like that as well, and as if reading my thoughts, he stood and motioned for us to go outside.

Not far from the house, he had built a pigsty from wooden poles where a few pigs grunted their contentment. About ten yards away, old Jacob and Pikanien were separating lambs from ewes in a pen of thorn branches, 'To keep out jackal, caracal and even leopard,' *Pa* explained.

Big cats came down from the mountains during the night and indulged in the kind of feast that was easy to catch and non-existent in the hills. He sighed, 'This is not Morgenster, but here, where the warm winds blow, we can start anew and give *Ma* a chance to get well.' The worry lines folded their secrets deeply around his eyes and forehead as if to say, '*This is just a dream.*' And how true that was, considering the ghost-like person in the bedroom.

We walked all the way to the gate, and the early evening's stillness smoothed out the worries of the internal wars we had to fight on our own. 'We are the lucky ones, Little Bird,' he said, and when he looked at me, his eyes mirrored the unspeakable atrocities of a war we were indeed lucky to have survived. He took my hand in a childhood gesture and turned to me, 'Now tell me the secret that keeps your thoughts far from here.' There had never been a time I could hide my feelings from him, and I sat down in the dirt road where tears could fall and words be said, and no one but us would know.

When dusk set in, he pulled me up and said simply, 'Let's see if your sisters are planning a wedding worthy of you.' My life's path had his blessing.

Around the dinner table, Lettie and Hannie struggled to contain their excitement about the wedding. Traditionally, Afrikaner weddings are times of great celebration and much eating and dancing, which can last for seven days or until the food runs out.

Invitations went out far and wide for our wedding, and the yard outside soon became overcrowded with wagons, horses and tents as they drew together for merriment.

'I have asked *oom* Hendrik Pretorius to bring his *pensklavier* accordion, and even old *oom* Klasie Bekker will be here to play the concertina. It will be a real *vastrap,* and we'll dance until dawn,' Ampie's excitement boiled over in long sentences. We had always made music at Morgenster, but I wondered how the more rural Bushvelders would approach the upcoming feast, especially since Ampie, who had travelled these outlying areas quite often, spoke with so much anticipation.

When lambs started bleating as usual in the early morning, Ampie saddled up for his return journey to Weltevreden, leaving Dirk and me with, 'Next Friday, Nelie. At the church.'

He shook hands with Dirk and patted his shoulder, '*Totsiens,* Dirk-man,' and with that, he swung his leg effortlessly over the pony's broad back. Our emotions kept us rooted to the spot until there was no sign of Ampie on the horizon.

'What will I do on Friday, *hê* Nelie?' Dirk said with the crack of adulthood in his voice. We walked back to the house, discussing his role in keeping our wedding rings safe until the pastor, *Dominee* Du Preez, asks for them.

Ampie said there would even be someone to play the church organ, leading guests who may be quite unaccustomed to singing with accompaniment. 'That would be grand, won't it, Nelie?!' Dirk enthused, and I marvelled at how an ordinary day could become one to enthral and remember forever.

Guests started arriving at Kameelfontein days before the wedding, and three days before the celebrations, there was hardly room to move in the yard or along the road to the gate, where campers started pitching tents. Everyone wanted my time, but Hannie came to rescue me from the festivities 'for a beauty sleep before the big day.'

Friday the 13th broke windless with the grandfather clock's tick adding a reassuring rhythm to what would soon become a scurry of busyness. It is customary in the Boer tradition for wedding guests to remain at the homestead rather than join the family at church. This meant they could stay up all night without worrying about falling asleep in church.

Looking out the window, I noticed that few had clothes appropriate for a wedding ceremony anyway, and my heart swelled at my good fortune to have a wedding dress fit for the wealthy.

Lettie thought it wise for me to get dressed at church to avoid dust and soil the horse might kick up. She combed my hair in an elaborate roll that changed my features so cleverly that two unfamiliar, calm amethyst eyes stared at me in the mirror. With shock, I recognised a youthful *Ma.* 'No tears now, Nelie,' Lettie recognised her too, 'She would want you to be happy. You are happy, aren't you?' I swallowed and nodded away the moment's sadness.

The most beautiful music met us at the church entrance. Our families waited in anticipation along the short aisle, scanning the dome-like structure long-necked to take in the newness of a church wedding.

We had become so used to congregating out in the open, under a tree or in tents during the war, that the formal setting made our union the special moment it was always meant to be. In front, Ampie's tall figure waited in black coat tails, a white shirt, and gloves – a handsome man who would share my life 'until death do us part.'

Tante Katrien's lace dress hugged me perfectly, and the satin bow's weight felt exquisite around my waist. Lettie made a short veil from off-cut lace she had sourced from Mosam's shop in town, which cast a dense mist onto the church interior and hid the tears that sprang to my eyes for no reason. But *Pa's* elbow guided my steps to Ampie's side.

I saw *Dominee* Du Preez's lips move, but heard none until Ampie said, 'I do,' and looked at me expectantly. I mumbled, 'I do,' and then Dirk offered the rings, which sealed our path together, 'For better or worse, as long as we both shall live.' *And that might be long or not long at all. Only God knew.*

Signing the wedding register with Jan and Truia's husband, Jacob Celliers, as witnesses, happened in a daze, and it was only when Ampie said, 'Well, *Mevrouw* Bergmann, shall we go home?' that I focused again on the present and dragged my heart back from Upington and the little riverside shack.

Ampie was real, and it was in the real world we had to live, not the wishful thinking of *if only.*

By the time we arrived back at Kameelfontein, it was late afternoon. While our buggy bumped happily towards the gate, guests started streaming from their tents, and with hats waving and shouts of, '*Hier kom die bruid!* Here comes the bride!' delivered the said bride and groom to the front *stoep.*

We had hardly stepped off when *ooms* Hendrik and Klasie started playing a foot-itching *vastrap,* that was sure to call the most reserved to grab a partner for this lively Boer quickstep.

The floor carried a white flour dusting to ease dancing, and without much ado, Ampie took me in his arms for a wild dance that had others shouting, '*Balke toe!* To the rafters!' and we turned and swirled with others with much merriment.

When nausea overtook me, it was easy to attribute it to dancing, but for the rest of the night, I drank ginger beer and hoped it would save the day.

By one o'clock, a drunk Ampie said we should go to bed, but once there, he fell asleep fully clothed. I let the beautiful lace dress fall to the ground and lay down quietly at his side. My husband, my child's father, and my child, conceived far from the bridal bed, were my constant companions during the night.

The festivities lasted eight days. Early on the eighth morning, *Pa* cracked his whip loudly all the way to the sheep pen and sang at the top of his voice until the party-faithful crept bleary-eyed from their tents. On his orders, Lettie, Hannie and Bettie set out the stale bread they had baked the week before and nothing else. It wasn't long before wagons were uploaded, and farewells said.

In the silence that followed, it felt strange to be idle. We sat together around the wood stove in calm companionship – the kind that only large families truly understand. Then *Pa* said, 'This was good. Now comes the hard work,' and I knew he was not talking about the clean-up. We felt deflated, and it was hardly dusk when we headed for our bedrooms.

Ours was a small room which probably used to be a storeroom in a previous life, but we were happy to have it to ourselves. In its dim cosiness, it was at last our time to explore each other's bodies; to love with the tenderness and respect that would sustain us until death do us part.

The next day, I saw *Pa* and Ampie talking animatedly out in the yard. Ampie was pointing north while *Pa* shook his head as if haggling over the price of sheep. That night, Ampie said, 'Nelie, I must find work; we have no money. People are poor, so I must find building work in town; maybe Nylstroom or Warmbaths, or even to the north where people are moving in larger numbers.'

We lay quietly, contemplating how it would affect our lives. A new marriage to nurture, a new environment to adjust to, a new baby to love and care for. To me, it also meant growing the baby without his scrutiny.

'You have to go, husband,' I offered, knowing I had both our extended families close by for support.

The next day, Ampie packed his bag and saddled his pony. 'Dirk and Gert will come with me,' he announced matter-of-factly, and with that, the mother/son bond between Dirk and me was casually broken as if it didn't matter at all.

I held Dirk for a long time, knowing adulthood would change and shape him. 'It is time, Nelie,' he said gruffly, turned on his heel and rode away without looking back. I was left on the path until my cheeks felt stiff and dry with too many salty tears shed over a time forever gone. One child gone and another to take its place.

While treading weary steps back to the house, what strengthened my resolve to do well by my child was *Pa's* words, 'It is our humanity and the pride our women carried throughout this war.'

Humanity and pride would sustain me while Ampie and Dirk were away.

In all the ranks of the 'Petticoat Commando' there was not one woman who had dared more, risked more, than the brave Queen of Holland when she dispatched her good man-of-war to bear away from the shores of Africa the hunted President of the South African Republic (Paul Kruger), to the refuge of her hospitable land.

The Petticoat Commando. 1901

A heat blanket hung over Kameelfontein in late April, keeping us inside from noon till four in the afternoon. It spread a quiet over everything winged, hooved and human, interspersed only by cicadas' *tjirr*.

'Best to give over, Little Bird,' *Pa* explained, stretching out on a *riempie* couch to catch up on sleep lost during the oppressive heat that shaped the night's sweaty discomfort. Even the children and menfolk had learned to rest during the day's heat. That brought stillness and contemplation to the homestead but didn't erase my longing for the joy of having women around.

Dirk, my steadfast companion, had grown into his own shoes and took our communal time with him. Bettie loyally insisted on staying behind when Hannie and Lettie joined their husbands on their return from hunting. Thereafter, the two families moved north, 'Where the trees grow dense, and meat is plenty.' The previously soothing birdsong became shrill, and the cicadas' *tjirring* was unbearable in Dirk's absence.

Bettie's sadness at losing Eva was as deeply felt, and she kept busy cleaning and dusting a house that needed no cleaning to escape the memory of a child's laugh. Even though I missed Eva and my sisters, it was in the simple tasks of gathering firewood or lighting a fire that I missed Dirk's quiet presence the most. For so long, he was my constant shadow, my wise old-man child, whose destiny became my responsibility.

Often, as pregnancy's discomfort robbed me of happiness, I imagined that not even the child growing in me could take Dirk's place.

But that was a childish notion which I should not have entertained.

War had already shattered traditional family structures with harsh determination, and it was up to us, the survivors, to forge new and stronger bonds to sustain ourselves.

It was on a day of intense sadness and longing that a dust swirl in the distance announced the arrival of visitors. Out on the veranda, where the heat was less oppressive, I straightened, took off my apron and called the others from their slumber. Few visitors had come by during the busy post-war rebuilding years.'

Maybe a neighbour in need,' Daan ventured, combing fingers through unkempt sleep-hair. It was several minutes before two riders came into focus. We waited outside like soldiers on parade, quietly and uncertain of what the moment would present.

The riders who dismounted were dressed in the familiar Boer khaki clothes and well-worn jackets – one sturdy and the other slight. It was only when they stood side by side to greet each other that I recognised our younger sister, Johanna. My legs felt weak, but she pulled me into a fierce embrace and would not let go.

We laughed and cried until *Pa* separated us with, 'This is a miracle! We thought you were dead!' and held her to his chest. A broad-shouldered young man with an easy smile introduced himself as Hermanus Heystek. Once we were seated around the dining table, he explained how he had found Johanna hiding in bushland close to Warmbaths, no more than 20 miles south as the crow flies, quite oblivious that the war was over.

'Nelie, I also met your husband!' Johanna told excitedly of meeting Ampie, Gert and Dirk in town, where they were busy building, 'A big hotel with many rooms.' Hermanus took up the story, and we learned how the three men took time to make sense of her journey, then clothed her in what they had, fed her and directed them to our family. 'What a day it must've been,' Daan said with a smile. For the first time since the war, happiness came to him as well.

I counted our family's pain in numbers – *Pa* lost a much-loved mother, two daughters whose whereabouts were still unknown, nine grandchildren, a baby not yet born, and a wife who was living in a hazy world between life and death.

Their death and disappearance represented our combined sadness that could never be erased.

But God gave us Bettie, Dirk and Eva, as well as an extended family through my marriage to Ampie. And my baby.

'God be praised,' *Pa* said as if reading my mind. Then the talk turned to our daily lives. Hermanus painted a picture of growth in Warmbaths and Nylstroom village. 'Ampie is building the Brown's Hotel,' he indicated its size with arms stretched wide, 'For thirsty and tired travellers on their way to Pretoria. And after that, they will build a bank in Nylstroom.'

Pa questioned him about his family, as is the custom among farmers. We listened with interest to his description of a family farm that stretched many, many miles across the Marikele Mountains, barely 30 miles north of Kameelfontein. The farm runs parallel to the Matlabas River until it meets with Bechuanaland, a British Protectorate in the north.

'*Oom*, the trees are different from here, and the antelope are tame and plenty,' Hermanus spoke with enthusiasm of a place untouched by war and hunters. 'Ampie said he would like to visit one day to see this for himself,' he finished.

In the week that followed, it became clear that this wish might become reality sooner than anticipated, as Johanna and Hermanus had eyes only for each other. And so it happened that Johanna travelled with Hermanus to meet his family, and within a month, we celebrated another wedding at Kameelfontein, albeit on a much smaller scale.

Our loss was magnified tenfold when Johanna left so soon after we had found her, but the light of adventure shone bright in the couple's eyes, and after a while, we accepted her absence and settled into our usual routine.

At the end of May, I felt the baby move for the first time. Like its conception, the first movements caressed my heart with wonder An excitement I hadn't felt before forced a blush to my cheeks, which didn't go unnoticed. Bettie watched me closely with knowing eyes, but their softness told their own story of long-forgotten joy.

'When, Nelie?' she asked one morning as I readied myself for a visit to the Bergmann farm. I held up enough fingers to cover the delivery time but could not meet her eyes. No words were needed to know that Ampie could not possibly be the father. Then she straightened her shoulders, shook her head determinedly and said, 'Over my dead body will you ride this horse.'

With *Pa's* help, we tethered the horse in front of the buggy, and we travelled at a leisurely pace to Weltevreden. At the Vlieëberge's highest point, we stopped so Bettie could look back on the valley with its camelthorn carpet cut in half by ancient wagon tracks. We stood in the buggy and stretched our necks to have a better look at the monotonous scenery, which nonetheless had its own beauty, if only one cared to look.

At that moment, a baboon barked nearby, followed by several others. The horse, which was content to trot up the mountain lazily, took off with such speed that Bettie and I fell forward against the canopy railing.

'Oh, dear God!' I heard her cry as she managed to grab my arm and somehow get a grip on the wooden beam. The horse's wild flight that shook the buggy side-to-side was totally obliterated by the pain that washed over me. In its fright, he eventually veered off the tracks and into a tree whose branches would not let him escape. Bettie's calm, which had sustained her during the war's tribulations, helped her make me comfortable, turn the horse around and retrace our steps to Kameelfontein, while pain took me to the dark of oblivion.

I woke on a cold morning with a winter's sun willingly shining its bleak rays onto my bed. Bettie was curled up on a chair next to me, fast asleep. There were dark circles under her eyes, and her normally tidy hair showed a change in her state of mind, reflecting carelessness and exhaustion.

On the bedside table, several of Lennon's medicines stood at bottled attention – Witdulsies, Paragorie and Levenessens – soldiers to remedy inflammation and heal wounds. My hands flew to my stomach and came back empty. Bettie's hand folded mine in its warmth, and she wiped the hair tenderly from my forehead, but I turned to the wall as loss washed over me – a loss stronger than any that war had ever dared throw at me.

'Be still, my precious friend, be still,' she said calmly, and when I did not respond, she swallowed hard and said, 'He is buried nearby, Nelie. You can visit him later.'

Pa once said there was not one woman who had dared more or risked more than the brave and dauntless young Queen Tomasina of Holland, who had helped our president escape during the war. She did not cry or lose hope, nor did she cry in a dark room. But I was not her. I was empty. First Edward, then Dirk, now my son. I refused to dare more and risk more! *Where are you in all of this, God? Where?!*

The loneliest people are the kindest. The saddest people smile the brightest. The most damaged people are the wisest. All because they do not wish to see anyone else suffer the way they do.

Anonymous

'**F**rom time to time, we are just sad, not bitter. Sad can be hopeful, bitter not. The kind of sad you feel now just takes time, *my suster*,' Bettie, who should know, said on a day the south-wind blew the last of the feather-like leaves off the camelthorns' wide branches.

Already there was a warm change in the early August air; a warmth not reflected in my heart, where bitterness had found a comfortable home. Nights were battlegrounds between sorrow and despondency, and by daybreak, anger came swooping down from the dark hours to claim the winner's trophy it was not entitled to.

For weeks, I spent time with *Ma*, listening to her laboured breathing, feeling at home in a room where death was a constant guard. She did not care or admonish me about my fights with God or the devil, whoever was uppermost in my thoughts. There, I felt safe to shout and cry. Until the day she sighed deeply and stopped listening. Then there was no more to say or shout about; only more to cry about.

'The Bushveld has no mercy,' *Pa* talked to himself while shaping a casket from camelthorn, 'But we can't let it take her dignity as well.' We understood what heat could do to a body. We had seen how quickly slaughtered animals became inedible and riddled with worms in the heat that was death's real enemy.

Bettie and I dressed *Ma* in *tannie* Botes's embroidered nightgown, which we had found in a trunk, and watched on as *Pa* gently lowered his wife of many years into the casket crafted with love, to rest in the coolest room.

Flies were already about, and we had to cover her with linen sheets until the casket was sealed for her final journey.

1903's spring came early on the wings of summer heat, forcing Daan and Jan to make haste riding north and south to spread the news of *Ma's* passing. Even so, it took three days before family and friends stood in a sea of black around her grave.

We sang songs from the Psalms – songs so well-practised in the concentration camps, that they fell from our lips with certainty and ease. But my heart was cold and distant. Death could force tears to my eyes no more. I found no deeper meaning in the Biblical words *Pa* read from Corinthians, 'O death, where is thy sting? O grave, where is thy victory?' But from a lifetime ago, I heard his more comforting words, 'When you have nothing more to lose, Little Bird, your soul will speak. All you must do is listen.'

We walked home in silence.

Pa Andries took to walking the veld and tending the graveyard until the soil lay obedient and tired under his determined hand. Looking from the kitchen window, two crosses stood forlornly by themselves – a large one for *Ma* and another with its feet planted in a small mound of soil.

'Who lies under the little cross, Nelie?' Dirk, who had travelled home for the burial, asked innocently. The answer would not cross my lips, and I looked away. Bettie came to stand behind him and wrapped her arms around his shoulders, which had broadened into an adult's.

'A baby, taken from his mother far too early, Dirkie.' She squeezed his arms, let go softly and walked away as quietly as she came, leaving the stillness as explanation. It came to him slowly. Like mist before the sun, the new contentment his eyes showed on arrival, faded into the sad old-man eyes he carried with him the first day we met. He leaned his head on my shoulder, and we stood in silence for a long while. *All we had to do was listen.*

Ampie, Gert and Dirk stayed one more day. Before they left, Ampie took my hand, and when dusk set in, we walked to the graveyard. There he knelt at the little mound and pulled me to his side. 'I would've come if I knew, my Nelie. He was mine too,' he said brokenly.

We cried together and clung to each other for the comfort owed us. In that moment, my baby's rightful father was right there, not wandering far-off lands in pursuit of his own happiness.

The horses were already saddled when Ampie fished a letter from his pocket. He had brought several letters from the post office in Nylstroom but had forgotten about this one.

I knew right away who it was from. Only two people outside the family knew where I would be. The others urged me to open and read it, but something so precious needed its own time and space to tell its tale. I waited until Ampie, Gert and Dirk had left and then found a quiet spot under a camelthorn where doves cooed their secrets in the branches above.

A few pages written back-and-front fell from the envelope, and my fingers shook in anticipation of the news so neatly penned.

Rooipad
Post Office Upington
Transvaal
28th day of August 1903

Our dearest Cornelia,

It is our sincere hope that this letter finds you in good health and spirits. We are well also but would be lying if we said we do not miss you and Dirk.

By now, you would be a married woman with a new life and a new focus. We hope your wedding was grand and that the wedding dress looked beautiful. Not a day goes by that we don't make one or another plan to visit you — this might even become true one day!

The letter then went on to detail the changes in the region, the British influence, the quality of oom Roelof's crops, and life in general. Edward was not mentioned until the last paragraph as if he were not important at all.

Oom Roelof ran into Edward in Upington a few weeks ago. He was gaunt and in a hurry, but the oom convinced him to spend some time at our place, and that's how we know that he's heavily involved in the war across the border in German South West Africa. There, he supplies goods to both warring parties, he said, but we could tell it's not the whole truth.

Oom Roelof spoke to him at length in private and said that Edward was, in fact, on the Nama's side, supplying, supporting, and fighting alongside the Nama freedom fighter Jakob Morengo in his heroic war against the German military.

We are scared for him. This war is not his and a dangerous mission, but we'll pray for his safety. He asked about you and spoke much about saving enough money to build your house at the river. We told him you moved north with your family but did not have the heart to tell him about Ampie and the wedding. He left with promises to find you and build a future together. We hope you are not disappointed in us for not telling the whole truth.

God be with you, Nelie-kind. Be safe and happy.

Much love,
Oom and tante Kleynhans

The sun shone brighter, and my heart felt lighter after reconnecting with these loving and kind people. Bettie was right after all – this kind of sadness takes time and patience. Now I knew for certain that moments of happiness do shine their light on the darkest moments.

The months went by in a hurry towards Christmas, which we spent with Ampie, Gert and Dirk, who came home for a week, and my in-laws, *Ma* Gertruida, Truia, her second husband and four children. Their belongings were already stacked high on two wagons for a journey which would bypass Nylstroom and end north-east in Pietersburg. Truia was becoming increasingly unwell, and the newly built hospital in town had a doctor on duty. As a bonus, the children could attend school for the first time.

After saying goodbye to Ampie and Gert, *tant* Gertruida took me aside and said, 'I have left you a gift in the kitchen. Time has denied me a chance to know you better, my daughter, but the gift has always been in my family, and now it will make you happy too. Use it often. There's something for Ampie as well.'

In the empty house, Ampie and I found a beautiful accordion on a soap-scrubbed table.

'That accordion belonged to my great-grandmother on *Ma's* side,' he said in wonder, 'and *Pa* Abraham had crafted the small table before going to war.'

The depth of *tant* Gertruida's love and devotion to the next generation of Bergmanns was contained in these simple articles.

But it also made me wonder whether she had a premonition that we would not meet again.

'I will learn to play the accordion, my husband, and at this table we will feed our children,' I promised in his embrace.

'And that we will, my wife,' he whispered in my ear, then rode away for the journey south.

'As individuals die every moment, how insensitive and fabricated a love it is to set aside a day from selfish routine in prideful, patriotic commemoration of tragedy. Just as God is provoked by those who tithe simply because they feel that they must tithe, I am provoked by those who commemorate simply because they feel that they must commemorate.'

Criss Jami, Killosophy

'**I**t has been a year,' Bettie counted the months since *Ma* had passed away, but for me, it was in the changing seasons that moments of deep sadness returned to be commemorated.

Those who had gone before me left this world when seasons changed, and each event that carried great sadness happened at such times. For this reason, *Ma's* death was just the last in a long line of sad events to remember and honour. I had already mourned our little boy anew when leaves were changing colour and evening breezes turned us towards a hearth's warmth.

As far as I was concerned, there was more comfort and hope in the changing seasons than commemorating dates of traumatic events. A season allowed breathing space and time to live through the sadness, and that is how my life took on direction and became meaningful again.

It was while living through the last year's sadness that I realised we had never named our boy. To me, he was just 'my boy.' *Ma's* gravestone already cast a solid shade in the afternoon sun like the solid, dependable person she was, while the little cross to its side stood skew in the wind, and the small mound of soil was scattered often by guinea fowl. But in my heart, the season had not yet arrived to give him a name and a gravestone.

On a sunny day, I found the menfolk mixing sand, stone and cement out in the yard, and when I asked, *Pa* said, 'It will read *Abraham Jacobus*, as it should,' pouring and smoothing a concrete slab. 'Now write it, Cornelia!' he said and held out a porcupine quill for the purpose. When I hesitated, he continued, 'Was he not worthy of more than a cross?'

He waited while my feet yearned to run and my fists refused to unclench, but the quill remained aloft for its baptismal duty.

After what seemed like an eternity, I came to accept that the season had finally arrived, albeit under protest, for our boy to become part of our family.

It was while erecting Abraham's gravestone the next day that Dirk rode in on a cloud of dust. If not for his distinctive brown-and-white dappled pony, we would not have recognised the handsome young man with the serious eyes – muscled and bearded, he towered over us all.

'I'll be hanged! Surely, it's not you, Dirk!' *Pa* exclaimed and vigorously shook his hand. It had been a year since we had last heard of or seen the three men, during which time we could only guess at their whereabouts.

'I can't stay long, *Oom*. I must keep the building works going in Pretoria,' he said, then looked down in discomfort, 'While Ampie and Gert are away.' He came to tell of Truia's passing and said he would be on his way within the hour. Death's darkness came to stand among us again, and the news was a reminder of how fleeting contentment and peace could be.

'The dead will not be more dead tomorrow, Dirk; there is no haste. Break bread with us and stay the night,' *Pa* took him by the arm, and we went inside.

Early the next day, *Pa* and I accompanied Dirk as far as Nylstroom. Our bags were packed for a short stay in Pietersburg, where the funeral would take place. At Nylstroom, Dirk forked off to the south, and we continued to the north-east. There was no question whether we would support and mourn with Ampie's family. War had already taught all Afrikaners to be one big family - to be loyal and support each other in the dark hours that were bound to cross our paths.

We travelled in silence. Here and there, *Pa* pointed out features of interest; scenes from *RéAndriese's* childhood tales. He had a faraway look in his eyes, and with each mile we covered, he withdrew more into himself. I remembered her wisdom, which so often guided my days, and wondered if he even cared to remember that time.

Closer to Pietersburg, the first citrus orchard came into sight and then stretched for miles next to the dirt road. *Pa* straightened and unnecessarily spurred the pony, which told me he had been transported to the time with *RéAndriese*. 'She told me about you, *Pa*,' I broke the silence. His eyes refocused as memories drifted away, reigning in the tired horse to a slower trot. I waited, wondering if he would tell me after all these years.

At Pietersburg's outskirts, he ran a weary hand over his face and admitted, 'I loved her more than I have ever loved anyone. Not even your mother, good woman that she was. I loved them both, but not equally.' Then he withdrew into his memory world again.

Truia's funeral brought a large extended family together. Friends and relatives came from all over Transvaal and the Orange Free State to pay their respects. A tent city grew on open ground close to the cemetery where friends and family could linger for days, as was customary for travellers from afar.

Ampie and Gert had plans to stay for as long as it took to formalise *Ma* Gertruida's parental guardianship of the four Kroch children.

'Jacob Celiiers would quickly drink through their inheritance, and besides, he's not their real father,' Ampie explained and added, 'Gert will stay behind to help *Ma*.' When I asked about Gert, he said not everyone could be a builder, and judging by his curt answer, I guessed the issue might've spilled over many times between them.

Truia's children stood silently next to the open grave, eyes stark and shoulders straight in obedience to a culture that reveals little of inner strife. I wondered how many years *Ma* Gertruida would be able to care for these children. The oldest was barely fourteen. My heart cramped when she bent with difficulty to straighten seven-year-old Rachel's wayward collar. Her journey was not nearly done.

Our last goodbye was not the last after all, but this one would be. We kissed and held each other tight for this final greeting.

The sun, which rose with heat in its heart, continued its journey until black-clad mourners had trudged back to their tents. On our way, we walked among many unmarked war graves, which added the sadness of Irene camp in my heart.

'Nothing urgent needs doing at Kameelfontein,' *Pa* announced early the next day and guided our horse and buggy north-west, away from where we came. The silence between us shifted from tense to expectant with each mile we ventured closer to a mountain range in the distance. Where trees met mountain, a blue haze demarcated a valley still hidden from sight. As we drew near, the scope of a lush valley with neat citrus rows lining its belly unfolded like a wonderworld. *Pa* brought the buggy to a halt, and I stood to take it in.

I longed to walk between those rows and feel the cool soil between my toes, but an invisible hand kept me standing, and I felt foreboding stirring between heart and mind. Then I heard memory's call, '*Come, walk with me in a citrus orchard, and you will go away a person better able to survive your own wars.*'

'We have to go further, *Pa*,' I urged. He didn't hesitate, but clicked his tongue, and the pony walked on, ears pricked and turning as if listening to an alternative command. Soon, we found ourselves between the lemon and orange trees. There, wheels had imprinted recent travels, and I wondered aloud if we might be trespassing, but the pony determinedly forged ahead as if we had no choice in the matter.

Even though it was midday, the citrus scent came to us on cool air, and I pictured a child darting between the trees like a little bird. How wonderful it would be to grow up among the trees that cast a scent spell on those who visit their grove. We passed an enormous lemon tree on our left whose branches hung unpruned close to the ground. I turned to see it better, but it slipped past without revealing more. Why would that one be unpruned, I wondered, as I searched for a memory that kept evading me.

Without warning, the orchard opened to surprise us with a scene so peaceful and beautiful that I could not breathe. *Pa* sat motionless. He, too, breathed in short, shallow gulps. Ahead, a Cape Dutch style farmhouse lay resplendent in its white coat. A windmill churned lazily to supply water for a garden drowning in masses of flowers. An old oak tree stood proudly among the beauty, and underneath a garden bench waited to be sat on. It seemed so much beauty was not even possible.

'I remember the house and windmill,' *Pa* spoke shakily, 'but the flowers are still young.' A middle-aged woman came from behind the house and stopped, surprised at our intrusion. A traditional *kappie* covered most of her face, and as she came to us unhurriedly, I felt a premonition stir wildly in my chest.

Pa stepped down slowly and waited. The woman took off her *kappie*, and at that moment the sun shone directly into her lion-eyes. I watched as if in slow motion, he kissed her on the forehead. 'Little Bird,' he said tenderly, smoothing her hair. She leaned into him and mouthed, 'Andries, my love.' Only then did the memory come to me: '*Where flesh meets soul, Nelie. The feeling only a few can recognise and even fewer can explain.*'

36 – The Lucky Ones

The years of our life are seventy, or even by reason of strength, eighty; yet their span is but toil and trouble; they are soon gone, and we fly away.

Psalm 90:10. The Bible

1905

'Moses, a man of God, said seventy, maybe eighty years is what we have. And I have already lived and toiled sixty years of strife and trouble. I will spend the remainder with *RéAndriese*,' *Pa* announced when we turned the bend towards Kameelfontein's gate.

For so many reasons, I felt like an orphan at that moment: My heart was torn in two when Edward had disappeared, Ampie and Dirk were somewhere that I couldn't picture, and the angel of death snatched Little Abraham, *Ma* and my younger sisters. Others had moved away and taken Eva with them. *Now Pa too?!*

The summer storm that shook our house that night stole the sleep I was hoping for. Big raindrops came hand in hand with thunder and lightning. A uniquely Bushveld odour of dust and grass-veld drifted in with the first fat drops that ran down from the thatched roof and landed on my windowsill. Sleep caught me thinking that rain could heal. Unanswered questions faded, and a calm came over me as I drifted off to a place that left no room for whys and why-not's.

The next morning, *Pa* confirmed, cup-in-hand, the Bushveld's ability to calm and soothe the senses with its smells, which seem to bombard us from every direction. 'Yes, Nelie, gone forever are the Highveld's sweet red grass and its sour grass stockfeed. Here, all that live and breathe get drunk on nature's elixirs.' A thought that did not sit unkindly with me.

If the Waterberg was as magical as Ampie seemed to think, its balmy winds had my consent to rustle my leaves, the camelthorns to shade my soul and its grasses to carpet a smooth path for our journey.

From the moment *Pa* and I set foot in the house on our return, it became evident that the space was occupied by more than three adults, a youth and two children. There was a sense of expectation that softened simple tasks. I saw it in the way Bettie's hips swayed as she swept, dusted and carried washing. I found her talking to the chickens and singing as she tended the pot plants. But the language she spoke was best observed in the lock of hair she let fall freely from a loose bun, and a few bodice buttons released from their demure guard-duty.

Daan and Jan's smoothed-over hair and careful word choice added to the sweet mystery of expectancy and unfolding courtship. At 19, my quiet young brother, Andries, was a keen observer who looked on and learned about life's ways from his older brothers.

'Who do you think will win, Little Bird?' *Pa* mused as we sat out on the veranda, relishing the beauty of a wooing dance that belonged equally to Daan and Jan. But it was no mystery to me.

I felt a deep sadness and compassion for Jan, who had lost everyone dear to him, but I feared this would not be his time for a new start.

At dusk, my prediction took shape when Daan shyly took Bettie's hand as they wandered down the road with no destination in mind. And that was good.

During a time when few were allowed to choose a mate, the love unfolding between Daan and Bettie carried its tenderness and wonder throughout the house. Most men who were widowed during the war simply rode up to a farmstead known to house eligible women and asked to 'combine our flocks.' In this practical, albeit unromantic way, motherless children gained a carer, and widows became part of a family with the means to provide for them.

'We are truly the lucky ones, Little Bird. Love chose us, and we chose love, but many thousands don't have that luxury,' *Pa* said, looking into the distance. He told of other men who travelled vast distances on horseback to find a companion.

'If we Afrikaners don't strengthen our own communities, the English will find a way to do it for us,' he said with bitterness at war's losses and the British immigrants' insistence on changing schools, businesses and the law. Irene Camp taught me the same hard lessons.

Even the simple act of finding a partner was not as simple when viewed in the bigger picture. *Pa* was right – we had to work together as a large cultural family to work together as a nation.

The following week was an up-and-down journey of 'what shall I do's' for the family. *Pa* sorted through his possessions, applying practicality so that a horse could reasonably carry them to Pietersburg. Bettie and I worked long hours preparing for her wedding, and through it all, abandonment's sour taste, which always seemed to follow me wherever I go, became my shadow. In the dark of night, I pondered the good and the bad until *tannie* Botes's Bible brought the answer to my restless mind. For so many years, I had resisted re-reading the documents and letters that she had stowed in its jacket, but now there was nothing to lose and no one to hurt by revisiting her life.

When I opened the letter, I could smell liquorice and Lennon's remedies. It lay patiently in my hands with a determination to be read again. The little note written by Paulus Botes was buried in its folds, and alongside, the Deed of Ownership to Section 334, Elandsfontein. I owned this land through our bloodline and her goodwill, which the Deed confirmed with a clear message, but it was Paulus's note that I had to make sense of:

> *When apple blossoms are no more*
> *Don't forget their promise,*
> *My Apple Blossom*
> *Be true to generosity*
> *Sand and tree belong to thee*
> *Give, give, give*
>
> *Your only love, always,*
> *Paulus Botes*

How disappointed would Ampie be to know that I've hidden my ownership while he was slaving away? And how could I be true to generosity and give, give, give, if all I've ever had to give was myself? I wrestled with these questions until the cock crowed the first time, and then the answer came to me in its simplicity.

I wondered how I could've missed it all along. The words flowed from my pen with ease as I wrote my own Deed of Transfer to Section 334, benefitting Dirk, my old-man child, God-given on a dry riverbed for our mutual healing. I sealed the letters and Deeds in a large paper bag and addressed it to Dirk Botes, giving him the surname he came without.

Daan and Bettie got married in the magistrate's office in Nylstroom, with his children's solemn eyes following the proceedings until the required documents were signed. 'The Government is granting small farms to landless farmers between Nylstroom and Potgietersrust; we'll make a life there,' Daan drew their path to married life.

Jan and Andries raised hats in greeting and solemnly shook their brother's hand in Afrikaner men's stoic way, then kissed Bettie and the children goodbye. They didn't waste time and hastily disappeared hastily into the newly established Land Council offices to secure their own land.

Pa and I travelled home in the company of flies and our thoughts. From Nylstroom, the two-wheel rutted path led north-west past Alma village, then Langkloof granary and the single-room post office perched behind it like a child's hastily put on Sunday hat. The road curved slightly to meet a T-junction at the foot of the Waterberg mountains. There, Loubad Road's right arm reached out towards the steep mountains through Sandrivierspoort Nek, and the left towards the Vlieëberg Pass and Kameelfontein.

The gods of providence were hard at work in our absence. Two horses stood tethered in front of the house, and we recognised them immediately as Ampie and Dirk's.

The open front door welcomed us with the smell of frying onions and loud banter from the kitchen.

A smile of approval played around *Pa's* mouth when he greeted them warmly. 'Now I can leave,' he declared and started gathering his meagre belongings. 'The sun is still high, and I should make good time,' he sealed his future, while my heart squeezed with sadness at the imminent parting.

Dirk stood close, and Ampie took my hand when *Pa* was ready to leave. 'Our years are seventy, and if we're lucky, eighty, Little Bird. Live them to the full,' he whispered in my ear - a wish for a long life and much happiness.

Then he left our little group without a wave or backward glance.

The years of his life by reason of strength could be eighty. Be their span but toil and trouble, they would soon be gone.

He needed to be with his lion-eyed true love.

37 – *Officially Killed*

Before the reward there must be labour. You plant before you harvest. You sow in tears before you reap joy.

Ralph Ransom

The autumn sunsets had become their typical deep red, spanning the horizon in broad strokes of vividness. That's when nausea waited for me between the rows of preserves, drying onions and garlic in the scullery. Straightening after it forced me double, a whisper of joy touched my lips.

Is this how life truly works? Did we first have to sow in tears before reaping the promise of joy?

I counted on my fingers, pulled the writing paper close and shared with *tante* Katrien and *oom* Roelof what I was not willing to share with anyone else yet, not even Ampie.

The big house's large rooms echoed their loneliness after *Pa's* departure, and with just three pairs of feet walking its polished concrete floors, there was virtually no need to sweep, dust or clean. And no need to knit for a baby that would arrive, God willing, in December's heat.

I waited a few more weeks to tell Ampie, but the secret was revealed before then when he found me bent over in the chicken coop. We just stood together in contented silence while the chickens clucked a simple congratulation.

How to tell Dirk about his farm kept me out on the veranda with negative thoughts – deceit, secrecy, and dishonesty foremost in my mind.

But it was Dirk himself who provided the solution, when he joined me one late winter's day with, 'Nelie, I have to go my own way.' His eyes told a different story, but his shoulders were set determinedly to be his own man.

I stroked his labour-hardened arm, and then he said, 'I have some money saved from building work and may ride up the Langkloof valley to find land.' I nodded when he explained that Ampie had recommended the rich soil around Tweespruit Creek for sowing. 'That's where he wants your family to live one day, too,' Dirk's voice pleaded for my acceptance.

I was happy.

'That is a good plan, Dirkie,' I said, patting the seat next to me. 'I will help you, but of my help you can never speak,' and outlined *tannie* Botes's gift, then stood to fetch the paper bag.

In the distance, Ampie's long legs were striding briskly home. 'Read it tonight and then take it to the attorney, Hendrik Kroep, in Nylstroom. He will certify everything. This is my gift to you, my son.' Dirk fumbled uncertainly with the bag but disappeared indoors before Ampie had reached the first step.

At sunrise, Dirk's horse stood saddled before breakfast porridge had time to stiffen and cook through on the slow wooden stove. 'I am off to the post office in Nylstroom,' he said, wiping his mouth, impatient to go before Ampie could say his usual second grace after our meal. 'I want to be home before dark.' *Tante* Katrien and *oom* Roelof's letter lay on the sideboard waiting to be mailed, and my heart sang as I pictured their faces at the news of our baby.

'Nelie, we will not argue about this,' Ampie said a week later in a tone that would not allow a discussion about visiting Section 334 with him and Dirk, even though his kind eyes spoke a contrasting message. At that moment, the sun shone on little Abraham's gravestone, and from where I stood in the kitchen, its unmistakable message reached me. The familiar pain of loss knotted my stomach, but I knew the desire to accompany them did not merit an argument.

Foreboding, my old friend, flashed an image of a life-weary woman on a rise looking across Tweespruit towards the Botes farm, a brood of young children clutching her dress. I caught my breath sharply and found Ampie's concerned face at eye level. I patted his hand reassuringly, but it was an act that did not reflect my true feelings.

Foreboding had never lied to me, and there was no doubt in my mind about its predictions. It was I who had to decide whether they were a hindrance or a blessing. The baby moved vigorously as if in sympathy, and I rested my hands on the growing mound below my ribs.

Late in the afternoon, the riders returned - their animated talk reaching me before the earthy odour of hot and sweaty bodies. 'We even climbed the cliffs on the Waterberg mountains' higher reaches!' he said.

'There were many falcon nests wedged between rocks and wild bees that would not let us near their hives! You should've seen it!' Dirk enthused, his eyes bright and full of wonder about nature's bounty. 'And there's plenty of water,' Ampie added.

In my vision, Tweespruit's nourishing waters flowed between two homesteads to complete the picture of a mother and children. I smiled at their happy faces and went to bed long before they had stopped planning where Dirk should build a house. I already knew where.

It was on a mild day in mid-October when a horse and buggy stopped at the gate as if unsure whether they were at the right place. A man stepped off to open the *bekslaner*, but those few steps were enough to recognise our visitors. I half-ran ungainly down the road, heavy body hampering any suggestion of speed.

'*Oom* Roelof!' I heard my voice run ahead in excitement to meet the older man before he could manage the troublesome gate, and when my legs caught up, he folded me in his strong farmer's arms and held me until *tante* Katrien could join us. *What a blessed day to see them again!*

'Steady on, Nelie,' Ampie tried to stop the flow of questions and excitement, which carried its own momentum, until after supper, when the old people's eyes started drooping.

We laughed our happy laughs, knowing there were so many more questions to ask and answer. 'We are in no hurry to go home, *kind;* tomorrow is another day,' *tante* Katrien said with the slightest concern in her voice, but I was happy and did not notice.

That night, there was no tossing and turning to settle a heavy body, but I woke early and lay, eyes closed, to relish the news and tales the old people brought from afar. In the kitchen, Dirk had already stoked the fire, and cups stood at attention for coffee, its aroma spreading through the house.

I found the four of them on the veranda, talking softly and waiting for sunrise. 'This is the best time of day in summer, because it's not all that hot yet,' I heard Ampie explain the seasons to people used to fierce summer heat and bitterly cold winters.

We waited expectantly for the magic of a Bushveld sunrise and the early call of pheasants and far-off jackal cries, which identified the area as a place ruled by nature.

I sat next to *tante* Katrien, who took my hand in understanding of nature's simple truth: its rhythm was the constant that brought calm and satisfaction to us humans, who, unlike animals, feel the intensity of isolation.

As the days came and went, we learned not only about Upington and its surroundings, but also about how the southern states were coping with changes brought about by decisions made in England and by people who had never set foot in Africa. *Oom* Roelof reiterated *Pa's* concern about our nation and how the new government's efforts would stoke the simmering hatred bound to persist in Afrikaner consciousness for many generations.

'We're too old to be touched by it, but your children and grandchildren will carry and nurture its results until it eats away at their core,' he ventured. It was up to us as parents to set a Christian example of forgiveness to balance the scales. And thát would be an extremely cumbersome task.

'Let us visit Abraham,' *tante* Katrien said evenly on a day when the sun hid behind the clouds' skirts, and cicadas fell silent for a well-earned rest. Now that we had settled into a comfortable routine with the country's big problems solved in our own humble way, I could recognise the concern she carried like a shield. We sat on the soft earth where a small fig tree Ampie had planted would one day cast its shade on *Ma* and little Abraham. From there, we had a peaceful view over the house, the *kraal* where *Pa's* cattle still congregated for a drink, and the Vlieëberg Pass in the far distance.

'Tell me about him,' she spoke into the silence of a graveyard, and I told of the sorrow that started at the Pass and delivered beneath the concrete headstone at our feet.

She patted my hand and said, 'Who knows the days of our lives and the trials of our hearts, however long those days may be, *kind*.' And I waited for the truth I sensed was buried deep, struggling to be heard. While her eyes took in the serenity of our surroundings, she said quietly, 'We had news from Edward. No, we had news about Edward,' she corrected while thumb and forefinger unconsciously rubbed together in a nervous dance. The baby moved suddenly in its cramped space, and again I felt foreboding's dread coming to interrupt the peace and quiet.

'I know the path of your love and how it has found new roads to travel, but my news will test the depth of the love you feel for Ampie,' she began the telling.

Then it spilled from her mouth in a torrent she was unable to stop until the last word flew away in a sigh.

The baby's movements grew more agitated as my disbelief deepened, but the truth waited for no one to reveal itself. I sat, stunned, at the cruelty of this truth, which changed my day, but happened on an ordinary Monday in late September, when Edward was buying cattle on both sides of the border between German South West Africa and South Africa.

'Farmers in Upington knew all along that Edward was supporting the Nama in their territorial war with the Germans. Food supply to the 'rebels' had been a thorn in the Germans' side and had to be curtailed at all costs, it seems,' *tante* Katrien led in the story. To do so, they hired two Boers of questionable character to lure Edward west across the border under the pretence of selling cattle. There, among the dunes in a remote and isolated part of the Karas Mountains, they shot and left him for dead where no soul ever sets foot.

'A day later, on September 26, a German patrol wishing to erase any complicity, found Edward, barely alive and in much pain. And like a dog, they shot and killed him with only the hot desert winds as witness,' she completed the horrific tale. '*Oom* Roelof went in search of Edward for a proper burial after word came through of his absence but returned after many weeks' fruitless search. We tried, Nelie; we tried,' she uttered brokenly to be the bearer of such sad news, tears blurring the hurt in her eyes.

'Of this secretive act no one will ever speak, Nelie-*kind*, but for your own sake and that of your family's future happiness, you have to allow space to accept that in this war-ridden world, we sow in tears before we reap joy.'

She held me until peace once again returned to *Ma* and Abraham's resting place.

38 – Life after Death

'Birth is the sudden opening of a window, through which you look out upon a stupendous prospect. For what has happened? A miracle. You have exchanged nothing for the possibility of everything.'

William MacNeile Dixon

From his first mediocre try to suckle, I knew our second son's character would fail to meet our expectations. The animal world's primal truth, that a parent always protects the weakling more than others, became imprinted in the way little Ampie was raised by his father from that moment.

Nothing was too much, no effort too great and no hour too early to shower attention on a baby with the longest limbs I have ever seen. I often found Ampie on the veranda with his namesake curled like a kitten on his lap – long arms and legs dangling in a relaxed acceptance of a firstborn's right to favouritism.

'Always measure your attention evenly, Little Bird. You are bound to dislike one or more of your children and favour others, but never let them know,' *Pa* had shared his wisdom. His lived example made me search among us siblings for those he professed to dislike. I could find none. And that's how it would be with little Ampie.

I could never allow my misgivings to overshadow the attention which by right should be measured evenly between the children we bring into this world. But Ampie had his own compass for child rearing.

'We should call him by his birthname - Abraham. It is confusing with two Ampies in the house,' I tried to douse the flames of one-eyed parenting, which I had often seen manifesting in those who shared names. But little Ampie remained *klein* Ampie, continuing the Afrikaner name-sharing tradition to the point of ludicrousness.

A few miles south of Kameelfontein, a few generations of the same family lived happily within the constraints of repetitive naming. In the years since I came to live here, I had not been able to tell with certainty who was who. It was not unusual to hear them speak of Old Gert, *oom* Gertjie, Gerrie, and *klein* Gert.

Their relationships also entwined: Gert's Gert, or Old Gert's Gerrie and many variations on the same name, but they knew exactly who they were talking about. At Morgenster, a generation of children came already named, denying *oupa* Dewaldt and *ouma* Susara the naming tradition. But *Pa* and *Ma* stayed true to it, going back two generations to do so. At least we knew who we were named after.

The utter sadness that shared my days and nights after *tante* Katrien's revelation left me without the desire to eat, sleep, dream or prepare for parenting a child who had no fatherly connection to his half-brother in the graveyard. I looked upon *klein* Ampie's rimpled baby face and felt no joy. It was *tante* Katrien who put him to my breast, who cuddled and spoke words of endearment to him.

'Ewes don't accept every lamb they bear, but in the nursing comes the acceptance, *kind*. That is nature. We will stay here until it happens for you, Nelie,' the good woman said sympathetically.

My heart was still cold, and a smile pretended on my lips when the old people started preparing to leave in early 1906. By then *oom* Roelof had ridden far and wide with Ampie and Dirk, exploring the countryside. When he pulled me to his chest in greeting, his whisper soothed my broken heart, 'We are your parents and will come again, Nelie.'

Days later, Dirk told of their explorations, which included a house design for Section 334 - one suitable for a large family. 'They will live close to us and be our parents again, Nelie!' he said with a new light in his eyes. Only then did I understand that nursing begets nursing, which eventually led to the acceptance of *Klein* Ampie.

Ampie assumed the unspoken lie that Dirk had inherited Section 334 from his grandfather, whom he believed to be of considerable means, enabling Dirk to build a house as well. 'And then I must leave to build and earn our keep, Nelie. This time north towards Bechuanaland,' he said with impatience to save enough for our own home.

Because Kameelfontein was a loan farm, the plan was for *klein* Ampie and me to join Dirk, together with all *Pa's* livestock. 'To live on your own farm, Nelie,' Dirk said quietly when Ampie's hoofbeats were swallowed by tree, shrub and grass.

We looked east across Tweespruit from his new house site, then sat on the smooth pretend steps to take in the tranquillity.

The Waterberg mountains sat protectively close and sent red milkwood, wild fig, hookthorn and wild seringa's scent down its slopes from the north. The veld around the house carried the most delicious medicinal odour of campher bush, *wilde als* and *buchu* herbs. Guinea fowl in the tall trees, bushveld partridge in the shrub and wild ducks at Tweespruit added their melodies to complete the image.

'What a fine farm this is; here I can live and die, Dirkie,' my thoughts escaped, and we continued planning a house with a fireplace and wide kitchen hearth where many pots could hang over its warm flames. Just that morning, Dirk and Ampie had taken me on a tour of the unfenced yard, but it was the *bakoven* they had built a few yards from where the back door would be that they were proudest of - a clay-brick oven with a vaulted roof and cast-iron door. 'Here we can bake bread and rusks, Nelie,' Dirk said with longing at the prospect of such delicacies.

Dirk started building his house in earnest, and a month later, we lit the first fire in the hearth. 'This is our home, Nelie,' he said, but I knew mine would keep watch over this one.

A few weeks later, Dirk arrived from Alma's post office with a letter addressed to Kameelfontein. '*Tant* Liena van Heerden in the post office said it's been lying there for weeks, but now that she knows where you are, she'll keep our mail until we need something from her shop or maize meal from the granary next door,' He explained elaborately. I could always tell when the menfolk had been to the granary or post office, as *oom* Jan and *tant* Liena were avid talkers who transferred their style to any visitor. Even Ampie, a man of few words, fell victim to it.

The letter, addressed to Ampie, was in *Ma* Gertruida's curly handwriting. But who knew how long he would be away, so Dirk and I read it with growing happiness. It gave directions to access Ampie's inheritance at Hendrik Kroep's offices in Nylstroom. Six years after his death at sea, old Abraham Bergmann's estate was finalised, and each child would duly receive £3-1-6, adding to their savings for Section 333, Elandsfontein. A few Pounds that Ampie did not have to slave for in the heat.

Land was selling at 2 shillings a morgen. With 12 pennies in a shilling and 20 shillings in a pound, the children could buy 30 morgen right away.

Dirk shifted behind me. 'Thank you, Nelie,' he said and hugged me in sincere gratitude for the 150 morgen that his feet would walk and which he didn't have to save for. I was happy that Paulus Botes's wish had come to fruition in a worthy recipient.

A postscript to the letter read, 'Your brother, Gert, is a big help to me. But sometimes I do wish he would take to work with more spirit,' hinting at the reason the brothers had parted ways.

Ampie arrived in November after spring rains had coloured the veld green. Dirk's first maize crop stood proud in a small field near Tweespruit. It took many hours of hard labour with unwilling oxen and hard soil for a humble yield. Like a first-time father, Dirk showed off his effort as they walked row after row, arms pointing the way to future crops. They came inside, where Dirk proudly took his mentor around the house and discussed the brickwork, then out to the wide *stoep* overlooking Tweespruit.

'Ampie says we should plant tobacco. The farmers at Vaalwater, on the other side of the mountains, had tried it, and all you need is good soil and water. Everybody smokes, everybody.' Dirk's eyes were sparkling with excitement. Ampie nodded and smiled his calm smile, 'I will learn all about it on my next travels and teach you when I am back,' he promised. That's how we learned that he would be home for a few months and then return to 'marula country, where antelope get drunk on its fruit.'

The months went by so quickly that April's cool came as quite a surprise. Ampie spent his days playing with *klein* Ampie and carrying the neck-wobbling infant on regular trips to Section 333. One sunny day, he took my hand, and we crossed Tweespruit, which had all but dried up in autumn. On a slight hillock, he turned me around and said, 'From here you will always see Dirk's house, Nelie,' and marked out a square, 'For our own house.'

Soon after, he returned to the far north Bushveld. I often had to take *klein* Ampie to the home site and stop his crying, for a sensible man had turned into an insensible father. I had time to plan the layout of a house that would be built with love and hard work. It was while I was standing in the 'kitchen,' that nausea overtook me, and while heaving hands on stomach, the wonder and promise of new birth struck me again.

It's not a mother's discomfort that matters, but the sudden opening of a window through which you look out upon a stupendous prospect.

At that moment *klein* Ampie looked up and smiled his father's slow smile, and I thought, *Yes, a stupendous prospect indeed.*

39 – A Truth We Should Live

'Don't worry that children never listen to you; worry that they are always watching you.'

Robert Fulghum

Andries Dewaldt began life as I hoped he would end it—calm, gentle to all, content despite the pain that brought him to me. I loved him instantly.

It was Dirk who paced the veranda and soothed *klein* Ampie's hysterical crying when labour surprised us sooner than expected. Dirk hurried to fetch *tant* Liena with *klein* Ampie cocooned on his back. He stoked the fire, boiled water, and followed *tant* Liena's midwifery instructions from behind a closed door. Naturally, baby Andries adored Dirk like you would a father.

By the time word had reached Ampie, where he was building a house for old man MaHerrie in the far north, Andries's plump little arms reached up from a sitting position. The dust and smells of a hundred miles came rushing with Ampie to the front door, hair and beard sprouting wild fingers in all directions.

'Nelie! Dirk! Where is my son?!' Ampie's voice flew before him to reach us in the kitchen, his eyes searching until they found *klein* Ampie playing nearby. And that's what it would always be like – *klein* Ampie first and second, and unless a good God intervened, the only. I held Andries tight and kissed his head where the downy hair parted in a cowlick.

Ampie's visit was one filled with stories of people who had braved the frontier regions where the Limpopo River cuts the border between the Transvaal Colony and Bechuanaland. Dotted many miles apart and spread over vast bushland teaming with wildlife, the number of Boers trying to make a living was growing steadily, but not enough to knit a community.

'Come with me next time, Nelie,' Ampie pleaded, and I could feel the pull of excitement and adventure winning the race with motherly concern and sensibility. 'It is hot, yes, but so beautiful with the different colours of vaalbos, knoppiesdoring, marula and rooibos trees, all growing together like a family,' he stroked my hand to emphasise the beauty.

I looked at our boys and nodded. They needed a father now.

For weeks, we heard about and got to know the people who lived on the north road over Rankin's Pass and Sandrivierspoort Nek, a steep pass over the Sandrivier range in the central Waterberg mountains, just a few miles to the east. He described Vaalwater village, where tobacco grew in neat rows on wet feet from the Mokôlô River, 'But everyone calls it the Mogôl.'

Ampie explained a local tongue's peculiarities, which moulded foreign names to suit a palate used to saying words the way they are written. Bulge River, the next village on the north road, naturally changed to a guttural Bul-ge-rivier. Apparently, Ampie had asked what the corrupted name meant, and old *omie* Koekemoer, who had lived there all his life, said, 'It is what wé call it, *broer*. The *Rooinekke* call the *boeppens* where the river turns, a bulge – *dom khakis!*' he spat out his disgust with the English in brown tobacco juice at Ampie's feet, some missing their mark to paint his *velskoens*. The picture was so comical that Dirk and I could not stop laughing. Ampie reluctantly joined in and said defensively, 'These people are rough, but I like them!' which held the promise of many more stories.

We followed the path of Ampie's building work. With so few farmers and little money forthcoming from the government for rebuilding a bankrupt people, his travels took him through wild country where some settlers 'live like the blacks in thatched huts.' On occasion, he came upon humble homes hidden on the fringe of civilisation, where children born out of wedlock played practically naked. Their skin tone identified a union between races frowned upon by others, and they have parents unequipped through a lack of a moral compass to guide and educate. 'These children will never see the inside of a church or school,' he spoke the words that would soon draw the lines pegging social standing in South Africa.

'Where the land changes from hilly to impossible-to-cross, a fork in the road leads to unnamed places in the Zoutpan- and Waterkloof Wards,' Ampie continued, outlining his path. 'I took the right first, which the map showed as Waterkloof Ward,' he said. It was a road lost and found many times between high mountains where aloes grow to the top, and eagles keep watch above the valleys.

On the larger rocks that jut out into nothingness, engravings showcase the lives of hunters whose bones had withered and crumbled over the ages.

He followed the snake of a large river that delivered him to a plateau where a few square daub-and-reed thatched houses stood forlornly on its banks. '*Hartbeeshuisies*, the locals call these. People who keep to themselves,' Ampie said, 'And from there I travelled west to camp at old *oom* MaHerrie's place in the Zoutpan Ward.' At this point, Dirk and I had to ask many questions, as we could not picture the veld's vastness or the people making a home where heat, snakes and antelope ruled.

In the second month after Ampie's return, he indicated there were still many stories to be told, which meant we would not travel north for many months.

During the day, the men spent most of the light hours preparing the fields for tobacco seedlings, which they were nursing and shielding from the cold of winter, and at night, Ampie entertained us with tales from a world not that far away but seeming years removed.

I watched Ampie's patience bloom as he taught Dirk the intricacies of growing tobacco from seed, his voice carrying the lessons to the veranda where I sat. I listened and learned that to reap the best rewards, the process must start with sowing good seed in soft, nutritious soil.

Here in the Langkloof valley, rabbits would feast on the seedlings' soft petals, so seed-stands with legs at least three feet high had to be built, filled with soil and then gently sown with seeds that could easily be confused with those of onions.

Their work-hardened hands worked gently to cover the tiny seeds with soil and spread a cheesecloth tightly to keep it moist. A time-consuming job that yields its reward seven days later. Give or take another thirty days, and the once fragile seedlings are ready to face the sun, and when they are about three inches high, they are strong enough to be transplanted in the prepared fields.

'That is when the hard work actually starts,' Ampie said with a laugh, straightening to stretch aching muscles. 'From then onwards, they need water every day, Dirk,' and he explained that tobacco grows fast, so that in three months' time, the first leaves could be picked.

Dirk was an eager student who soaked up the minute details, especially how the leaves should be hung by their feet in the cellar they had built for this purpose at the beginning of June.

'Soon, I will build my own on our farm,' Ampie said as they cleared a wide tunnel that ran at an angle deep underground. It was secured and strengthened with a clay-brick wall and opened into a chamber big enough for a grown man to stand upright. There, metal hooks ran on wires on the ceiling for shifting the tobacco bundles to breathe – a place where one could get drunk on the intensity of odours.

During these activities, I tried to ignore a growing midriff. With no tell-tale nausea, I could avoid acknowledging another pregnancy for a while, but this was a childish wish, unbecoming of a mother of two. By the time Dirk and Ampie were transplanting the seedlings – one poking holes with a stick and the other securing plants three feet apart – I was preparing for an autumn baby.

One evening in late October, Ampie swung *klein* Ampie on his neck, Dirk carried Andries, and they guided me towards the tobacco fields, 'To see the fruit of our labours,' Dirk said proudly. We walked the rows, which sat at least four feet apart, 'So that the east winds can dance here to avoid rust.' The plants' aroma was all around, like the *buchu* and *wilde als*'s scents that intoxicate. And so I learned about crops that would never survive in the Highveld cold at Morgenster.

The days became warmer, and the nights unbearable as the sun shifted to rob us of the cool valley breezes. How I longed for *tante* Katrien's motherly touch and *oom* Roelof's practicality! But even though my heart ached for news from Upington, it was silence that accompanied the south winds.

'Something has happened to them, Dirkie,' I voiced my concern on a hot day in early 1908 when my 26 years were not enough to find my own guidance. 'They will come,' he said without conviction. What came was a letter from Black & Horn, Attorneys at Law in Upington – a notification of inheritance payable to Cornelia Jacomina Bergmann, only daughter of Katriena and Roelof Kleynhans of the farm Rooipad, District Upington. Included were two death certificates. *Oom* Roelof's stated natural causes, and dated two days later, *tante* Katrien's cause of death was noted as heart failure.

'A broken heart,' I whispered, and my own tears flowed in warm streams, taking with it any feeling from a heart that felt as if it would never heal.

After two days of not knowing or caring whether the sun rises or sets, Dirk came to sit with me.

In the comfortable silence that always seemed to hang between us, he said, 'They will always be with us, Nelie. We may not be able to see them anymore, but we can try to remember what we had learned from watching them.'

This calmed my heart.

To watch and learn was infinitely better than being told. Both excelled at that.

This was their truth; the truth we should live for our own children.

40 – *Rebuilding a lost Life*

'Perseverance is the hard work you do after you get tired of doing the hard work you already did.'

Newt Gingrich

1908/1909

Bent over a wash barrel at Tweespruit, the household's never-ending bundles of dirty clothes and diapers tried hard to break my back. But the hard work that consumed my days had nothing to do with scrubbing, rinsing and hanging out what we had toiled in. No, the hard work happened in my head.

One question kept repeating itself: How did I end up a slave to the dullness of daily chores when the dreariness and strife of concentration camps had tried and failed to douse the flames of my heart? It seemed the answer would never come.

When little Lettie was born hand-in-hand with the first sunrays on a day God had specially dedicated to her, I saw not the milky-blue eyes and downy skin's beauty, but counted the hours it requires to make soap from beef lard over an open fire, the time it takes to teach a child and bend their will to accept the acceptable, and to survive. To survive in a world surrounded by men.

Tante Katrien and oom Roelof may have regarded me as their only daughter, but a daughter to whom nów?

When Lettie was six months old, and Andries delighted us on unsteady legs, Ampie became restless. Shortly after, a bundle of necessities to survive beneath the stars started growing under the seringa tree where a swing he had built for klein Ampie hung idle in the child's pursuit of a father who could not say 'no.'

'If we pack enough maizemeal and stampmielies, we can live well in the wild, Nelie. I will shoot for the pot, so no one goes without meat,' he said in a tone that did not invite counterargument. In my mind's eye, the crushed maize stampmielies and porridge were already bubbling, unappetizingly bland.

Months of campsite living, reducing child rearing to a few do's and many don'ts, did not excite me either, but 'For better or worse' was a promise before God and man that I could not avoid now. 'Then we'll live under the stars,' I agreed and started a wood fire outside in preparation for the soap we would need.

Many pails of water found their way into a big three-legged cast-iron pot, and Ampie went around to the outlying farms gathering as much lard as he could for the time-consuming process of soap-making. This was freely given in the expectation of a sizeable bar of boerseep for their own laundry needs. After three days of stirring lard and water under a harsh sun, the process was finished. First, the lard had to be melted, after which I added caustic soda at intervals to finally separate the dregs from the oily mixture. Soapmaking is best learned by watching the process unfold, as a boerseep recipe is written in memory and shaped over a long time.

By the fifth day, my legs, face, and arms were burned to an unhealthy red, and the soap stood crisscross on the veranda to dry. The constant effort to keep toddlers and a baby from an open fire honed my nerves to a sharpness that boiled over into anger and a disquiet about the journey.

A few months after the fact, we received word of my brother Andries's marriage to someone called Maria Engelbrecht. Dirk stared off into the distance with the letter in his hand, then dropped it on the table with, 'We should have been invited – it's not that far.' That closed the door on any get-togethers between siblings and cousins. Sadly, our family tree will have fewer branches, as they will be born and remain faceless names to us.

The necessities under the seringa tree grew into a sizeable heap, helped in no small measure by Dirk, who found many pressing commitments in the valley, which resulted in him returning with frivolous gifts.

Coincidentally, his outings led past the Van Heerden's granary, post office and shop for 'Anything you may need for the road, Nelie.' Ampie was more attuned to Dirk's sense of duty at a time of all-consuming packing, child rearing and never-ending chores. 'She is quite pretty,' he referred to Jan and Liena van Heerden's daughter, Santjie, home from school in Pretoria.

My hand hesitated mid-air, wiping away the sweaty markings from a forehead damp with fighting nausea, and leant heavily against the plastered walls' cool sturdiness in the passage.

I missed the signs of love-language altogether in the drabness of my days. I knew it was unfair to transfer my feeling of helplessness to others, but if only young women knew the cumbersome life they were so eagerly signing up for, they might not enter it so young.

An unfriendly breeze found its way through the front door and took me back to Irene Camp's struggle and the swirling hot wind gusts that covered everything in dust and seemed to magnify our helplessness. Instead of happiness for Dirk, waves of despondency crashed over me, and a body so awfully tired of sharing space with another being.

On Dirk and Santjie's wedding day, a package was waiting for me at the Van Heerden's post office. 'I put it aside, Nelie, my hartjie,' Liena said, gesturing towards the granary which was swept and cleaned for a traditional Boere opskop dance party - quite unrecognisable in its festive coat. When we stepped inside, the concertinas and guitars were already playing to an audience impatient to have a good time.

Liena measured me up and down, then made a place among the trestle tables laden with baked goods. 'Here, this is a good place to rest a while,' she said quietly and wiped stray hair from my face. Her concern was kindly cushioned in helpfulness.

Soon, the granary was filled to the brim with guests, music fit for a Boer wedding, and children happily mingling with and dancing among adults. Klein Ampie disappeared between swirling dresses and shiny shoes while Andries and Lettie watched on, big-eyed in the delight of a colourful show.

'Dance with me, Nelie!' I heard the voice of too much peach brandy, before the long fingers identified a husband usually given to sobriety. 'Come, wife, where we're going, there will be no dancing,' Ampie said louder than intended, and I left the little ones in someone's care to waltz away on a wave of nausea in the arms of the stranger who stole my husband.

The early morning's fresh air was no help to clear heads, as our buggy clanked along in tandem with hoofbeats towards Elandsfontein. The horse found its own way home when Ampie's hands, slack in drunken sleep, let the reins go.

But sleep was the last thing I could give in to with Lettie cuddled in my arms, and Andries curled at my feet. Klein Ampie was riding the tides, squashed in between two unsynchronised adult bodies – one rigid in worry and the other relaxed in mindless slumber.

'There comes a time when we see our other half with new eyes, Little Bird,' Pa had tried to explain the moment when a wife or husband recognises a partner's faults. But did it have to come so soon into our marriage?

Without a care for my circumstances, my thoughts turned to what kind of husband Edward would have been. Such thoughts ensured that on a day of celebration, sleep passed me by like the rains which did not come in 1895, 1896 or 1897. Like those dry years' stinginess, I knew with certainty that many nights to come were bound to be sleepless.

I heard it first as a faint bleat and then a chorus of sheep in distress so close that I threw off sheets and rushed outside in the half-moon's pale light. Sheep outlines lay together with those of wilde als, buchu, and campher bush. On their sides, they lay in their hundreds like the round tolbos, guarding emaciated bodies among the wooden shrubs that would not sprout green for a few seasons.

'Oh, God, what has happened to our sheep?!' I shouted to the dry wind, but God took his mercy with the winds that chased dust clouds up the mountain. I fell to my knees at the riempie bench to support a body heavy with child.

Did you not have me drink from this bitter cup of drought and death before, God?! How can you ask me to do this again?!

The three children's cries found me stiff and cramped out on the veranda. 'Pa is sleeping, and I am hungry!' klein Ampie cried his hunger to ears not wanting to hear, nor to nurse or feed another human being for as long as I lived.

But this was what God had put before me and what must be done. I straightened and looked towards the veld where sheep lay dying mere hours ago, but the sun shone its heat brilliance on Dirk's tobacco fields and Tweespruit in the distance. The sheep had disappeared.

For a moment in my dream, I was taken back to the unforgiving drought that struck Southern Africa, when locusts and rinderpest were wreaking their own havoc. Antelope and cattle carried the virus over a land with few physical borders, and where they fell, locusts came in dark swarms to strip the last plants which drought had managed to avoid. By the time the horrors had passed, the plague epidemic had killed millions of even-toed animals to Morgenster's north and south.

Pa had seen the signs of the dreaded rinderpest before in countries to the north. There, animals died in an instant where they stood, mucus streaming from eyes and nose, as the sickness swept the land at an unheard-of speed. 'I'm locking the gates,' he announced with concern cutting his brow in two. 'No one leaves, and no one enters,' he warned and quoted the Bible on the run, 'God brought plagues on Egypt as a warning to obey Him.' We grasped the seriousness of the sickness in his unwarranted lesson. When its reign was over, Morgenster was one of a few farms that became a food source to a community devastated by hardship. From our animals came the rootstock to rebuild many a herd.

In all that time, we never doubted God's goodness and the promises to his people. Why would I doubt now? I stood, dusted my knees and held my arms wide for the blessing of three healthy children, and when they breathed their sleepy breaths in my hair, I felt the warmth of motherhood spilling over me.

Perseverance is the hard work you do after you get tired of doing the hard work you already did. I will persevere.

Part Six: Frontier Peoples

41 – To the Frontier

'Letting there be room for not knowing is the most important thing of all. When there's a big disappointment, we don't know if that's the end of the story. It may just be the beginning of a great adventure. Life is like that. We don't know anything. We call something bad; we call it good. But really, we just don't know.'

Pema Chödrön

The package stared at me with silent accusation from its vantage point on the sideboard. The sender's address sat in bold, curly letters on the side, like *ouma* Susara's crochet web pattern.

When the last spoonful of porridge had found Lettie's willing mouth, Ampie walked in, carrying the scent of freshly laundered clothes and Williams' Shaving Soap – his new nickel-box soap that had appeared on the washstand after a trip to Nylstroom. That was one of many happy days.

Ampie explained the soap's virtues enthusiastically while wiping smoothly shaven cheeks ear-to-ear, 'It cost just four pennies! And it will stop the old cut throats' burning.' Then, like a magician, he pulled from his pocket the tiniest perfume bottle, thin and straight and clear as water. On its flat side, it read, *Héliotrope Blanc*. His grey eyes were laughing with delight as he unscrewed the cap, releasing its sweet, powdery scent close to my nose. 'Now we are kings and queens,' he sing-sanged and promptly danced me around the room. From that day, I dabbed a drop of *Héliotrope Blanc* behind my ears in the mornings and felt like a queen who did not have to do washing, ironing, childminding, cleaning, or scrubbing.

The boys' hungry demands were just faint sounds to my ears now when Ampie came to stand behind me, his strong arms finding me in a gentle embrace. 'My queen,' he whispered like the old Ampie who courted with few words and gentle manners.

Thís was the man whom I willingly replaced Edward with. I turned to hold him close for the good man he was. I might have imagined that he was thát drunk at the wedding, who knows?

'When, Nelie?' Ampie pointed to the package, whose origin was announced to whoever saw the elaborate writing. I waited for the answer to find my lips, but knew it sat in my heart. If I opened the package, it would somehow make real *tante* Katrien and *oom* Roelof's death, and I was not ready to let them go, not yet, not for a long time. And maybe not ever.

Ampie ran his hands over my arms like you would a child who fell and hurt themselves, then said quietly, 'It is easier if you do not see them go.'

I saw *Pa* Abraham slide overboard and into the blue ocean that had robbed his people of a grave to name him by. It was Ampie who had to stand witness to that cruelty – a son old enough to fight a war, but young enough to cry for a father who passed away early.

We opened the package together. Inside, wrapped in layers of brown paper, lay a few articles that seemed quite insignificant given the old people's wealth. What stared at us was a cookie-cutter, a wall plaque proclaiming God as praiseworthy, a well-worn apron, and a potato masher that could easily last another hundred years' daily use.

'The vultures took the valuables,' Ampie said, 'but these things, few as they are, hold true value for their owners.' His sensitive explanation gave meaning to what lay on the table in their simplicity. So little, but so much!

'I will use it often,' I fingered the cookie cutter's rough edge and let my hands slide over the potato masher's handles. 'The plaque would look good above a sideboard,' I said and bent to smell its scentless flowers, which carried the warmth of *tante* Katrien's home to our hearts. 'It will hang in our own home one day,' I murmured and wrapped it again for a time when it would look down on our family.

'We are leaving next week, Nelie,' Ampie announced that evening as we sat around *Pa* Abraham's table at dinnertime. I rubbed my stomach absentmindedly, and he understood that the journey would have many stops and take a long time. 'The baby will be well,' he said and explained for my peace of mind that he would plan our travel to camp at day's end, close to a farmhouse and a woman's care.

We started packing for two adults, three children and a baby who may or may not be healthy.

The survival skills I had learned at Irene camp made choices easy. Days before our departure, I stocked the *huisapteek* with all the Lenons ' medicines Liena van Heerden's little shop could provide. My needlework and materials were packed, and preserves, jams, pumpkin, corn and soap were lined up like soldiers in their wooden crates. 'We would need more than two oxen for this load!' Ampie announced, but the arguments died on his lips when faced with my stubborn silence.

We left two days later, before sunrise. The children sat behind our seat, protected by a canvas canopy, and Ampie's trusted pony was tethered to a wagon straining under its heavy load. A few pots and pans hung beneath its belly where they would remind us at night that we share a 'bedroom.' But we would be dry and safe from mosquitoes, snakes and wildlife in a space under the wagon which Ampie had fitted with canvas walls, rolled down for our protection, 'Like a real bedroom, Nelie.'

The first night revealed the reality of a cramped bedroom. With no breeze and pots and pans for a roof, we shared the space with six pairs of little feet. But we were together on an expedition that saw *klein* Ampie's excitement boil over in *oohs* and *aahs* most of the day.

Once, a fully-grown kudu bull leisurely crossed our path as if to say, 'These mountains are my home. Yóú play by my rules.' The boy's questions hit us in a multitude of *whats* and *whys*, but most had to do with the kudu's curly horns. Ampie answered each patiently, preparing the next generation of hunters to be kind to nature and thankful for its bounty.

Our journey was slow, following the general direction of Ampie's previous travels. After four days' heat and flies and three nights' discomfort, we made camp on the banks of the Mokôlô River at Vaalwater, where tobacco plants grew close to the water. At dusk, we bathed in its lukewarm water, which felt like oil on my skin. Its flow was as relaxed as we were, and when I lay on my back, our baby's movements made lazy circles on the calm surface. With at least two months to go, the little legs kicked as strongly as a full-term baby's.

Maybe it would be another boy or perhaps a strong girl like *Ma*!

There was no road to speak of once we had chosen a north-westerly direction towards Zoutpan Ward, leaving the north-east route for later.

The road towards Waterkloof Ward was a much more cumbersome trek, which snakes through the mountains to where Ampie had made acquaintance with the strangely quiet frontier farmers.

Each day was a picture of lives lived extremely differently from ours. At times, we skirted old, run-down buildings that would have been home to people long ago and followed faint wagon tracks leading north. 'Families are the ones who need wagons, Nelie,' Ampie tried to ease my concerns. I knew there would be others living north, but who were they, and would they be friendly when we did meet?

Then the day arrived when Ampie could not find a farmhouse to camp close by. The going had been particularly tough between the mountains, and the four oxen had struggled to work as a team between gravelly soil and deep sandy patches. The children cried and whined all day in their cramped space, and my body ached after the wagon's jarring attack.

That was the day our baby stopped kicking. I waited all night for the familiar movements, but when pheasants and guinea fowl announced dawn, labour's first pangs had taken their place.

Be calm now, Nelie. Be calm. What would you have done if this were Irene Camp?

What came to me was a vision of Bettie's strong hands delivering babies in the harshness of dust, rain and tents sizzling in summer and freezing in winter. She could deftly encourage mothers at the end of endurance to keep going when it was clear there was no hope of a safe delivery. And in their moments of utter despair, kindness took over those hands to coax a dying baby back to life.

Once, after delivering live twins preordained by circumstances to a grave, she rested her head against the tent pole, exhausted, eyes closed, and sweat streaking her hair in wet strands. 'It is not only God's grace that gave them life, Nelie,' she answered my questioning eyes. 'It is Hé who gave my hands power to replace my cold heart,' and in that confessional moment, we were back at the riverbend, exchanging Eva for a baby that would never suckle again. And here I was at my own riverbend, so desperately in need of Bettie's hands and kindness.

A calm came over me like a warm coat in winter, as Ampie, shaking with shaking hands, boiled water and followed my directions to get ready for pain and struggle.

And how we struggled between those god-forsaken mountains – prayers asked, then shouted, and having to accept help was not forthcoming.

It was a day when the mountains expectantly waited to echo a mother's raw cries as she says farewell to a precious baby and lets go of dreams and a part of her soul that could never be restored.

The evening's cool came to rest among us while Ampie read haltingly from Psalm 23: 'The Lord is my shepherd; I lack nothing....... Though I walk through the valley of the shadow of death, I will fear no evil; for You are with me, your rod and staff comfort me.'

I felt no comfort.

Klein Ampie, Andries and Lettie sat with us under the wagon - big-eyed like abandoned puppies, cheeks painted with dry dust-tears. They knew not what had happened but accepted, with a child's innocent trust, that all was well in a parent's comforting presence.

Even though I did not have their accepting hearts, there was comfort in holding onto the thought that, in the face of a big disappointment, letting there be room for not knowing when or how we will heal is the most important thing. We don't know if that's the end of the journey. It may just be the beginning of a great adventure.

42 – The Bushveld

I am so tired. I have grown old from being serious. I have grown ill from being serious. I want to laugh at myself. I want to forget myself. I am so tired.
Kamand Kojouri

1910/1911

Nothing in my old life prepared me for this new life of seemingly endless expectation and soul-deadening loss. Not even Irene Camp's unfathomable heartache had touched my being with such sorrow as the silent cry of a lifeless baby.

At night, when the Bible's comforting words spoke through Ampie's calm voice, I heard all and accepted none. I listened with a hardened heart to the story of Job, who had seven sons and three daughters, thousands of sheep, camel, ox, and many servants, and I lay in Ampie's arms without joy. I knew that I was unquestionably different from Job - I had reason to deny the Word's truth.

Which god in their mercy would gift a life of never-ending toil and sadness and shallow baby graves?

The further north we travelled, the more wooded the veld became. Our days and nights became spaces of heat and thirst with cicadas endlessly trilling their pleasure at our discomfort. Each morning broke with nature's cries, but never early enough for *klein* Ampie's hungry mind. A host of antelope tracks sat criss-cross around our wagon, and the s-bend snake journeys were clearly marked in the sandy patches, often only a few inches from where we slept. 'Mamba and rinkhals,' Ampie said matter-of-factly, but he took to battening down the canvas with care before bedtime.

While we counted time in the many brilliant sunrises and red sunsets, I felt increasingly distant from the happiness I once knew. It was easy to live a life cocooned in my head while at the same time answering the constant stream of children's questions or doing daily chores. I often thought about the time after *Pa*'s return from Pietersburg with a lemon tree. A time when *Ma* started most sentences with, 'Excuse me, what did you say?' cocooned in her own thoughts, yet functioning well as a parent.

The children's delight at eating around a campfire never waned, and that was where Ampie revealed himself as the best storyteller. Mosquitos sang their blood-thirsty songs and came at us in waves, but an open fire's smoke kept them at bay while Ampie told stories, real and imagined, until the last child had fallen asleep; most often *klein* Ampie, who was a dreamer since birth.

We learned about generations of Bergmanns and the paths they had travelled since arriving in the Cape on a creaking boat from Germany in the 1700's. 'All the way from Hamburg,' he said, and we dreamed of far-off places, which, for *klein* Ampie and Andries, were just beyond the nearby trees. Lettie just laughed her happy laugh and snuggled close in my lap.

But happiness elusively kept its distance from me, and Ampie's concerned eyes followed my every move. 'There are things that death cannot touch, my princess,' he said in his quiet way after yet another sleepless night, then cupped my hand between his. We breathed in the veld's earthy smell, carried to us on the cool morning air.

'The special time when our hearts grow,' *Pa* used to say. But my heart felt cold and not ready to hear about the things that death cannot touch, even though I knew the answer well.

'Tell me about your forebears,' I heard my own voice, but I had no desire to know more. That is how it happened that Ampie told about German immigrants who crossed oceans for a fresh start.

'The first forefather, Abraham, arrived in Cape Town as an unmarried soldier in 1707 from Hamburg, but must have had misfortune, as he died young at 36. Well, not before he married and had three children. His only son, Abraham Junior, was only three years old when the father died, but at least he lived to 41, leaving behind seven children.'

At this, Ampie laughed and winked as if we should hurry up and have more ourselves, and for the first time since our baby's passing, I could appreciate the humour.

How Ampie remembered the dates, I do not know, but perhaps it was all part of being a good storyteller.

Next in line was a Carel who had turned 18 before old Abraham passed away.

'Nobody knows when Carel died, whether his was a long or short life,' Ampie said.

'But it carried the heartache of losing a wife in childbirth and having to marry a second time so the stepmother could look after the only baby – little Abraham Johannes.'

From here onwards, I felt like monkeys who gorge themselves on ripe marula fruit and become drunk on its fermented juices. Who could keep pace and remember all the Abrahams, their many wives and many, many children?

'Wait, Ampie, I need to rest first before you finish this story,' I said wearily, but could tell he was walking in his forefathers' shoes, and there was no stopping him, so I sat back and tried to listen carefully. It wasn't such a long stretch between 1781, when the next forefather was born, and sitting under the wagon in 1910.

The forefather must have lived a good life with his wife and seven children in Tulbagh, the most beautiful wine-growing region in the Western Cape, where he was a farmer. From this marriage, Petrus, who worked and married into a good family, was born 96 years ago.

I straightened so quickly at the story's next turn that I felt faint. Ampie rushed forward, but I pushed him away with, 'This cannot be true!' But it was – Petrus Bergmann had 18 children between two wives! 'Their offspring would have walked past each other and not know they were related,' I shivered and thought, *Nothing much had changed since Petrus was born.* That could well be the future I was destined to endure. Could any one mother have a child each year? I was young enough to have my share of 18!

'Oh, wait, Nelie, I'm only at my grandfather Abraham's birth in 1840 now,' Ampie tried to stop me leaving. 'He had six daughters and just one son to carry forward what, I think, then became the family name. That son was my father, *Pa* Abraham Jacobus, whom we buried at sea.' At this, he turned away and busied himself adjusting the canvas roof. Then he said with a crooked smile, 'And look, here I am, brother to four sisters and father to a brother who has no need for my guidance.' In that awkward moment, I understood his generosity towards *klein* Ampie and the need to tell stories that keep long-gone family alive. There are, without question, things death cannot touch.

'Tomorrow we'll be about as far as we can go, my queen,' Ampie promised when the children woke in quick succession.

'For now, we'll accept what the day brings.' And the day brought more heat, more flies, and more marula trees. After weeks on a diet of meat, rusks and maize porridge, the yellow fruit that lay in their delicious hundreds under wide-spread branches was 'Sunday pudding!' *klein* Ampie and Andries shouted to the birds above.

The four oxen refused to move during the day's heat, and nobody complained about that. Together, we fashioned a canvas roof attached as a lean-to for shade. The multitude of shrubs and trees which coloured the air with scented brush were best appreciated from our *riempie* chairs in the shade. We took in the calm it offered, which felt alive at the same time, as if many eyes were watching - this I would soon recognise as unique to the terrain.

'The Bushveld,' Ampie read my mind, and went on to tell how he had heard the name for the first time from *oom* MaHerrie after days' hunting on horseback. They were covered in bloody scratches from the willowy buffalo thorn tree, which grew so densely that their zig-zag branches and double thorns marked them as vicious, yet effective antelope protectors. A contented smile played around his lips as he relived the excitement of what was new and unique, and it stirred a place hidden deep in my heart – a yearning and slow awakening of the same excitement. My eyes misted over as he looked askance, took my hand and leaned back to take an even deeper breath, this time marked with contentment.

The oxen's rumps seemed to have fleshed out in the weeks since we had turned west towards Zoutpan Ward. 'The grass is sweeter here, Nelie,' Ampie declared, bending to inspect the curly-leafed *soetgras* more closely. 'This is good country.' A knot formed in my stomach as I took in the veld's vastness and no humans to tread its soil.

'No, not altogether empty,' he squinted towards the horizon, then pointed to a thin white smoke spiral ahead. 'Zoutpan's salt pans,' he explained the efforts of a few hardened men – the Smiths – who toiled all day scraping salt into hessian bags for a pittance. By nightfall, we made camp between the thorn trees not far from what Ampie said was 'A flat expanse, shiny white in daylight.' The change in trees from tall to medium to small and thorny was remarkable. As far as the eye could see, sickle bush held hands and built a thorny wall, so much so that there was just one track leading towards the pans.

'We will leave tomorrow morning. There is no water or shade here, but we might meet the Smiths and talk a bit,' Ampie explained. 'Only the antelope come here to lick salt, not snakes,' he teased.

When at last the children were asleep after running up and down the salty surface endlessly, we lay down, tired of travel and discomfort. Each one's thoughts took their own direction and intensity. Mine stayed close by. *Was I really still so unspeakably tired? Had I grown old or ill from being serious?*

I did not know if I still wanted to forget myself and drown in the sorrows of being human, but I could not say anymore that my heart and soul were altogether tired. I touched Ampie's shoulder and listened to his breathing.

Yes, there were things death could not take away, especially here among those who loved me and whom I loved.

43 – Settlers, Animals and Veld

"There will come a time when you believe everything is finished - that will be the beginning."

Louis L'Amour, 1908

Eva's plaintiff cries stirred me from a deep sleep. Our horses stomped their impatience at being tied up among the sickle bush on the cold riverbed where Edward and I tried to shield her between us.

'There is no milk, Eva, shhhhh...!' I said softly, holding her tighter. A feverish cheek touched mine with damp fingers. But Edward took the intimate moment away, shaking me roughly and calling, 'Cornelia! Cornelia, wake up now!' and I sat up so quickly that my forehead bumped him on the nose. Blood streamed in vivid spurts and ran over his mouth and chin, but his laughing grey eyes remained untouched. Then he stole Ampie's deep rumbling laugh and pinched his nose to stop the bleeding.

'Nelie, a rolling pin is easier to swing; there's no need to head-thump me!' His voice became serious, and I came fully awake. 'You must have dreamt of Eva. Did you have a vision that she was harmed?' Ampie had accepted my sense of foreboding a long time ago without asking any questions.

I was thankful he did not share my ability to know the unknown – how would knowledge of Edward have changed this kind man? Would he have believed at all that I loved him and not my first love?

We lay back against the pillows and listened to the calming sounds of children laughing in the distance while ours were still fast asleep. A newborn baby was crying much closer. We shot up and dressed hastily to follow the cries through the sickle bush, which were determined to steer us in a fool's direction without revealing mother or baby. 'It was so close,' I panted shallowly like old Soldaat after a chase.

Circling the next thicket, the salt pan suddenly opened in white brilliance. Ahead, humans of all sizes and shapes were scrabbling around its fringes, and large, fat-bellied hessian bags marked their salt-scraping efforts.

'Where were they hiding last night?' Ampie wondered aloud and scanned the pan's breadth west to east.

That's when my eyes fell on her. Staring into the distance, a woman sat a few yards away, suckling her baby under a sickle bush – its meagre shade hardly any protection for mother and child. We moved closer.

'Good morning, *Mevrouw*,' Ampie raised his hat in greeting, and two eyes totally void of feeling looked our way. I had seen these blank, pitiful eyes before in Irene camp. It was a picture of extreme struggle, as if there was nothing more to life than hardship's blandness. The woman wore a dress that had known better days and seen more water and soap in a previous life than it did in recent months. Ten dirty toenails pointed heavenwards. A threadbare blanket whose colours had faded into the indeterminate, pretended to shield them from a carpet of *khaki duwweltjies* – the paper-thin brown thorns which covered open spaces.

Nothing, from the old *kappie* that hung tiredly around her face, the strangely pale baby, the emotionless eyes, to the hunch on her back, told of happiness. The hair on my arms stood up, and the supernatural stirred the air. We had to get away from this dreary place.

'Ampie, we have to go!' My voice was a whisper as I turned and ran back the way we came. It was Ampie who caught and steered me in the right direction, and adjusted my *kappie* before we joined *klein* Ampie, Andries and Lettie under the wagon. I did not need to explain my feelings; Ampie understood the otherworldliness of Zoutpan's salt pans with one quick measure. 'We will move on as soon as the children are fed. I will speak to Smith another day,' he confirmed and started saddling his pony to lead the oxen at a faster pace.

An overgrown two-track trail led straight north among marula, mopani and knob-thorns, leaving the sickle bush behind in their effort to shield the pans and their secrets from inquisitive eyes. Foreboding hovered around me like dust in a sandstorm, but at dusk it settled, and we made camp under a big baobab tree that towered over a fresh water pan nearby.

'Yóú name this place, Nelie,' Ampie tried to lighten the mood, and explained that in all his travels in the surrounding areas, this was the first and only baobab that he had come upon. I thought for a while, then settled on Kremetartpan – a name that accurately describes the baobab and pan. 'It will be a compass for travellers,' I said, 'A beautiful place where the night-owl can sing its lonesome song.'

That night, foreboding came to me for the first time as a welcome visitor. In my vision, I saw three wagons travelling slowly north.

From up high, three smiling women waved to us on their way past the baobab where we stood, and three men cracked long whips in the air, loudly talking to each other like old friends sharing good times. I watched them on their slow journey, and as the last wagon rolled past, I recognised *klein* Ampie with a black dog trotting alongside. I looked again at the women and recognised myself on the wagon, surrounded by four children. She smiled a slow smile of happiness and waved. I waved back.

Sleep evaded me after that, and I listened to the owl who sounded mournful yet wistful. Previously, visions had left me tired and wrung out, but this time I felt uplifted and eager to get going.

'And now, my queen, why the haste?' Ampie asked hesitantly early the next morning, afraid to break the spell of positivity as I impatiently stoked a fire.

Between stirring porridge with a determined hand and stoking the fire, I told him about my dream, which he accepted without comment. We ate, thanked the Lord for his blessings and gathered the children who were already playing among the low scrub.

That evening, we camped under an old marula tree a few hundred yards from the track. All around, tree types that I had never seen before dotted the landscape. The veld sloped westward into a thick stand of buffalo thorn. 'The locals call it *blinkblaar-waggen-bietjie* thorns,' Ampie explained that their shiny leaves may look harmless, yet the double thorns hidden underneath would hook and keep you stationary for quite a while. 'Not easy escaping their claws, so best to avoid them altogether.' I felt safe from predators close to their thorny protection. The next morning, only small duiker spoor tracked past, confirming my feeling. What turned my blood to ice and kept the children under the wagon was a snake track as wide and thick as my arm, leading north towards open ground.

Ampie became deadly pale after following the track into the undergrowth. 'Black mamba,' his voice turned husky with concern, and we started packing up with more haste than at Zoutpan. The sun was already overhead by the time he had finished the tale of a black mamba which he and *oom* MaHerrie had encountered, 'Not far from here.'

He told of a snake, 'As long as the wagon and thick as my forearm,' at an anthill where they had planned to rest and have a bite after hunting the entire morning. The grey snake came out of nowhere, head lifted as high as a fence pole and swaying side-to-side in front of them. '*Sit still, neef,*' *oom* MaHerrie spoke without moving lips, and they sat there, not daring to blink until the snake lowered its head and headed for a hole.

At that moment, the dogs came back from their hunt, heading off the mamba from its home. 'I have never seen anything like that, Nelie. This snake struck so many times that I could not even count them, then disappeared into the hole just as fast. *Oom* MaHerrie's dog was dead before we could find the bitemarks,' he said with so much concern that I held Lettie a bit closer.

With fits and starts, I learned about a nervous snake named for its black mouth. A snake that would rest at night and hunt in the early morning or midday, whose home was permanent and filled with family members, old and young, and who could grow up to fourteen feet and slither faster than the average adult human could run. 'But who would be able to kill these terrible snakes?!' The question escaped my constricted throat, and Ampie finished his tale with another that he and *oom* MaHerrie had witnessed from the safety of their horses.

'We saw a honey badger fight the swaying mamba, and after he had been struck many times, the badger jumped forward and bit right through the snake's body just below its head.' I was aware that badgers have such thick fur and tough skin that a swarm of bees might attack them with no effect. But a mamba?! 'Yes, Nelie, we must get away from these thorny flats; this snake has its home here and will kill to protect it. Vaalbos is not a good place,' he named the area.

From here onwards, the wagon tracks north were hardly visible, but with eyes on the sun and scanning the bush for tall tree beacons, we set up camp during daylight at an incline in the road that must have been a pan many lifetimes ago.

'A time before hunters had dared the bush where leopard still roamed, and lion came hunting south across the dry Limpopo River from Bechuanaland,' Ampie filled in the blanks. But here I didn't feel unsafe, not like Vaalbos's snake fields. Before long, the children were throwing stones and picking berries. 'Sweet cross-berries,' I learned.

We walked the hard-baked surface, which now revealed itself as a large indentation half the size of Kremetartpan at the baobab. Heat crept up our legs from the dry surface where the sun stored it during hot days, but a pleasantness accompanied it, drawing us to the middle. There, Ampie possessively pulled me close to dance a slow waltz.

The children came running, shouting excitedly, each with a block-patterned tortoise in their hands. Even Lettie toddled along, holding a tiny, slowly wriggling tortoise close to her chest. 'There many!' Andries shouted in our faces with his boy voice, holding up five fingers, then changing hands to hold up five more. Ampie laughed delightedly, rubbed Andries's head with, 'There many, many, ey Andries?!' and took a little outstretched hand to be dragged along to several shallow holes. 'Tortoise nests,' Ampie said in wonder, and I guessed, like me, he had never seen tortoise nests before. I had heard that they are commonly found near a water source, so could there be water under the surface?

The sun set like a ball of fire, and the dark came on instantly. 'That is how it happens here in the Bushveld,' Ampie sounded content. Listening to the crickets talking to each other when everyone was already sound asleep, a peace came to sit in my heart.

Here, where the earth's goodness reached up to greet us; here, the time came when I stopped believing everything was finished.

Between Skilpadfontein's tortoises, I found my new beginning.

44 – Finding Purpose

'We have two lives, and the second begins when you realize you only have one.'

Mario de Andrade

Should birds look down with knowing eyes on the five of us, flat on our stomachs on the pan's brackish surface, what would they think? That we are scratching for food and water as they do, or learning to be like monkeys who use all fours for transport? Or would they have a deeper understanding of our actions, which dictate that the human spirit needs places where nature has not been rearranged by man's hand?

Skilpadfontein abundantly served up such a place at sunrise, with various spoor left at our front door during the night.

'The wild becomes wild because wé make them wild, children,' Ampie explained, antelope's presence so close to our wagon. 'That is the reason I hunt for food on horseback many miles away.' And it was why, here at ground level, four pairs of dirty heels and many more hoofprints belonging to our unconcerned neighbours were facing me.

The morning's lesson required us to follow the tiny scratch marks of the tok-tokkie beetle, which rises earlier than others to reach a few dewdrops on grass petals. 'They run as fast as a duiker to get the best food, and then they tock and listen, tock and listen,' Ampie finished in a child's language the lesson of how male tok-tokkies tap rapidly with their abdomens to find a mate and wait impatiently for the female's answer.

The ancient pan was lined with its tiny markings, and in the near distance, we could still hear some tapping their mating song. If we were intent on not disturbing their daily pattern, these hard-shelled black beetles would live on this pan forever as the Creator had intended. Before long, the children were squealing with delight at having found the beetles. Andries wanted to know where they lived and where their babies were sleeping, so Ampie crouched and duck-walked them to the pan's edge, where the grass was denser.

There, after an intense search, they found the tiny hollows and small yellow eggs that the mother lays among the grass.

'That is their food once they have hatched,' I heard Ampie using every opportunity to teach them about nature's rules in the only school that matters to children of the veld.

That morning, a gentle breeze whispered me awake. It felt cooler than usual and found its way over our warm bodies under the wagon where Ampie had tied up the canvas walls the night before, 'Because it feels safe here.' And it was.

There was abandon in the children's play. Even the oxen grazed leisurely on *soetgras* close to us, and the pony contentedly swished the annoying flies away. 'Animals know,' Ampie verbalised my feelings. There was a softness and mystery about Skilpadfontein that invited us to a towering knob-thorn close by. When we stood in its sparse shade, goosebumps deliciously crawled down my back. 'You should build a house here, Ampie.'

What you build in the sweat of your brow, my heart will call home.

We stood together, looking out over the veld. As far as we could see, tall trees pointed their arms heavenward, and birds crossed the sky in their daily business of feeding chicks and surviving in an oppressive yet soothing heat. 'I do not understand it either, Nelie, but this is the Bushveld which called to us; now we have to find the answer to its calling,' he read my mind.

When we had first arrived at Skilpadfontein, our biggest need was water, as it is anywhere in the north-western Transvaal. The brown water we scooped from the Bulge River many, many weeks ago, was for cooking, drinking and an occasional face-wipe. The oval metal washtub remained unused on its hook in the wagon, and the children wore little more than pants day in and day out to save on washing.

Thoughts of Irene Camp's dreadfully unhygienic living visited me every day, but once we had settled at Skilpadfontein, I took to watching the birds' flight paths like in days gone by. 'You will tell me where the water is,' I spoke to myself, and when I was sure which direction their morning and evening flights took, Ampie saddled his pony and discovered a deep rainwater pool, a few miles away towards the west.

The bush grew so prolific that the wagon would never have been able to venture closer, and it was up to us to carry water for drinking. Ampie carried the tub on his head like the black women we saw at Vaalwater, and set it up close to the water, 'but far enough so we do not dirty our drinking water.'

There, we boiled water and filled the tub halfway every second day, bathing from young to old in the same water, changing the next day to old-to-young so that everyone had a first turn. But we could bath, and that was a special indulgence!

We camped at Skildpadfontein for months before 1911's winter. On a crisp morning in May, Ampie started packing up, 'Because the oxen have to work off their fat behinds.' He made a game of harnessing them to entertain the children who had forgotten all about travel's long days and the tediousness and sameness associated with a slow journey. All along, he kept whistling tunelessly as if harbouring a secret. At six, *klein* Ampie picked up on it and was like a fly to jam around Ampie. '*Pa, waar gaan ons, hê Pa?*' he nagged to know Ampie's plans, but not until we were ready to leave, did Ampie explain that winter is hunting-for-*biltong* time in the Bushveld. 'Otherwise, blow-flies lay their eggs in the *biltong* while they dry and you will have none to go with your porridge, *seun*,' he said, which just resulted in many *what* and *how* questions about *biltong* and why we eat raw meat.

The father, who had spent so much time away from home, now patiently shared the knowledge he had acquired of a region which had already stolen our hearts. He walked to the nearest ox and demonstrated to three eager faces from where the best *biltong* would be cut, and elaborated on the salting process, then hanging and air-drying the long strips of meat.

Faint were my memories in this moment of *tante* Katrien and *oom* Roelof, of Langkloof and the war and the lives it claimed. But fresh were the memories of Edward that very morning, when nausea overtook me. My heart ached at the bittersweet memory of little lives lost on the path of life.

The sour in my mouth made me wonder about a human's capacity to bury the memory of a love that was so real, so strong, that the danger of war meant nothing at the time. Yet, since then, I could pretend Edward's lonely death on a sandy slope did not touch me and merely belonged to history.

It felt as if I was looking through someone else's eyes at my family, like I had two lives - one distant in memory's haze and another still in progress.

What touched me deeply now was this new life growing in and around me. What was real now was a loving family, not the sweet memory of a life lived before.

I knew, as sure as the sun's light and warmth which touched us each day, we have two lives, and the second begins when you realize you only have one.

Part Seven: The Power of Peach Brandy

45 – Self-inflicted Misfortune

Quiet minds cannot be perplexed or frightened, but go on in fortune or misfortune at their own private pace, like a clock during a thunderstorm.
Robert Lewis Balfour Stevenson, 1870's

Since peach brandy had made a stranger of Ampie at Dirk's wedding, my thoughts had a subtle strain etched into them, especially when men found reasons to come together 'for old times' sake.'

The moment we were perched on the wagon, the familiar discomforting thoughts returned, spurred on by Ampie's declaration.

'There is no better friend in the Bushveld than *oom* MaHerrie.' What tied my stomach in knots was his eagerness to meet up with someone he shared hunting history with. People might call it dread or fear, but to me it was a particular foreboding I could not name. For the moment, the children's excited chatter diverted my thoughts to less ominous places.

In front of us, the two-track road wound its way north until another faint track crossed it west to east at a place where trees, shrubs, grass and animals melted together in a most beautiful picture. Alongside, a grassy pan that stretched far into the distance, drew all living beings for sustenance – drinking, feeding and feeding on each other. Here, the soil became loose and thick, sapping the oxen's energy. Tall coarse grass grew among the sweeter *soet-* and *krulgras,* and the cross-berry bushes the children loved, seemed to grow everywhere - their shiny red-brown berries an invitation to a multitude of birds.

Ampie rode alongside the wagon and pointed out the diverse trees. The marula's dark green was interspersed with the grey of what he called the vaalbos, 'but,' he said, 'All the Bantu who live here call it the môgônônô, so it's better to do that. They do not speak Afrikaans. And the cross-berries are in fact marêtlwa. Say marêtlwa, children,' he repeated, and they echoed the name in chorus like children in school.

Lettie was a few months shy of two and copying our every word, relishing our delight when she spoke a short sentence and dragging the 'r' like those born in the Cape province. *Klein* Ampie was the wild one who loved nature's way of cancelling human rules in favour of its own, helped along in no small measure by Ampie's ignorance of a first son's mistakes. But what surprised us was our quiet Andries's ability to imitate bird sounds. His older brother tried to outdo him, squeezing his bottom lip to whistle until his face was red and his lips cracked. Still, he failed. It did not surprise me when *Klein* Ampie became so enraged that he fell on the ground, kicking and screaming like a toddler.

I looked on and continued with my work, ignoring his outbursts. My heart warmed when Ampie, in a rare rebuke, said firmly, '*Seun*, take your *kettie* slingshot and shoot a few fat pan pigeons – you are a good shot; leave Andries to do what he is good at,' and with that, the matter of giftedness was resolved.

Andries could sit under a tree, head tilted heavenwards, listen to whichever bird made itself at home in the branches and then pitch his voice perfectly or whistle to the same tune. Many times, he even fooled us adults. From the hornbill, pigeon, go-away bird and *mossie*, to the guinea fowl who came to roost in the trees at night, all seemed to be his favourites.

His ability to mimic others was a reminder of the dedication required to craft a table from wood, sew a dress from imaginary patterns or build a house with precision – these examples abounded on both sides of our family.

Our going was leisurely, with frequent stops to talk about the animals and birds, so much so that often a whole day would pass before we covered a few miles. I was glad, because this was our family's time. My thoughts turned to my own childhood and *Pa* Andries's gentle patience, which turned stories into facts to be remembered forever. From their eagerness to learn, I judged that our children would always belong to nature – bound to it with affection and understanding.

For days, we camped under two enormous marula trees close to the crossing. Ampie had something new to show us all the time, and often he would wake us to listen to unusual sounds or to show what the veld delivers only at dawn.

We learned quickly to be quiet for these treats.

One morning, we woke to the faintest of sounds. With finger against lips, he motioned us to keep quiet, and there, mere feet away, a steenbok was grazing on the cross-berries – quiet in her shyness and subtly hidden in early morning's grey. She stepped daintily around a small boulder which suddenly came alive and started suckling - mother and child so close, that I could see their long eyelashes and black noses moving up and down as the ewe nibbled on the dew-laden leaves and the tiny fawn quenched his thirst.

We held our collective breath as the mother lifted her head and looked straight at us with dark, wide-set eyes, studying her two-legged visitors with such intent that there was no mistaking who intruded on whom. Her large ears turned constantly to make sense of us. Except for white around the eyes and pasted between the chin, chest and underbelly, her golden-brown shoulders stood as high as my knee – a perfect example of God's artistic creation. Then Lettie sneezed, and in an instant all that remained was our memory of a moment shared.

'That was good, wasn't it, children?' Ampie whispered his awe at such an unexpected gift.

'I can shoot it with my *kettie*,' klein Ampie announced to the veld and demonstrated with an invisible slingshot.

'But they did not speak,' the imitator in Andries said wistfully, and before we could focus on parenting, the boys were arguing about animal voices like a cockerel with hackles raised in mock-fight. That's when I first noticed Andries's tenacity and unwavering conviction in what he believed was right. In the heat of the moment, our quiet boy drew his four-year-old self up and on steady legs pushed the much taller firstborn back, his eyes fixed intently mere inches from his adversary's with, 'It.. did.. not.. speak!'

That was also the first time I noticed the coward in *klein* Ampie. And so did his father. We did not speak of it, but from that day, it was always the two Ampies against everyone else, in the way nature demands that the weaker be protected at all costs.

The next day, Ampie said we should keep moving for another day before returning to the crossing to follow the tracks east towards *oom* MaHerrie's farm, Biesiepan. He wanted to show us the furthest point he had been to on his previous travels.

'Sand, thornbushes and tall trees are everywhere,' he said, and I wondered why we should see it as well, but we loaded the wagon and travelled a half-day to the area he described as 'Groot Doornlaagte.' I was surprised at how quickly the scenery changed from beautiful at the crossing to unappealing a few miles north.

Being with child left me hot and miserable, and it was with relief that we rested in a few môgônônô's shade. Ampie walked back and forth among the trees, a frown deepening as he circled back. 'Nelie, people have camped further on. I found two wooden pegs with WH burned into it,' and because I must've seemed dumbfounded, he continued, 'The government had already sold this land. If we want to build at Skilpadfontein, we must make plans to buy it, and fast, before another farmer claims it.' To me, finding evidence of people camping was a good thing. More people meant the new Union of South Africa was looking after its own, and not by the hated English far across the sea.

'Yes, *neef* Ampie, the government has sold farms to a few families to live here in the wild. Kolbooi, my *kaffer*, came to tell about that,' *oom* MaHerrie said when we arrived at his place after a two-day journey which saw Ampie whip the oxen and drive them at an unaccustomed pace. The large man with big hands and kind eyes welcomed the children and me into the home Ampie had built.

A yellowed photo of a wife long departed hung in the *sitkamer* above a sideboard now covered in a generous layer of dust. Along the passage walls, antelope trophies hung in their multitude, among them some which I could not name. From curly kudu and long gemsbok to short duiker, and the buffalo horn's large, muscly black arms – years of hunting expeditions looked on mutely at the new arrivals.

Nothing in the house spoke of cleanliness or hard work, and without reason, I took a deep dislike to the older man with a fleshy softness spreading around his waist.

Around the dining table that night, we ate bland stew and maize porridge, which Kolbooi's wife had prepared over an open fire outside the back door. The house had a wood stove built into a nook, which Ampie had placed cleverly so there would be a draft taking the sting out of summer's heat.

It was obvious from the dust layer that the expensive stove, which must've been transported with great difficulty, was not used. 'A waste of time after Anna had passed away,' *oom* MaHerrie said from the doorway, hinting at a more respectable time in his life. In my mind's eye, I saw *Pa's* weak efforts to cope after *Ma* had passed away, and my heart softened towards the man whose humanness was centred in the one who belonged to memory.

When the children were asleep head-to-toe on single beds, which had not felt the warmth of children's bodies for a long time, we three adults sat outside at the fire, braving mosquitoes in the evening's quiet. The black couple had left for home by then, but not before leaving a large earthenware jug close by – its sour contents announced potency and predicted headaches for quenching a soul's thirst with marula beer.

I did not have to feign being tired, but left to sleep with Lettie. I could hear the men's happy voices late into the night, and I placed my hands protectively over the knot in my stomach, thoughts swirling like dust on freshly ploughed fields. I drifted off to sleep thinking, *Keep a quiet mind and do not be perplexed or frightened, Cornelia, for the good Lord will protect in fortune and misfortune.*

All I could do was to live at my own private pace, like a clock during a thunderstorm.

46 – Ellisras Ward

'O God, that men should put an enemy in their mouths to steal away their brains!'

William Shakespeare, Othello

1911's winter came and went.

Drinking marula beer and brandy became nightly rituals for the men who now counted three after a drifter appeared from the bush late one evening. 'From Betchuanaland Protectorate,' he announced importantly. His unkempt hair and beard were set on a ripe-smelling body that carried the odour of little water and a hot sun. He kept the men entertained with many stories of 'The black land up north.' Stories that became more interesting and daring the longer they lingered around the fire.

As the beer took its toll on the younger men, *Oom* MaHerrie visibly relaxed and took on the role of storyteller rather than drinking partner. But this failed to reassure my mind, which was fraught with worry, and my body, growing heavier and more vulnerable. '*Kinta*, it is time to call me *oom* Hendrik,' he offered as an invitation to share concerns in a woman's absence. I realised I had misread his character altogether and gladly accepted the offer. And so began a friendship built on kindness.

The man who had been first to wake in the morning a few months ago now struggled to get out of bed by nine. So did the drifter who slept on the veranda until noon. Kolbooi's loyal heart saw to it that Ampie was fed, but the drifter was left to snore in a drunken haze.

It was not unusual for the children and me to be done with our daily chores by the time Kolbooi and his wife, Pula, had dished up a second breakfast for the disgruntled Ampie, yet they could have put down ashes for a meal, and it would have been eaten without complaint. Not that the Tswana were inventive in their cooking, no, it was usually just porridge, boiled eggs and tasteless meat stewed until it was grey and unappetizing.

No hand of mine would serve the weak of will, and even though I tried a few times, my unwilling hands trembled in their refusal. From then on, I prepared food for *oom* Hendrik, the children and myself and left Ampie and the drifter to Pula's fare.

No matter how often I urged Ampie to return home before the expected birth of our child in December, he seemed incapable of feeling the same concern. In his beer-fogged state, he missed the emotional undertone connected to losing a baby on an arduous journey. On one occasion, when I tried to force an answer, he became angry, and his eyes took on a look that I've seen before in physical fights between men. I did not ask again, and neither did I sleep soundly again.

Using eyes and signs to communicate, Pula made her own concern known. She kept pointing west, then to my stomach with an expression só urgent, that I realised she had felt the loss of more children than the men cared to know about. One morning in November, she refused to leave the kitchen even though *oom* Hendrik spoke harshly and ordered her to sweep outside.

It was Kolbooi who translated her signs into Setswana. The dishevelled men could hardly take it in, but I followed the signs and melodious tone which worked together to tell his story. I listened intently and was struck by Kolbooi's repeated use of *'Mmelegiši'*. Exasperated, he slapped his forehead with a whip-sound and said, *'Êê, batho a Modimo!'* pointing heavenwards. Thát I felt. God was surely watching the seriousness of this dreadful situation unfold.

'Kolbooi is talking about the people who had bought the farms to the west,' I said and looked accusingly at Ampie, who did not have the clarity of mind to focus on much else than his headache. 'Soon, Kolbooi and I will have to start walking west if you do not wake up and stop drinking!' I brought my hand down hard next to Ampie's plate. He looked shaken, but it was doubtful whether he could react.

However, at that moment *oom* Hendrik came home from the cattle *kraal* and summed it up in a few sentences. 'Maybe the new farmers – the Kühns, Harmses and Van Rooys - are now camped on their own farms. I think they named the farms Zandpan, Stockpoort, Witkop, Groot Doornlaagte, or was it Hoornbosch? I do not recall.'

At this, Kolbooi and Pula hissed their displeasure and beckoned me outside. There, stick in hand, Kolbooi drew the road west to the crossing and beyond.

A family took shape in the loose sand, but it was the tall woman whom he repeatedly stabbed with the stick, saying *'Mmelegiši.'*

Then Pula made soothing sounds and rocked back and forth as is the way of black women when carrying babies cocooned on their backs. Kolbooi followed up by holding three fingers in the air and circling the sun's path three times. A midwife living three days away! How could it have taken me so long to understand the simple message! The baby made an arduous turn that forced me to double, but relief at understanding flooded my body, and the baby calmed down. It was the first week of December.

I fetched writing paper and wrote a simple letter to 'The mother of the house.' Who knew if she was even able to read?

Pula's earthy smell wafted over my shoulder, and I guessed at her awe of the written word as it flowed from a lead pencil. How unlike were our worlds – I could make meaning in word and script, and she used the ancient tools of sign and sound, yet I sensed an intelligence and desire to learn in those dark eyes. I followed the few sentences with drawings of a heavily pregnant woman and wrote Biesiepan Farm underneath. Pula eagerly took the note from me, and toddler-on-back disappeared west, using the transport she knew best.

Six days later, a buggy stopped in the shade out front. A tall woman in her 50's stepped off and strode with careful yet determined tread to our veranda while Pula negotiated with much difficulty the simple task of getting off the tiny metal boot. 'They normally walk everywhere.' The woman said kindly, but when she noticed my stare, she shrugged to acknowledge the white man's insensitive customs, which dictated that blacks do not ride up front in a buggy.

With outstretched hand, she said, '*Tant* Anna Kühn,' and I took it, instinctively knowing that I could trust her to deliver a baby out in the bush. We talked about prior pregnancies and held hands in the silences that marked little lives lost. She judged the baby's position with experienced hands and declared, 'Three more weeks. I will rest the horse tonight, go home tomorrow and come again before Christmas.' My mind was at ease.

It was time to clean the house front to back – a task I had neglected in the false belief that this baby would be born at Langkloof. Pula eagerly washed the cement floors in the main house and smeared liquid dung on the outbuilding's floor.

I packed away years' worth of unused articles that so obviously belonged to a woman fond of needlework, leaving them untouched where they had last been used. Only a hardened soul would not feel sympathy for the old man who wanted to keep his mate's memory alive. Here, in the house of cobwebs and dust, a new life stood a chance of adding the joy so long forgotten and stirring responsibility and care into the men's beer-slackened hands.

True to her word, *tant* Anna stepped into the house with purpose four days after Christmas, even though her feet, crippled by large, painful bunions and arthritis, dictated a slow pace. That night, without much fuss or crying and even less pain, a chubby-cheeked baby boy joined our family. Gerhardus Petrus Benjamin, we named him after a forebear in my family. His serious expression reminded me of *oupa* Dewaldt, who had deep insight and a strong character. Would it not be a miracle if that became baby Petrus's inheritance?May he never change when life's struggles interfere.

My fervent wish was that his calm would fill the holes in my heart left by brothers who had gone before. A soft breeze drifted over us, lifting my spirits.

Fatherhood lessened Ampie's drinking, but the drinking spell, which had already lasted so long, could be broken only if we broke its hold. We had to return to Langkloof.

At the end of January and with Ampie not showing any intention to leave, Pula, the children, and I gathered our possessions and loaded the wagon while Kolbooi searched for the oxen. He made sure they were ready to move at the first crack of the whip. But still Ampie slept on in a drunken haze.

At sunrise, Kolbooi, Pula and all their children stood like soldiers at the ready, the young ones wide-eyed about the new activities. 'Why do we have to go, *Ma?*' *klein* Ampie and Andries whined. In a child's accepting, without question, way, they had made this their new home and did not anticipate being separated from their black friends, 'In a million-million years!'

Lettie cried in sympathy with the boys, but I made them say goodbye to every child by name. When I came to Pula, the stoic woman awkwardly held my hands in her work-hardened ones.

'*Sepela gabôtsê, Mma,*' I heard her say, but in the moment, I had no words of farewell. I loosened my apron and placed it in her hands, and searched my pocket for the lead pencil, then folded her fingers around it.

Kolbooi helped the children onto the wagon, and I went inside for one more try to wake Ampie. It seemed not even the devil could wake him, but I persevered. Nobody would want children to witness the embarrassing picture that liquor could paint.

'*Tot wedersiens,* Kolbooi!' I called from the wagon and cracked the whip. Ampie's horse snorted his displeasure at being tied to the wagon. It was impossible to read Kolbooi's eyes, but he lifted his threadbare hat in imitation of the white man's habits.

Kolbooi and Pula's children ran alongside the wagon until we turned west towards the crossing, but Pula remained motionless where we had left her. Then we heard her ululate a long, wavering wailing - a sound that meant sadness, joy, regret and celebration all in one. I cracked the whip needlessly with, 'Come, Rooiland! Bonte! Faster, you lazy beasts!'

Two grieving women's heart-songs disappeared in the children's crying while Ampie settled in a grey world, slack in dreamtime. I knew then the journey would not be measured in miles.

Infant Petrus was happily sleeping in the wagon's roll and dip. And I? An anger that had taken hold weeks ago grew and festered in the place where tolerance should have sat. From being both mother and father in a stranger's house came new emotions. For too long, the Nelie of Irene camp had been hiding, ensconced in the happiness a family brings. But the drinking? For that, I did not sign in front of witnesses on our wedding day.

At the crossing, the wagon creaked and bumped over the grooves other wagons had made in the pan's clay soil, now dried by the bushveld sun into a rock-hard surface. It shook Ampie to his senses. He sat with a start and looked around, hair sticking out in all directions. 'No, no, Nelie! Turn back. I must build at Waterkloof Ward!' he half-shouted, fumbled with his hat, and gracelessly got off the wagon. I watched him fall and felt nothing.

Where animals, birds and trees had formed a beautiful picture a few months ago, the heat left its mark in brown grass, tired trees and the hornbill's occasional call. It took effort to turn the wagon in a wide circle among shrubs and thorn trees, intent on leaving their mark on us.

Ampie found his feet and led the oxen onto the track from where we came, losing his footing a few times while my inner devil wielded the whip for needless speed.

A dry river's sandy shores stopped our two-day trek east. Its usual angry course was clear in bent-over trees and flattened grass, but now a few green pools were the only evidence of summer rain upstream. Just like Ampie had described long ago, a few reed-and-daub houses spiralled smoke from low-slung thatch roofs and skew chimneys. Further north, a cluster of brick homes outlined the makings of a village. Closer to the riverbank, corn stood yellow and dry in the heat while a few Boer pumpkins lay ready for the picking, and along the road, children played in the dust.

I thought of the pencil in Pula's hand, and how this place's loneliness could have been captured now to cement the moment. There was hardly a page left of my Croxley paper, as the urge to sketch animals and birds had called me often on our way here. Like the drawings I kept private in the button box Edward had given me, so was the call to mirror nature on paper hidden from my family. *Pa* knew. *RéAndriese* knew. And the button box knew. And as if to say, 'I know too, *Ma*,' Petrus looked on with his serious eyes.

Questions about building in this lonely place had to wait until resentment had died down. Ampie set up camp with trembling hands, carrying a scowl and a thirst for more than water.

The sympathy I should have felt was swallowed by one thought only: *Why do men put an enemy in their mouths to steal away their brains?*

For that, I had no sympathy.

47 – Round-trip to Vaalwater

'When we least expect it, life sets us a challenge to test our courage and willingness to change; at such a moment, there is no point in pretending that nothing has happened or in saying that we are not yet ready. The challenge will not wait. Life does not look back. A week is more than enough time for us to decide whether or not to accept our destiny.'

Paulo Coelho

A week was more than enough time to decide whether or not to accept my destiny. A father's sweet talk and love alternating with anger-fuelled times were the choices that seemed to predict our family's destiny.

No sooner had we woken the next day than an unsettled Ampie wandered over to spend time with our neighbours. 'The building work is a police station at Vila Nora,' he pointed east on his return, 'but we will stay here for a while.' For the first time, we had a heated argument about staying where the mosquitoes gathered in their thousands at night, and where no good food was to be had apart from the sun-baked pumpkins. He became so angry that he stood trembling inches from me, hands balled at his side. But I was defending our destiny and would not back down. Then he stabbed me on the chest with a finger and said, 'Know your place, Cornelia!'

I understood my place was to be quiet. Was this the price I had to pay for our children's sake, and would I , Cornelia of Irene camp, meekly accept Ampie's authority? She waved a finger of warning at him - she knew her place. 'To fight for your children is worth every angry word, Little Bird,' I heard *Pa*'s voice and found strength in his wisdom.

At nightfall and still in a foul mood, Ampie left to sit with the nearest family. Soon, the call of friendship with such unlikely people became clear in the loud voices and the sour smell of marula beer, which drifted on the wind.

The next morning, I made sure there would be enough water, maize meal, and *biltong* to last until we reached Vaalwater, fed the children, and took them for their ablutions behind a *blinkblaar-waggen-bietjie* bush nearby.

'I cannot do it,' Lettie wailed and kept looking behind me. There was no patience left in me on a day already swarming with flies and a fierce sun picking at our white skins, but I looked around to satisfy her and found many pairs of dark eyes watching us, their goods perched in bundles on their heads.

With trousers around his ankles, *klein* Ampie lost his footing in the excitement of seeing his friends. Behind the children, Pula and Kolbooi's white smiles lit up their black faces. I let go of Lettie and threw my arms around the woman who spoke no Afrikaans but knew my language. She inspected my effort to bind Petrus behind my back, clicked her tongue disapprovingly, then untied him and reworked it with practised hand.

I needed no words to explain what was clear to anyone. Kolbooi took the oxen and Ampie's horse down to the water and returned to harness the draught animals for travelling east towards Vila Nora, a police outpost. I doused the fire, settled Lettie and Andries on the wagon while *klein* Ampie was rolling on the ground in a mock fight with Kolbooi's son, Johannes, whom he adored for his bird-hunting skills. I handed Kolbooi the whip, took up the reins, and the wagon started creaking slowly towards the only river crossing. There, the sand was firm, allowing the oxen good traction.

I did not look back as we followed the track. Life sets us a challenge, and it's up to us to face it.

Two days into our journey, the track between the boulder and the cliff became less arduous and opened onto level ground. We made camp under a big tree with mountains to our north and south, and when a few rabbits Johannes and *klein* Ampie had snared were roasting on red-hot coals, we noticed another fire flickering in the distance. Could it be the police outpost? Kolbooi disappeared into the dark, and long after the children had fallen asleep, he returned, imitating a rider carrying a pistol and holster – without doubt the policeman at Vila Nora. The fear of being alone in the wild with Kolbooi's *knobkierie* and the .22 our only protection, subsided, and the night seemed more welcoming.

We woke to Ampie sitting outside our wagon enclosure. There were no words between us, and my heart told me there would not be any for a long time. We reached the farm, Clermont, where the Vila Nora police building was supposed to be erected, but the only police presence was a tent pitched in a clearing.

A pole outside made space for a horse, and maize porridge was hissing and puffing over a wood fire. A man in his forties appeared, wearing neat khaki clothes and sporting the whitest beard I had ever seen on such a young man. The pride with which he carried himself instantly demanded respect.

'No, *neef*, I was promised a room, but if you are the builder, it will have to be a stone building,' Nel, the policeman, announced, his mouth pursed in disbelief. There was no building material. The rocks would have to be fetched from the nearest mountain, and 'Payment is made at the police station in Nylstroom.' A determined look came over Ampie's face, and instinct told me we would have to stay with him or move on alone. He stomped off towards the mountains to fathom how boulders could be moved towards the building site.

I remembered Dirk's words, 'You can do anything, Nelie; do it, and God will help you,' which decided our pre-dawn pack-up and trek south towards Vaalwater – a white and black family together setting foot on untrodden paths. Nel rode with us until the Palala River crossed our path, then held my hand long in greeting with, 'This is a difficult path, *Mevrouw*, but stay close to the river until reaching Melkrivier. I know people there. Farmers travel more often between these little villages and Vaalwater, and you'll be safe on the road. God be with you,' he said in a thick accent and with pity in his eyes.

Many moons of hardship later, we arrived at 24 Rivers close to Vaalwater. Ampie had spoken fondly of spinster sisters, Edith and Molly Fawsett, English women who had made South Africa their home and lived on the isolated farm. Being close to Vaalwater, the last outpost serviced weekly by government buses doing mail deliveries to and from Nylstroom, they had reason to feel safe and comfortable on their own. And so did we, after their warm welcome and hospitality, which included Kolbooi and his family. 'Stay and rest, sister, you have endured much,' they invited us into their lives.

With little fanfare, they prepared a meal, stoked a boiler for hot water and made beds. Kolbooi and Pula withdrew into their otherness, but accepted food and water with cupped hands like you would manna from heaven.

Klein Ampie, Andries and Lettie had never seen a porcelain bath, and sat quietly in the warm water until I started scrubbing weeks' worth of grime from behind ears and between toes. The sweetest aromas wafted from a bar of hair soap that Edith showed me to use. 'Not the tart-smelling Pine Tart Soap,' she said, but when she noticed my ignorance, she followed it with, 'This came all the way from India's spice markets. They have been making hair soap for a long time.' For this, the children sat still and watched with wide eyes.

Later, I learned that Edith had spent her savings on buying the farm and was living off what was left. A smile never left her face as she watched our little family's delight in discovering what life had never offered before. By the time Petrus had had a bath, the others were asleep. As I lay him down, Andries said sleepily, *'Dankie, Mammie.'* The simple thank you of a child was enough reward for our suffering. I stood by his side for a long while, stroking his silky, clean hair until the tears had dried on my cheeks.

It was indeed true; there was no point in pretending that nothing had happened or in saying that we were not yet ready. The challenge would not have waited.

I slid down in the warm water, which swallowed all the cares accumulated on the long journey. Tomorrow I might have to face another challenge that will not wait forever.

48 – A Farm to Cherish

'For I know the plans I have for you,' declares the Lord, 'Plans to prosper you and not to harm you, plans to give you hope and a future.'

Jeremiah 29:11. The Bible

1912

Edith and Molly Fawsett's pleas to stay on at 24 Rivers tore my heart in two by its sincerity, intensity and perseverance.

The children, now exposed to a world of indulgence, expected a similar lifestyle on Section 333's empty plains. No explanation could colour in the bleak picture of life in a wagon and the bitterly cold winters at the Waterberg mountains' foot. The children's interpretation always brought them back to, 'And I will be first to bath in our white bath,' even though I tried to tell them that bathing would be in Tweespruit's freezing waters. Kolbooi and Pula mutely accepted that nothing would ever be the same among people who do not speak their dialect or share their customs. But go, we had to.

The air was crisp in late July and frost hard beneath our feet. It lay in white sheets on the oxen's backs when Kolbooi cracked the whip in a final goodbye to the beautiful place we had called home for so long. The children's cries accompanied us for many miles on the south-west road to Vaalwater.

A single parent's loneliness and doubt sat heavily on my shoulders and did not ease until we reached Vaalwater village, where the green tobacco plants were replaced by winter's fallow fields. The Mokôlô River had lost its summer flow and now meandered slowly, and in places there were only a few deep-water holes with mist hanging thick over its surface until late in the morning. There would be no camping on its cold banks, and the oxen obediently travelled the last few miles on exhausted legs.

If only there were a railway to get us across the mountains. But there wasn't, and it was up to our travel-weary selves to get back to Langkloof. Old *oom* Bergmann's planning ensured a 197-morgen haven for his children and grandchildren, albeit only a promise of ownership in the distant future.

The oxen had no choice – there was one dusty road snaking between a few dozen forlorn houses, stretching from Sandrivierspoort Nek and the north where we came from. Leafless trees added to the feeling of abandonment. The children were quiet for the first time since we had left 24 Rivers – their uninterested eyes taking in the nothingness.

A hundred yards along, and to our surprise, there was some activity on an open plain where a few wagons were drawn back-to-back. Women in traditional Afrikaner dresses and wide-brimmed *kappies* were stirring maize porridge and speck *kaiings* in big three-legged pots. Their activities seemed quite out of place in the sleepy village, but then my eye caught sun-burnt menfolk shovelling and digging behind the wagons.

Klein Ampie and Andries were already on the ground running with their black friends, following their noses to pork rind and speck's rich odours which drifted on the breeze. Kolbooi tied the in-spanned oxen to a dikbas tree's rough trunk. Its fragrant imitation-pear flowers tried hard to lift our spirits amid the drabness of winter dust and cold.

I sat there, taking in the homely scene of teamwork and the scents of earth and wholesome food that reminded me of the homes I had belonged to. My heart ached with such ferocity for times past that it froze the picture in time, and tears came unbidden to eyes so inexpressibly tired of witnessing the sadness that life brought forth. I cried quietly for everything that had been and everything that could and would still be.

'Nelie! Nelie, *klim af, my sussie*,' I heard from far away, and I leaned into the shoulder next to me. I did not care about the sun on my face or the people around. I only wanted to be here, leaning on a shoulder, not having to think about or worry about others.

I closed my eyes and heard children laugh, oxen swish their tails, and someone breathing deeply, taking time to remove my *kappie* and wipe my face with rough hands that smelled of soil and hard work. 'All is well; we can climb down now,' I heard and opened my eyes to look into Dirk's, so close, so calm and reassuring.

In the Afrikaner's practical way, the women had set up *riempie* chairs and ladled enormous helpings of porridge and *kaiings* for everyone, unobtrusively ensuring there was a seat for me. 'It is a nice day,' an older man said, then rose to shake my hand, saying, 'Koos Labuschagne.' When women bent their heads and folded their hands, he prayed over our simple meal, thanking an ever-giving God for his grace and mercy. We ate in silence.

Later, I learned that the men were preparing space for a railway platform, as the plan to extend the railway line from Nylstroom was well on its way, and all should go well, if only the *'verdomde'* countries overseas could keep out of each other's hair. That was the first time I became aware of world affairs and the troubles that could draw our new Union into an unwanted conflict so soon after our own.

When dark set in and the others had retired to their own wagons, Dirk sat with me until the coals had greyed over. 'Now we can go home, Nelie,' he remarked and took my hand like he used to. He explained that Santjie was home caring for their son, Antoon, born in 1910. 'But the good Lord has not blessed us with more children,' he said quietly, and I felt a sense of shame for having so many children and the resentment I had been feeling for being with child so often.

From my serious child from a distant life, I learned to be humble, thankful, and silent before our God, who knows the road ahead.

We went to bed and left before dawn the next day. Ampie's absence waited unexplained for the right moment.

Two days later, we arrived at Langkloof, crossing the dry Sterkspruit where I wondered again how an insignificant-looking creek could turn into a monster that could sweep away to an early grave anyone brave enough to enter its brown waters in summer. Equally surprising was the drab winter veld which would magically change and put on lush summer clothes to draw animals, birds and insects from far and wide.

'Atop the Waterberg mountains,' Ampie had said, 'Is a different world altogether.' There, mountain seringa, lavender, and peeling-bark trees grew alongside teaks, sometimes on the open plateau and often in horizontal clefts and around cliff-side caves.

It was there, exploring the overgrown clefts, that he had to climb like a baboon and run for his life when the strangest animal backed out of a small cave, quills pointing to its rear in defence and rattling in anger at Ampie's intrusion.

He learned a valuable lesson in survival at that height when the porcupine charged and drove him up the krans into a wild bee's nest. A fearsome adversary, he was fortunate to escape by wallowing in an evil-smelling rock pool, which lay stagnant from summer rains, and without which its frequent wild visitors would perish. There he lay, nose barely above water, until the bees had calmed down and flown away in pursuit of their daily tasks.

'I am sure *Pa* had stood there before putting in a request for our farm, Nelie, because once you have seen the mountain and valley's beauty, you know God is near and will protect all who walk this land,' Ampie's attempt at describing the breath-taking views rolled over lips not often given to many words. But that felt like a lifetime ago, and even though the mountain's beauty would always be there, my heart came back to Langkloof forever changed.

The delight in getting to know Santjie and Antoon was medicine to a broken heart and a spirit stretched to endure what so many Afrikaner widows had to endure after the war – the loneliness, the lack of money and resources, the anger at not having a choice.

Dirk and Kolbooi took our wagon across the dry creek crossing and set it up on the hill where Ampie and I had once selected a house site. Under a tall tree, they pitched a tent alongside the wagon and let the old oxen roam free. The pack-mule chose its own patch of grass and went about settling in in a leisurely way, never worrying about what had happened yesterday or what may happen tomorrow. Our first night was filled with winter's peace - crickets chirping and jackal and baboon barking their own song. We were happy on the land, '*Oupa* had bought for us.'

Guinea fowl woke me before sunrise while the children were still asleep. I remembered frost's beauty, which comes to blanket the veld and went outside to feel the stillness it brings. And there, not five feet in front of me, Ampie sat quietly – frost hard on his wide-brimmed hat.

He came to me with sorrow written in deep lines around his mouth and eyes.

And I took the gift of love that was meted out, for the Lord knew the plans He had for me.

Part Eight: Langkloof

49 – A Place of Contentment

Only you have a certain fragrance that can touch others in a way that they feel compelled to take their own journey within and find their own medicine.

Corina Luna Dea

The following twelve months echoed the happy times Ampie and I had before the hated *mampoer* peach brandy turned him into a bully. A bully who had forgotten what marriage vows, 'to honour and love' and 'for better or worse, as long as we both shall live,' mean.

The strangest thing about liquor is that it plays hide-and-go-seek with people. Before, on days when Ampie drank, the children knew to hide so as not to endure his unwarranted wrath, and on sober days, the kind man I had married lived peacefully among us, being attentive, playing with the children and working hard in accordance with the Bible's teachings: 'In the sweat of thy face, shalt thou eat bread.' Since the day he had waited in the bitter cold outside our tent, he had not once tried to buy or brew *mampoer*, and I became calm in the warmth of his love.

On a Friday after Ampie's arrival, Santjie invited the older boys to play with little Antoon for a few days. With their string of black friends tagging along, the invitation was hardly cold when their excited laughter disappeared across Tweespruit towards our friends. The quiet they left behind was deafening.

'Now, pack a bag, and in there must be your prettiest dress. Do the same for Lettie and Petrus – we are going to Nylstroom,' Ampie said in a secretive tone.

Once camped close to the beautiful Witkerk where we got married, he declared, 'Petrus and Lettie will be baptised tomorrow at *Voorbereiding*' - a sermon which serves as contrition and preparation for Sunday's communion to honour our Lord's sacrifice. There was an apology in every word for trekking in the wilderness when they were born.

I had never felt nearer to Ampie than during the sermon when he held Petrus close to his chest, and his tears mingled with the baptismal water that was sprinkled liberally on Petrus's downy forehead. Many a woman dabbed eyes, overcome with emotion in the presence of such love. As if reading my feelings, the pastor dedicated our children to an Almighty with the hymn, 'Nearer my God to thee.' It was a fitting end to an emotionally charged sermon. The congregants, sensing a spiritual strengthening in the moment, repeated the last strophe, *Nader my God aan U,* with feeling and gusto. The less cumbersome Afrikaans words rolled easily off the tongue without the difficult High Dutch pronunciations of times past.

The next day, on our way back, Ampie spoke about his anguish at losing his family; the fearful search for our *spoor* on roads so seldom travelled, and the physical hunger which was only matched by that of his soul. Here in the telling, he held my hand as of old, in a promise to never let go of us again. I believed him.

A year later to the day, World War I broke out on 28 July 1914. Distance and isolation kept us safe and ignorant of how the upheaval would change the world for four long years. We knew from experience that those at its core would forever be changed people.

That afternoon, I found Ampie out on Dirk's ploughed tobacco field looking south from its higher position. Far away, dust clouds from what seemed more than one wagon rose against the distance's blue. 'They will be here tomorrow night,' he said, and we returned home to prepare for visitors. As the early winter dusk closed in on us, we could see a rider scouting ahead of the wagons, which had most likely by then camped for the night far away towards Alma. We guessed they would slowly make their way across the veld the next day. By the time the rider had dismounted, our lanterns and a fast-burning fire were lighting a path for anyone unwise to travel in the dark.

At first, we did not recognise the bearded man in dusty clothing, but then he spoke with a distinct timber to his voice, which Ampie recognised from long ago. 'Albert Schoeman, *my ou maat!*' he greeted the friend from his youth and shook his hand vigorously. To me, this connection was layered in distant memory. I faintly remembered the tall man and his family from church get-togethers in Lichtenlburg, but to be truthful, he was more a friend of Ampie's family than mine.

'He was barely 12 when their menfolk went to fight in the Boer War,' Ampie whispered after we had convinced Albert that only fools would travel on horseback during a dark moon. He single-mindedly wolfed down the rabbit stew and porridge I had prepared, then the men spent a few hours discussing life's tribulations on the road. I wondered how they could profess to know the difficulties of such travel when their experiences were so far removed from what a woman faced daily - feeding, clothing, and rearing children without a permanent home.

Sleep overtook me when my thoughts drifted to the *why* of an instant dislike, I felt for the man I hardly knew. Was it in the granite of his light-blue eyes or the subtle way he avoided talking to me directly? I drifted off with *Pa*'s long-ago warning, 'Never trust a man who cannot look you in the eye, Little Bird.'

We woke to cold coals and ash, and a hollow where Albert's body had made its imprint. 'Tonight,' Ampie predicted the travellers' arrival, but I went about my day as if Albert had never stopped by. An hour before nightfall, four wagons made their way to ours and were drawn into a *laager* so that humans could camp in its protective arms, and the oxen could feed freely towards the green surrounding Tweespruit. Two wagons carried machinery, and the others were sleeping quarters. A young woman, heavy with child, slowly climbed down from the lead-wagon. Her struggle to find a foothold urged me forward to hold her arm, and when she looked into my eyes, a kinship flowed between us that I instinctively knew would be lifelong.

'Come, *my suster,* sit here,' I helped her to the fireside where Ampie had made space for our best *riempie* chair so she would be warm and comfortable. Albert introduced her as his bride, Katrien, and the others as they appeared from a heavily laden wagon, 'My brother, Jacob, his wife Grietjie, and children, *Groot* Tommie, Mienie and Anna,' skinny teenagers with hard work and hunger sitting around mouths strangely quiet in the company of adults.

I was overjoyed to have company and did not care about the men doing nothing but talking, hunting, or walking the valleys and mountains. I cared about the two good women who held their tongues among men and talked endlessly when alone with women. Their journey was long and tedious, during which the two brothers found work as State water contractors.

They drilled for water to help rebuild farms lost during the scorched earth war policy – a lucrative contract that contributed greatly to savings for the farms they hoped to buy in future.

I wondered why everyone looked thin and hungry yet ate large helpings at our table.

Dirk, Santjie, and little Antoon joined us many evenings, bringing steenbok and wild rabbits Dirk had caught in snares. There was always a good supply of rabbits when seasons changed, as young wheat shoots on the fields drew them in so that their natural carefulness evaporated into the cool night air.

After a month and beyond the full-term date for Katrien's delivery, talk among the men started drifting towards, 'When we buy farms together.' Dirk took me aside with, 'Nelie, I do not trust these brothers. They eat too much and talk big about what they own, but their children are scrawny and their wives quiet,' he echoed my fears.

On an especially cold and frosty night, I was woken by Katrien's crying. When I reached their wagon, she was fighting labour pains by herself while Albert sat outside at the dying embers. Grietjie and I rushed into their wagon at the same time as Katrien wailed, 'Lord, do not take this one!' Grietjite shook her head sadly, confirming what I suspected. This was not a first baby.

Irene Camp taught me many lessons, but Bettie's was the best: How to deliver a baby in distress and help a mother who had lost her will to live – now was such a time.

I climbed down, went up to Albert and shook him by the shoulders. 'Albert, stoke the fire and get hot water going, *man*. Do it now!'

He seemed dazed, then said, 'Do not let him die! Not my son!' My anger became white-hot in the face of his disregard for a good wife who may lose her life. I pushed him off the *riempie* chair with all my might just as Ampie appeared sleepily from our tent, taking in the situation instantly. He motioned me towards the wagon and hastily stoked the fire, repeating a task associated with our own loss so long ago.

In the wagon, prayer seemed the only option to save two lives, and Grietjie and I prayed fervently while trying all the measures known to us to do so. Katrien's life had hardly begun. *But a life in service to whom? Albert? A stillborn baby?*

We kept up our desperate efforts until a tiny baby, the colour of the sky, was born and started mewing like a kitten. We sagged to our knees, and Grietjie mouthed a silent prayer to thank our God, the giver of all life. In the dark of that night, a miracle happened, and we were witnesses. Who could ever forget it?

Outside, Albert was waiting anxiously, but when I said God in his mercy had saved Katrien and their little girl, an indifference came to sit in his eyes. Then he walked away. At that moment, my heart hardened towards him, and a protectiveness towards Katrien took hold.

Soon after the baby's birth, it became clear that Katrien harboured a deeper strength I had not noticed before. She became adamant that little Sofie would be baptised in Hartebeestfontein, where she herself had been baptised, confirmed in church, and married. Nothing, not even heated words, could sway her.

They left by train from Nylstroom to return a few months later. Katrien, with her church membership certificate firmly in hand, now had a determined demeanour about her. You had to be slow of mind not to recognise that a new Katrien was directing her life. She had discovered her own fragrance that could touch others in a way that they must take their own journey within.

When talk of buying a farm together came up again, she was the first to say we should buy separate farms in the Bushveld, which Ampie had described as having beauty in every tree, animal and bird. Grietjie and I nodded and started packing essentials.

When Ampie asked how so and why now, I reminded him that 'Skilpadfontein is waiting for us. That is our journey we are compelled to take.'

He did not argue, and we left a week later.

50 – *Rekindling old Friendships*

Walking with a friend in the dark, is better than walking alone in the light.
Unknown

1915/1916

The road north seemed much shorter the second time round. Many more wagons, cattle and horses had since travelled the two brown tracks as they wound through valleys, over open ground, crossing rivers and creeks and skirting mountains until we reached Zoutpan's salt pans. On the way, the women and children became eager students of what we had learned about surviving the veld's dangers and demands.

At the pans, Kolbooi and Pula remained behind on the day Ampie intended to show his friends what salt pans look like. Grietjie's son, *Groot* Tommie, could not get enough of talking to the salt scrapers, but his shy glances at two girls his age were a clear intention giveaway.

Again, I felt unease among the pan-people and searched for reasons to be at our wagons. There, Johannes was playing in the shade with four-year-old Petrus. When I asked about Kolbooi, Pula and the other children, he took on the typical Tswana non-committal bearing - no answer was ever going to be forthcoming.

They had disappeared without trace from a place I felt compelled to leave as well.

Upon my urging and against the Schoeman brothers' wishes, the rooster Grietjie had insisted on bringing along, marked the time to leave the next day.

Like the first time we had camped close to the pans, we left before sunrise, even though the brothers, quite unaccustomed to women deciding the day's events, complained about it to Ampie. He did not say a word but fitted the oxen's yokes for the last leg of our journey to Skilpadfontein. I secretly enjoyed the moment and loved him for remembering how efficiently and wilfully a woman could travel on her own, as well as the consequences thereof.

Before leaving Langkloof, the three men had visited the Landdrost's offices in Nylstroom, where they obtained paperwork and directions for pegging land with the intention of buying. It was a simple process: In the presence of an independent witness, such as an unacquainted farmer, a farm's size could be determined by a rider who must peg four beacons during daylight hours. It made sense to do so in summer when the days are longer.

The first night we camped at Skilpadfontein, the men spread a rudimentary map of the area showing which farms had been made available to prospective farmers. They pored over this for hours, and by then, the glint of greed was fully set in the brothers' eyes. By the time we served coffee and rusks, they had whipped themselves into a dreamworld, imagining their ownership of whatever had not been claimed in the Bushveld. Ampie only wanted Skilpadfontein, the place where our dreams were centred.

I looked over his shoulder, and with fresh eyes, it was immediately clear that the brothers' wish for much land at low cost could be fulfilled if they shared beacons and at least one fence line.

'You will save money on fencing in future by sharing a fence. Until then, should your cattle cross over to neighbouring land, it is a friend's,' I offered. Ampie was immediately taken by the idea, but the brothers grumbled and shifted in their seats without giving credit to the source of inspiration. After much discussion among themselves, they eventually decided on two farms, which they named Vaalbos and Rooibokvlei, bordering each other and not too far from Skilpadfontein.

'There is no sense in getting angry, Nelie; these are men who had never learned to think of others. Theirs was a hard world,' Ampie excused their behaviour, but I wondered how, even though sharing that hard world in war, he had a soft core, and they did not. And for that matter, we women, too. Instead, we chose love and compassion.

Within the week, old *oom* Callie Kühn stood witness in the haze of dawn at a central beacon of piled stones, first at Skilpadfontein and then hastily south to the brothers' beacon where they milled around on restless horses. While Ampie was marking our borders, the two men mounted and rode off in opposite directions to peg their farms.

At 2s 6p per morgen and long daylight hours, they rode in at dusk on exhausted horses, many thousands of morgen richer. *Oom* Callie printed his name laboriously on three Deeds of Sale, thereby sealing the families' future of fortune or failure.

So it came that Ampie started making clay bricks sourced from Skilpadfontein's pan, where the children had found the tortoises. While these dried in the summer sun, he scoured unclaimed farms for *ouklip* – the rocky ingredient for a concrete floor - and chalk or limestone deposits that could be used to bind sand in the absence of cement. That he found on a stretch of land, he promptly named Kalkpan. A much larger deposit lay in the low-lying areas of Witkop, a farm belonging to old *oom* Callie and *tant* Anna Kühn, the midwife responsible for little Petrus's safe delivery.

'Our house will not have dung floors that you have to smear often,' Ampie proclaimed and patted my bulging stomach, heavy in its expectation of another baby. I was content in his caring.

Truia was the first child born in our new, albeit modest home. This time, *tant* Anna Kühn asked for someone else with less painful hands to deliver our baby, and Ampie rode the few miles to Grietjie's at Rooibokvlei, where he found her ready to leave at a moment's notice. She seemed strangely pleased to leave behind a home where two families lived together in what could only have been described as a house of tents.

A while after Ampie had delivered Grietjie home safely, he told about finding the older brother, Jacob, stick in hand, counting thin strips of *biltong* hanging overhead. 'So that the children do not steal them,' the older man said in answer to Ampie's silent question. I could tell it upset a man who would go hungry to provide for his family. 'A stingy man will die hungry,' he ventured with distaste, and it was clear that no deep friendship would develop between the men as it had for us women.

We regularly visited the Schoemans, always taking produce from the vegetable garden Ampie had planted behind our house. Skilpadfontein was our heart-home – a place we found in happy times and now made happy with the laughter of five children who roamed far and wide to discover the delights of a bush that never stopped giving.

Building work increased as government funds began to flow through. But that dried up quite suddenly in 1916.

Whichever way we looked at it, the reasons did not come to us, and Ampie stayed home for long stretches.

On a sweltering day late in the year, a farmer rode in from the south, dressed in a buttoned-up waistcoat and jacket like an office worker. Ampie recognised his manner and speech as belonging to subsistence farmers near Nylstroom and Warmbaths. This took me back to Irene camp and the spiteful fights between women from those areas. Soon, we learned that he worked as a State agent recruiting black men for the war effort in Europe. It also became apparent why he carried a certain shiftiness when he looked at Johannes, now a strappy ten-year-old.

Instead of inviting the man for coffee as was his habit, Ampie stood hands-in-pockets outside, shook his head multiple times and pointed south from where the farmer came. The message was not lost on me, and apparently not on Johannes either. As soon as the man turned his back, Johannes disappeared among the trees in a north-easterly direction from where Kolbooi and Pula's family originated.

Judging by the agent's thinly veiled brutality, Kolbooi would be forced to join the war as a labourer. By the time the horse's hoofbeats had disappeared north, an unsettled feeling had taken its place.

'I want no part of this war – one was enough,' Ampie said with a far-off look in his eyes. The following days, we went about our tasks with hardly any conversation, lost in the what ifs that are always present in times of war.

So far from civilisation, we were unaware of the 25,000 blacks who volunteered or were coerced into travelling to France. There, without choice, they were treated like slaves at its wet and gloomy ports and the Western Front as part of the South African Native Labour Contingent. What did we know about these heartless measures out in our bush-world?

'I am a builder, Nelie. Loosen your heart from this place so we can move to Langkloof, where there would be more work,' Ampie explained shortly after, with pain in his voice at having to let go of the place we had built together.

I searched my heart until late at night and realised that Ampie was right – work would be more plentiful close to Nylstroom. Besides, our children needed a proper school, not only the veld's teachings.

Klein Ampie was as wild as the black children with no regard for discipline, and there was no church we could attend, no doctor, nurse or shop for essentials. I pounded maize like many generations of black women before me, with sweat and aches marking my effort, and chopped wood like a man when Ampie was away.

In a way, our lives were like those of frontier people all over the world, but to me, living simply was acceptable only because it afforded love and security in our home. When that was absent, as for Katrien and Grietjie, life was primitive and harsh. It was clear we had to go. At night, I cried for Katrien and Grietjie, who had no such choice, and Ampie understood my tears.

The unease which followed the State agent's visit must have spilled over into the larger Bushveld area. Those without any property started their search in earnest. It was not long after that a friendly, thick-set man dismounted at Skilpadfontein – his clothes spoke of wealth and proper care. 'Vermaak,' he introduced himself with a firm handshake and came to the point right away, '*Neef, niggie*, I am here to buy your farm,' and over coffee and rusks, we shook hands with *oom* Vermaak, and in doing so, we broke our connection to Skilpadfontein. Hope of a future at Langkloof took its place.

With the instinct that comes from living close to the veld, Johannes waited outside the back door on the day we were due to *trek* south. Our quiet five-year-old Petrus was beside himself with joy at seeing his friend again, and cried for a long time, talking gibberish Setswana-Afrikaans until *klein* Ampie teased, 'Petie *is 'n aapstert*, Petie is a monkey, whê, whê, whê!' But Petrus was happy.

For a long time and many miles past Rooibokvlei and Vaalbos, my own tears would not cease. Katrien and Grietjie accepted our decision stoically, conditioned over the years by unfeeling men to accept life's challenges rather than fight them. I hated these men for it and did not bother greeting either, convinced their touch would find a way to contaminate and force me to put it in words. No, it was best not to shake their hands.

Katrien and Grietjie were the kind of people God had put on earth to shine a light in our lives. With them I could walk in the dark, which was infinitely better than walking alone in the light.

Once past the salt pans, Ampie spoke what he understood to be the truth about the families at Zoutpan. How he knew, I could only ascribe to his quiet way of watching and learning and understanding the unsaid. 'These pan-people live as one large family, Nelie,' he said, and in this one sentence lay the explanation for the young mothers who were not quick of mind. Their babies' intelligence would never overcome the challenges of schoolwork – the weaker genes simply passed from one generation to the next.

This dreadful situation left me breathless and worried for people caught in situations where choice was not an option, and where choices were made far outside acceptable social norms. It disturbed me to know it was happening in our world. Did these people not have any boundaries?! Ampie patted my hand as if to say, *You cannot change this, Nelie. Menfolk make the rules here.*

Soon, we reached the fence separating the pans from the farmland. There, outside the pan's evil radius, Kolbooi, Pula and all their children waited, white smiles shining brightly against dark skins. With no social rules guiding them into our world, they knew through lived experiences the difference between good and bad and how to manage it.

Their close walk with the supernatural kept them from the pan. These were our friends who would walk with us in the dark.

51 – Onward and Upward

In fact, we say that an intention is good, that is, right in itself, but that an action does not bear any good in itself but proceeds from a good intention. Whence, when the same thing is done by the same man at different times, by the diversity of his intention, however, his action is now said to be good, now bad.

Peter Abeland

1917

So few recollections of my life as a little child at Morgenster remained that when my namesake was born in a far-away war's third year, no matter how desperately I tried to marry her image with a memory of my little self, all that was left were glimpses and feelings.

I reached for memories which had become hazy in their long-ago time - the swirling mist on the dam, the smell of sheep, of snow as it falls on dry leaves.

My mind travelled back to a time when my nose reached just above *ouma* Susara's yellow stinkwood table, and what that brought back were instances when foreboding brought with it both good and bad as a warning.

I looked at Cornelia, little Corrie, who was laboured into the world from an exhausted body and an undetermined foreboding that sapped my last reserves. *Ma* Sophia's tired eyes were there too, watching the struggle between want and need, and nodding when need won. *Onward and upward, Nelie*, they said.

All that memory could offer on that day was an unease, its origin at the time quite without substance or reason. After all, Ampie was able to find building work, we had enough to eat, and the peaceful valley was balm to our travel-weary bodies. Cows, mules and donkeys grazed the veld, and we had clothes to wear. Then why the unease?

We returned to Langkloof, happy to build a home overlooking Tweespruit and Dirk's house in the distance. The older children merely exchanged one playground for the next without complaint. Until *klein* Ampie, Andries, and Lettie had to start school.

School was a five-mile walk towards Moerdyk Gedenkskool – a newly-built single room at Sandrivierspoort Nek's foot. There, beyond the curve where Sterkstroom's waters turn east to follow the mountain range, the school sat peacefully on its banks.

Ampie accompanied the children on their first day and cautioned the boys to look after Lettie on their way back. The second day, *klein* Ampie was nowhere to be seen, and the sun was looking down from four fingers above the trees by the time Ampie had found him hiding behind an anthill. That was the first time his belt came off for an obstinate, favourite child.

I watched from a window as father and son settled the matter – one held by the scruff of his shirt and feeling the wrath of a father who recited studies' merits and virtues. I heard the language of frustration with a grown child that was 'lazy' and 'ungrateful' and 'would not grow into an honourable man' – each characteristic followed by a swing of his long arm.

Not long after, three heads disappeared behind the trees towards school, and a father came to lean against the big tree out front. I joined him, and after a while, put my arm around his shoulders. 'It had to be done, my husband,' I tried to restore peace. He nodded, but the pain of having to discipline a beloved child filled his eyes with sorrow.

A distaste for the deed changed him that day, and I realised that I did not know much about Ampie's upbringing. Were they disciplined severely, as most children were in those times, or was there a softness and empathy for children's need to test boundaries?

He never spoke much about his family, and I had to judge them as fair, forthright and hardworking, based on Ampie's actions. I also knew that facing strife and challenges was not adequately demonstrated to him and his siblings, blurring the line between love, responsibility and what is right. When his own children were born, it prevented him from being a fair parent and from showing all children equal attention. I could not say for certain whether this was how it worked, but in my world, *Ma* and *Pa* had shown, in word and deed, what had to be done; nothing ever seemed too difficult to overcome.

On a given day, *klein* Ampie brought home a letter from the schoolmaster summoning a parent. It also happened to be peach time in the valley. 'A new cling-peach from the Highveld,' *oom* Klasie van Jaarsveldt at the river's bend said while filling a grain bag with yellow peaches for our family - the bag bulging with its fragrant contents. Later, Lettie told of the silence on their way home; *klein* Ampie, subdued for reasons unknown, and she and Andries following quietly, lest attention turn to them. 'But the peaches smelled so good,' she said and lifted her nose as if they were still following Ampie and the peach scent.

Preserving peaches is a craft most women on the Highveld learn from a young age, using stone-fruit that grows best in its cold climate. I sent for bottles at Dirk and Santjie's, then filled the bottles I could lay my hands on, and still there were peaches left over. Meanwhile, Ampie was mulling over and did not share what the teacher had discussed. I let it be, knowing he would speak when there was a plan for whatever pained him.

That lasted a week, after which he sent a reply to the current teacher, Mister White, a leftover British appointment from the 'Anglicise the Boers' post-war time. These were cruel and hard teachers who tried to beat every Dutch and Afrikaans word out of students. It was the *'why'* that did not make sense to farm children, who were unable to understand enough English to grasp the reasoning behind it. Who would ever speak to family and friends in the *Rooinek's* language anyway?!

The next day, both Ampies disappeared towards the mountains and Andries and Lettie went to school by themselves, this time on a donkey to save shoes and time. When the sun was hovering over Dirk's house in the west, and the two school children were home, shoulders hunched after a day's demands, husband and firstborn's excited descent from the mountain could be heard long before dusk brought them to the *stoep*.

Late that night, lying in the crook of Ampie's arm, he said, 'He does not take to book learning,' and that was the only explanation I was ever going to get. In its avoidance, it robbed me of further sleep, as I wondered what a twelve-year-old would do on a farm where not much farming happened.

In the week that followed, each day started with the Ampies taking off for the mountains, and Andries and Lettie heading to school.

With only Petrus, Truia and baby Corrie to tend to, the days became quiet, except for an ever-present premonition that something unpleasant was about to happen.

Johannes and Petrus carried water from Tweespruit, gathered firewood and eggs, while Pula swept or washed clothes, and Kolbooi milked cows and helped Dirk in his effort to plough our field closest to the creek. 'This war may last a long time, Nelie. You need maize and corn on the land, and pumpkin, potatoes and watermelon in the pantry. We may have to feed ourselves in the lean times to come,' Dirk tried to repay Ampie's help with tobacco farming.

But the truth was wandering the mountains with father and son.

On such a day, I remembered with a start the quarter-bag of peaches in the pantry. In the busyness of our days, I forgot about it, but where the bag should have been, only a dust sprinkling marked its presence. I stood there for a while, thinking on whose desire for the delicacy would be greatest, but decided the answer lay not in hunger.

I followed our family's movements over the last week, but they had skirted the pantry while two rode off towards Nylstroom and came back with knapsacks full of 'farm implements.' Yet search as I may, those implements were nowhere to be found. That's when foreboding chilled my bones, forcing me to take note of Ampie and *klein* Ampie's activities, which, I realised soon enough, were always secretive and discussed in hushed tones.

As children, we used to say, 'When not pretty, be clever,' and that memory stood me in good stead now. Johannes's love of freshly baked bread made him an eager spy, willing and able to follow father and son without being noticed. He needed no more than a day to report the 'tokoloshe' – a shiny big-bellied ghost with curly arms, that 'spits' and 'eats peaches' - hidden upstream in the mountain's lower clefts. My day turned from light to dark.

Soon, the *tokoloshe* made itself known to our household when Ampie returned from his 'farming' in a foul mood, unsteady and unreasonable. 'Petrus! Petrus! His slurred shouts could be heard all the way from Tweespruit, and our quiet boy came running, eyes wide in fright. 'Tomorrow you will herd the big bull and cows up the mountain and stay there until I send for you!' Ampie ordered harshly.

I knew not what to say to a loving husband turned devil in a day. There was no arguing with him about a six-year-old alone on the Waterberg plateau, looking after twenty animals for months with no protection or skills to sustain himself.

'Ampie, he is too young!' I tried again, and then he hit me full in the mouth so that I fell backward over the bedframe. He kicked the linen chest with a dull thump and stormed outside like a bull enraged.

Corrie cried inconsolably, but the house fell silent in the face of the enormity of what had happened. The children huddled in our bedroom door, and when I tried to rise, a sharp pain shot up my back and forced me face-down onto a bed that had thus far only known love. Even if I could, sadness kept me there while Andries and Lettie took care of the little ones.

As the hour became late and cold had settled animals and birds to sleep, Petrus came to stand next to me. 'I am big now, *Ma*. I will go,' he said close to my ear, and in his boy-voice I recognised the man he would become – the quiet peacemaker, always given to good intentions.

We say that an intention is good, that is, right in itself, but that an action does not bear any good in itself but proceeds from a good intention.

And I could not love our quiet boy more for the sacrifice he was willing to make for peace at home.

52 – Schools and Teachers

The boundaries which divide Life from Death are at best shadowy and vague. Who shall say where the one ends, and where the other begins?

Edgar Allan Poe

1918 – 1921

For three months, Petrus grazed our animals on the windy mountain plateau where sweet grasses grow, far away from the ever-growing livestock herds down in the valley. For three months, I argued and pleaded and took beatings from a man who seldom revealed his true self through the brandy waves, all to no avail.

The day Petrus left in the dust of animals unwilling to *trek* uphill was bitterly cold. I bound and adjusted the canvas that was to be a shelter, so the precious *biltong,* crushed maize and extra blanket lay comfortably against his back. With a pocketknife, tin cup and plate inside a small three-legged pot, the stocky boy came to lean against me once, then put on his hat and whistled for his young dog, who, like Johannes, never left his side. This time, Johannes had no choice but to stay on the farm 'to earn his keep.' We could not understand such cruelty, least of all the black boy who watched on, eyes wide in his inability to grasp the white man's ways.

Seeing the lonely little figure disappear in the distance, set my heart in a cold place where I had never been before. *Look up from whence your strength comes,* the Bible echoed its message hollowly. But my heart drew comparisons between the stone-hearted Schoeman brothers and Ampie, and I did not like the results.

By September, the two Ampies wrapped up the brandy still when, no matter how far they searched for peaches, none were to be had. We smelled the two before they came into sight – the acid odour seeped from pores and soaked through clothes so dirty that they fit to be burned. Without a greeting, *klein* Ampie slumped over Petrus's bed, and as the sun fell on his cheeks, adulthood showed itself in a downy beard.

I felt angry, ashamed and hollow to look at a dishevelled husband and son who could not escape the open-mouthed stares of the little ones.

I had the unpalatable task of making excuses for what was inexcusable.

The first spring rains brought Petrus down the mountain, ashen-faced and thin like the reeds around Tweespruit – the cattle lowing in discontent at having to return to withered and unappetizing winter grass. When he stood in front of me, I was reminded of Dirk's old-man eyes on the day we had met in the lost river. Hunger, suffering and disillusionment with the hand that was dealt him stared at me. I held him close, and after a while, he started telling of his struggle to cook even the most basic food – *kaboemielie* crushed maize – and to keep a fire going where the wind blows furiously for no reason.

'*Ma*, I tried,' his voice trailed off after an attempt to explain his lack of knowledge. 'I wasted the *kaboemielies, Ma*, because I did not know I should not have filled the pot,' he said about the crushed maize, which only requires a handful for a meal. 'I had been looking after the cows from sunrise, and when I came back that evening, the pot had overflowed and killed the coals,' he remembered tearfully, and continued, 'Johannes never came. I waited and waited.' We cried together, but I did not have the heart to tell him that Johannes had sneaked away, taking more food at night, and that Ampie had caught him and made him pay for his 'disobedience.'

However, before long, the two friends were playing along Tweespruit's banks as if Petrus had not been away for months, their joyful laughter carrying happiness.

World War I ended in November. Although expensive, coffee, tea and sugar were always available at Jan van Heerden's store, but now they were in short supply and soon after dried up. Life became one long, miserable plodding from one day to the next. Once pleasurable jobs became chores, and I started resenting having to do child minding, cleaning, and cooking with few resources, wondering where the next meal would come from. How our lives could change in such a short time, I was unable to fathom.

But soon it was peaceful in our home again when the two Ampies had devised ways to produce citrus brandy and then stayed in the mountains for weeks at a time. The children fell back on their old ways of hiding when an unreasonable and drunken father came home. Everyone except Petrus, who watched on defiantly and was beaten as a result. He became familiar with the harsh language of a drunkard and learned to dislike liquor in any form.

Not even the loss of another child born months too early could shake Ampie from his stupor and unreasonable behaviour, while in the background *klein* Ampie became his mirror image, ordering the other children around without lifting a finger to ease our load. I carried the sadness and loss alone and adorned the tiny grave with *buchu* leaves and wildflowers – a little girl who lay close to their scent but would never know their beauty. Again, it was Pula's quiet presence that brought my heart to centre and brought me to a feeling at peace.

In 1919, Petrus went to school for the first time, and even though he was not old enough for school, Truia snuggled up to him on the donkey's uncomfortable back, eager to be away from a house that harboured pain and discontent. My heart ached to know she would face the hated Mister White at such a tender age. 'We will look after her, *Ma*,' eleven-year-old Andries promised. I doubted that would be possible, but I wanted her far away from Ampie's drinking.

A week into the school term, Ampie was sitting outside under the big tree when the children came home earlier than usual. It was a day marked with calm and glimpses of the old, kind Ampie. It seemed as if he was looking forward to the children's return, and when the boys helped Lettie and Truia to dismount, a smile played around his pipe. He called to them. At that moment, a breeze lifted Truia's skirt where a few blue marks snaked around her thin legs. By the time she stood big-eyed in front of him, the boys had circled her for protection. But Ampie spoke softly, 'Show me your legs, Truiatjie. You too, Lettie, and you, and you,' he made all four turn around. From where I stood at the kitchen window, the blue and purple lines peeped in angry patterns from beneath pants and skirts. My breath caught at the beatings' measured cruelty. Ampie took the boys aside, and they talked quietly at length.

By the time the children had had their porridge the next morning, Ampie's horse was saddled, and he waited patiently alongside. His eyes, however, told the tale of anger. It was Andries and Petrus who later relayed the day's happenings, each falling over the other to fill in the details with relish. 'And *Pa* went up to Mister White and asked him if he was the *Rooinek* teacher who beats little girls.'

And 'Then he took him behind the school by the neck.....' and 'Beat him around his buttocks with the hippopotamus hide sjambok until he cried like a baby...' and 'Yes, *Ma*, like a baby!'

Apparently, Ampie told the teacher that, should he lift his hands again to hit a child for speaking Afrikaans, he could expect a beating só severe that he would regard this one as mere child's play.

The next day, Mr White did not turn up for school, and the children had to go home early. That was a good day in our home too. Except for *klein* Ampie's surly manner, we laughed and joked until long after bedtime.

Short were our celebrations, though, when a tough-looking Afrikaner teacher with a wild beard and even wilder eyes introduced himself to the mixed class as *Meneer* Van Rafenswaay. Like an August wind, six younger versions of him rushed into the already full room, pushed the little children off their seats and made themselves at home with much noise. By the day's end, Andries, Lettie and Petrus knew everything there was to know about the family. 'The church pays this one,' Andries's voice carried the disrespect that was already etched on the others' faces. 'And he is *woes, Ma*!' Petrus tried to explain the teacher's angry ways, but it was our naturally mellow Lettie who indignantly painted the picture best, 'All his brothers lifted our dresses, and he did not stop them!'

A slow fire started burning in my chest, and I knew it would have to burn for a while before I could be sure what to do. We so desperately needed a teacher, but a mean one? And that, one of our own?!

By now, the two Ampies were busy cutting tobacco, which came from Dirk, Kolbooi and Johannes's hands. The crop was poor and meagre, as the summer rains disappointed and the soil depleted. With *klein* Ampie, an unwilling helper, and Kolbooi, who was poorly due to an illness that resisted all my healing efforts, it took a long time to harvest and hang the tobacco.

No, *Meneer* Van Rafenswaay was the kind of problem best solved by a mother.

It required time, patience and planning to dream up revenge. Often, I had to remind our children that I was still working on a plan to improve things. In that time, food became increasingly scarce. For a second year, big rain clouds drifted in from the west, skirted Langkloof and rolled their cottonwool over the mountains to rain in a far-off place.

The animals became scrawny and looked to us with sunken eyes for food that was not to be found. Some lay down exhausted and never got up again. Some vanished altogether, and when I asked, Johannes was the one to tell that, 'The *baas* sold it,' to a wealthy family towards the Vlieëberge.

It did not take long to know that the money paid for overpriced sugar to feed a hungry brandy still. But Ampie's absences suited me well. When famine came knocking, as it did, a loaf of bread was as precious as the water we drank. Every Monday, Andries went to school with a loaf that robbed our children of a second meal, but I hardened my heart. 'Tell *Meneer* if my cloth comes back, he'll have more bread,' I promised and made sure it was well-wrapped in the bleached flourbag cloth.

At the end of the third week, Lettie cornered me in the pantry with '*Ma*, what is in the bread?' We just looked at each other with happy eyes, as the boys were quick to tell that all the Van Rafenswaays were spending a lot of time outside to relieve themselves, and when inside, they looked 'yellow' and tired. That's when Andries started spreading a rumour about poisonous plants that grow everywhere in times of drought and boosted the rumours with tales of unhealthy vapours in the lower valleys. With a famine truly bringing us to despair in 1921, the Van Rafenswaays simply packed up and moved north towards the isolated Waterkloof Ward.

Even though the older children's eyes asked many questions, I could never share what Kolbooi and Johannes had taught me: It is impossible to taste ground ant eggs. Half a teaspoon causes discomfort; more causes a walk to the other side.

But who knows exactly how much after all, as the boundaries which divide life from death are at best shadowy and vague, especially when it applies to a child's wellbeing.

This time, the boundaries were clear.

53 - *Poorer and Hungrier*

Anguish often causes us to physically crumple in on ourselves, literally bringing us to our knees or forcing us all the way to the ground. The element of powerlessness is what makes anguish traumatic. We are unable to change, reverse, or negotiate what has happened. Anguish always finds its way back to us. After going through such things, your bones are slightly different than they were before.

Brené Brown: Atlas of the Heart

Starting on a Sunday, one thousand, nine hundred and twenty-three years after the birth of our Lord, the new year seemed to have the same ingredients as those preceding it – the poor became poorer and hungrier, and the rich held onto their possessions and money.

Dirk and Santjie's labours on the land, together with supplies from her family's shop, assured food on their table, which they ate sparingly. Dirk's advice saw pumpkin, onion, corn and maize stored in our pantry that, after so many months of hardship, were nearly depleted.

After countless arguments, unnecessary aggression, bare shelves and empty plates, Ampie started looking for building work as far as Pretoria, but for a nation still struggling to find its feet after WWI, there were many contenders and few opportunities. The brandy still was gathering dust, as *klein* Ampie rode off with his father on most occasions. On their return, his shaking hands bore the signs of a weakling who drank away every penny he had made through hard labour. Each time they returned, he seemed more like his father. I started looking over my shoulder to escape what violence might creep up on me, and once again, Langkloof became a place of fear and unhappiness when the two Ampies were around.

On the day Petrus and Andries brought home a bony, stringy-fleshed rabbit they had caught in a snare, nausea overtook me at its rank smell. They watched me with concern, then took off with Johannes, the .22 and a hessian bag towards the mountains. When dusk set in, they returned, smiling through lips double their size and hardly able to see through eyes swollen shut, but their offering lay on the table in brown honey-comb blades of goodness.

'And there's a duiker at the back door, *Ma*,' Petrus announced proudly, then returned the .22 to the gun-rack. Between the two, they hung the duiker in the tree outside and came back with kidneys and liver, 'For our feast tonight,' and handed the intestines into Johannes's eager hands.

I closed my eyes and could smell the fatty intestines' deliciousness roasting over coals, the way only Pula could do without burning its delicate casings. Two hungry households would be feasting on the boys' labours tonight, I thought as he disappeared like a springhare in the dark.

It was Andries's privilege to say grace over our food and the family, but by the time 'We thank you, Lord, for the bounty we have received' left his swollen lips, the girls were crying quietly and would not touch the onion-and-liver dish, which was indeed an unexpected bounty. 'Because then it will be gone,' Truia said between sobs with child-like logic.

It was a particularly hot summer. Andries and Lettie were in their last year of school and making plans for their future. In the afternoons, the children came home with red faces and empty water bottles. No amount of talking could get Truia to wear her *kappie;* she was as stubborn as a mule. 'She had water from Sterkstroom too, and I saw Klein-Jan Viljoen relieve himself upstream just last week!" Petrus expressed his frustration with a headstrong sister. Ten days later, Truia could not get up, and when I took her hand, it was clammy and cold even though her body was hot and sweaty. Her eyes drifted from the roof to the door and back without focus. I lifted her arms and legs one at a time, but the left arm and leg moved without purpose or strength.

Oh, dear God – how did this sickness come into our lives?!

For days and many long nights, Pula and I bathed Truia in steaming water and added as much mustard as Petrus could beg and buy in the valley. A polio outbreak happened once when I was young, and that was during a hot summer when people swam in the river and did not bother to defecate far from the stream. Out of desperation, some mothers had tried various elixirs and home remedies, but the one that proved to prevent lung paralysis was frequent hot mustard baths. Why that worked, no one could tell.

Truia recovered in the bedroom's isolation but was forever burdened with a withered and growth-stunted left side – a child who had to learn to walk, eat and talk again. But she was alive.

The year crept forward slowly, with its focus firmly on the struggle to survive, felt by everyone, especially the animals who grazed on unpalatable *suurknol* and the odd bitter weed. The children reported seeing sheep eating stones, as nature forced its will on man and beast, who suffered greatly. Everyone except the older Italian couple who had been living along Sterkstroom's banks since 1902. Vito and Minento Bari had arrived with enough money to buy a farm outright and to have an adventure, 'To-a de south and-e not-a de Egypt and-e Tunis,' *tante* Minento told anyone who wanted to know why two Europeans ended up in the Waterberg. A childless couple with hearts of gold.

On a day when despondency bent me double, and bile was the only food a new life could force out of me, Vito Bari secured their buggy under the big tree and helped *tante* Minento down the narrow steps. She scanned the room and, in her practical way, stirred the coals to life, made tea, and casually handed me mine with, 'A bambino, yes?' but her eyes did not miss the empty pantry or the threadbare clothes blowing in the wind. By the time they were ready to leave, my heart was in a better place. We embraced like old friends with a promise to visit soon, which was just a week and arms full of clothes and food later. We cried together while the baby kicked with joy at such generosity.

Andries finished Standard Six – the highest grade at school - at the end of November and announced that he would be leaving to work at the South African Railways, which had been expanding rapidly across the country. 'A job that pays well, *Ma*, and one less mouth to feed,' he pointed out, looking at my heavy body, but the guilt of leaving his family at this time was hard to miss. Yet, it was the same family dynamics that forced him to fend for himself.

The day after Andries's departure, Rachel Maria was born – small enough to fit in a shoebox and light enough to hold with one hand. Our seventh living child was born with a father who was not by my bedside. She brought with her the struggles of a malnourished, distressed and colicky baby, so much so that the night hours became hellish nightmares and daytime a war of worry and need.

The day indifference came into my heart was bound to happen, and it happened in the second month. I looked at the red, screaming baby and felt nothing but irritation.

My tired hands changed her diaper, not when needed, but when remembered. Her clothes became sour from spilled milk, and where she slept next to me in the double bed, the sheets reeked of unwashed bodies. Sometimes I was aware that other children were present, but mostly they took care of themselves.

I did not even notice that Petrus and Johannes had disappeared with two donkeys. But on a sunny day, shortly after, when birds were singing in the trees and bees buzzed among the wildflowers, *tante* Minento came into the bedroom, looking like the picture of Jesus that hung on the *voorkamer* wall. A colourful halo pretended above her head, and a sympathetic smile looked down on me where I sat in bed with Rachel. 'Petrus, he call,' is all she said.

I do not know how it happened or how much it cost, but by the time I sat in the zinc bath, the house smelled of cooked food, and the older children's happy voices drifted in from outside. Baby Ralie was fast asleep in a basket, and *tante* Minento was scrubbing my back, making soothing Italian noises.

Around the dining table, which was loaded with the most delicious food, she took my hand, made a cross for her faith, and announced that Ralie would go with her until she was stronger. I did not argue.

And so the weeks became months, then years, that passed without highs and lows, but the highs of my heart were overshadowed by the lows of an anguish that took over my senses. To understand the hills and valleys of my emotions, I often went out to our nameless little girl's grave not far from home, where the wind, trees and birds spoke in soft tones. There, I could make sense of my life - how the me in me had disappeared altogether in the burden of trying to raise good children without the help of a father who moved between being a devil and a loving angel. I questioned why the aches of an old woman plagued the battered body of one young enough to climb mountains, yet too old to climb the steps of my own home.

By 1926, I came to understand that longing for a child given away out of necessity and carrying the torch for so many others could cause us to physically crumple in on ourselves, virtually bringing us to our knees and forcing us all the way to the ground.

There were good times, too. It was a good year for building, and Ampie made good money.

On 7 May 1926, he travelled to Nylstroom to buy Section 333 of the freehold farm Langkloof - 197 morgen, 200 square roods, held under certificate of partitian title. 'This is good, wife,' he said proudly, but I smiled and felt no joy.

For many months, Ampie stayed at home and was once again the man I had married. That was, until *klein* Ampie joined our household and they rediscovered the mountain path to the still.

Two years later, on 24 January 1928, Ampie bought Portion D of the quitrent farm, Goedehoop, a sizeable 145 morgen (204 square roods), held under a Deed of Transfer. 'Now our children have an inheritance,' Ampie declared and started making bricks to enlarge our house. This time, he added a *stoep* and bathroom with a white bath and basin, which was transported on a wagon from Nylstroom. The *voorkamer* became the kitchen and was so big that there was space for a piano, which came from Warmbaths to stand proudly in a corner.

It was the piano that started calling me, even though the darkness in my heart spoke louder and won most of the time. It was while sitting on the *stoep* one balmy day that *Ma*'s voice came to me so clearly, that I sat up with a start: *Cornelia, listen to its call!*

There was no one around, so I went inside, opened the piano and breathed in its unique ivory smell. The music came from deep inside where hurt, pain, joy and happiness combined to help stiff fingers find their path. I heard its call and obeyed.

And so did Petrus. After he had finished Standard Six in 1927, he took the reins of farming firmly in his hands. Using every resource Ampie's money could buy, he planted tobacco, corn and maize on much enlarged paddocks which he and Johannes had cleared by hand and ploughed with young, strong oxen. They worked from sunup to sundown, not resting until a task was done.

I marvelled at how dissimilar our boys were. Whenever Andries came to visit, he and Petrus became the boys of their youth, scouring Langkloof's cliffs for kudu, rooibok and eland, or holding each other's feet while dangling upside-down from the cliff-edge to reach wild-bee nests – looking death in the eye over the abyss. Like two overgrown boys, mischief landed them in hot water with the young sergeant at the newly established police station at Sandrivierspoort Nek.

There, Petrus once spent a cold night behind bars when caught red-handed hunting eland and kudu while it was prohibited. This did not serve as a deterrent but a source of merriment between the two.

And then there was *klein* Ampie – always ready for a fight, always lazy and never a brother to the others.

The only farmer who could claim Langkloof was Petrus. And in him, the Bergmann musicality ran strong. After a long day's work, he would open the piano and sing a song while working out the chords. His clear voice stayed true to pitch, and soon the girls and I would join to complete the day.

Not long after, a distinct call came to me. It was with shame that I remembered my promise to Ampie so long ago: *I will learn to play the accordion, my husband, and at this table we will feed our children.*

When a wholesome quiet descended on our home after the girls had left for school, I brought the accordion from its wardrobe hiding place and started learning to make music for the person I was then – beautiful and soft, touching my soul, where anguish was never far away. It was music fitting to honour *Ma* Gertruida's love and devotion to the next generation of Bergmanns, which was contained in a simple musical instrument. After the day's music practice, I left it in full view on the small table *Pa* Abraham had made before going to war. Maybe the next generation would feel its pull too.

Tante Minento was a good, albeit old, mother who often brought Ralie for visits. Soon, however, we realised that it was painful for Ralie to be away from 'home.' Like most older parents' children, she spoke with a higher pitch, never went without shoes or a knitted bonnet, and seldom played with her siblings. She became an old person in a child's body, but she lacked nothing. From her first day at school in 1928, Vito drove her to school in Nylstroom, sitting like a little pigeon on its perch in the first automobile that had ever driven on the Waterberg's wagon tracks.

Like *tante* Minento, he was besotted with this only child and waited under a tree all day for school to end, then worked until long after dark to finish his farm work. Ampie and I argued whether to leave Ralie in their household, but in the end, we agreed that we could not change, reverse, or negotiate what had happened. God gave the older people a purpose and reason to live and gave Ralie the best life any child could hope for.

But agreeing on something and living with the decision was not a guarantee that we truly accepted it. It was in the long nights that the ghosts of such decisions kept me awake for hours, and soon there was no sleeping at all.

That's when the truth came to stay permanently: Anguish always finds its way back to us, and when it does, our souls and bones are slightly different from what they were before.

54 – In Sickness and in Health

Strange crawling carpets of the grass, wide windows of the sky; so in this perilous grace of God, with all my sins go I. And things grow new and I grow old, though I grow old and die.

The Collected Poems of G.K. Chesterton

The strangest sense of longing came over me in 1928.

Nightmares started invading my dreams, and as soon as that happened, premonition woke and urged me to make sure the children were tucked in and the doors locked. Afterwards, a half-sleep followed, filled with visions and thoughts of my dear friends, Katrien and Grietjie Schoeman, so far away. All the time, Edward's blue eyes were present - lonely and sad in their long-ago haziness yet watching my dream movements like a magistrate judging a case's merits.

Ampie came to stand with me at the washstand, where my mirror image looked back at me with sunken eyes, lined black with sleep-deprived worry. 'What is it you want me to do, my princess?' he asked like the loving Ampie of old and nodded when I indicated travels to the north.

For months, peace and quiet had been measuring our days at Langkloof. Gone were the years of drinking and heavy-handedness that had shared our home. The violent husband disappeared the day fruit brandy brewing ceased in the lower mountains, after which moody *klein* Ampie packed a satchel and left for the unknown without a goodbye. For months thereafter, we carried and wrapped ourselves with apprehension, careful not to disturb the wholesomeness. A peace reigned which Corrie and Truia had never experienced in their young lives, and our hearts were full because of its unexpected goodness.

The only reminder of a violent time was the constant back pain I carried from one too many beatings. Petrus's ever-watchful eyes, which kept the unhappy memories alive by always being protectively near me, added to the pain. His childhood was forever scarred, and his future etched with a distaste of overindulgence.

Sunrise found Johannes, Ampie and Petrus loading the wagon with goods fit for a long absence.

Kolbooi, slow in old age, oversaw the loading. After two days' packing and many trips across Tweespruit with instructions for Dirk, we went to bed, tired and excited to leave behind the monotony of homelife. True to his nature, Johannes did not comment on our travels, but by day's end, he was ashen faced, doing most of the heavy lifting. 'It is a long journey, Johannes,' I reminded him, forcing his brilliant white smile to the surface - his family was longing for their soul people too.

The young oxen Ampie had bought at Nylstroom's saleyards were fighting the restraints of their new role in front of the wagon. But by the time the sun was overhead, and Ampie had steered them north-west at Sandrivierspoort Nek, they had made their peace and were pulling together.

Once we had left behind our valley, each whip crack seemed to increase Corrie and Truia's expectations of the journey. Lettie, who postponed wedding plans to relive fond childhood memories at Skilpadfontein, spent all her time answering the girls' never-ending questions.

We made camp near the stone rondavel police station where Petrus had spent, 'The coldest night of my life,' for ignoring hunting restrictions. How Andries laughed about his brother's discomfort and having to borrow five Pounds, so he did not have to spend several more nights under a threadbare blanket in the cold, round hut. The memory of their youthful laughter and larrikinism made Andries's absence more noticeable, and Petrus's silence bore witness to this knowledge. He stood and disappeared into the dark with Johannes to gather firewood. Their companionable voices' low hum drifted over the quiet like a salve for my weary soul.

The stars hung low in a dark sky and lit the mountains with that unique African crispness, which could easily lead travellers astray.

'I saw a ghost, *Ma*,' Truia whispered wide-eyed from where she sat curled up next to the fire – her shrivelled body twisted awkwardly to the side. 'There are no ghosts, Truia,' Lettie explained, 'And no graves here in the wild where lost souls would walk at night.' But I heard it too. Johannes and Petrus were to our right, and Ampie was snoring softly in the tent, but the sound of movement and animated conversation came from behind through the pass. I held up my hand, and we waited, turning our heads slowly to find the 'ghost.'

Nothing.

Then Corrie and Truia screamed in unison, and there, not ten feet from us, a white ghost moved slowly towards us, its shiny eyes and long legs heading straight for our camp. Ampie came running, gun in hand, and the girls' screams echoed from mountain to mountain when the ghost reared on its hind legs and came down hard on the stony ground.

'Who goes there?!' Ampie shouted and aimed at the moonlit movements.

'Whoa, Spook, whoa!' a voice tried to calm it while we clung to each other behind the fire. Petrus and Johannes rushed open-mouthed into the light with armfuls of wood, then dropped it and leapt over the fire, hooting and howling with the joyous laughter of their youth, as they led Andries and his white horse into the light.

Looking in from outside, the eerie moonlight could easily have turned shadows into ghosts, but our ghost was the missing link on this path of remembrance. My heart beat happily until sleep took over.

Soon into our journey, the changes since we had last travelled this road became evident. Even though the Schoeman brothers had stopped by at Langkloof at least once a year to offload animal skins for leather hawkers, they never spoke of these changes. Their main purpose was always to sell corn, maize and animal fat in Vaalwater. With the extended rail now reaching the village, a larger mill was built next to the line, and animal fat could be uploaded for delivery to a soap factory in Pretoria.

Never once did women and children accompany them, and never once did they respond to the question why. Although I had received the occasional letter from Katrien, their day-to-day lives were a mystery to me.

The seldom-trodden road north was now a wide strip maintained by the Roads Department to accommodate a railbus that ran once a week to the border crossing between South Africa and Bechuanaland at Stockpoort.

'It goes both ways where the road forks at Slangfontein, *niggie* – one to Waterkloof Ward and the other to Zoutpan Ward. But we don't call them that anymore. People talk about Soutpan, Ellisras and Steenbokpan now,' a farmer offloading maize said when he noticed my surprise.

But I was unable to imagine how 1908's faint wagon tracks could change so rapidly to smoothe the way for rubber wheels. 'Many changes, *Mevrou,* many changes. The bus goes north-west first, stops at Fancy Halt where there's a little post office, then on to Stockpoort.

It cuts through to Ellisras, where more farmers have claimed a piece of land next to the river, and then back to Vaalwater.' The farmer was in a talkative mood and rocked back and forth on his heels to confirm his importance. 'Yes, now people will start farming and taming those wild places,' he said, looking at his gun in a way an experienced hunter would. I thought about the doe-eyed steenbok who shared our camp at the crossroads of Groot Doornlaagte, and my stomach cramped at the thought of losing such beauty.

True to the tale, the road was fit for more than oxen, mules and horses. Close to Slangfontein, where the road forks, a pall of dust could be seen ahead, and soon a big bus came lumbering downhill, taking up most of the road. The oxen were determined not to pull together and wouldn't pass the smoking, roaring beast. It took all Andries, Petrus and Johannes's strength and many cracks of the whip to calm them, but only after the driver switched off the engine did they manage to move past their fear. We left the diesel smell behind and made camp quite a distance from the road, where baboons barked, and jackals yodelled their displeasure at things not belonging in the veld.

We arrived at Vaalbos late in the afternoon. The house, which I had never seen, sat calmly in the sun's last rays. Chicken, duck and geese greeted us outside in a yard swept smooth to the point of barenness. 'Wait outside,' I told the menfolk, and Lettie and I entered with trepidation through the back door into a kitchen. One room led straight into the next, where we found Katrien in bed, 10-year-old Maria at her side and young Janneman standing uncertainly in the corner. The laughter of three younger children could be heard deeper in the house.

'*My sussie!*' she mouthed, a smile spreading around a face so swollen, I could hardly recognise it as that of my friend. There was no mistaking her pregnancy's advanced stage. With practised hands, Maria wiped her mother's face and with a nod to Janneman, he disappeared outside. Later, we could hear him and our boys herding the sheep and watering the donkeys and oxen. Through the window, I saw Johannes chopping wood. I watched how Petrus, Andries and Johannes took over everyday tasks while Ampie left with a pail to do the milking.

With shock and dismay, I realised there was no father in this house except for eight-year-old Janneman. And the mother was just ten years old!

We made camp a short distance from the house, but I remained in the room with Katrien. Once fed, Lettie took the exhausted Maria by the hand and put her and the younger ones to bed, then slept in a nearby chair. Maria mutely shook her head when asked about her father, but Janneman said shyly, 'He and *oom* Jacob have been away for a long time.' In that sentence lay my dislike of the brute who caused this situation.

A woman this ill should not have been with child again.

The next day, I could hardly get up, but Katrien's delirious dreams ignored the pain in my back and my stiff fingers. The stove was already lit, and two black women with toddlers, Danie and Hermien strapped to their backs, were sweeping the yard, nodding and talking to Pula in the singsong of their language while little Katrien played nearby in the shade.

As I looked on, they straightened and waited. A long-armed young man rushed to the back door, with angst and sadness spread over him. His pale-blue eyes were level with mine, and in them I saw a carer's concern and love.

'*Tante*, it's me, *Groot* Tommie of Rooibokvlei. *Ma* died this morning,' and with that, the hacking cry of one unaccustomed to grief escaped from deep inside him. My world stood still. Two strong women diminished to nothingness by a life of strife, want and struggle – one on her way to the grave and the other already there.

I took *Groot* Tommie in my arms, and we stood there for the longest time while the black women ululated softly for the goodness of others lost too soon.

We buried Grietjie in the family graveyard while a husband and brother-in-law were at a place other than next to the grave. The black women insisted on staying behind with Katrien, while we honoured a life that was mostly ignored by an unfeeling husband.

By nightfall, it was evident that Katrien's baby would wait no longer, but the strength needed for the task lay not with her. After two days of fighting death, she gave up the fight. Between Lettie, me, and Maria, we forced a healthy baby into the world. We thanked our God for that miracle and prayed over Katrien's soul.

It was wide-eyed Maria who shook my arm with, '*Tante* Nelie, *Ma leef!*' And when I struggled to my feet, Katrien let go of the dark, blinked a few times and breathed deeply. She was alive!

We stayed on for another month until the two Schoeman brothers' return, and when I was sure Katrien could manage with the help of young Maria.

It was Ampie who warned, 'Nelie, my princess, we must go home. You are ill and not getting better,' which echoed the worries I carried from sunrise to sunset and many a night hour too. We had to say goodbye.

'This is farewell, my friend,' Katrien said brokenly – a truth clear as spring water. We were two damaged people – one forever unhappy and shackled to an unfeeling man, and the other living with the physical pain born of drunken violence, but happy in the world around her.

Our feet, so long ago, trod the strange hope carpets of a life bound by promise and looking with expectation into the wide windows of the sky. Where did so much hope go in so few years?

We cried for an eternity until our souls were happy to part. Petrus leaned from his saddle, raised his hat in greeting with the promise, 'Soon, Maria. I'll be fetching you soon,' and then we were on our way. Our wagon chose the road south to Langkloof, where we belonged, and the journey was made bearable on down pillows and the warmth of my family's love.

The next four years, pain became my constant companion, and my bones crumbled in on me until my back was bent, and the stranger staring from the mirror was old and weary of struggle.

Often, Edward looked over my shoulder, and many times it was *tante* Katrien, *Ma* or Grietjie who joined me there. Sometimes our babies' milky scent swirled around my bed and filled my heart with a warmth that only a mother would know.

By 1935, Petrus regularly disappeared north on his bicycle, and soon there was talk of marriage. 'Maria is the woman who will make you happy, my boy,' I shared my wisdom, but secretly I worried that the kind-hearted girl would inherit her father's iron will.

We hardly ever saw *klein* Ampie, and finally, I was able to close my heart to him. Ralie was happy and well cared for at *tante* Minento's, and Lettie and Andries were secure in their own marriages. Ampie, in his changed state, would take care of Corrie and Truia until they, too, had found their purpose.

But in the dark of night, I had to admit to myself that the days of my life could only be measured by months, not years.

The pain of old injuries became one with my spine and crawled into my head at night, when rest should have taken away the burden, but made it worse.

Ampie took to sleeping in a chair next to me, ready to fetch whatever I needed. 'Everything I have ever needed has already been given to me in life,' I told him, 'I do not need earthly goods where I am going.'

He insisted on taking me to the hospital, and I recognised his guilt for the years lost at the brandy still. 'I am happy here, Ampie. This is my home,' I often reminded him, but the day came when he rode his horse so fast to Vito's house that it became lame. Vito drove his car with shaking hands and wild eyes to Pretoria, where doctors prodded and pricked their way through tests. They would not listen to my protestations, so I lay back and let them. For three months.

There, in the quiet of my room, I could relive my life. And there was much to relive. I was happy that it was my time to dream.

'*Ma*, come sing with me,' Petrus said, sitting at the piano, and I pulled up a chair to sit next to him. His clear voice started the Sunday with a Dutch hymn that *oupa* Dewaldt used to sing while carving each chair for the yellow stinkwood table:

Abide with me; fast falls the eventide
The darkness deepens; Lord, with me abide
When other helpers fail, and comforts flee
Help of the helpless, oh, abide with me

'Why this one, my boy, and why today?' I asked. 'Because it is your special day, *Ma*. It is the fourteenth day of April 1935 – the day God has dedicated to you,' he said kindly. His grey eyes changed into the blue of Edward's, then to the grey of Ampie's, and then the hazy blue of all our babies, one after the other. And I thought:

In this perilous grace of God, with all my sins,
I have been abundantly blessed.
And even though things grow new, and though I grow old,
How good a life was this.
Though now, I grow old and die.

I closed my eyes.
This was my life, and the special day God had gifted me.

Bibliography

Anglo Boer War. (2022). Retrieved from:
    https://www.angloboerwar.com/

Armstrong, H. (1980). Camp Diary of Henrietta E.C. Armstrong.
    Experiences of a Boer Nurse in the Irene Concentration Camp, 6
    April-11 October 1901, ed. by T. van Rensburg (Pretoria, HSRC,
    1980)

Australia for Everyone. (2021). The history of Sydney, Victorian Era.
    Retrieved from: https://www.visitaustralia.com.au

Australian Government. (2022). About Australian Stories. Boer War.
    Retrieved from: https://www.gov.au

Australian Government. (2023). About Australia. The Boer War.
    Retrieved from: https://www.australia.gov.au/about-
    australia/australian-stories

BCCD. (2022). British concentration camps of the South African war
    1900-1902. Irene. Welcome Trust

Biggins, B. (2004). Anglo Boer War. South African units. Brabant's
    Horse. Retrieved from: https://www.AngloBoerWar.com

Brandt, J. (1913). The Petticoat Commando/Boer women in secret
    service. Mills & Boon, London

Curson, P. (2012). *Border conflicts in a German African Colony: Jakob
    Morengo and the untold tragedy of Edward Presgrave.* Arena Books,
    Edmunds, UK

Curson, P. (2014). Namibia: A young Australian's war. Newsmakers

Hobhouse, E. (1902). The brunt of the war and where it fell. Read
    Books, London.

Hurstville Heritage Inventory. (2020). Hurstville Railway sub-station.
    Retrieved from: https://www.studyres.com/doc/6889855/hurstville-
    heritage-inventory-georges-river-council

Lexicon of terms and places connected with the campaign. (1912). The
    Transvaal War.

Madsen, C. (2004). Canadian troops and farm burning in the South
    African War. Canadian Military Journal, *Vol 6*(2), 49 – 56

Magaliesberg. (2023). Retrieved from:
https://en.wikipedia.org/wiki/Magaliesberg

National Museum of American history. (2022). Liners to America Atlantic crossings. Retrieved from: https://americanhistory.si.edu/on-the-water

NSW Government. (2022). Hurstville Public School, strive for success. Retrieved from:
https://hurstville-p.schools.nsw.gov.au

Pretorius, F. (2011). The Boer Wars. Retrieved from: www.bbc.com

Smithsonian, National Museum of American history. (2022). On the Water – Atlantic Crossings – 1870 – 1969

Sole, T. E. (1968). The Südwestafrika Denkmünze and the South West African campaigns of 1903-08. Military History Journal, *Vol 1*(3)

South African History Online. (2011). Emily Hobhouse. Retrieved from: https://www.anglo-boer.co.za

The Blue Post. (n.d.). Past lives of the near future. Retrieved from: www.thebluepost

The Maritime Heritage Project. (2022). RMSS Zealandia sailings 1800s, 1900s from San Francisco to Hawaii to Australia. Retrieved from: https://www.maritimeheritage.org/passengers/RMSS-Zealandia.html

Van Warmelo, J. (1911). The War Diary of Johanna Brandt, ed. by J. Grobler. Protea, Pretoria, (2007). Published camp reports; Cd 819, pp. 28, 58-61, 120-123, 235-241, 351-355; Cd 853, 62-66; Cd 902, 69-73

Wayne, M. (2013). Past lives of the near future: Hurstfield – Act 1 (1875-1975). Retrieved from:
https://pastlivesofthenearfuture.com/2013/09/11/hurstfield-act-i-genesis-1875-1975/

Hester lives in Australia with her husband and two hounds. She was born in South Africa and grew up surrounded by wild animals and exposed to the intimate culture of oral storytelling. She is a specialist in personalised teaching methods with a PhD in Education.

Hester educates through storytelling, using the magic of informal narratives to reach young and old. She writes for neurodivergent children, who find it difficult to learn through traditional teaching methods, while delighting adults with extensively researched historical fiction.

She believes each story retains a part of her soul.

Find Hester: www.hestergarner.com
Instagram: drhesseven
Facebook: Hester Garner Author
Amazon: amazon.com/author/hestergarner-author
BookBub: Hester Garner

Contact Hester: drhesseven@gmail.com

9 781763 669208